PORT MOODY PUBLIC L
D0209769

NIGHT WORK

FORGE BOOKS BY DAVID C. TAYLOR

Night Life
Night Work

NIGHT WORK

DAVID C. TAYLOR

A TOM DOHERTY ASSOCIATES BOOK
NEW YORK

This is a work of fiction. All of the characters, organizations, and events portrayed in this novel are either products of the author's imagination or are used fictitiously.

NIGHT WORK

Copyright © 2016 by David C. Taylor

All rights reserved.

A Forge Book
Published by Tom Doherty Associates, LLC
175 Fifth Avenue
New York, NY 10010

www.tor-forge.com

Forge® is a registered trademark of Tom Doherty Associates, LLC.

The Library of Congress Cataloging-in-Publication Data is available upon request.

ISBN 978-0-7653-7485-1 (hardcover)
ISBN 978-1-4668-4344-8 (e-book)

Our books may be purchased in bulk for promotional, educational, or business use. Please contact your local bookseller or the Macmillan Corporate and Premium Sales Department at 1-800-221-7945, extension 5442, or by e-mail at MacmillanSpecialMarkets@macmillan.com.

First Edition: April 2016

Printed in the United States of America

0 9 8 7 6 5 4 3 2 1

For Priscilla, Susannah, and Jennifer, with love

ACKNOWLEDGMENTS

Thank you to my agent, Lisa Gallagher, for her continued enthusiasm and her smart and useful suggestions on the story told; to Tom Doherty, Bob Gleason, Linda Quinton, Elayne Becker, and the team at Forge, for their support and encouragement; to Jane Herman, for the clarity of her copyediting; to Emily Mullen, for her diligence and her patient responses to my flood of inquiries and suggestions.

To all my friends, ink-stained wretches, who get up every morning to face the interesting mystery of the blank page.

All men dream: but not equally. Those who dream by night in the dusty recesses of their minds wake in the day to find it was vanity, but the dreamers of the day are dangerous men, for they may act their dreams with open eyes, to make it possible.

T. E. Lawrence, *Seven Pillars of Wisdom*

PART ONE

HAVANA DREAMS

1

"They're going to kill me. Do you know this? Do you understand? If you take me back, they will kill me." Echevarria stubbed his cigarette butt into the corpse of his hamburger in the Miami airport coffee shop. "*Paredón*. You know what that means? *To the wall*. It's what they say when they come to take you out to shoot you."

"You told me," Cassidy said. He was reading the sports section of the *Miami Herald* to avoid talking to Echevarria. He didn't like him. He hadn't liked him when he picked him up in New York at The Tombs for the extradition, and he didn't like him any better after being handcuffed to him off and on for twenty-four hours. He was one of those arrogant shits who had no understanding of his effect on others. He viewed the world through the narrow crack in his own forehead and assumed that everyone saw the same things he saw, that anything he said or did was acceptable.

Echevarria had been chained to a rail in a Tombs interview room when Cassidy came in with one of the grubby, overused manila envelopes that held a prisoner's belongings from the time of his arrest. On the front of the envelope was a list of names written in different hands and later crossed out, a history without details of men processed through the system.

"Who are you?" Echevarria demanded. He had an accent, an undercurrent of Spanish.

"Detective Michael Cassidy. I'm escorting you."

Echevarria looked Cassidy over as if inspecting meat. Cassidy was just under six feet tall and weighed a hundred seventy pounds. He had broad shoulders and a narrow waist, unruly black hair, and a face of planes and angles as if the bones were trying to break through. He was restless, intense, with a motor that always ran at high speed. He suffered the examination without comment while he looked over the man he was to return to Havana on a murder charge. Fausto Echevarria was in his mid-thirties. He was tall and round-shouldered. His thick black hair was combed straight back from a high sloping forehead. He had a heavy red mouth and carried himself with his head tipped slightly back so that he looked at the world down his prominent nose. He wore an expression of mild disgust as if everyone around him smelled bad, with no understanding that the rot might be his own.

"Give me my things."

He held out his hand and Cassidy put the envelope in it. Echevarria took out a thin gold watch with an alligator band and fixed it to his handcuffed wrist. He removed a gold pen, a leather-bound notebook and matching checkbook and put them in the inside pocket of the tan linen suit he wore. Cassidy lit a cigarette while Echevarria checked his wallet.

"A hundred dollars is missing. Someone stole."

Cassidy took the wallet, counted the money in it, and checked the property list from his pocket. "You had six hundred when you came in."

"Now I have five hundred."

"Your suit's been cleaned and pressed. Your shirt's been laundered. Your shoes have been shined. You have a fresh pack of cigarettes. You probably didn't eat jailhouse food. That's where the hundred went." Jailhouse prices. An orderly or guard doing business.

"Are you calling me a liar?"

"I'm entertaining the possibility."

It did not get any better as the day went on.

Echevarria complained about the squad car that took them to Idlewild Airport, and Cassidy had to admit that it stunk of piss, puke, fear, and the disinfectant that failed to burn those smells out, but the man had killed three people in Havana and had tried to shoot the New York cops who arrested him. Did he expect to be transported in a limousine? Echevarria looked out the window as they drove east toward the Midtown Tunnel. "They say New York is the greatest city in the world. I say it's a shithole."

It was going to be a long trip.

• • •

"Extradition escort is crap duty, man," Orso had said. "They're sticking it to you again." They had been at the curved bar at Toots Shor's that evening, a warm refuge from a December night with an arctic wind off the river. The bar crowd was three deep, and most of the tables were occupied. The joint was alive with laughter, shouts to newly arrived friends, the hum of conversation, the clink of ice in glasses, boozy good cheer as 1958 drew to a close. "They give escort duty to the stumblebums, the lushes, the guys treading water till retirement. They keep giving you shit details, 'cause they want you to quit." Tony Orso was a big sleek man, over six feet tall, and more than two hundred pounds. He was dressed in a tailor-made dark wool herringbone suit, an off-white silk shirt, and a maroon Countess Mara neck tie, an outfit that must have set him back six months' salary. Cassidy never asked him where the money came from. Maybe he had a rich aunt.

"I'm not going to quit. I like being a cop."

"Yeah, I know you're not going to quit, but they don't. They think you hate being a cop, 'cause you don't do what other cops do. You don't take the money. You don't look the other way. You don't give a shit what the brass thinks. It's been a few years, but they all remember you threw Franklin out a window. Twice. No other cop's thrown another cop out the window once. Nobody wants a loose cannon in his precinct, so they run you through the different departments. They give you the assignments no else wants, the shit ones, or the ones that are too hot, might burn someone's career. The only reason they don't stack your ass and set it on fire is they think you have juice. Nobody knows where it comes from. Nobody knows who your rabbi is in the Department, but everybody's heard the rumor. Don't fuck with Cassidy. He's got juice."

"If only they knew."

Franklin was a Vice Squad lieutenant who Cassidy had thrown out of a hotel window when he caught him torturing a prostitute who had tried to quit working for him. He had thrown him out another window six months later when he discovered Franklin was blackmailing Cassidy's sister, Leah. Franklin had survived, but tossing him had solidified Cassidy's reputation in the Department as a wild man and had given rise to the rumor that he had a powerful rabbi protecting him, because no disciplinary action had been taken against him. The rumor was unfounded, but it had the same effect as having protection, and some people stepped wide around him.

Orso raised his hand, and Al, the bartender, brought two fresh martinis.

"Tony, you want to get another partner, go ahead. No way you're going up the ladder as my partner."

"Fuck you, another partner. Who do you think I am? Besides, I like all these fucked-up assignments. If it goes bad, you catch the shit. If it goes good, I get some of the glory. I'm having fun. I don't give a shit about promotion. I'll put in my twenty, take the pension, and then set about the business I was made for."

"What's that?"

"Making women happy. Speaking of which, the only good part of this escort duty is you're going to Havana. I hear they've got so much good looking cooze down there Marilyn Monroe would be the dog. What'd this Echevarria guy do?"

"Killed three guys."

"Who?

"I don't know. What's it matter? Three guys."

"Fuck him. He deserves what he gets."

• • •

Echevarria leaned forward from the backseat. "How much money do you make in a year, Detective? Four thousand dollars? Five thousand?"

Cassidy ignored the question.

"I will pay you five thousand dollars to let me out at the next corner."

The patrolman driving flicked his eyes to Cassidy.

"We're going to Idlewild, Officer. No stops."

"Ten thousand. You give the driver what you want."

"You don't have ten thousand dollars on you."

"I'll write you a check."

Cassidy laughed.

"No, no. We go to my bank. Irving Trust on Fifty-seventh. You go cash the check. Ten thousand dollars. We drive someplace. I get out. You tell them whatever you want. I overpowered you. I had friends stop the car. Ten thousand dollars."

The car stopped at a light. The driver looked at Cassidy again. Cassidy looked back at him until he dropped his eyes. The light changed, and the car went on.

• • •

"I only fly first class."

"Not on New York's dime."

When the seat belt light went out, Echevarria lit a cigarette and rang for the stewardess. "Bring me a double rum," he demanded in a way that made her clench her jaw. When she brought it with the bourbon Cassidy ordered, he tasted it and said, "This is not Cuban rum. This is Puerto Rican. You think I don't know the difference?"

"It's all we have, sir."

"I don't drink this shit. Take it away. Bring me a double gin and tonic." He thrust the glass at her. Cassidy saw that she wanted to say something, but her training checked her. She turned and stalked up the aisle.

"You've got a way with people, don't you?"

"Her job is to bring me what I want. Why should I beg?"

The arrogance faltered at the Miami airport police unit when Echevarria understood that he would spend another night in a cell, but it was only for a moment. "Why are you doing this? Where are you going to go, some sad little place with bedbugs, no air-conditioning? I'll buy you the best room at The Fontainebleau, a room you cannot afford on your cop's salary. I'll buy you dinner there too. Like you've never eaten. Wine. Twenty dollars a bottle. Have you ever had twenty-dollar wine? I'll buy it for you. There's no reason to stay here. This is stupid." He emptied his pockets reluctantly onto the receiving desk.

The cop on duty was a gangly redhead named O'Hara. He had big knuckled hands and bony wrists, and he wore black cowboy boots with his uniform. He led Echevarria to a holding cell, pushed him in, and locked the door.

"I'll see you tomorrow," Cassidy said.

"Anything special with him?" O'Hara asked.

"Feed him and water him, and stand well back. He talks an awful lot of bullshit. You listen to him for five minutes you're going to want to reach in and slap him silly."

He caught a taxi to the Fontainebleau where he had reserved a room, took a shower, and then went out to Joe's and ate stone crabs and drank a twenty-dollar bottle of Puligny-Montrachet. He went back to the hotel and lay in bed in the dark room and listened to the thump and hiss of waves on the sand eight floors below and waited for sleep to come. He had been running on empty for weeks, wired on coffee, cigarettes, and booze. If he slept, there were bad dreams of running and gunfire, hard, bright, ugly images that disappeared so quickly when he woke gasping and panicked that he could not capture one of them. He had had vivid dreams since childhood, dreams in which he was both asleep and awake. Days, weeks, or months later he would be somewhere in the city, and he would recognize that this was what he had dreamed, this street, that person; an overheard conversation as he passed two people in a doorway; that window with the three women behind it; that man with the oily smile who beckoned him from an alley mouth. The dreams were random. Sometimes they came true, sometimes they did not, but disappeared to wherever dreams go. For years he tried to find markers in them that would allow him to separate the prophetic from the run of the mill, but he could not, and then a few years back something had changed. He had walked a dark street one night, and as he walked he understood that he had dreamed these moments, dreamed the walk, the dark night, the danger that lay ahead in the shadows. The dream had predicted this, had warned him, and because of that warning he had been able to kill the man who waited in the darkness to kill him.

For a while after that, the prophetic dreams had come often, and he had been able to hold on to them after waking. Usually they predicted something mundane, an unlooked-for meeting with an old friend, the recognition of a room as he entered that he had only seen before in a dream, a conversation in a restaurant, but they had also helped him solve the murder of a young woman found dead on the ice at Wollman Memorial Rink, and to track down a serial killer. He had begun to think of the dreams as a talent, a resource, something that he could develop. Through his brother, Brian, he had found a sympathetic neurologic researcher at Cornell Medical College who had run tests and found nothing out of the ordinary, no explanations. "We don't know the capabilities of the human brain. We do know that we use only a fraction of its capacity." He had asked Cassidy to keep notes on all his dreams and especially on the ones that came true, and he had done that for a while, but then the dreams changed. They became more fragmented, more chaotic, and he woke unable to remember them.

For the last few weeks, sleep had come hard, and the dreams were harsh and splintered, and they left him with feelings of dread and impending loss, but with no understanding of what it was he was going to lose.

That night Cassidy dreamed of Dylan—Dylan, his lost love, who had not troubled his dreams for years. *He was in a tunnel, a place he had never seen before, dark and oppressive, claustrophobic. A line of figures shuffled past him. They were pale and insubstantial, the color of faded roses from head to foot. They scuffed by heads down, identical, featureless. Then one raised its head, and it was Dylan. Gunfire, and the figures began to fall until only she was left standing, eyes wide and pleading.* He awoke drenched in sweat, gasping for air.

• • •

In the morning O'Hara was still on duty. "Overtime. I'm trying to pay off a goddamn boat I bought. A friend told me a boat's just a hole in the water into which you piss money. What'd I know? I'll go get him. He offered me five grand to let him go. I might've done it if I could've figured out the story."

"He offered me ten."

"Shit. For ten I would've done it and taken my chances."

O'Hara brought Echevarria out. Echevarria's suit was rumpled. His hair was mussed, and he was unshaven. He wouldn't meet Cassidy's eyes and he avoided looking at O'Hara.

"Did you feed him?" Cassidy asked.

"Jailhouse oatmeal and jailhouse coffee. I wouldn't call it food, and he didn't eat it." He took Echevarria's personal effects from a drawer and slid them across the desk and Cassidy saw a look pass between them.

"I'll feed him. We've got time. They canceled our flight, mechanical trouble. I'm waiting to see what they can get us on."

"Uh-huh. Sure. Good luck, then." O'Hara was suddenly eager to see them go.

"You all right?"

"Yeah. Yeah. Sure. Fine. Just beat, man. Just beat. Too many hours on, not enough hours off."

Cassidy read the evasion but let it go. He snapped the cuffs on and led Echevarria down to the coffee shop. The booths were hung with tinsel. A small plastic Christmas tree crowded the cash register at the check-out desk. Their waitress wore a Santa hat with a soiled white fringe. Christmas was still a few days off, but the spirit in the Miami airport was already worn out.

Christmas—the children ripping the paper off carefully wrapped packages in their eagerness, the adults quietly satisfied giving and receiving well-considered presents, the Christmas dinner at Leah's table, the only one big enough to accommodate the entire family. The toasts full of humor and love. Cassidy would miss it this year.

He had already bought presents for his brother, Brian, his sister, Leah, their children and spouses, and for his father and stepmother and had left them in Leah's care. He loved being with his family, but Christmas was rough. He usually accepted, even prized, that he was alone, free of responsibilities to someone else, but Christmas highlighted what he did not have. When he got the assignment to extradite Echevarria, he put in for vacation. Who knows what might happen during ten days in Havana? He might get laid. He might turn a corner and fall in love.

Echevarria complained about the booth Cassidy chose, the service, and the food when it came. The coffee was swill. His hamburger was overcooked. Cassidy's eggs were disgusting.

"Fifteen thousand dollars."

"I don't need fifteen thousand dollars." Cassidy put the paper aside.

"Don't be stupid. You're a cop. You make no money. Everybody needs fifteen thousand dollars.

Cassidy shook his head.

"Okay. Twenty."

"Get up."

"Why?"

"I have to buy cigarettes."

"Twenty thousand. I have it in a Miami bank. We can go there now."

"Do me a favor, Echevarria. Shut up." Money did not tempt him. He had grown up in a household that had money. His mother inherited hers from family holdings that got their start when Boston was still a village. His father made his in the Broadway theater after a brief, lucrative career running booze during Prohibition. Neither had any reverence for the stuff. His mother spent hers wildly to show contempt for the hard, narrow, tight-fisted rules of her upbringing. His father spent his, because what the hell, there would always be more tomorrow. When his mother killed herself, Cassidy inherited more money than he thought he would ever need and his indulgences were few. He liked to buy art from the studios of the artists he knew who worked in Greenwich Village where he owned an apartment from which he could see the river. He liked to eat in good restaurants. He hoped that when he got older some perverse and expensive passion would kick in so that he could fling money around like confetti. Somebody once said that money was for throwing off the backs of trains. Maybe he could work up to that.

There were few people traveling at that time of day, and the concourse was not crowded. A boy of about ten walking with his parents noticed the handcuffs and pointed. "Look, Mom, Dad, a bad man. Look." His mother hushed him and pulled him along, but the boy kept looking back over his shoulder as they went, drawn by the mystery of evil.

Echevarria, wrapped in thought, made no comment, but a minute later he slowed and pulled on the handcuffs and Cassidy stopped. Echevarria's face was pale and his voice was tight and harsh. "Do you think I'm kidding you? *Paredón.* This is what they will do to me. This is where you take me. To the wall."

"You've been extradited to stand trial for murder."

"Trial? There will be no trial. They don't need a trial to send you to the wall."

"Maybe you shouldn't have shot those guys."

"You think this is about the men I killed?" He snorted. "They were nothing. Peasants, hired gunmen, *nada.* They have killed many themselves. They would have killed me. No, they don't kill me for them. Nobody cares about them."

"Their mothers, brothers, sisters, lovers?" Cassidy said it mildly.

"Their mothers are whores. Their sisters are whores. Their lovers are whores. Their brothers are the same as they are. The reason they are going to kill me is that I stole from a bigger thief than I am. The second biggest thief on the island. The first is, of course, President Batista. Do you know who the second is?"

"No." Cassidy tugged on the cuffs and started walking again.

Echevarria stopped talking while Cassidy bought cigarettes at a newsstand. He offered one but Echevarria waved it away impatiently and pulled him out into the concourse so he could go on. His face was pale and he was sweating from his urgency. He looked around quickly to see that they were not overheard. "General Roberto Fernández Miranda." He waited expectantly, but he saw that the name meant nothing to Cassidy. "He is President Batista's brother-in-law. He has the concession for all the slot machines in the casinos and bars. He owns the parking meters in Havana. Do you know now much he makes from the parking meters? Half a million dollars a month. From parking meters. *Coño!* Half a million a month."

"So you took some of it and killed the men who were protecting it."

"He owed me money. He refused to pay. He thought because he was a big man he did not have to pay. This is the thinking of peasants when they get power. My family came to Cuba in 1705 with a land grant from King Felipe number five. Batista and his people are jumped up *negros* from the cane fields, greedy shits without honor. They put on suits and think they are no longer monkeys."

"You're an unpleasant bastard, Echevarria. Stop talking to me." Cassidy had never met a criminal who could not rationalize what he had done. And why did men think killing was a simple solution to a complex problem?

"You won't help me."

"No."

"All right, then." He nodded as if something had been decided.

"Detective Cassidy?" A young woman in an airline uniform looked from Cassidy to Echevarria as if unsure who was the handcuffed, who was the handcuffer.

"Yes."

"We've found you a flight. It's the Tropicana private charter, but I've explained the circumstances and they've agreed to take you. We'll have to hurry. They're holding the plane for you. I've had your bag put aboard. If you'll follow me." She was blond and pretty and wore a light blue cotton uniform of a broad-shouldered, quasi-military design, and she walked fast, her heels clicking on the linoleum floor. She had a smile that went on and off like a light. Every once in a while she would throw a look over her shoulder to make sure they were still with her. The smile would light. Her eyes would find the handcuffs. The smile would snap off.

"I have to use the men's room," Echevarria said.

"There'll be one on the plane."

"No. Now. I have to now."

The young woman from the airline stopped and flashed her professional smile to cover her mild embarrassment. "If you need to use the facilities, there's time. The gate's at the end of the corridor. I'll meet you there." She smiled and went away.

Echevarria paused at the men's room door to let Cassidy go first. Cassidy put his hand on the door to enter.

Politeness suddenly from this arrogant shit? The look between Echevarria and the jailor O'Hara. Cassidy hesitated. Echevarria's hand slammed against his back and shoved him toward the door. Instead of resisting, Cassidy went with it and crashed the door, yanking Echevarria with him.

There were three of them in the men's room. One man was on the left next to the sinks under a mirror. Another was near the urinals on the opposite wall, and the third was waiting behind the door. The one by the urinals held a small automatic. The one by the sinks showed no gun, and the man near the door had been rammed back when Cassidy crashed through. The one with the gun brought the pistol up. Echevarria, surprised by Cassidy's lunge through the door, staggered as he came into the room, and Cassidy used the momentum to sling him by their handcuffed wrists into the gunman before he could pull the trigger. Echevarria's weight knocked the gunman back into the urinals. He hit his head and went down, and the gun spun away across the floor. Cassidy snatched his gun from under his arm as the man by the sinks tried to get a pistol from his pocket. It caught on the cloth, and before he could untangle it, Cassidy stepped forward in the small room, dragging Echevarria by the cuffs, and touched his gun barrel to the man's forehead.

"Don't."

The man's eyes crossed as he looked at the gun.

"Drop it." The man dropped the pistol, and it clattered on the tile floor. Cassidy shifted his aim to the man behind the door. The door had hit him in the face. He was crouched by the wall whimpering with his hand covering a smashed nose while blood ran down his chin. When he saw Cassidy point the gun, he raised his hands and stood up, and Cassidy could see that he was not more than sixteen years old. The man on the floor by the urinals moaned. Cassidy kicked his gun into one of the stalls and pulled Echevarria to his feet. The adrenaline was burning out, and he could feel shakes coming on in reaction. He ground the barrel of his pistol into the side of Echevarria's neck. "Who are they?" His voice sounded harsh.

"Cousins. They live here."

"You paid the jailer to let you make a call."

"Yes," in a defeated voice.

"You, what's your name?" Cassidy said to the man by the sinks.

"Javier."

"Javier, pick up your gun. Two fingers by the tip of the barrel. Do you understand?"

"Yes. I understand." He had a thick Cuban accent and his voice was tight with strain. He was slim and not more than five feet six inches tall. He wore a white shirt and black trousers. His black hair was oiled tight to his skull and a neat, narrow mustache was a black line on his lip. He looked at Cassidy with a mixture of fear and anger.

"Bring it to me. If you do something stupid, I'll shoot you."

Javier crouched and picked up the gun by the barrel tip and carried it to Cassidy, who put it in his jacket pocket. "Go get the other one in the stall. Same deal." The man on the floor shifted. Cassidy kicked him. "Lie still." Javier brought the second gun to Cassidy. "Does he have a gun?" Cassidy gestured toward the boy with the broken nose.

"No."

"You, turn out your pockets. Slowly." The boy obeyed. "Lift your shirt." There was no gun tucked in his waistband. "All right. The three of you into that stall. Shut the door. Stay in there for five minutes."

"You are not going to call the police?" Javier asked.

"No." If he called the Miami cops he'd be held up for at least a day.

"We had to do it. You know this?"

"Why?"

"He is family. They will kill him if you take him back."

"He killed three men."

"Men of no importance."

"They were important to somebody, and he has to answer for it."

The man on the floor must have hit his head hard, because he wobbled when he tried to stand. Javier and the boy helped him into the stall and closed the latch.

"Okay. Let's go."

He sensed the tension rise in Echevarria. This was his last chance. He was steeling himself for it. Now or never. Cassidy held his eyes and pressed the gun barrel against Echevarria's side. The courage went out of him, and he slumped. Cassidy tugged on the cuffs, and Echevarria went with him. He opened the door and stepped out into the corridor. He pulled Echevarria toward the end of the corridor, stopping to drop the two guns he had taken from the Cubans into a mailbox.

The young woman from the airlines was waiting at the gate. She flicked them with her smile and said, "Have a nice flight." The gate agent took the tickets from Cassidy and they walked out into the afternoon glare. The sun was still high in the sky, and the temperature was in the seventies, forty degrees warmer than New York the day before. They crossed the tarmac to where the plane waited in heat shimmer. Bright script on the fuselage read *TROPICANA SPECIAL*. They went up into the DC-6, and the attendants began rolling the ramp away as they went into the plane and the stewardess shut the door and then showed them to seats at the rear.

The plane was full. Most of the passengers were men, and most of them were drinking. Maybe some of the women aboard were married, but probably not to the men they were with. This was party time. They were headed for Havana, out of the loop of their normal lives. There were no rules. One of the women spotted the handcuffs. She was a tall brunette in a tight skirt that hobbled her at the knees and a tight gold shirt that strained to hold her breasts. She swayed down the aisle carrying a drink in a tall glass and tapped on the handcuff chain with a long red fingernail while she leaned in to examine Cassidy with eyes as wide as an owl's.

"Have you been a bad boy?" Her breath was warm and smelled of rum.

"No. I'm the good boy. He's the bad boy."

"What'd he do?"

"You know those tags on mattresses that say 'Do Not Remove Under Penalty of Law'? He removed one."

She blinked while it penetrated. "You're kidding me. You're a kidder, aren't you? And you're kidding me."

"Cross my heart."

"Kidder."

"What's going on here?" He gestured at the plane, the party, at the man with an orchid clenched between his teeth as he danced in the aisle.

"The Special? It's from the Tropicana Club. They send it for the high rollers. You know, to get them in the mood."

"Hey, Alice, come sit down," a man called from near the front of the plane.

"I'm coming, Georgie." She slapped Cassidy on the shoulder, said "Kidder," and stilted away up the aisle on high heels, looking like something from the original blueprint for sex, her ass swaying just a little more than it had to. She checked once over her shoulder to make sure Cassidy was getting the benefit.

I've got to get laid. Maybe that's why I can't sleep. It would be worth the experiment. Even if I didn't sleep, at least there'd be something for the effort.

The engines revved, spat smoke, the propellers flicked and then blurred into their rhythm, and the pilot came on the intercom to welcome them aboard the Tropicana Special and to announce in a western twang that "it's time for all you good folks to strap this plane to your bodies so we can take off for Havana and have some fun."

• • •

"May I bring you a drink, Detective?" The stewardess smiled and bent over enough to let Cassidy look down her dress.

"I'd like a martini, dry, on the rocks, a twist, if you have it."

"And for your, uh, um," she struggled with it. "Would he like something?"

"Please bring Mr. Echevarria a Cuban rum on the rocks. A double. Thank you."

She went to the back of the plane to fill the order. At the front of the plane a small stage was set where a few rows of seats had been removed. A man in a bolero jacket and skintight pants got up on it and sang a suggestive song about rum and a woman and a beach and the moon.

The drinks came and the stewardess went away. The singer finished his song, and three women in split skirts and bikini bras got up and did a dance that would have been banned in thirty of the forty-eight states, and a couple of the passengers got up and tried to match them until they were shouted down.

A man rose from a seat near the woman who thought Cassidy was a kidder and walked back to perch on the arm of the empty seat across the aisle. He was in his late thirties, Cassidy guessed. He was about six feet tall and had a boyish Irish face and thick hair that looked like he combed it with his fingers. He wore linen trousers and a dark blue cotton shirt open at the throat, and he had the easy open manner of someone comfortable in his skin, a man with some power and used to wielding it without second thoughts. He raised his glass in a toast and took a sip. "The lady up there says you're a cop."

Cassidy nodded and said nothing. Handcuffed prisoners drew people the way animals in the zoo did—proximity to danger, but the danger caged.

"Do you mind if I ask what he did? I kind of didn't believe the business about the mattress tag."

"He killed some people."

"How many?"

"Three."

"Uh-huh." That didn't seem to bother the man. Maybe that was one of the benefits of having power. People died, you lived. "Why'd he do it?"

"You'll have to ask him."

"Why'd you do it?"

Echevarria pulled at his drink and looked at the man with a flat stare. "Go fuck yourself."

The man laughed. "Yeah, you're right. Prurient interest about another man's misfortune. But I can't do that. It's against my professional code. See, I'm a senator, and the code says we fuck other people, never ourselves. What happens when you get to Havana?"

"There'll be some cops meeting the plane. I turn him over to them, spend the night, the next day I'm on vacation."

"A vacation in Havana's not bad duty."

"You know Havana."

"I do. I like Havana. I get down here a couple of times a year. Fact-finding missions for the good of the Commonwealth, of course. And the fact is there is nothing a man could want that Havana cannot give you." He grinned. "Where are you from, Detective?"

"New York."

"Nothing I can do for you, then. You're not a constituent. I'm sorry."

"I'll have to struggle along without you, then."

"I'll buy you drink. They're free."

"Thanks, I've got one."

"Okay. Nice talking to you. See you around." He went back up the aisle, stopping to talk to people, touching others on the shoulders, offering a sip of his drink to a pretty woman. His laughter carried to where Cassidy was sitting. A man who took life in big bites, Cassidy thought.

• • •

When the plane landed, the stewardess asked Cassidy to wait until the rest of the passengers were off. Maybe they thought someone coming off The Special in handcuffs would kill the party spirit. The young senator paused by his seat. "Where are you staying?"

"I don't know. I haven't thought about it."

"There's the Hilton. American owned, if that's important to you. To me, what's the point? You could be in the Miami Hilton, the Los Angeles Hilton. I like the Nacional. It's got a casino, of course, but if you're really looking for that kind of action, the Tropicana's the place to gamble. Besides, they flew you here. You might as well give them the custom."

"I'll give it some thought."

"You don't gamble?"

"Not for money."

"See you. Have fun." He went on, youthful and confident, worlds to conquer.

Fresh air blew in through the open door, soft and tropical, and carrying the smell of the ocean and the scent of flowers Cassidy could not name.

Two soldiers were waiting at the bottom of the ramp, a colonel for command presence and a sergeant to do any heavy lifting. They were dressed in gray military uniforms with polished leather belts crossing their chests and pistols in polished leather holsters at their waists. The colonel was a tall man in his late thirties. His uniform was severely tailored to emphasize his slimness. His cavalry boots gleamed. He had a narrow, tanned face with a pointed chin and a nose like a hawk's beak. The sergeant was a big man, thick through the chest and shoulders, heavy-legged. Coarse black hair like wire forced its way out from under his hat, and his face was flat and broad with small dark eyes set deep. Indian blood. A gray Jeep was parked near the fence, a driver behind the wheel.

The colonel smoked a thin cigar, which he waved genially at Cassidy as they started down the ramp. Cassidy felt the drag on his wrist as Echevarria held back, and heard Echevarria suck in breath. He jerked on the cuffs to move him. He wanted this over with now. He wanted to be free of Echevarria. He looked forward to being in Havana, anonymous, solo, no rules, no responsibilities. *Who knows what he might find? He might even get lucky.*

"Detective Cassidy, yes?"

"Yes." Cassidy shook the colonel's hand.

"I am Colonel Diego Fuentes. SIM."

It sounded like "seem" to Cassidy. "Seem?"

"Servicio de Inteligencia Militar. Military Intelligence. Yes?"

"You're not a cop? I was expecting cops."

"True, I am not a member of the Havana Police Department, but in our system my duties often overlap theirs. In this case, the men this *cabron* killed were soldiers, therefore the case falls under our jurisdiction." He showed Cassidy even white teeth in a smile that did not reach his eyes. Then he stepped around to face Echevarria, who waited at the base of the boarding ramp.

"Ahh, Señor Echevarria, *bienvenido.*" He punched Echevarria hard in the mouth. Echevarria cried out and stumbled back, pulling Cassidy with him. The punch split his lips, and blood flowed and he buried his face in his sleeve to staunch it. Fuentes stepped forward, fist cocked to hit him again.

Cassidy blocked him. "No."

"Please?"

"He's my prisoner. You don't hit my prisoner."

"You're in Cuba. He is in Cuba. In Cuba I do what I want."

"Uh-uh. He's my prisoner until you sign for him. Please don't hit my prisoner."

The big sergeant shifted and put a hand on his gun butt. Cassidy held Fuentes's eyes. He did not know how far the colonel would push it, or how hard he'd push back. *Why? Why for a shit like Echevarria? Because he's my prisoner.* He waited.

The muscles in Fuentes's jaw bunched and jumped. He licked his lips. He glanced at his sergeant.

Cassidy waited.

Fuentes took a deep breath.

Was it coming now?

Fuentes let the breath out and smiled and made a throwaway gesture. "Of course. Of course. You are right. We are civilized men. We must adhere to the rules. We must obey the proprieties." He smiled and waved toward the waiting Jeep. "Come. We'll go to La Cabaña and sign papers. I will relieve you of the burden of Señor Echevarria. You will stay in Havana, yes? You will see what a wonderful city we have. Anything you want. You tell me. I will arrange."

They started for the Jeep. Cassidy noticed that the sergeant fell in behind them, but there was nothing to do about that.

Fuentes prodded Echevarria with a finger like a gun. "You are a lucky man, Echevarria. You have an American to protect you. Of course we are all lucky to have America as our friend. All of Cuba. Where would we be without our big brother to watch over us, to tell us what to do, to sell us Coca-Cola? Poor little Cuba without America, eh?"

He was smiling all the time, but Cassidy could hear Fuentes's anger burn just below the surface of the smile and the cheer. He recognized anger. Anger was no secret to him. It coiled under his skin. He listened to its whisper all the time.

• • •

The fortress of La Cabaña crowned a two-hundred-foot hill on the eastern side of Havana's harbor. Centuries under a tropical sun had yellowed the stone blocks of its massive walls. Old cannon stuck out from the embrasures. It was a place of power from which men ruled until other men breached the wall and threw them out and took the power and waited for the men who would come to throw them out. The endless cycle.

It had been a prison for two hundred years. How much blood had soaked into its stones? How much more to come?

Cassidy saw Echevarria stiffen as they approached the gates. Nothing good waited for him here. All that he had fought for, connived for, killed for was going to turn to ash behind these walls.

Fuentes signed the papers at a scarred wooden desk in an office deep underground at the end of a cold stone cellblock built into the fortress walls. The two electric lights were dim yellow and did not penetrate the shadows in the corners. The air smelled of earth and damp. It was a place that would suck hope from a strong man. Cassidy countersigned and stowed the papers in his jacket pocket. He unlocked the handcuffs. Echevarria rubbed at the red circle on his wrist. He was diminished now, driven inward, hopeless. Cassidy had seen it before with prisoners when they felt the walls close around them, heard the key turn in the lock.

"Is he my prisoner now?" Fuentes asked.

"Yes."

"*Paredón!*"

The Sergeant slammed Echevarria back against the wall. Echevarria's eyes went wide. Fuentes drew his pistol, stepped forward until the barrel nearly touched him. Echevarria put his hands up as if he could ward off what was coming. Fuentes shot him twice in the face. He sagged down, boneless and broken, and left a smear of blood against the wall. His shattered head leaked a thick, dark pool onto the stones of the floor. The room stunk of cordite. Cassidy's ears rang from the pistol blasts. Echevarria's last look, a plea, a horror, would be with him for a long time. He did not like the man, but the brutal suddenness of his death shook him. There one moment, then gone.

Fuentes touched the dead man with the toe of his boot. He looked up as if mildly curious about Cassidy's reaction. The gun dangled, but it was still in his hand. Cassidy looked back at him. *Give him nothing. Show him nothing.* There was nothing to say, nothing to do. That moment at the airport when he had stopped Fuentes from hitting Echevarria had led directly to this. It was a demonstration for Cassidy's benefit that Fuentes held the power here. Did Cassidy have a greater responsibility for Echevarria's death than he should have had? Yes. Was there anything he could do about it? No. Not right now. Maybe the time would come. In the war he had seen how casually men destroyed each other without thought or compunction. Shouldn't that have scrubbed the capacity for surprise out of him? Yet it still shocked him when it happened.

"Sergeant Lopato will have someone drive you into the city. Wherever you want to go." Fuentes put the pistol on the desk and lit a cigar. He gestured toward the body on the floor. "This was justice."

"A funny kind of justice."

"He was tried in absentia and sentenced to death. Would it have been better to lock him in prison for a year, to let him think about it every day? One more day gone. One more. Closer and closer it comes. This was a kindness. I hope someone will be so kind to me if my day comes."

"I hope so too."

Fuentes drew on the cigar and let the smoke filter out of his mouth. He smiled. "Good-bye, Detective Cassidy."

Cassidy followed the broad back of Sergeant Lopato along the corridor. Dim light came from caged bulbs widely spaced in the vaulted ceiling. The stones seemed to press in and down, but the tropical heat did not penetrate. The doors to the cells were thick wood, banded with black iron. Small, barred observation windows pierced them. Hands clenched some of the bars, white fingers on the black bars, but the interiors of the cells were dark and he could not see the faces of the prisoners.

A door clashed open somewhere ahead of them, and a file of prisoners came into the corridor behind a warder who swung a three-foot billy club from a leather loop on his wrist. The prisoners shuffled, heads down, the walk of the defeated, resigned to their lot, beyond hope. Their sandals scuffed on the worn stone floor. They wore light cotton pants and cotton shirts once red, now faded to rose from years of use. They shuffled along without raising their heads, and suddenly he was haunted by the dream he had had the night he had spent in Miami, the dim tunnel, the shuffling, rose-colored, featureless figures.

The last one in line was slighter than the others. As they passed, Cassidy noticed that the prisoner's close-cropped hair was copper red. She raised her face and looked at him without recognition, her face as he had known it, as it had lived in his dreams and memory, but older now, drawn and tired, scared.

Dylan McCue, spy, lost love, dead these past four years. Or so he had thought.

• • •

Cassidy followed Sergeant Lopato up narrow stone stairs, along another dank stone corridor, and up broad stone stairs, worn down by centuries of shuffling prisoners, and into the sunlight. He saw none of it. He saw only Dylan's face, worn, blank-eyed, beautiful. *Was it Dylan? How could that be possible? Why was she here? How did she get here? Was it Dylan? Was it? Yes, it was.*

The sunlight and heat after the dim coolness of the cell block woke him to where he was. He stopped and looked around. The wide parade ground of the fortress; worn paving stones with grass growing in the cracks; the massive wall rising twenty feet to the broad parapets; prisoners cutting grass, herded in groups by warders carrying batons, overseen by men on the walls cradling rifles. The prisoners wore loose shirts and pants made of unbleached cotton the color of dust. Why had she been wearing a red shirt? Segregation in prison was not usually a good thing. It often meant you were a danger to people, or people were a danger to you. Was that it? What the hell was she doing here?

Lopato stopped when he stopped and watched him without expression.

"Do you speak English?"

No change of expression. He looked like a man who could not be provoked by the blow of an axe.

"*Habla Ing—*" He was stopped by Lopato's abrupt nod. "The prisoners we saw with the red shirts. Why the red shirts?"

Lopato looked at him with obsidian eyes, calculating whether the question was worth an answer. "Politicals. *Communistas.* Very bad ones." His voice was surprisingly high and reedy coming from that massive head. "*Condenados.*"

Condemned.

Cassidy spoke Spanish, but now it seemed important to keep that information to himself. There had been a Spanish housekeeper in the brownstone on Sixty-sixth Street for five years who was paid extra to speak to the children only in her language, and he had spent two summers working on a ranch in Mexico. His father felt he needed to learn the discipline of hard, physical labor.

"What will happen to them?"

"*Paredón!*" He smiled and pointed a finger like a gun and pulled the trigger. "*Paredón.*"

"When?"

"*Yo que se.*" Lopato shrugged as if it was of no importance. "Tomorrow. The next day. Next week. *¿Quien sabe*?" Who knows? What did it matter? Condemned was condemned.

2

The car was a four-year-old Buick painted gray, the color of most SIM cars. The driver was a young corporal with severely cropped hair and a rigid posture. He drove with his hands at ten and two and had a delicate touch on the brake and accelerator that produced a smooth ride. Cassidy sat wedged in a corner of the backseat, ignorant of the scene that passed the windows, deeply tangled in the last time he had seen Dylan nearly five years ago. They had been on a Russian ship steaming out of New York Harbor. Cassidy's father, Tom, caught up in the McCarthy witch hunts, was being deported, returned to Russia, a country he had fled as a teenager. Cassidy had boarded the ship at its New York pier to try to get his father off before the ship sailed. He had failed. Dylan, Cassidy's lover, a KGB agent, held them with a gun until her superior, a man named Apfel, came into the cabin to decide their fate. Then she had changed her mind. She killed Apfel. Her story would be that Cassidy and his father overpowered them and shot Apfel. To make it work, Cassidy had hit her, hit her hard, split her mouth, hit her again and knocked her down, and then he and his father had jumped into the harbor and had been fished from the water by a pilot launch, and the ship, with Dylan on it, had steamed away. For years he had feared she was dead, that the story had not held up, that she had paid the price the KGB extracted for failure or betrayal. Now the Cubans were going to do what the Russians had failed to do.

Suddenly the car was as confining as a cage.

Cassidy told the driver to stop. He would walk the rest of the way to the Hotel Nacional, and the man could leave his suitcase at the desk. The driver protested. He had been ordered by Sergeant Lopato to take Cassidy to the hotel. Nothing had been said about dropping him in town. Lopato was not a man to disobey. It would be better if he delivered Cassidy where he had been told to deliver him.

When the Jeep stopped at a red light, Cassidy got out and walked away, leaving the driver no choice.

He walked along Calle 23, La Rampa, through Vedado, the high-rent district west of Old Havana. The shop windows displayed clothes and jewelry you could buy in New York made, more attractive by the absence of tax for visitors. The street was crowded, and the language he heard most was not Spanish, but English. Havana was an occupied city, occupied by American tourists dressed in colors never found in nature. The cafés and bars were filled with afternoon drinkers having loud fun. It was an expanded version of the party on the flight over. Here none of the normal rules applied, and when you went home, anything that might smudge your conscience was forgotten, wiped clean by the ninety-mile flight across the water.

Two young women in bright cotton dresses sat together at a café table at the edge of the sidewalk, nursing tall scarlet drinks with fruit in them. Cornflower hair and blue eyes, teachers from the Midwest, or maybe that was just his fantasy. They looked at Cassidy and smiled an invitation. Was he going to be part of their adventure? He smiled back and shook his head. They shrugged, oh, well, and looked to see who might be coming next.

Havana. A man could have a good time down here, as long as he didn't think too much about the uniformed men with submachine guns on the corners.

No matter what the local newspapers and radio said about successful military operations in the Sierra Maestra, no matter how many speeches Batista gave about the imminent defeat of the "small band of Communists" in the hills, the uniformed men with submachine guns were not there to protect the merchandise in the windows along La Rampa, not there to politely explain to the furniture maker from Des Moines how to get to the Tropicana so he could unburden himself of his money at the roulette wheel, not there to suggest to the boys from Delta Kappa Epsilon where they might find the finest whores, nor to guide the advertising executives from New York to the club where women performed athletically with a large man and a small donkey. They were there because of Fidel Castro and his rebellion. Castro's death had been announced by Batista, but he had been resurrected by Herbert Matthews of the *New York Times*, who found him very much alive in the mountains and took photographs to prove it. Very embarrassing for Batista. So, more soldiers on the streets, more late-night raids, fists pounding on doors, frightened men and women bundled into cars and taken to La Cabaña to discuss what they knew about the misguided rebels who were threatening everyone's prosperity. More bodies leaking blood in the early-morning gutters, more corpses bumping with the tide against the seawall in the harbor.

The big lobby of the Nacional was hushed and cool, the light golden and comforting under the massive beams of the ceiling. The thick walls shut out the city and the heat. The desk clerk was deferent and eager. Cassidy's bag had arrived. It had been taken to a room overlooking the sea. Would that be all right? Perhaps he preferred the other side. Some were disturbed by the sound of the waves on the Malecón.

No, he preferred the ocean side.

Wonderful, anything he wanted. Any friend of Colonel Fuentes. But behind the smile and the eagerness was wariness. Who are you, friend of Colonel Fuentes? How much trouble do you bring? It was an indication of the colonel's reputation and power.

The elevator was already full when Cassidy entered. American tourists in bright resort clothes, three elegant silver-haired women conversing in Spanish, and two men who got off on Cassidy's floor, men who sparked Cassidy's cop radar. They both wore cheap tropical-weight suits, rayon shirts, and wide, hand-painted ties. They had the hard-eyed, lumpy faces of men who had been hit more than once and would probably get hit again. They weren't tourists. Cassidy had seen men like this in holding tanks or waiting for the desk sergeant to fill out the booking slips. What were they doing here? He knew that one of the Hotel Nacional's owners was the gangster Meyer Lansky. No surprise that some of his thugs would have rooms here. The hell with it. It was none of his business. He wasn't on the job here. They stopped at a door down the corridor from his.

Cassidy's bag was in his room. There was a bucket of ice and a bottle of Bacardi rum and a bottle of Johnny Walker Black Label on a tray near the closet, anything for a friend of Colonel Fuentes. He poured rum over ice and stood looking out the open window. The air was warm and soft and smelled of tropical flowers, burning charcoal, salt, and diesel. The ocean crashed white on the breakwater of the Malecón. There was something familiar about the broad boulevard, the massive blocks of stone, and the spray that rose above them, something he should remember, but he could not get ahold of it.

The sun was setting, and the western sky was a riot of orange and purple. He could see over the city and harbor to La Cabaña on the hill. The last rays of the sun turned the stone walls red.

Red. Condemned.

When? What had Lopato said? Tomorrow, the next day, who knows.

No. That could not happen. He would have to think of something very smart to get her out of there, but if he could not think of something smart, he would do something anyway, wouldn't he? What had he said to the Senator on the plane when he asked if Cassidy gambled? Not for money.

He drank the rum and stood by the window and thought about the prison, about entrances and exits, about how far the cell block was belowground, how thick the doors were, which cell she had entered. He tried to remember how many guards and warders he had seen and whether the warders had been armed with more than wooden batons. How would he get in? How would they get out? Evening turned to night. The rum went down in the bottle. Maybe a change of position would spark something. Maybe if he lay down on the bed.

Something woke him. A thump. A bang. Something. He lay in the darkness and listened. Was that a scream from somewhere outside? He got up and went to the window. Cries rose from below. He opened the window wider and looked down. People milled outside the hotel. Smoke curled from one wing. A siren wailed in the distance and was joined by another and then another. He checked his watch. It was only nine o'clock.

He opened the door and went out into the corridor. Guests from other rooms were in the hall talking to each other in tense, bewildered tones. He heard the word "bomb" in Spanish and in English, and Castro, and rebels. A door opened along the corridor and the two men from the elevator came out and went down the hall to find out what was going on. They had pulled their door mostly closed when they left. Cassidy nudged it open with his toe and looked in. A movie camera sat on a table near the far wall. It was pointed toward a rectangle of glass in the wall. Cassidy recognized it from his time in Vice, a camera, a one-way mirror, and people on the other side unaware that they were being filmed. So who was it and who wanted the leverage the film would give?

Cassidy crossed and looked through the one-way. In the next room, the young senator from the plane was on the bed straining through improbable gymnastics with two young women, one the color of dark honey, and the other of chocolate. They all seemed to be having a good time. As

Cassidy watched, one of the women glanced at the one-way and then shifted to be sure the senator's face was clearly visible.

"What the fuck are you doing in here?"

The two men from the room were back. They looked angry and dangerous. One had a knife or razor scar that ran from his ear to his chin. The other had the thickened eyebrows of an ex-pug. "Who the fuck are you?" Scar tissue asked.

"Nobody. Just passing by. Saw the camera and thought, cool, guys are in the movie business. I always thought it would be cool to be in the movie business." He used the talk to close the distance on the two men. He figured the pug would be the more dangerous of the two. He'd know how to hit, and he'd know how to avoid getting hit.

"The movie business? What are you, a wise guy? What, you walk into someone's room, no one asked you?"

"Sorry."

"Fucking right you're going to be sorry."

Cassidy swept up a ceramic table lamp and smashed it against the side of the pug's head and then backhanded the wreckage of the lamp across the scar's face. When his hands went up to defend himself, Cassidy kicked him in the balls, and then turned to see how the pug was doing. He was on his knees on the floor, dazed and bleeding from the ear. Cassidy kicked him in the head, and he fell over, unconscious. He turned back to the man with the scar. He was bent over, holding himself and sucking for air that would not come. Cassidy punched his head with the remains of the lamp, and the man went down hard. It took a minute to tie their hands with lamp cords, and then Cassidy took the reel of film out of the camera and left the room.

The people in the corridor were at the far end where a window looked down on whatever was happening below. Cassidy went to the door next to the room with the movie camera and knocked. There was no answer. He slapped the door hard a couple of times with the palm of his hand.

"Go away." Muffled by the door.

"Senator, you've got to get out of there."

"We don't want any." Muffled giggles.

Cassidy banged again. "Senator, it's Michael Cassidy. The cop from the plane. You've got a problem."

The door opened. The Senator wore a towel and had a drink in his hand. "I'm very busy, Mike. I'm doing a little fact-finding in here."

"Uh-huh, well you're fucked and you're fucked." He held up the reel of film. The senator seemed to understand what it meant. His face turned serious. "I'm in room five-oh-six across the hall," Cassidy said. "I'll buy you a drink." The senator nodded and went back inside the room.

Ten minutes later he knocked on Cassidy's door.

"Do you know who owns this hotel?" Cassidy poured some scotch into a glass, added ice, and passed it to the senator, whose hair was wet from the shower.

"No."

"A couple of people, fronts, but mostly Meyer Lansky. Do you know who that is?"

"Sure. He's a gangster."

"Yeah, well, he's *the* gangster. Some people call him the Mob's accountant. Some say he's the brains behind all the illegal gambling in the States. He's got Batista in his pocket and Batista's given him license to run gambling in Cuba. He's one of those guys who thinks long-term. The film, the girls, you, that's long-term thinking. It's always good to have some weight with a U.S. Senator. Maybe assigning you a room with a one-way mirror wasn't coincidence. Where'd you find the girls?"

"They found me in the bar." The senator grinned and shrugged at his own gullibility. His eyes were wary, but he didn't seem badly shaken by anything that had happened. Maybe he was one of those people who was used to people cleaning up after him. Maybe he was one of those men who liked to walk to the edge of the cliff just to see how high the fall might be. "What about you? Are you thinking about long-term benefits?"

Cassidy tossed the reel of film to the senator. "You should burn this, unless you collect them, reminiscences for your old age."

The senator bounced the reel in his hand as if weighing it. "You think I'm an idiot, don't you?"

"I haven't thought about you at all. I saw what they were doing. I didn't like it, so I stopped it."

"Okay. Thanks." The senator waited to see what came next.

"You're welcome." Cassidy headed for the door.

"Where are you going?"

"Downstairs."

• • •

The lobby was full of people, some in bathrobes, some in party clothes. The lights of ambulances and fire engines and police cars flicked through the glass of the doors and windows and painted the walls in streaks of red and blue.

Outside, the fire trucks and ambulances and police cars were parked at angles. They had come fast, and the men in them had gotten out fast, but after that they had discovered there wasn't much to do. An explosion had blackened the façade of the casino wing, and the glass had blown into some of the ground-floor windows, but that was the extent of the damage. Flashbulbs flared. Cops and uniformed SIM officers stood talking in clumps. A group of firemen put more energy than necessary into extinguishing flames in a grouping of small ornamental palms.

A cop grabbed Cassidy's arm and pushed him back toward the other tourists. Cassidy gestured toward the group of uniformed officers bunched near the casino entrance. "*Estoy con el Coronel Fuentes.*" The cop stepped back and touched the brim of his hat and nodded.

Fuentes seemed unsurprised to see him.

"What happened?" Cassidy asked.

"The bomb went off before she could get it inside." He nodded toward where Sergeant Lopato crouched by a young woman who lay on the sidewalk. Light from the hotel windows fell on her. She wore a yellow party dress. The dress was dark with blood. Her left side was heavily bandaged. Blood had flowed from under her and pooled at the raised sill of the entrance. One foot still wore a green high-heeled shoe. She moaned, and Lopato leaned close and said something to her. She moved her head from side to side, either in refusal or in pain.

"It blew her left arm off," Fuentes said. "Clearly she meant to carry it into the casino. Maximum damage, hey? Dead tourists. Innocent Americans killed. The outrage. The terror. Now the tourists don't come. The economy suffers. The new order rises. The old order falls. A good plan when you're sitting with your Communist friends in a house by the beach drinking rum and making revolution. Who would look twice at a pretty girl in a pretty dress carrying her purse into the casino? No one. We want pretty girls in the casino. And what is she thinking as she comes here, hey? She will walk in and leave the purse under a table, maybe the roulette table, play a few spins, and then walk out. Maybe she plans to stop on the Malecón to watch, and then home to her friends, full of excitement. The description of the explosion, the noise, the fire, the screams of the capitalist oppressors. And she is the hero. A good plan. Only one problem. A bad timer, or a bad fuse. The stupidity of amateurs."

A doctor had been standing nearby trying to get Fuentes's attention. Fuentes ignored him. Finally the doctor could not wait any longer. "*Coronel* . . ." He lifted his black bag to show Fuentes.

"No. No drugs. Not until she speaks to my sergeant. Give her drugs, she goes to sleep. She wakes up in the hospital, she has courage she does not have now." He said it in English for Cassidy's benefit.

"She's going to die if you don't let me attend her."

"She came here to kill. If she dies, she dies. So what?"

The girl cried out, a high wail that trailed to a whimper. It sounded like a plea.

"If she lives," Cassidy said, "you can question her again and again. If she dies, you get nothing."

"Your professional opinion, Detective?"

"Yes."

"Thank you."

Lopato stood when Fuentes approached him. The two men talked together in low voices. Then Lopato squatted by the girl again and asked her a question. She did not respond. Lopato put his hand on the blood soaked bandage that covered her ruined shoulder and squeezed.

The girl screamed.

Some of the firemen walked away quickly.

Lopato leaned down and asked her something again. When she did not answer, he clamped her shoulder. She screamed again. Her feet drummed on the terrace stones, and she died.

Fuentes looked over at Cassidy and shrugged.

• • •

He did not think he would sleep. And then he woke and somewhere in the night an idea had come. He examined it in daylight. It seemed half-baked, but it was all he had, so he went to look for the senator.

Cassidy found him eating breakfast in the dining room. The senator looked freshly showered, rested, and serene, as if nothing that had happened the night before had touched him. He indicated the chair opposite him at his table. "Sit down. Have some breakfast. I recommend the papaya, and the coffee is wonderful. I don't know why you can't get a decent cup of coffee in the States."

A waiter came and poured coffee for Cassidy, took his order, and went away.

"I guess you heard what all the excitement was about." The senator mopped egg yolk with a piece of toast. "A rebel bomber blew herself up, one of Castro's people, they say."

"Yes. I saw her."

"I hear she was pretty."

"Not when I saw her."

"They can't win. Batista's got a big army, well equipped. We've been supplying them and training them for years. I don't think a bunch of rag-tags are going to beat them."

"Maybe."

"Maybe?"

"She must have known she could die doing it. She must have known the bomb could go off while she was still there."

"And?"

"Do you think there are any men in Batista's army who would blow themselves up for him?"

The senator pushed his plate away. "That's an interesting thought. Dedication over equipment. Commitment beats heavy weapons."

"The American Revolution."

"Yeah, yeah. I get it. It doesn't always work. Mostly God is on the side of big battalions. That's the gospel up in Washington. Still, an interesting thought."

The waiter brought Cassidy's food, scrambled eggs, a piece of papaya, a fried plantain.

"I apologize for last night. I insulted you. You did me a service and I asked what you wanted in return. It comes, I suppose, of working in a town where nobody offers anything for free. I'll scratch your back if you'll scratch mine. You begin to think everyone acts that way. Sorry."

"Forget it. And at the risk of disillusioning you, I need your help."

"Come on." He looked a little angry.

"The world's full of disappointments."

"Yeah, yeah. What do you need?" He was not happy.

"Are you really down here to do some fact-finding?"

"That's what it says on my schedule and on my receipts."

"Are you busy today?"

"Maybe a cigar factory in the afternoon. We've still got a couple of tobacco growers down near the Connecticut border. Some of them sell wrappers to the Cuban cigar makers. Why?"

"Do you know La Cabaña?"

"The fortress across the harbor next to El Morro."

"It's a prison. I need to get in there."

"Sure. Why?"

"I have to get someone out."

That didn't seem to disturb him, but it made him pause. "Who?"

"A woman."

"Uh-huh. What's she in for?" The interest of a born conspirator began to show.

"I don't know. Politics. But whatever it is, they're going to kill her."

"So what's happening here? Are you following your dick or your brain?" This from a man who had done both.

"Both."

"You know her."

"Yes."

"Ahh, like that, huh?" A man who liked women and understood what that could do to you.

"Yes."

"Why do you need me? You're a cop. They'll let you in, won't they?"

"If I go in with you, they'll be looking at you. No one will pay attention to me."

"Once you're in, what do you do?"

"I don't know."

"This is a hell of a plan."

"I'm not strong on plans. I'm more likely to bang around and see what happens."

"Uh-huh, just grab and hold on tight." It seemed to intrigue him. Maybe being a senator wasn't exciting enough.

Cassidy said nothing. The idea sounded ridiculous to him. What did it sound like to the senator?

"So I go to the authorities and tell them about my abiding interest in prison administration, or history, or something. I form a group. We go in. You do what you do, and then we get caught. That's not really going to be a help to my political career."

"No."

"Last night was last night. That's over. I owe you, but this? Why should I do it?"

"No reason at all."

"I suppose it has to happen fast."

"She's on short time."

Cassidy lit a cigarette and smoked while the senator thought about it.

"A goddamn stupid thing to be doing."

"Yes."

"We could try for this afternoon. I'll get some people together. I'll have to make some calls, find out who can give us permission."

"Thank you, Senator."

He grinned. "If we get caught, my father's going to kill me."

Cassidy went shopping on La Rampa. He bought a cheap briefcase and stored his purchases in it and went back to the hotel and lay on the bed and wondered if he would be alive at the end of the day. It was a thought that had come often in the war. If you examined it from all sides it would paralyze you. Better to stuff it back in the box and go on. What else was there to do?

They left the cars in the shade of the high wall inside the gate and followed their guide, a slim, clerkish lieutenant with a wisp of a mustache and an impeccable khaki uniform, across the heat of the parade ground, the cut stones smooth and warm underfoot. The office of the Commandant was cool. The ceilings were high, the windows deeply recessed in the thick walls that displayed old photographs in frames of stern officers in elaborate uniforms, swords at their sides, artillery squads firing small field guns, soldiers on parade shouldering rifles from fifty years ago. The Commandant, General Castillo, was a happy round man, with a round head like a soccer ball painted with oiled black hair parted in the middle as if with a razor, a round belly, round wire-rimmed glasses. He was delighted by an excuse to show off his command. He greeted them with small cups of strong dark coffee and thimbles of brandy served by mess men in white uniforms, and gathered them around a large map of the fortress so he could explain its construction and history. Jack and his friend George, a senator from Florida, three aides, serious young men in seersucker suits with close-cropped hair and horn-rimmed glasses, all poured from the same mold. And two secretaries. Claire with Jack, tall, athletic, blond, with the high cheekbones of a model and long red fingernails that had never seen a typewriter. Alice with George, the pneumatic brunette from the plane from Miami, who swatted Cassidy on the shoulder in the lobby of the Nacional while they waited for the cars and said, "Ooh, I remember you. The kidder from the plane. What happened to the guy?"

"I ate him."

She laughed and swatted him again and leaned a heavy breast against his arm for a moment. Perfume, musk, and body heat.

General Castillo carried a riding crop and used it to proudly point out the interesting features of his fortress. His English was accented, clear and colloquial. "Started in 1763 and finished eleven years later under the reign of King Carlos III. The fort occupies nearly twenty-five acres and it could have housed six thousand men in time of war. However, the fort was never involved in a battle. Do you know why? Strength. It was clearly such a powerful fortress that no one ever had the courage to test it. To guarantee peace, you must have great strength. It is weakness that invites attack. There is a lesson here that America knows well. It is America's strength that keeps the Communists quiet. Without that, they would be on our beaches and at our throats." He slapped the map with the riding crop. "Now, we are here. Here are the barracks. Here are the stables, though we do not keep horses anymore. Here is the magazine where we still keep explosives and ammunition." He turned to his audience and threw his arms wide. "Welcome to Fortaleza de San Carlos de la Cabaña. Now, let us go out, and we will walk, and you will ask me questions."

Sun-warmed stone. Well-clipped lawn around a sundial. Young soldiers, their uniform shirts off, suspenders over bare torsos, playing soccer on a strip of grass near freshly painted barracks. Squads doing close-ordered drills under the bark and lash of sergeants. Flower borders along the paths. No sign of prison, of condemned prisoners in rose-colored shirts. General Castillo was not going to spoil his visitors' day by showing them that. He led them west, away from the area Cassidy had seen the day before when he had delivered Echevarria to the mercy of Colonel Fuentes. The sun was hot on his back, and his hand sweated on the plastic handle of the briefcase.

He followed the tour for a look in the magazine to see the stacks of brass howitzer shells, crates of hand grenades, old wooden shelves packed with new cardboard boxes of small arms rounds. "Please, Señorita, it is best not to smoke in here. Boom!" A few minutes in the armory to admire the water-cooled .50 caliber machine guns on their tripods, the racks of M-1 rifles and Thompson submachine guns left over from World War II and supplied by the government across the straits for little more than their cost, an act of friendship. A trip to the battlements to inspect the black iron cannons that pointed out through the embrasures and had waited for a hundred years to take on any brig or frigate that might sail in to test the harbor's defenses. At the next corner, Cassidy hung back until the others disappeared, and then walked away.

He went back to where they had left the cars and stopped there for a moment to try to reconstruct where Fuentes's Jeep had taken them the day before. That road, or the one that went to the right? Why hadn't he paid more attention to where they had gone the day before? All right, that way, if not, then think again.

He walked quickly, not so fast that someone would remark on his pace, but with purpose, a man with a briefcase and a place he had to be, perhaps a bit late, or maybe he just wanted to be on time. Nothing remarkable in that. No reason to pay attention.

Two lieutenants in SIM uniforms stood talking and smoking outside an office door. They watched him cross the plaza. One said something and pointed toward Cassidy. Would they call him over and ask him what his business was? It's the prerogative of power to stop someone and demand an accounting. What's the point of having the power if you don't demonstrate it? The other one said something, flicked his cigarette away, and turned back into the building. The first one watched him for a while. Was he worth the trouble? No. He followed his friend inside and Cassidy walked on.

The road slanted down between gray walls. At the bottom three narrow roads, little more than alleys, branched from a small square. Which one? He had some vague memory that the Jeep had followed the one on the left. A hundred yards along he discovered he was wrong. The road made an abrupt right angle that no Jeep could have navigated. He went back and tried the one on the right.

The walls rose high above him, and the stone roadbed was in deep shadow. He was a hundred yards along when he heard gunfire. He stopped to listen. It had not been the individual shots of men on a firing range, but a ragged volley of half a dozen rifles. Moments later he heard three spaced shots. Snap. Snap. Snap. Coups de grâce. First the firing squad, and then three pistol shots to make sure. His heart jumped.

The narrow street widened out into a plaza. On the left he recognized a building, a long two-story block of cut stone with deep-set barred windows and a red tile roof. The wooden double doors were banded with black iron. The cellblocks were in its basement. Gunfire rattled from somewhere past the end of the building. It was followed by two spaced single shots.

Four civilian workmen in cotton jumpsuits came around the corner. They carried a ladder, paint buckets, and long-handled brushes, and they walked fast with their heads down. They knew Cassidy was there, but they refused to look at him, and they hurried into the narrow road, eager to get away from whatever was happening past the end of the plaza.

Cassidy touched his gun at the back of his belt under his jacket. What the hell was he going to do with it? Six shots against a firing squad with rifles. If it came to that he might do better to shoot himself.

Beyond the building the wide pavement ran through a low wall to broad steps. The steps descended into a wide, dry moat that was backed by the exterior walls of the fortress that rose thirty feet from its floor. This was part of the old defense architecture. If you breached the outer wall you were faced with the deep, wide moat. If you made it up from the moat you faced the thick walls of the cellblock. If you made it past its defenders you were channeled into the narrow high-walled street where no more than five or six men could walk abreast. If you made it down the street, maybe you deserved to have the fortress.

Voices came from the moat, but Cassidy could not make out what they said, only that some of it had the weight of command. He moved to where he could see. Uniformed soldiers carried the bodies of two men in rose-colored shirts from the wall where they had been shot to a truck. The tailgate was down. They heaved the bodies like sacks up into the truck bed to lie with the three who were already there. The soldiers of the firing squad leaned on their rifles and smoked cigarettes and talked. Colonel Fuentes and Sergeant Lopato stood together in the shade of the wall. The facing stones of the wall were bullet shattered and pocked from years of executions. New blood darkly oiled the pavers at the foot of the wall. One of the soldiers came back from the truck and sluiced a bucket of sand onto the blood pool, and flies rose in a cloud.

Fuentes handed Lopato a piece of paper, and Lopato crossed the moat and disappeared from view. The colonel took a leather case from his pocket and selected a thin cigar. He rolled it in his fingers, bit off the end, lit it, and blew a plume of smoke into the still, warm air, a man taking a break from a tedious job. He started to turn, and Cassidy stepped back. Fuentes was one of those dangerous men with antennae others did not have. He heard what he should not hear, sensed the unseen threat in a vague shift in the air.

Cassidy waited until he heard voices and then moved to where he could see. Below him Lopato and a guard escort led three men out into the sun. They were all dressed in the faded red shirts of the condemned, and two of them appeared to have already passed out of the world. They stood slumped, heads down, slack and dull, as if uninvolved in what was happening. The third man was slim and straight and charged with energy. He shook off the hands of the soldiers who escorted them and marched to the wall. He inspected it for a minute as if reading the history of men who had died here in the scars and gouges. Then he turned and scuffed the ground with the side of one shoe to clear it of pebbles and broken stone so that he had a solid, level place to stand. He waved as if to say, come on, come on. What are you waiting for? Here I am. The soldiers pushed the other two forward. They went as long as there was a hand on them and stopped when the hand came off. They turned when their escorts pulled them around by their shoulders. They did not raise their heads, and they paid no attention when the man in the middle spoke to them, offered them comfort and courage. At Fuentes's command, the firing squad shouldered their rifles and aimed. The brave one raised a fist and shouted *"Viva la revolución!"* The volley cut him off, and the three men were driven back against the wall. They crumpled onto each other and lay entangled and unmoving. The firing squad grounded their rifles. Colonel Fuentes, still smoking his cigar, took his pistol from its polished holster, walked to the bodies, and shot each one in the head. Sergeant Lopato called a command, and men stepped forward to carry the bodies to the truck.

These were the men from the dream of Dylan surrounded by featureless rose-colored figures falling at the sound of gunfire.

There was a corporal on duty at a counter just inside the big entry door. He looked up when Cassidy came in, but before he could speak, Cassidy flashed his badge and held up the briefcase and said, "*Documentos importantes para Coronel Fuentes,*" and rushed on by as if the fate of the nation depended on rapid delivery of those papers. He braced for the command to stop, but it did not come. He went down the worn stairs to the coolness of the lower level and stopped by the wooden door that led into the cellblock. He put his head against the wood but heard nothing but the thump of his own heart and the pulse of blood in his ears. He pushed the big iron handle down and eased the door open. There was no one on the other side.

He opened the door wide and stepped through.

"*Oyé.*" A guard he had not seen rose from a small desk in an alcove next to the door. "*¿Quién es usted? ¿Qué quieres?*"

"Estoy buscando Coronel Fuentes." But Cassidy could see that the man did not really believe that he was looking for Colonel Fuentes. The guard put his hand on his gun. Cassidy stepped in and slammed the briefcase against the man's head. He bounced against the alcove wall and stumbled forward, and Cassidy hit him twice in the face and once in the throat with his fist. The guard sprawled across the desk, gagging for air. Cassidy jerked the big .45 automatic out of the man's holster and hit him hard on the side of the head, and he slid to the floor. Cassidy dragged him around and crammed him into the kneehole of the desk, and then stood and listened for sounds of alarm. He heard nothing.

Down the block eight cell doors stood open. Eight empty cells, eight dead men. He tried to remember which door led to Dylan's cell. Where had he been when the prisoners came in the day before? She passed him without seeing him when he was about here. And then he had turned and watched as the prisoners took up positions, in front of their cell doors. Which was hers? *Think. Which one? That one or that one.* The twelfth, thirteenth, or fourteenth from the end. Somewhere in there. There was no movement behind the small windows in the cell doors, no hands grasping the bars, nothing that would draw the attention of Lopato and his men. Maybe they'll go by me. Maybe they'll forget.

A door banged open at the end of the cellblock and light flooded in and Sergeant Lopato and two soldiers entered. They stopped just inside the door, blind in the dimness of the cellblock after the sunlight. Cassidy stepped into the guard's alcove and thumbed the safety off the .45. He should have checked to see if there was a round in the chamber. Too late now. The sound of the slide would draw them. Lopato opened the next three cell doors. Two men stepped out without urging, but the soldiers had to go in and get the third. They pulled him out of the cell. He made no protest, did not struggle, but his legs did not work, and they had to drag him through the sunlit doorway while Lopato herded the other two.

When the door closed, Cassidy searched the desk in the guard alcove and found a ring of keys in the top drawer. How much time did he have before Lopato was back? They take the men outside. They put them against the wall. The squad is brought into place. Fire. Maybe two minutes after the gunshots, six or seven minutes in all. He went down to the three cells he thought might be hers and called out, "Dylan. Dylan, where are you? Dylan." Fingers gripped the bars of the cell where he stood, but they were a man's hands. "*¿La mujer, adonde esta?*"

"Allí, en ese lado." A gesture with his head.

Cassidy stepped to the next cell. "Dylan. Dylan, are you in there?" No answer. He ran through the keys with clumsy fingers until he found the right one and opened the door. A dim caged bulb in the ceiling showed him the cell, eight feet by twelve feet, the pallet on the floor, the toilet bucket, and Dylan standing with her back against the wall, braced, wide eyed, hands curled like claws.

"It is you." Her voice sounded rusty. "When I saw you in the corridor yesterday, was it yesterday? I thought I was hallucinating. I thought I was finally going mad. But it was you."

"Yes."

"How? Why? It can't be." She stepped forward and touched him to make sure he was real.

"I'll tell you afterward. We don't have time." He opened the briefcase and took out the clothes he had bought that morning on La Rampa, a dress, underwear, the clothes of a tourist, a silk scarf to cover her distinctive hair, and rubber-soled shoes in case they had to run. "Put these on."

She looked at him for a moment as if trying to grasp what he had said, and then pulled off the rose-colored shirt and cotton pants and began to dress.

God, she was thin, and there were bruises on her arms and back where someone had beaten her.

He stepped to the door in time to hear the ragged volley of the firing squad. A couple of minutes until Lopato came in for the next group. "Hurry."

She came out of the cell tying the scarf over her hair and took the keys out of the lock and stepped to the next cell and began to search for the key that would unlock it. "What are you doing? We have to go."

"I can't leave them in here."

"Dylan, we have to go now. They'll be in here in a minute."

"I can't." She had the door open and was working on the next. She got lucky and opened it with the second key. Now there were two men with rose shirts in the corridor, and she handed each of them some of the keys and told them to get to work. Cassidy took three keys and moved up the line looking for the doors they fit. Soon there were twenty men in the corridor, and their voices rose as they talked about what to do. One of them moved to the door to the killing ground and slid a bolt across to lock it.

"They're not going to make it."

"They'll try, and if they don't, well, it's better than sitting in a cell waiting for them to come take you. Do you have a gun?"

Cassidy handed her the .45 he had taken from the guard. She passed it to the man from the cell next to hers. They hugged, and as she pulled away, she said, "*Suerte, hombre.*" He smiled like a man who knew that all his luck was behind him. Someone tried the door from the killing ground, and the man turned and fired a bullet through it. Someone outside yelped with pain.

Cassidy hurried Dylan up the stairs and out into the plaza. Gunfire sounded from below the wall. The soldiers there would be firing back through the door. He led Dylan to the narrow street, and as they turned the corner he looked back in time to see four soldiers and Sergeant Lopato come up the stairs from the killing ground. A shot came from the front door of the prison building. One of the soldiers spun and went down, and the others threw themselves flat and began to return fire. The men in the prison block were not going to get out, but they would buy Cassidy and Dylan time. How long before the general alarm was raised? How long before they blocked the gates?

The two drivers were standing in the shade by the cars smoking and talking. Cassidy led Dylan to the one closer to the gate. The driver flicked his cigarette away and walked over.

"We have to go now," Cassidy said.

The driver looked around. "And the others?"

"They'll be a while. You can come back for them."

"Are you sure?" Did he hear the distant snap of rifles?

"I'm sure." Cassidy put his arm around Dylan's waist, and she leaned in and kissed the side of his neck and rested her head on his shoulder. "I'm sure."

The driver nodded and smiled. "Ahh, yes. Of course. Of course." He understood the urgency of love in the afternoon. He opened the back door and ushered them in with a flourish, got in behind the wheel, revved the engine to show his appreciation of the need for haste, circled the plaza fast enough to make the tires squeal, and drove out through the gate.

Dylan put her head against his chest. He could feel her body shake. He felt her tears through the cloth of his shirt.

3

Cassidy asked the driver to take them to the Nacional, but Dylan had him pull over on La Rampa, and they got out and watched him drive on. "They'll know you were at the hotel. They'll go there first." She led him around a corner and hailed another taxi and asked the driver to take them to the old town and to drop them at the Cathedral plaza where they walked through the beggars displaying their wounds and deformities. She warded off the vendors who took her for a tourist with a smile and a shake of the head. They turned down an alley where the old stucco buildings leaned toward each other and laundry in all colors hung from the wrought-iron balconies and got on a bus and rode ten blocks with the people headed home from work. At a corner where the bus turned, two gray police cars nosed together into the curb. Four young men, college age, stood facing a white wall, their hands high, their legs spread, as the cops patted them down. The people on that side of the bus turned away from the windows. Cassidy and Dylan got out at the next stop and he followed her down narrow streets that smelled of grilling meats, flowers, the sea, and open drains. Music played from radios near open windows, drums and guitars, brass and maracas, a heavy tropical beat. She walked with purpose, and he followed without comment. He was in her world now, the covert, the clandestine, and she would lead them where they had to go.

She stopped at a wide arched gateway on a narrow street near the port and reached in through the slats and fiddled with something until she got it right and half the gate swung open and he followed her into a courtyard. It was paved with worn cobblestones and surrounded on three sides by a two-story building and on the fourth by a high wall and the gate they had entered. The building was old, the stucco discolored and broken in places. The ground floor under the two wings had been built as stables, but now they were crowded with cars in various states of repair. Pieces of car bodies, fenders, doors, bumpers were piled in corners of the yard.

Someone beat on metal with a hammer in one of the stalls.

• • •

"Your descriptions have been on the radio. Very accurate because, of course, your hair is easy. We should do something about that. And him too. Very accurate. Hair, height, weight, everything. Someone was paying attention. Who is he?"

"An old friend."

He waited for more but Dylan gave him nothing.

"We must do something about your hair, Selena. I'll ask Veronica. She works at a hair place for women."

Selena, the cover name she was using.

The man's name was Tomas. He was broad and thick and bowlegged, and his dark face was cheerful until you got to his eyes. His English was good, learned, he explained, during six years he worked as a mechanic for a Ford dealer in Fort Lauderdale. He carried a shotgun up from the garage and put it behind the door where it would be easy to reach. His hands were ingrained with oil and dirt even after scrubbing in the stone sink in the kitchen on the second floor. There was no sign of a woman here. The sink was stacked with dirty dishes. The towel he used to dry his hands was gray. The windows were opaque with years of stove smoke. One of the counters was littered with bits stripped from cars, radio tubes and knobs, a gearshift, unidentifiable pieces of metal, a wind wing in its frame. The wood table where they sat was scarred on the edges from where people had rested cigarettes.

Tomas lit a Chesterfield and blew smoke at Cassidy. "You're sure of him?"

"Yes."

He shrugged. "Okay, then. On your head if it goes wrong." He took a long barreled .38 revolver from his waistband and put it under a cloth at his elbow and got up and found an unlabeled bottle in a cabinet above the old kerosene range and poured rum into mismatched tumblers. He served them bread and plates of olives and hard cheese and small grilled fish. Dylan ate as if she had not seen food in days. Tomas ate the fish with his fingers, crunching heads and all and washing them down with rum.

"Two more got out, they say. But no names yet. If they're ours, we'll soon know."

"And the rest?" Cassidy asked.

Tomas shrugged. Dead or recaptured. What else was there? The phone rang and Tomas answered it. "*¿Si?*" He listened for a while and then hung up and came back to the table. "Big search. SIM, soldiers, police. It's too dangerous to move you now. So tonight we hide you here. Tomorrow we get you out of Havana."

He led them back downstairs to one of the garages where a 1952 Chevrolet Bel Air waited with its hood open. A blanket lay across the driver's side fender to protect the paint from tools. The valve cover, carburetor, air cleaner, and other pieces Cassidy could not identify were on a workbench against the wall. "Valve job," Tomas explained. Cassidy helped him roll the car back to the door. The floor underneath it was caked with oil and grease. Tomas scrubbed some of it away and then screwed a handle into the hole he had cleared, and pulled. A section of the floor tilted up on counterweighted hinges. There was a ladder leading down into a pit. "Wait," Tomas said. He went down into the pit and opened a low door at one end and ducked in. A moment later a light came on in the room beyond the door and he reappeared and climbed back out. "A good place. They will never find you here. You'll be safe."

Or trapped in a hole, Cassidy thought.

"I'll bring you food and something to drink. I'll push the car back over, but even so there is just enough room to open the trapdoor and crawl out. Just in case." In case something happens to me, he meant, a man who lived with that daily reality, the midnight knock on the door, the car with darkened windows, the room where men waited with questions.

They went down the short ladder into the pit and then into the room at the end, and the trapdoor thunked down as Cassidy lit a cigarette and took in the hideout room. It was not much bigger than the cell Dylan had left. A mattress took up half the floor. There was bucket in the corner, a wooden stool and small wood table on which Tomas had put a plate of ham, some cheese, half a loaf of bread, a bottle of water, a bottle of rum, two glasses, and a knife. A bare bulb glared from overhead.

She studied him carefully in the silence of the room, and then smiled. "You haven't changed, Michael. You look the same."

"So do you."

"Liar."

Her face was thinner, and there was a shadow of something that had not been there before, sadness, or pain. Her eyes did the same shift from blue to green, depending on the light, green now, and fathomless, eyes to drown in. There was a thin white scar at the corner of her mouth. He touched it with his finger and she did not flinch. "Did I do that?"

"Yes." She touched it with the tip of her tongue. "Every time I looked in the mirror I thought of you. Where were you? What were you doing? Were you even alive?" She took his cigarette from his mouth and took a drag and gave it back to him, an intimacy from when they were together in New York four years ago. "Did you think of me?"

"Yes."

"A lot?"

"Yes. A lot."

"Do you believe in Fate, Michael?"

"Not much."

"They were going to kill me today, and then you came and got me. It has to mean something."

"What?"

"I don't know. Something." She accepted the glass of rum he offered and lit a cigarette off the burning coal of his. "I always thought I would see you again before I died, but lately I began to lose faith that it could happen. I know that at the end of it in New York you believed I came to you because my superiors ordered it, because they needed to know if you had the photographs. It was like that in the beginning. But by the end, I loved you for me, for you, and this morning all I wanted was to see you one more time before they took me to the wall."

Almost five years ago the murder of a Broadway dancer who turned out to be a blackmailer had led him into the middle of a KGB operation. Dylan had been sent into his orbit to find out whether he had discovered the blackmail photographs that were to be used against men high in the U.S. power structure. The unintended consequence was that they fell in love. When Cassidy blew up the operation, Dylan was pulled back to Russia. After that, there was silence.

"You could have gotten a letter out, just to let me know you were all right."

"What for? You hated me."

"No."

"You were so angry."

"I got over that." There had been anger, but it burned out until all that was left was loss. "Tell me what happened when you got back to Moscow."

They sat down on the mattress with their backs against the wall, a tin ashtray between them and the rum bottle within reach.

"At first they weren't sure they believed me, and then even if they did believe me they didn't like it much. The operation had failed. Apfel was dead and beyond their displeasure, so they took it out on me. Reeducation." A shadow passed over her face. She chased it with a smile. "It's amazing the things you can learn about yourself if they are pointed out forcefully enough."

"But they decided you were all right." He lit another cigarette.

"They decided I was too valuable an asset to throw away. An American trained from an early age. So they started me out again. Small things. And they put temptations in my way. I met people who were willing to share their unhappiness about life in Russia. I met people who could help me make money if I would help them. I was offered chances to go abroad. I understood what they were doing, so I reported them all and, after a while, they began to think I was all right."

"So they sent you here."

"Yes. I speak Spanish, and they wanted to test my commitment in a controllable situation. I've been here six months. Why are you here? Why did you come to Havana? Except, of course, to save me."

"I brought a prisoner down. He'd been extradited for murder." He told her about Echevarria and what had happened to him. She was unsurprised.

"Colonel Fuentes. Sometimes there was no firing squad, just him and his pistol one by one. Sometimes you're taken outside. Sometimes he does it in your cell, and then other prisoners are made to clean it up. He used me for that, on my knees, scrubbing the stones. He called it woman's work."

"Why were you in La Cabaña? What happened?" He passed her the cigarette.

"The usual things that make an operation go wrong. A blown tire. An army truck stopped to help the poor woman with her car in the ditch. But one of the soldiers knew the man with me. They'd been in school together, not friends, and he had heard that the man had gone into the hills with Castro. They searched the car. There were guns under the seats and in the trunk."

"A KGB operation?"

"What do you think, Mike? Do you think I came as a tourist and decided to smuggle guns because I was bored? I am who I am. I do what I do. I was sent here to help a revolution we believe in."

"All right."

She hesitated. "Sometimes I find it hard to believe in the people who say they believe the same things."

"Okay."

"Think of how hard it is for me to be with a Capitalist Running Dog, a lackey of the fat cats of Wall Street." The twitch of a smile.

"Good point." Did she feel the low current of tension he felt? What was it? The memory of an intimacy only lovers share. Was it there in the way she looked at him, or was he imagining it?

She stretched till her muscles cracked. "God, what a day. What did someone say? Nothing concentrates the mind like the prospect of hanging. Dead this morning. Alive tonight because of you. Until now I never knew how good a cigarette could taste, or rum. I never knew how much I liked being alive." She stretched and yawned. "I have to sleep. You don't get much sleep the night before they're going to take you out and shoot you." He moved so she could lie down on the mattress. As she drifted toward sleep she said in the soft sleepy voice of a child, "Michael, would you hold me, just hold me?"

• • •

A noise in the darkness woke him. Dylan was spooned against his back. Her breath came and went in a slow, calm rhythm. The noise came again, a distant clang of metal, and then a scraping sound. Someone was moving things in the garage above. He felt around next to the mattress until he found where he had left his holstered gun. There was more scraping and banging. Were they looking for the hidey-hole? Did they know they were there? What about Tomas? Dead? Forced to give them up? He rose and groped in the darkness until he touched the wooden chair. By feel he wedged the back of it up under the doorknob, a futile gesture. If they knew where the hideout was, a chair against a door wasn't going to do much good. He thought of turning on the light to see what other resources he might find, but he did not want to wake Dylan. If things were going bad, she would know it soon enough. Let her sleep.

Waiting is hard for an impatient man. After a while he pulled the chair away and opened the door to the darkness of the pit. The sounds from above were louder now. He heard voices but they were too muffled to know what they were saying. If they lifted the trapdoor, he would rush them. Six shots in the revolver, maybe enough if he surprised them.

There was more banging and scraping. Someone yelled in pain. The noises slowed and then stopped. It was quiet. Maybe they'd gone. Maybe they hadn't found the trap. Maybe they were waiting for him to poke his head up. He counted to three hundred, but no one came and he heard no more. He went back into the room and wedged the door with the chair and lay down on the mattress. Dylan breathed slowly and regularly next to him. He put the gun on the floor where he could reach it easily and lay in the darkness and tried to sleep.

• • •

At dawn Tomas, his face bruised and cut from the night's inquiries, led them away through the narrow streets of the Old Quarter. Shopkeepers wet down the pavement in front of their stores. The sun was till too low to bring much heat, and the morning smelled fresh. Cassidy wore the cotton pants and shirt of a worker, and Dylan wore a shapeless cotton dress. Tomas had not found the woman who was to dye her hair, so she had hidden it as best she could under a kerchief. She carried a basket on her shoulder to shield her face. At a glance she looked like one of the many women hurrying to work or to the market before the choice bits were gone. They crossed a small plaza with a waterless fountain in the center, its broken-nosed angel perched on a chipped and tilted pedestal. On the wall of the church nearby someone had started to paint *Viva La Revolución*, but it ended in a scrawl and a smear of red, and the body of a young man lay in the gutter below it, his blood mingled with the paint. A priest in a black cassock came out of the church followed by two men carrying a door, and as Tomas hurried them through the plaza, Cassidy looked back to see them roll the dead man onto the door and carry him into the church.

Tomas left them in the care of a woman named Marta at a small brick sugar warehouse near the old city wall. He shook hands with both of them and wished them Godspeed. He had been lucky with the searchers, he said, and maybe it would pass to them. They had been regular police, not SIM, and while they had punched him a few times out of habit, their hearts had not been in it, or in the search. Someone had reported that they had seen a man and a woman who might have fit the description of the fugitives going down Tomas's street, and the cops were checking every house, but the years had taught them to have little faith in eyewitnesses.

Marta was a black woman, six feet tall, and over two hundred pounds. She wore a man's one-piece coverall with the sleeves chopped off, and men's shoes with the toes cut open to ventilate her feet. She called Cassidy and Dylan *my children* and seemed unruffled by the problem of moving the fugitives. She smoked a pipe stuffed with harsh, coarse tobacco while they drank bowls of sweet milky coffee and ate a breakfast of fried bananas and bread at a workbench at the rear of the warehouse. She loaded them into the back of an ancient truck under a mountain of burlap bags destined for a sugar refinery. The truck's springs had worn to nothing, and they felt every bump and jolt as it banged and rattled over the old cobblestone streets, and the dust from the burlap filtered down. They were saved from suffocation by a metal shelf that jutted out over them from the back wall of the truck bed and gave them room to lie together and breathe. There were two checkpoints. At the first they could hear Marta banter with the soldiers. They knew her, knew her routine runs, and their search was cursory. At the second one, the voices were hard and commanding. They made her get out of the cab and let down the tailgate. The truck rocked as someone got up into the bed and began searching. Cassidy dug his gun from his pocket. The searcher would stop, grunt with effort, move, stop, grunt with effort, move again, working his way up the truck bed. Something banged and scraped along the metal shelf over them. It banged and scraped again. He was probing the pile of bags with something metal. A bayonet? Something rammed down through the bags, and Cassidy pushed back against the wall of the truck. The thing withdrew and rammed down again, and Cassidy heard Dylan gasp. Someone shouted a question and the searcher called back, "*Nada.*" Nothing. The truck rocked as he clambered to the back and jumped down. Moments later it sagged to the left as Marta climbed back in the cab. She slammed the door, slammed it again to make it stay, ground the starter till the engine caught, clashed the gears and set off with a jerk.

"Are you all right?"

"Yes. Fine." Was something in her voice?

"Are you sure?"

"Yes."

The whine of the tires on smooth pavement put him to sleep, and he woke when they turned off and slowed. The road that bumped under them was dirt and stones, and the truck rocked along, pitching and jouncing, and then stopped.

Voices.

Hands pulled the burlap sacks away. Cassidy and Dylan came blinking into the sunlight. They were in a farm clearing. The truck was parked near a small house made of scrap lumber and tin. A goat tied to a banana tree grazed at the end of its rope. Chickens pecked at the dirt of the yard. Ten men waited at the back of the truck and watched them curiously. They were young, and they were bearded, some more successfully than others. They wore mismatched fatigues. Some had boots. Others wore sandals made of tire treads. Nine of them had rifles slung on their shoulders. The tenth carried a Thompson submachine gun, a symbol of rank.

Dylan stumbled getting down from the truck, and then gasped with pain when Cassidy took her arm to right her. The sleeve of her dress was dark and sodden with blood. They cut the sleeve away to reveal a nasty gash from the probing bayonet across her upper arm. The blood had stiffened the cloth in the wound, and when they peeled it away the cut bled again. Marta wrapped it tight with a piece of cloth offered by the farmer's wife from the shadow of her doorway.

"She needs a doctor," Cassidy said.

"She needs to get away from here," the man with the Thompson said. "We all need to get away. We are too exposed here. The army patrols use this road." His Spanish was hard for Cassidy to understand. It was spoken back in the throat with a lot of dropped consonants. His name was Armando, and he was the leader of this band by whatever alchemy it is that makes some men follow and some men lead. He was thin, light boned, with a sharp nose, and thinning black hair cut ragged by someone with an unsteady sense of style. He wore gold-rimmed glasses and looked like an accountant who had put aside his books to take up a gun. He was very sure of himself, a good thing in a war leader, or deadly for his followers, depending on where he led them.

"Is there a doctor where we're going?"

"There are people who know wounds."

"Let it go, Michael. I'll be all right."

"You have a gun," Armando said. "You will give it to me." He held out his hand.

"I'm going to keep it."

"No. We do not know you."

"You know her. She knows me."

"We know *of* her. We do not know her. We must be careful. People come to us saying they are for the cause, but there have been betrayals. There are others who will decide who you are, but I need the gun."

They walked for more than two hours, first through farmland, cane fields, and scrub forest that had been cut over more than once, and then, as the land rose, on narrow paths through thickening jungle. The men talked as they marched. Their rifles remained slung on their shoulders. They walked close together with no scout out on the point to run the trail in front of them.

Cassidy dropped back to walk with Armando.

"Do we have much farther to go?"

Armando looked at him suspiciously. "We will be there when we are there."

"Does the army patrol this area?"

"Yes. Sometimes."

"Maybe I should have my gun back."

"Why do you think you need your gun?"

"You have no scouts out. No one's walking point. If we run into an army patrol, most of your men will be dead before they get their rifles off their shoulders."

"This is what you think?"

"Yes."

"We are past the time of needing advice from Americans. We are a people who can stand on their own feet without the help of Uncle Sam."

"I'm sure you're right. I'd like the same chance. If we meet a patrol, I want to be able to defend myself."

They walked in silence for a while.

"You were in the American army?"

"Yes."

"During the war?"

"Yes."

"And you saw fighting?"

"Yes."

"Much?"

"As much as there was from D-Day until the end."

They walked on.

Dylan looked back to see what he was doing, and Cassidy walked up to join her.

"What was that about?"

"Small-group tactics. They should have somebody walking point in case there's trouble waiting up ahead, and they should have someone walking drag in case there's trouble coming up from behind."

"And?"

"Nothing. He's going to do it his way."

"They're a proud people."

"I hope it doesn't kill them. And us."

The trees closed in overhead so that they walked in shadow and occasional shafts of light. Without the sun, the ground was soft and muddy and the air was thick with moisture and smelled of decay and of tropical flowers Cassidy could not identify. Birds called, and occasionally an animal scrabbled away in the underbrush.

Armando walked up past them without looking at them and spoke to a man at the head of the march. The man nodded, unslung his rifle, and jogged up along the trail and disappeared around a bend. Armando stood by the side of the trail and spoke to the men as they passed. When Cassidy reached him, he handed him his revolver without comment.

• • •

The clearing held six crude huts, and a large, ramshackle house of wood and tin with a front porch supported by stumps and pieces of stone. It was an old farm mostly reclaimed by the jungle. When the patrol came out of the trailhead, three men and a woman got up from where they were cleaning rifles on a blanket by a fire. People came out of one of the huts, and a man and woman left the garden patch they were hoeing. They all wore fatigues, and the men were bearded, and they rushed the incoming patrol with shouts and hugs of greeting.

A man stood on the porch of the house and watched. He was about thirty years old, Cassidy thought. His fatigues were neat, and he wore polished army boots. He was a big man, over six feet, and heavy through the chest and belly. He was as dark as any man Cassidy had seen, so dark that his skin seemed to absorb light. He did not come down off the porch to join the noisy celebration. He waited for them to come to him.

Armando started for the man on the porch, and when Cassidy and

Dylan started to follow, he checked them with a gesture, and two of the men from the patrol came to stand near them with their rifles held across their chests. Armando went up onto the porch, and as he did, a woman came out of the house and joined the two men. She was not much over five feet tall and a hundred pounds, but wiry and strong-looking, with coarse brown hair tied back with a piece of red cloth. She stood with a hand on the big man's arm and stared out at Cassidy and Dylan while they listened to Armando's report. The big man glanced at them occasionally while Armando talked and at the end he shook the smaller man's hand, clapped him on the shoulder, and ushered him off the porch. He said a few words to the woman and gestured to Cassidy and Dylan to come up.

"My name is Antonio Gonzales. I am deputy commander of this unit of the July 26th Movement." He did not offer to shake hands. He did not introduce the woman. His eyes were brown, large and liquid, and the whites were shot through with blood. "And you are?" His voice was deep and indicated little real interest in their answers.

"Selena Perez," Dylan said. "I've been with the Portillo group in Havana."

"There is no Portillo group. They were taken. They were in La Cabaña. They were executed two days ago. We received the news by radio."

"I escaped with this man's help."

"Only you?"

"I don't know. We were told two others got away."

He turned to look at Cassidy. "You have a gun. Please give it to me."

Cassidy took the gun out of his pocket and handed it butt first to Gonzales. What was the point of refusing?

"Your name? He examined the pistol briefly and then handed it to the woman who tucked it in her belt.

"Michael Cassidy."

"Why are you in Cuba?"

"I'm a police officer with the New York City Police Department. I brought an extradited prisoner to Havana."

"Who?"

"A man named Fausto Echevarria."

Gonzales looked at the woman. She shook her head. She did not know the name.

"He wasn't one of yours. He was wanted for murder. He killed three men guarding some money he was trying to steal."

"And how did you meet this woman?"

"I saw her when I brought the prisoner to La Cabaña. I recognized her as someone I had known in New York. I learned that she was going to be executed, so I got her out."

"Just like that?"

"No. It required some work."

Gonzales raised his eyebrows in disbelief and looked to the woman to see what she thought.

"Were you lovers in New York?" The woman asked.

"Yes."

She nodded as if that explained a lot. "Still, a fantastic story."

"The truth."

"Perhaps," she said.

"If I'm not who I say I am," Dylan said, "how would we have known who to contact to get out of Havana? How would we have known how to get here?"

"You say you're Selena. Perhaps you are. Perhaps you're not. If you're not, then who are you? A member of SIM? So you get one name from Selena before she dies, and that takes you to the mechanic. And the mechanic takes you to the woman, and the woman takes you to Armando. And now you're here, and so the mission is almost complete."

"And if we work for SIM, how do we let them know where we are? Ask to borrow your radio?"

She considered it seriously. "No. That would not be part of the plan. But my story is no more fantastic than yours."

"There are people in the hills who have met me, who know me. I have been in Fidel's camp too, six months ago. There are people who know me."

"Fidel is in the Sierra. We are here."

"There are people."

"Perhaps there are. We will see."

"Maybe if we spoke to the commander of the unit," Cassidy suggested to Gonzales.

"I am the commander of the unit," the woman said with a thin smile for his mistake.

They were locked in a windowless storeroom in the house. The door was stout, but the walls had gaps between the slats, and some of the floorboards were loose. If they wanted to get out, they could, but there was a man posted behind the house, and there were two dozen armed men and women in the camp to run them down. There was a sleeping pad in one corner with a pitcher of water and two mismatched glasses next to it.

"Three cigarettes left." Cassidy offered her the pack.

"Let's smoke one now and save the rest."

"I don't think she likes me much." He lit the cigarette, took a drag, and passed it to her.

"You insulted her. You took a look at the great big man and the little woman and you decided he had to outrank her. You thought that she was just there to keep his bed warm and to speak when he wanted to rest his voice. Women can lead as well as men. Maybe better."

"No argument from me."

"And fight just as well. A gun's not that heavy."

"I, for one, am happy to turn the whole business over to you. I'll stay home and cook and do my nails." He took the cigarette back. "Are there really people around up here in the hills who can vouch for you?"

"I don't know. Maybe. People get moved around. People die. You can't blame them for being careful."

"I can if they take us out and shoot us."

"It's what they should do." She saw his look. "It is. It's what they should do. Their responsibility is to the cause. If they can't confirm who we are, it's smarter to get rid of us rather than risk the group."

"Stop trying to comfort me." He handed her the cigarette. "Here. Finish it. Those things can kill you."

She laughed. He lay down on his back on the floor with his head pillowed on his hands. She stubbed the cigarette out and came over and sat down next to him. "I'm glad you showed up. Have I mentioned that?"

"I am too, though I'd prefer to be in the Hotel Nacional waiting for room service." Cassidy touched her hand, and she inclined toward him, and he thought, *Here, now it comes.* And then she pulled back and got up and went and poured a glass of water and drank it with her back to him.

At night they slept back to back on the pad. He turned over in the dark and put his hand on her. After a moment she moved just enough so that it fell away. Was she awake, or had she moved in her sleep, unaware of his hand? He did not know.

• • •

"What are they doing?"

He was looking out through a crack in the wall. "Cleaning weapons, checking equipment. They must be going out on patrol soon."

They had been in the storeroom for three days. Someone brought them food and water twice a day. In the mornings there was coffee. On the first day one of the women had come in to examine the cut on Dylan's arm. She was a sturdy, happy woman named Conchi who pulled the wrapping from the wound slowly and carefully after softening the dried blood with warm water and she hissed as she pulled the cloth free, as if the pain was her own. She talked constantly while she worked, one of those people who shared her thoughts with whoever was in range. "My father worked in the mill for many years, crushing the cane to make the juice. He was killed in an accident there, an accident with the machinery. My brothers were told to come get the body, but the foreman would not let them bring him home in one of the mill trucks, so they had to carry him home in a wheelbarrow. And then there was no money, so they left school to work. The bosses do not care if you give your life for their profit, but the revolution will change all that. The revolution is for the people." She washed the wound carefully with soap and water and covered it with a poultice of tobacco and other leaves and bound it with a clean cloth. "One brother is in New York. He owns his own taxi and has an apartment with two bedrooms. Do you know Brooklyn? This is where he lives. One can do this in America, but it is very hard for a man to have his own taxi in Cuba unless you can pay the bribe for the license. My other brother, the younger one, they caught him painting a message on the wall of the town hall, and they shot him. So I came to the hills to learn how to fight. The revolution is the hope of the people. The revolution will give us democracy." She came back each day to check the wound and seemed pleased with what she found.

The woman commandant was named Pilar, and she came each day to interrogate them. Each day she led them through their stories and checked their answers against her notes from the day before.

"You say you showed the guard at the door your badge and said you were going to deliver something to Colonel Fuentes, and he let you go by."

"I was moving fast. He didn't have time to see the badge was from New York."

"And there was only one guard at the door and one in the cellblock."

"That's right."

"But the day before, when you brought Señor Echevarria, there were many more guards."

"Yes."

"Where were they when you went back? How is that they were not there to stop you?"

"There were six men in the firing squad. Perhaps they were the guards from the cellblock."

"And you thought that one man could go there, to this prison, to free a prisoner."

"I had no choice."

"Yes. That's what you said yesterday."

"And the day before."

"Yes." Her tone was always neutral, betraying neither belief nor disbelief. "Had Portillo's wound healed, or did he still limp?" This was a new question for Dylan.

"I never saw him limp. He never spoke of a wound."

"No?"

"No." Maybe that was a test. Maybe she had passed, maybe failed.

"When the car tire blew and the car went into the ditch, how long before the army truck you speak of came?"

"Half a minute, maybe. They came around the bend from the other direction."

"How did they find the guns?"

"I told you before."

"Tell me again."

"I was trying to help Antonio out of the car. He had hit his head and was dazed. Some of the soldiers went around to see the people who had been riding in the backseat and were now standing by the car. One of them knew Antonio had gone into the hills. They searched the car and found the guns."

"Was Portillo in La Cabaña?"

"He was in the cell next to mine." Wearily. "The last I saw of him was after we opened the cells. Cassidy gave him one of the guard's guns."

"Did Colonel Fuentes interrogate the prisoners?"

"Yes."

"Did he interrogate you?"

"Yes."

"What did he want to know?"

"Who I knew outside the Portillo group. How many other groups were there in Havana. Where we were going with the guns."

"What did you tell him?"

"I told him I knew nothing of these things. I told him I had gotten a ride in the car, because I wanted to see my friends in Las Palmas and they said they were going there."

"Did he believe you?"

"No. Have you found someone who can say who I am, who can vouch for me?"

"If we find someone, you will know."

If, not, *when*.

• • •

"After New York, when I was first back in Moscow, there was a man in the cell next to me. He worked for Aeroflot. I don't know what his job was, but it allowed him to travel outside the country." They were sitting side by side with their backs against the wall sharing a cigarette Conchi had left them, waiting to be tired enough to sleep. "People who could travel were often asked to do things, deliver a package, pick up an envelope, become friendly with a counterpart in a similar business. They weren't spies, but they were known as *friends*, people who could be counted on for small tasks. He had disappeared in Paris for three days, had lost the package he was supposed to deliver. They didn't like that, and they wanted to know why. He said that he had met a woman, and they had gone to the shore. He had forgotten the package on the train. He told the same story every day they questioned him, over and over again. It was too stupid a story to make up, or maybe it was meant to look that way, and therefore it was smart. They couldn't decide, so they liquidated him just to be sure."

They finished the cigarette in silence.

That night she turned to him on the mat and put an arm around him, and he turned to her, and they pressed together, no words spoken. She cupped the back of his neck with one hand and tugged. He kissed her and felt her mouth open under his and she pressed her body against him. He pulled her shirt up and slid his hands into the warmth of her back and down over the swell of her ass. They undressed each other as they kissed, awkward and fumbling as if they had forgotten how buttons worked, and kicked away the last of the cloth and found each other, went into each other as if they had never been away, as if time had not passed.

• • •

"They're going out," Cassidy said. It was the blue of early morning before sunrise. Dylan got up from the mattress and came to crouch beside him and look out through a crack in the boards. The patrol was forming up in the center of the clearing. Most of them were carrying packs. "It looks like they'll be out for a while."

Armando, the clerk who had picked up a gun, led the patrol to the trailhead and down into the jungle. Nine people were left in the camp, Gonzales, Pilar, three men, and Conchi in the clearing and a fourth man on watch at the back of the house. Pilar and Gonzales sat together on a log near the remnants of a cook fire and talked.

When Conchi came in half an hour later, she was quiet and somber. She checked the wound without speaking. She put a small bottle of rum and a few cigarettes on the table, an offering, a comfort, and left without meeting their eyes.

"They've made a decision," Dylan said.

"Yes."

Her face clenched, and her eyes veiled as she absorbed what this meant. If you did this work, it was always there that it could end like this, but it was a thought kept tucked in a dark corner. Now it was out in the light. She looked at Cassidy, and he wondered how his face looked. Did it show anger or resignation?

They stood when they heard the scrape of the key in the lock. They had been sitting with their backs against the wall, touching at shoulders, hips, and thighs, sharing the cigarettes and rum Conchi had left, speaking of little, quiet talk—do you remember this day in New York when we went there, did that, the Italian restaurant on Hudson Street, the way the rain looked on the river from the apartment windows, Carlos Ribera destroying the sculpture that wasn't quite right?

Now they did what they had talked about. Cassidy stood against the wall next to the door. He had broken a leg off the table to use as a club. Dylan waited with her hand just above the door handle. Why go easy?

The door handle moved. Dylan grabbed it and jerked the door open hoping to pull whoever it was into the room under Cassidy's club. A hostage, leverage, someone to bargain with. A forlorn hope.

The doorway was vacant. Pilar and Gonzales stood back out of reach. A Thompson submachine gun was small in his hands.

"Please," Pilar said. "There has been a decision." She stopped as if she had lost track of what she had prepared to say, or maybe she understood it was not necessary. "We will give you time to make your peace."

Cassidy looked at Dylan. She shook her head.

"Now," he said, and let the table leg drop. Pilar nodded without expression and stepped back to let them leave the room.

He took Dylan's hand. Maybe there would be a chance when they went outside.

Gonzales opened the front door of the house and led them out. The morning sun slanted into the clearing. Cassidy could smell the smoke from the cook fires and the rich green smell of the jungle. Birds called, and there was a whisper of wind in the trees. Conchi and the two remaining rebels stood near a fire watching them. A coffeepot was wedged on stones above the coals. Cassidy had a sudden ache for the taste of coffee.

Pilar gestured, and they followed Gonzales down the steps and off the porch. Dylan's hand was tight in his. The steps creaked as they went down them. He could feel the pebbles in the dirt under his feet. A beautiful day. Life all around.

He saw movement at the trailhead. The patrol coming back?

No.

He yanked Dylan's hand, dragging her to the ground.

The first shot hit Gonzales in the chest and spun him, and the second and third hit him in the side, and he was dead as he fell. He was the farthest from the trailhead where the soldiers first appeared, but maybe they had targeted him because he carried the submachine gun and they worried about it. Pilar froze on the top step, and they killed her there. Bullets ripped overhead and kicked up dirt as Cassidy and Dylan scrambled under the porch. More slammed into the wood above them as they wormed back under the house. The man on guard at the back of the house ran toward the front. They could see his legs as he turned the corner. He stopped abruptly, crumpled, and lay in the dirt with his rifle a few feet from his outstretched hand. Cassidy looked out into the clearing. Conchi was facedown in the fire and one of the rebels lay across her legs. The other managed to fire a couple of shots that checked the rush of soldiers. Then he was cut down.

Cassidy and Dylan belly crawled under the house through the cobwebs and dirt. Shots banged into the walls above them. They crawled out the other side and ran across the ten yards of clearing with the house between them and the soldiers and plunged into the jungle. They kept going until they were well away from the house and then went to ground.

• • •

The afternoon sun filtered through the trees, throwing light and shadows on the bodies sprawled in the mud of the trail. They had been dead for a long time, probably since within the hour of when they had left the camp that morning, and the birds and insects and small animals had already begun the work of cleanup. The ambushers had stripped them of weapons and had turned their pockets out, maybe searching for the intelligence prizes of identification or indiscreet diaries, notes of plans, but also because looting is the privilege of the victors. The ambush site was easy to read. The army had been in cover on the high side of the trail with a clear field of fire. They had put blocking positions at either end of the trail section to prevent flight. The thing must have been over in seconds, the sudden blast of shots, the confusion and screaming. Then they came down and finished off the wounded one by one with a bullet to the head. Armando lay on his back in the middle of the trail, his arms crossed on his chest. A bullet had smashed one lens of his glasses.

"Nobody on point. All bunched up together again. Walking down the trail like a Sunday-afternoon stroll. What did I tell them? Why didn't they listen?" Why did their carelessness make him angry? They were people he had known only a little, people who had looked at him with suspicion. Why should it matter to him that they had thrown away all that they were and all they ever would be?

There was no way to bury the dead, nothing to be done. They set off down the trail. An hour later they ran into a patrol of bearded men in mismatched fatigues. The leader embraced Dylan and said, "Selena, we heard you were in the mountains. We came to find you."

4

Carlos Ribera's house was in Vedado, a suburb of Havana developed for the rich in the mid-1800s. The house looked out to the sea and was cooled by ocean breezes, God's benefit to those who could afford the real estate, as Ribera sometimes remarked, invoking a deity he dismissed as irrelevant to the anarchist he professed to be. Entry from the crushed shell drive was through massive, iron-strapped wooden doors into an airy, two-story front hall with a wide marble staircase that curved up to the floor above. The hall led to a big interior courtyard paved with Italian tiles where a bronze dolphin balanced on its tail and spewed water from its mouth into a round pool where lilies floated. There were plants in clay pots, flowers of every color, and three palm trees whose green crowns overgrew the red tiled roof. And there were Ribera's sculptures. Some were abstract tangles of metal and wood, some stone heads, roughly chiseled, the features beginning to appear as if forcing their way out to the surface of the stone. And there was one startlingly realistic bronze nude of a woman.

Ribera had been Dylan's employer in New York five years ago, and Cassidy had met him then. She had welded his metal sculptures with a skill learned as a child while working in a Russian tank factory during World War II. Ribera, a Cuban, was a self-declared Marxist-anarchist, and a self-declared genius artist. He had worldwide reputation as a painter and sculptor. It was harder to tell about his politics. He took positions to provoke and to annoy, to tip people off balance about who he was and what he truly thought. He had told Cassidy in New York that he was not a Communist, that the dictatorship of the proletariat was just another dictatorship, but he had provided cover for Dylan and the KGB officer who ran her cell. Two days ago, when they had come down out of the mountains,

Dylan had led Cassidy to Ribera's house. "We'll be safe there," she explained, but she did not explain the KGB's relationship to Ribera.

• • •

"My great-grandfather Oscar Mena built the house in the 1850s," Ribera said. The evening was a time for iced rum drinks in the courtyard, Dylan in a light silk dress she had found in the closet in their room, and Cassidy in linen trousers and a cotton shirt, softer than any he had ever worn, which, by some magic, fit him perfectly. "It was a time when the people with money were moving to Vedado. The streets in what we now call Old Havana were becoming too crowded, too egalitarian. What was the point of having money if you were to be jostled by the great unwashed every time you left your house?" Ribera raised a hand, and a serving man in black trousers and a white shirt brought a new silver pitcher rattling with ice and beaded with moisture, and took away the one from the table in front of them. "Oscar had made a great deal of money. He was in the sugar trade when the economics of slavery made that very lucrative indeed. Nothing better for the profit margin than owning the labor." He smiled to indicate his irony.

A serving woman brought a plate of grilled shrimp and lime and left it on the table without a word.

"Great-grandfather Oscar was something of a revolutionary himself, though not, my dear," a nod to Dylan, "one that you would have approved of. Spain was going to enforce its laws against slavery, and Oscar and his planter friends who depended on slaves thought it might be a good idea to annex Cuba to the Confederate States to prolong their way of life. He was encouraged by the woman who held his heart in her hands in those days, an American widow from New Orleans."

"What happened?' Dylan asked. She ate a shrimp and threw the tail over her shoulder where it was pounced on by one of the house cats. It was a habit she had picked up from her host.

"There was an uprising. They took an armory in one of the towns south of the city with the full expectation that the general sent to attack them was on their side. It was a miscalculation. They had offered him a title if they won, Duke of Havana, or something. The other side offered cold cash. He turned out to be more a pragmatist than a romantic."

"And Great-grandfather Oscar?" Cassidy asked. "*Paredón*?"

"No, no. He was much too grand, related to too many people, and much too rich to shoot. He paid a large fine, which expunged his transgressions, and they asked him not to do it again. He died upstairs in his bed at the age of ninety-three." He stood. "Let's go eat. Livia has done something fantastic to a small tuna. You have never tasted anything like it."

Carlos Ribera was a big man, thick through the shoulders and chest, with a big, square head, heavy chin, bold nose, and a tangle of gray and black curls. His powerful hands were scarred from work with metal and sharp tools. He dressed in guayabera shirts and linen trousers and leather sandals with perfect confidence that his informality would be acceptable wherever he went. His house was overrun by servants. In the days they had been there Cassidy had tried to figure out how many, but he discovered new ones daily. Dylan, champion of the proletariat, was uncomfortable with that, but Ribera laughed off her protest. "I give them employment, shelter, medical benefits, education, things they cannot otherwise have until after the revolution. Do you want me to throw them into the street to protect your democratic sensibilities?" He laughed at that absurd notion and poured her more wine. He was a man who worked to evade classification.

Ribera had fought in Spain against Franco's Fascists, and when Cassidy asked him about it, he dismissed it with a few words and a wave of his hand as if to say all wars are the same in their details. "It taught me that you can be on the side of right and still be beaten, that force can defeat ideals, that courage is not always rewarded, bitter truths that I wish I had not learned."

Their room on the second floor was vast. It had a high ceiling and eight-foot windows that looked out toward the sea and let in the cooling breeze. The floor was dark tile, and there was a gigantic four-poster bed with mosquito netting. A grouping of chairs and a sofa waited in front of a tiled fireplace. The closets held clothes that fit. The bathtub was big enough for both of them, and the towels were large and soft. They made love in the big bed and slept tangled together, and when they woke there was always a tray outside their door with a silver thermos of coffee, because, Ribera said, it was uncivilized to have to come to breakfast and talk without at least a cup of strong coffee to start the engine.

Cassidy carried coffee back to the bed. Dylan stretched till her muscles cracked, pushed herself up against the pillows, and took the cup. "God, I could get used to this."

"What are the poor people doing today?"

"Hey." Mild outrage. She took a sip. "Even the coffee tastes better here."

"Careful, your proletariat sensibilities are slipping."

"Don't tell. I consider this a loop out of my real life. I'll be back to the other soon enough."

It was the same for him—his life in New York was a distant insubstantial dream. His vacation lasted until January third. Then what would happen? Best not think about it.

He took the cup from her and put it on the table.

"What are you doing?"

"Getting back into bed. I want to go over the dialectics with you, make sure I really understand them."

"Ooooh, I love it when you talk dirty." She slipped down in the bed, and he pulled the sheets up over their heads.

• • •

Ribera's studio was a large, airy, one-story stucco building at the back of the garden. It was fronted by big French doors that opened and wide skylights that pierced the ceiling. Cassidy lay on an old, plush, much-stained sofa, smoking a cigarette and watching Ribera work on a large canvas under one of the skylights. Ribera stood back from the easel and studied the painting, and then picked up a palette knife from the paint-smeared table next to him, slid it through a drift of red, and stroked a bold, broad line on the canvas. He stepped back to study the result, sighed contentedly, and threw the palette knife on the table. "I'm a genius." He picked up his burning cigar from the ashtray and drew on it till it burned to his satisfaction. "So, the cop and the KGB agent together again. If there is a God, he has a wonderful sense of humor."

"You knew she was here."

"Yes. She came by when she first arrived." Ribera waited for the questions he knew would come.

"Are you still working for the KGB?"

Ribera laughed and waved the accusation away. "I never worked for them. I helped them in New York by giving Dylan a place, but I did not work for them." A distinction that was important to him.

"Is Castro a Commie?"

"Michael, Michael, Michael, you've been infected by the American need to reduce everything to black or white. Democracy or communism. America or Russia. For us it is not so clear, and sometimes the enemy of your enemy is your friend."

"And America's your enemy?"

"America has used and exploited us for fifty years. It has propped up dictators and supported repressive regimes so that American companies could have a peaceful marketplace here. Your country doesn't give a shit for us. It cares only about the money you can make off us."

"Do you think the Russians love you?"

"They don't have to love us, and we don't have to love them. You don't have to love everyone you go to bed with. Sometimes you just need the screwing."

"Hope the Russians don't give you exactly that."

• • •

New Year's Eve.

They drove downtown in Ribera's stately old Packard limousine with the chauffeur, Miguel, behind glass. The streets boiled with people. The cafés and bars overflowed to the sidewalk. A conga line, twenty men and women, hands on the hips of the one in front, led by drums and guitars and gourd rattles and a man wearing a papier-mâché head of a bull, came out of a side street and blocked traffic as they snaked across and followed the music into the open courtyard of a house hung with garlands of flowers. Through the tinted windows of the Packard, the scene had an underwater quality. Uniformed cops with submachine guns stood in groups at the intersections. Army trucks waited in the plazas, their backs filled with soldiers sitting with guns upright between their knees. SIM Jeeps cruised. For days there had been rumors of a final push by the rebels. It was a song that had been sung before, but it was not going to spoil the fun.

• • •

"No one will look for you on New Year's Eve, and if they do, they certainly won't look for you in the places I go," Ribera said with an assurance that made protest seem craven. They ate at a restaurant in Old Havana with wooden tables, beneath framed sepia photographs of cane workers in ragged straw hats, portly men on horses overseeing them, sailing ships in Havana Harbor, a garden party with women in long dresses shaded by parasols, and men in suits and Panama hats and staring stiffly at the camera.

The food was described by Ribera as the food of the people—*moros y cristianos, ropa vieja, camarones empanizados, picadillo, platanos*—accompanied by two bottles of 1929 Château Latour that Ribera carried in a wicker basket, definitely not a wine of the people. The owner, a thin, smiling woman with hair escaping from its bun like tendrils of gray vines, hugged him when they arrived. He had to stop to hug and kiss people at half the tables on the way to his own. The waiters and waitresses greeted him as a friend. Platters came hot from the kitchen. Water glasses were quickly refilled. A raised eyebrow would bring someone immediately, but no one intruded without being called.

The restaurant was full. Glad cries greeted new arrivals. Conversations were shouted from one table to another. Occasionally there was the sound of breaking glass. There was something desperate beneath the celebration. A dance on the rim of the volcano.

Two men came out of the kitchen and stood near the door until Ribera noticed them. They wore guayabera shirts and cotton pants. They were in their twenties, and they looked out over the room warily. They both were bearded, but their beards were trimmed. Camouflage for a trip to the city? Ribera excused himself and went to talk to them. He took an envelope from his pocket and handed it to one of them. The men nodded and went back into the kitchen and Ribera returned to the table and poured the last of the wine into their glasses but said nothing about the men and their mission.

When they left the restaurant an hour later, they heard gunfire. Maybe blocks away, maybe in the next street. Six or seven shots fired quickly, a pause, the ripping reply of a machine gun, then silence.

• • •

"Castro is the first real hope for the people in my life. Oh, many have promised, of course, but in the end it's the same old story. They talk about The People. They win the election, and suddenly the people are reduced to their friends, their cousins, others with money and power. It will come as a surprise to you, I'm sure, that power tends to corrupt. They get a little taste, and then they want more." He smiled at Dylan and patted her hand. "Not Castro. Of this, I am sure."

The Packard moved implacably through the streets. Other cars seemed to give way to its majesty.

"He is a democrat, a true democrat."

"People say his brother Raúl and that Argentine, Che, are Communists."

"Fuck people who say this. These are rumors spread by Batista and by people in the American business community who have been feeding off Cuba for a long time and don't want to stop. No, no. He is a democrat, a true democrat. You will see."

Dylan looked away and said nothing.

The traffic slowed ahead of them. They crept along at a crawl. Barrels had been placed in the street to funnel cars through a slalom to a roadblock, a striped wooden barrier manned by uniformed police who peered into the cars as they stopped. A pickup truck had been pulled to one side under a streetlight, and two men in work clothes stood by while soldiers searched the back. The Packard advanced car by car.

Dylan shifted nervously in her seat. Cassidy put a hand on hers. He looked out the side windows picking out escape routes, checking for cover. Just in case.

"This is not for us," Ribera said. "They are not looking for rebels in limousines. This is routine." But his fingers drummed on the armrest.

The Packard rolled forward a few yards and stopped again. There were two cars in front of it. The one at the barrier was a high prewar Chevrolet with a bulbous trunk. One of the cops talked to the driver through his open window. He pulled away and walked to a gray sedan parked at the side of the road. A moment later Colonel Fuentes got out and walked to the Chevy.

Dylan's hand clenched under Cassidy's, and she drew breath in a hiss.

"He knows us," Cassidy said. "He was Dylan's jailer at La Cabaña. He knows us both."

"Mmmmm" was Ribera's only response.

The car behind was on the Packard's bumper. There was no way to go but forward.

Fuentes looked in at the driver of the Chevy. The man passed him papers. Fuentes read them, and then handed them to the cop at his elbow and said something. The cop spoke to the driver. After a moment, the Chevy backed up until it touched the bumper of the car behind it. It turned as it went forward, backed again, turned again, maneuvered out of line to a place by the curb. The car in front of the Packard moved forward to the barricade. The Packard followed.

Fuentes walked back to the gray sedan. He leaned against it and lit one of his thin cigars as he watched. The driver got out of the Chevy and opened the trunk, and two soldiers began to search it.

Dylan opened her purse. A small silver automatic lay next to her compact and lipstick. "If he comes to the car," she said.

"Are you armed?" Ribera asked Cassidy.

"No."

"It will not be necessary, but here," Ribera opened a wood-paneled compartment under his armrest and passed Cassidy a Smith & Wesson automatic. "Do nothing unless . . ." There was no reason to finish the sentence. Cassidy jacked a shell into the chamber, made sure of the safety, and slipped the pistol under his thigh.

Soldiers pulled the barrier aside and the car in front of them drove ahead. They replaced the barrier and the Packard stopped just short of it. The chauffeur rolled down his window to talk to the corporal in charge. The man leaned in the driver's window enough so he could see into the back through the partition glass. What did he see? A middle-aged man displaying all the signs of wealth and privilege, and his two younger companions dressed for a party, people he had deferred to all his life. He pulled his head out of the car and gestured for the soldiers to move the barrier.

Fuentes flicked away his cigar and started toward the Packard. He raised a hand to hold the car where it was.

Dylan dipped her hand into her purse. Cassidy touched the gun under his leg. Ribera shook his head and rolled down the window. He leaned so he blocked the view into the backseat. Fuentes stopped a few feet from the car and touched his hat brim in salute. "Señor Ribera. I thought I recognized the car."

"Colonel Fuentes, isn't it?"

"At your service." Pleased to be recognized.

"Is there trouble? Should we be worried? My friends and I were going to go to The Tropicana to see the New Year in. Perhaps we should just go home. What do you recommend?"

"Do not spoil your evening. We have reports of hooligans in the city, but we are not concerned. Still, we have to take precautions."

"Of course."

"Would you mind if we had a look in your trunk?"

"In my trunk?" Just enough edge to his voice to show his displeasure.

"Please, Señor Ribera, it is no reflection on you. But your car has been parked. Perhaps the chauffeur stepped away for a moment. Perhaps the chauffeur has sympathies you are unaware of. It's just a precaution."

"Of course." To the chauffeur, "Miguel, please show the officers the trunk."

"And perhaps," Colonel Fuentes said. "I might have the honor of meeting your friends."

The chauffeur opened the door to get out of the car.

Fuentes took another step toward the car smiling in anticipation of a graceful social moment.

Dylan said "Shit" under her breath and cocked the pistol in her bag. Cassidy held the gun along his thigh. Dylan would take Fuentes. There were six soldiers and cops near the barrier. What were the odds?

Anger and shouting from near the searched Chevy.

Three men had gotten out of the backseat of the car. They were milling uncertainly. One of them was a man Ribera had talked to at the restaurant. A soldier ordered them to get back in the car. The man yelled something Cassidy could not make out. Fuentes turned and looked toward the Chevy.

One of the men by the Chevy pulled a revolver from under his shirt, extended it at arm's length and shot the soldier nearest him. The other men ran. A soldier stepped up behind the gunman and shot him in the back and the man slammed up against the car and tried to turn. The soldier shot him again. Some of the other soldiers began to fire. Someone in the Chevy started the engine and the car jumped forward. Its windshield exploded. The car careened off a lamppost and slammed into a police Jeep. Soldiers fired into it as fast as they could.

"Miguel," Ribera commanded. "Get in the car. Drive."

The Packard pushed the barrier aside, but no one paid attention to them. Through the back window Cassidy saw one of the rebels stumble and go down. He struggled to get up. Colonel Fuentes stepped to him and shot him in the head. Then the car turned a corner.

"Did anyone get away?" Ribera asked.

"I saw one man go down the alley."

Ribera rubbed his face with his hand and sighed. It was the first sign of distress Cassidy had seen from him.

"Well, so, we go on."

• • •

If there was a revolution rising in Cuba, the news hadn't penetrated The Tropicana, or maybe the people there were just going to ignore it until it stuck a gun in their faces. Laughter, the tinkle of ice in glasses, music from the band playing outdoors where the stage shows took place, the rattle of dice and the roulette wheel ball's clicking, the clash of slot machines, and the squeals and shouts of the winners. Many of the men wore dinner jackets, the women wore furs and jewels, and they had the avid, eager look of people determined to have fun before the bubble burst and they found themselves back in Peoria.

Ribera left them in the lobby where living trees grew up past the parabolic concrete arches that formed the ceiling. "You'll excuse me. I have a tradition, a New Year's Eve poker game. We have been playing for twenty years, the same men. I have most of their money, but I want it all." He laughed and clapped Cassidy on the shoulder. "Please sign my name to any bills." He turned away into the casino, which was handily located next to the lobby so that people who wanted to contribute their money would not have to waste time looking for the tables.

Cassidy and Dylan went through rooms of arched glass to the outdoor terrace, *Bajo las Estrellas*, Under the Stars, and danced to the music the band swung out over the polished floor. She moved with a grace he admired, and he didn't step on her feet, because she knew when to get them out of the way and how to make it look like part of the dance. He could feel the long muscles of her back under the thin silk of her dress. Sometimes on a turn his thigh would press between hers for a moment of intimacy. He pulled her closer, and she leaned her head against him. Her hair smelled of the expensive shampoo in Ribera's bathroom, and she wore a perfume as light and mysterious as a half-heard whisper.

She looked up at him and smiled. "I'm very happy. Is that wrong? Is it wrong to be happy and dancing while people you know are dying in the hills?"

"There are always people dying in the hills. We were almost there ourselves. Now we're dancing. Maybe their turn comes next and we get what they have now."

The music stopped and people left the floor. Cassidy and Dylan found a table under a spreading tree and ordered daiquiris. The lights dimmed. The music started again, but the rhythm was different now, deeper, throbbing, and when the lights came back up, the floor seethed with dancers, tall women in fantastic headdresses of fruit and flowers, bras with red nipple covers, feathers at their shoulders, bikini bottoms, and shoes with impossible heels. The men with them wore skintight pants and red shirts with ruffles in blue and yellow, and they danced as close to sex as they could get with their clothes on, and after fifteen minutes went off to wild applause.

A waiter came to their table with a bottle of champagne and two glasses. "We didn't order this."

"No, Señor. The gentleman did."

Cassidy looked to where the waiter nodded. Frank Costello waved from a table where he sat with three other men and four women.

"Who is he?" Dylan asked.

"An old friend of my father's. My godfather."

"The men he's with are gangsters, hoodlums." He looked at her in surprise. "I was briefed, Michael. I didn't come to Cuba without knowing who was who. The little one is Meyer Lansky, a Jew, supposed to be the smart one, the brains of the Mob. He made a deal with Batista in 1952 so that he and his friends could control the casinos in Havana. The funny thing is, Batista brought them in to clean up the gambling. He understood that more tourists would come to play if they knew the games were on the up and up. The one with glasses, the one who looks like an accountant, that's Santo Trafficante. His father was from here, but he grew up in Tampa. His family ran the *bolita* there, the lottery, and prostitution, gambling. I don't know who the big one is."

"Joe Stassi. He used to be just a low-level Mafia hood in New Jersey and Florida, maybe killed a few people for them. He's been down here a long time. We think he's the Mob's day-to-day manager. Costello and Lansky go way back, but I thought Costello was pulling out of the game. A year and a half ago one of the other bosses decided it was time for Frank to step down. He sent a guy over who shot Frank in the lobby of his apartment building. He only grazed him, but the word went out that Frank was putting in his retirement papers."

Costello beckoned.

"He wants you to go over."

"The Prime Minister of Crime, according to the papers. I grew up calling him Uncle Frank. Do you want to meet him?"

"No. I don't need to meet a gangster."

"I'll be back in a minute."

Costello stood up as Cassidy approached, hugged him and kissed him on the cheek, and then turned him to show him off to the table. "My godson, Michael Cassidy. Tom Cassidy's boy. Meyer, we went to that play last year when you were in the city, house seats down front, best seats in the house, the musical with the tall blonde you liked. That was Tom's play. Michael, Meyer Lansky here, Santo Trafficante over there. He's part owner of this joint. What a show, huh? You never seen anything like that on Broadway. Joe Stassi, lives down here, works for some of us overseeing the casinos." He didn't introduce the women who sat with them. They were part of the décor. But the one sitting next to Stassi spoke up for herself.

"I know you. The kidder. Boy, you really kicked over the anthill that day."

"How are you, Alice?" The last time he had seen her, she had her hand in a Florida senator's pocket while General Castillo showed them around the fortress of La Cabaña.

"I'm great. I'm never leaving Cuba again, ever. Paradise. And I've got my little Adam right here." She clutched Stassi's thick arm and leaned her head against his shoulder. He looked at Cassidy and raised an eyebrow. *Dames. What are you going to do?*

Costello touched Cassidy's arm and jerked his head in invitation toward the bar. Cassidy looked over to where Dylan sat.

"A couple of minutes," Costello said. "She'll be all right. Broads don't mind being alone."

A man in skintight red pants and a yellow ruffled shirt came onto the floor to juggle flaming batons. He was assisted by a tall, nearly naked woman whose job it was to strut on high heels and point to the wonder of what he was doing. Costello and Cassidy found room at the end of the bar. Costello ordered a daiquiri. Cassidy asked for a Bacardi añejo on the rocks.

"What are you doing with those guys?" Cassidy asked. "I thought you got out."

"A guy's got to make a living. I kept a couple of things. I thought you were only coming down for a day or so. That's what you told me," Costello said.

"I'm taking some vacation time."

"You were bringing a guy down, you told me. What'd he do?"

"He killed some people."

Costello nodded. Things like that happened. "You're a smart guy, Michael. You keep your ear to the ground. What do you hear about this Castro guy? Is he a Commie?"

"I don't know, but a guy I know who knows him says no. He says he's a democrat, a socialist maybe, but a democrat."

"Uh-huh. I don't get it. Batista's got an army, all the modern equipment, and he can't get a bunch of guys out of the hills? What the hell? What's Castro got, a few hundred men. Batista's got thousands."

"Maybe Batista doesn't want it as much."

"Yeah. Maybe. You'd think the guy with the most guns would take it. I don't know. Do you think Castro's going to win?"

"Yes, I do."

"We've got a lot of investment money tied up in Havana. A socialist? I guess we can live with that. He needs us as much as we need him. Maybe more. Without the tourists, without the casinos to pull them in, without the profits, his economy goes in the toilet."

They talked some more, about what Cassidy's father was doing, a new play for Broadway, about the Yankees and the coming season, could they repeat as World Series winners? They made promises to meet for dinner in the city, promises they would not keep.

"What did he want?" Dylan asked.

"He wanted to know whether I thought Castro would win. He's worried about his investments."

"What did you tell him?"

"I told him I thought he would."

They were dancing when the bandleader took the microphone and announced that it was midnight and offered *Feliz año.* Dylan kissed him, and said "Happy New Year" and kissed him again. She put her arms around his neck and he put his around her waist and pulled her tight, and they stood there among the cheering people, some cheering for the passing of the old, and some for the coming of the new.

As they went back to their table, a whisper burned from table to table where Cubans sat. *Se fue. Se fue. Se fue.*

Ribera found them. His face split in a grin, and his arms were wide to embrace them and all that was about to happen. "He's gone. He's gone. The son of a bitch Batista took off from the airfield at Camp Columbia. He's gone. We won." He looked happy and stunned, the way one does when the impossible, long hoped for, happens.

While they waited outside the lobby for the Packard, Cassidy watched Meyer Lansky, Santo Trafficante, Frank Costello, and Joe Stassi get into separate cars. Trafficante carried two heavy suitcases. The men looked grim, but Alice, still in a party mood, spotted him, blew him a kiss, waved, and then followed Stassi into the Cadillac.

They rode down into the city in Ribera's Packard with the glass lowered between them and Miguel, a gesture to the new democracy. Caravans of horn-blowing cars clogged the avenues. People rode their fenders waving Cuban flags and banners marked "26" to commemorate Castro's July 26th Movement. Crowds milled in the streets celebrating. People attacked the parking meters that lined the curbs with pipes, axes, crowbars, baseball bats, and battered their heads off.

"The parking meters were owned by Roberto Fernández Miranda. Do you know who this is?" Ribera asked.

"Batista's brother-in-law," Cassidy said.

"And a most hated man, an asshole. He owned the parking meters, and the slot machines, even the little ones that gave candy and prizes to children. It is said he made half a million dollars a month. Can you imagine?" It was the same tone of awe Echevarria had used when talking about Miranda's monthly take.

When they turned a corner, two men ran across the street in front of them. For a moment they were pinned in the glare of the headlights, startled like animals, faces stretched by terror. They wore SIM uniforms, and one of them carried a big, chrome automatic. They turned away from the light and fled down the sidewalk. Their pursuers ran into the street after them, and Miguel had to stop to let them pass. There were at least twenty of them, young men for the most part. Some of them carried clubs, and they howled as they ran, an ancient cry of blood pursuit. More men appeared from an alley and the SIM officers were trapped against a building between the two groups. The one with the gun fired and two men went down, and then the mob overwhelmed them. Clubs rose and fell, rose and fell and the headlights threw grotesque shadows on the wall.

Then it was over. The men stood and parted, drew back from the bloody bundles on the sidewalk. One of them held the chrome automatic. Another pointed at the car and said something, and others turned to look.

Cassidy sensed the danger. "Miguel, *atrás*."

When Miguel looked back to scope his path of retreat, his face was taut with fear. He tried for reverse as the men stepped off the sidewalk and started toward them. The gears ground and clashed, caught, and the car stalled. Miguel turned the key. The starter whirred, but the engine did not catch.

"*Suavamente, hombre. Con cuidado.*"

But Miguel was too scared to do it gently, to do it with care. The starter ground and ground, and the battery whined down in protest, and through the windshield they could see the men approaching. They came slowly, steadily. The one with the pistol walked in front as if the gun had given him the authority to lead.

"I'll talk to them," Ribera said and put his hand on the door handle.

Cassidy stopped him. These men were not going to talk.

Dylan unsnapped her purse and took out the small automatic.

The starter ground on as the battery weakened.

"We should run," Ribera said.

"It didn't work for those guys," Cassidy said.

The engine caught, sputtered, and caught again. Miguel clashed the gears, searching for reverse.

The leader of the mob raised the pistol and fired, and a bullet clanged somewhere in the body of the car. Miguel found reverse and lifted his foot from the clutch as the engine whined high. The car lurched backwards. The gunman fired again, and the windshield starred and a piece of glass blew into the backseat. The car rocketed back. Miguel jerked the wheel, and the car slewed around the corner as the man fired again. The bullet slammed into the car body, and then they were around the corner. Miguel kept his foot down, and they ran backwards down the street and into a small plaza. He slammed on the brakes, clashed into first, wrenched the wheel, and shot the car up a side street, and they were gone.

"*Coño,*" Ribera said. "That was close."

"I guess they didn't recognize the People's Packard limousine," Cassidy said.

For a moment there was silence, and then Dylan laughed. Ribera chuckled and then roared, and soon they were all laughing, Ribera until he choked, Dylan till she cried, Cassidy until he gasped. They would stop, and then someone would say People's Packard limousine, and they would start again. Miguel, forlorn of English, kept glancing in the rearview mirror to gauge their madness.

• • •

The word went out, and the cars began arriving at Joe Stassi's house around one in the morning. Gunmen checked the cars at the bottom of the drive and then waved them on to park near the house where men with submachine guns stood in the shadows and watched the drivers and passengers unload heavy suitcases and carry them into the house. By two in the morning there were twenty men in the living room drinking and smoking and talking in quiet voices waiting to be told what to do next by the four men in the dining room. Meyer Lansky, Frank Costello, Santo Trafficante, and Joe Stassi stood talking by the window while a team of accountants from their casinos counted the money that had been brought to the house and stacked in piles on the tables.

"Just in case," Lansky had said. "We don't know this guy Castro. Till we do, it's better we keep the money where he can't get it." The others had agreed and the casinos had been stripped of cash and checks.

"Jesus, have you seen what they've got in there?" Doreen asked. "I've never seen so much money." The women had been told to go into the kitchen and make sandwiches and coffee. All the Cuban servants had been sent away.

Alice dabbed at a spot of mayonnaise on her blouse with a wet dish towel. She picked up a plate of sandwiches and pushed through the door into the dining room. The men at the window turned to look at her with cold eyes. "I thought you guys might be hungry. Ham and cheese, roast beef, chicken salad."

"Put 'em over there," Stassi said with a gesture toward a sideboard. She was careful not to look at the money on the tables pushed together at the center of the room, but she could see it from the corner of her eye as she turned, mountains of greenbacks, and the open suitcases on the floor where the money went as it was counted.

"Do you guys need anything else? Can I make anybody a drink?"

"Beat it, Alice. We'll call you if we want something."

She could feel their eyes on her as she went back through the swinging door to the kitchen.

"Did you see it?" Doreen asked. "Jesus, there must be ten, twenty million dollars in there. I wouldn't mind slipping a couple of stacks up my skirt when no one's looking."

"It'd be better than the other things going up there lately," Marsha said. "Forget about it. Those guys love their money. Like a dog with a bone. You don't want to put your hand in there. Don't even think about it."

5

Cassidy dreamed of walking by a blue-green tropical sea. Waves beat against slabs of stone and spray blew high over a stone wall. He walked a broad, unfamiliar pavement. A car stopped in the distance and Dylan got out and started toward him—Dylan, beautiful, vivid, alive. Of course she was alive. He knew she was alive, and some part of him was aware enough to reach out in the bed and touch her. So why did the dream insist that she was alive?

Dream logic.

When she was close she said something he could not hear. He started toward her. She waited but he did not get nearer to her. He kept walking, but he could not close the distance.

Dream geography, dream reality.

Again she said something he could not hear. She waved and Cassidy ran toward her, but he could not close the gap. A man got out of the car and stood near her. He said something to her, and she turned and walked to the car. She looked back at Cassidy. He ran harder, but she remained at a distance. Just before she got into the car with the man, she lifted a hand to him, and then the car drove away, and she was gone.

Cassidy woke with his heart racing. The dream was still close enough to touch, and he remembered that he had dreamed it before, dreamed it a number of times in the months after Dylan had gone away on the Russian freighter and he had not been sure that she had survived what waited for her in Russia. After a while he stopped dreaming it. After a while he believed that the dream was a wish, not a prediction. But she was alive. She was with him. So what was the dream now?

The sun looked over the tile roof and into the window. It was after ten.

Dylan was not in the bed. When Cassidy went downstairs, the maid who brought him coffee said that Dylan and Ribera had gone down to the city an hour before. The maid wore an armband that said "July 26." She could not stop smiling.

The celebrating mobs had wrecked the Hotel Nacional casino. They had smashed the windows replaced after the bombing the week before, had dragged slot machines outside and hammered them open, and had attacked the gambling tables with axes. If they could not have revenge on Batista, the people would revenge themselves on the casinos that had made him rich, the symbols of the corruption that had elevated a few while crushing many. There was nobody in the wreckage, but the same clerk who had checked Cassidy in manned the front desk. He remembered that Cassidy had been sent by Colonel Fuentes and treated him with the sullen contempt the new order allowed him, but he went and found Cassidy's bag in the storeroom behind the desk and only overcharged him for four of the nights he had not used his room.

Cassidy stopped at a café on La Rampa that had tables on the sidewalk and ordered a cup of coffee. People in the streets banged buckets and sticks, impromptu percussion in celebration, and the cars honked wildly and flew the red-and-black flags of the 26th of July Movement. The waiter who brought the coffee said he heard that Che was already in the city. Moments later an armored car appeared around the corner and ground slowly down the street on its treads. Bearded men in fatigues rode the fenders and the roof, their rifles slung or held across their thighs. Los Barbudos, the waiter said with awe and ran out into the street to join the crowd that surrounded the armored car. They looked like the men Cassidy had seen in the hills—thin, worn, ragged—and they stared around them at Havana with a mixture of wonder and pride. The people around the car reached up to touch them, to capture some of the magic. Two pretty girls were hoisted to the roof to kiss the heroes, to the cheers of the crowd. The city was electric with hope and joy.

• • •

"Fidel's going to appoint Manuel Urrutia Lleó provisional president. The doctor's a good man, and his appointment will show the world that they do not have to fear a dictatorship by Fidel. He wants no part of government office." Ribera poured more wine in their glasses. They were eating a late, cold dinner at the table in the kitchen, a chicken from the icebox, a thick cold potato omelet, and a salad Ribera had thrown together with the casual deftness that marked everything he did. "You can feel the electricity in the air in the city. This is the beginning of something great, something that will inspire the world. And I am proud to be part of it." He thumped his chest with his fist.

Dylan was subdued and said little. She picked at her food, but pushed her glass forward whenever Ribera picked up the bottle.

"Did you see them?" Cassidy asked her.

"Who?"

"The people you went downtown to see."

"Some of them. Some won't arrive until tomorrow."

"And Fidel?"

"Nobody knows. He's in Santiago."

"Che is here," Ribera said. "He is at La Cabaña. And Raúl will come tomorrow, they say."

"La Cabaña?"

"It is not the same, Cassidy."

"No. Of course not."

Dylan gave him a look, said she was tired and was going to bed, got up and left the table.

Cassidy rejected the cigar Ribera offered in favor of cigarettes. They drank dark smooth añejo rum and strong coffee, and for a while they smoked and drank in silence, listening to the night sounds, the rustle of palm fronds against the roof tiles, the distant rush and ebb of waves, the calls of night birds, and the occasional pop pop of shots from downtown, someone celebrating, or someone in trouble.

"She's beautiful," Ribera said.

"Yes."

"Very straightforward, very clear. This is unusual in a woman. Men are often clear. Women are often, what? Opaque."

"Maybe we just don't see them clearly."

"Of course we don't see them clearly. They don't want us to see them clearly. They like the mystery. They are the mystery. Look at us. We have pricks between our legs, there for all to see, nothing hidden. What do they have between their legs? Chaos."

"Jesus, Carlos."

"Don't laugh. And don't be so goddamn Anglo-Saxon. Don't try to solve the mystery. Don't understand it. Embrace it. Love it. To hell with figuring it out. Go with the romance. Ride it like a wave. You should stay here."

"In Havana?"

"Yes, in Havana. We will make you a latino and a socialist. You will be a much better man for it."

"What would I do?"

"You'd be a cop. An honest regime will need honest cops. If such a thing exists, you might be one of them."

"I like New York. I don't know if I could live anywhere else. It's in my bones."

"Yes, but she's in your blood. And she's here. Have you thought about that?"

"No. I've tried not to think at all. I've tried to live one day at a time."

"Well, at least in that you're showing some latino sense. Perhaps there's hope for you, Cassidy."

He went up to their room braced for a fight the look she had given him seemed to promise. Dylan was standing at the window smoking a cigarette. The moon was high, and the light silhouetted her body through the thin cloth of the robe she wore, the swell of her hips, the long curve of her legs. When she turned at his entrance, the robe slipped open and she did not bother with it.

"Where've you been?" A mild, low voice.

"Talking to Ribera."

"I was waiting for you. I thought you'd be right up."

"You said you were tired."

She stubbed the cigarette out and stepped toward him. "I said I was going to bed. Why is it that men always hear the wrong signal? We say go, and you hear come. We say come, and you hear go."

"Men still live in the cave and respond best to grunts and sharp blows to the head."

She put her arms around his neck and pressed against him. He could feel the heat of her, the soft push of her breasts and the ridge of her pubic bone, her thighs against his. She kissed him. Her tongue probed his mouth. She tugged and stepped back and he went with her, and when the bed hit the back of her knees, she went down on it, pulling him with her without giving up the kiss. Her robe fell away easily, but they struggled to get him out of his shirt and pants without breaking from each other, and when that was done, they went at each other hard, as if there was no time left in the world. And then again, slowly, rising to peaks and pulling back, and rising again and again.

• • •

Havana, January 2, 1959.

A call for a general strike. All businesses were closed as the city waited for the appearance of Raúl Castro and Camilo Cienfuegos, heroes of the Sierra Maestra sent ahead by Fidel while he waited in Santiago for the proper moment, for the hero's welcome. Cassidy stood in the mob at the Central Park downtown as the first trucks filled with rebels rolled through to ripping cheers, flags waving, shots fired in the air. On the corner opposite he could see the bullet-pocked façade of the big department store building where Los Tigres, the private army of Senator Rolando Masferrer, made a stand the day before. A man next to Cassidy saw where he was looking and clapped him on the back and waved at the building. "Were you there? Did you see?"

"No."

"I was there," the man said and showed him his bandaged forearm proudly. He wore a madras shirt, khaki pants, and sandals, and he had a Thompson submachine gun barrel down on a strap over his shoulder. He wore the fuzzy beginnings of a beard, the new fashion in Havana. "We stormed them from two sides, and they could not hold us out. We hunted Los Tigres through the building like rats and killed them all," he said cheerfully. "I myself killed one in the ladies' department, and he went to hell with a woman's girdle on his face." He laughed and offered Cassidy a cigar and insisted he drink from the bottle of rum he pulled from his back pocket, and when the next group of trucks entered the square, he righted his gun and fired a burst into the air.

Cassidy worked his way through the crowds and out past the Hotel Nacional to the Malecón, the broad esplanade and seawall that stretched from the mouth of the harbor in Old Havana to the suburb of Vedado. He found a café with outdoor tables, deserted except for a bored elderly waiter, and ordered a coffee and a beer. He lit a cigarette and listened to the thump of the waves on the breakwater. Occasionally a fan of spray would rise above the wall. The surge and ebb of the swell was a peaceful rhythm after the riotous celebration downtown, a well-deserved celebration earned in blood. He thought about how men would fight for freedom, kill and die for it, and then let it slowly leak away in time. Maybe it would not happen here.

He alternated sips of hot coffee and cold beer and lit another cigarette and got up and walked to the seawall. He looked out over the green-blue water and then turned to look along the Malecón, the broad slabs of fitted stone curving away along the seawall, the clear bright water. Suddenly he realized he was back in the dreamscape of the night before, the same dreamscape from years ago. What exactly had he seen in the dream? He reached for it but it slipped away.

He paid for his drinks and walked along the Malecón toward the intersection where Dylan said she would meet him. He was a few minutes early. Calle L ran in a straightaway for blocks, and he leaned on the wall and looked down it and waited. Here the dream feeling was even stronger than it had been at the café, and it reminded him of the dreams he'd had as a child, when he would wake with the dream still working in him, and he would know that he was awake in his own bedroom, but the dream would still hold him, and he would still be in it and awake at the same time. Sometimes he would get up and splash cold water on his face and that would bring him out of it, and sometimes it would not, and he would lie in bed, scared to go back to sleep, afraid that the dream would overwhelm him.

A Buick Roadmaster sedan turned a corner four blocks down and slowly drove toward him. It stopped twenty yards short of the Malecón. The driver cut the engine. The only sound was the surge of the waves against the stones at his back. The sun glared the windshield and he could not tell how many people were in the car. The passenger door opened and Dylan got out. She raised a hand to him and then leaned down to say something to someone in the car. She walked toward him, straight and tall, her copper hair bright in the sun, her stride long. His heart rose as it always did when he saw her. He pushed himself away from the wall and smiled, and she came to him and kissed him and took his hand and led him back to the wall so they could sit. The car remained on Calle L pointed toward them, the driver invisible behind the sunstruck windshield.

Dylan took the cigarette from him, inhaled, and blew a plume of smoke, a sharing he had always liked. "It's beautiful here, isn't it?"

"Yes."

"Where did you go this morning? Did you go downtown?"

"Yes. I was down at the Central Park. Wall-to-wall people."

"They're so happy, aren't they? They worked and fought so long, and now they have it, finally."

"Have what?"

"Freedom." *Don't be stupid,* her look said.

"Yes. I hope they know how to keep it."

Her jaw clenched. "Don't be like that. This is not a day to be like that."

"No, you're right. No need for that."

She touched his hand. Apology accepted. They sat for a while without talking, and finished the cigarette between them. She took the last drag, flicked the butt over the seawall, and turned to look at him with her face set.

"I have to go."

"Go where?"

"Santiago."

"Where Fidel is."

"Yes."

"Why?"

"I'm needed there."

"By Fidel?"

"By the people I work for."

"The KGB?"

"Michael, please."

"Shall I come?"

She searched his face to see if he was serious. "I don't think . . . I'm not sure that would be a good idea. No."

"The KGB might find that confusing." Did she think this was going to be easy?

"Yes."

"When will you be back?"

"I don't know. It depends on so many things." She made a futile gesture with one hand.

He could not let it go. "I have a month's vacation coming. I could call the Department, put in for it, stay here until you come back."

"I don't know. I'm not sure that's a good idea." She twisted away from him and looked out to sea. The car door slammed. A tall, broad-shouldered man in his thirties stood by the driver's side door. He wore fatigues faded from washing and from the sun, and polished combat boots. Dark glasses shaded his eyes. His hair was as pale as ice and cut short. He had the high cheekbones and chiseled face so often found among the Slavs after centuries of mixing blood with conquerors from the east. He stood quietly, with his hands at his sides, the pose of a man at ease, but there was a tension in him. When he raised the cigarette he was smoking, Cassidy saw that the first two fingers of his left hand were gnarled and twisted as if they had been badly broken and never properly set.

"Your driver wants to go."

"Yes." She shook her head. "No." She gripped his arm hard enough to hurt. "He's not my driver. He's my husband."

He never saw that one coming.

"Say something."

"What the fuck am I supposed to say?"

"Say you understand."

"What do I understand?" Did she think he was going to help her with this?

"I thought I would never be allowed to leave Russia again. I thought I would never see you again. All that was over and done. And then you found me. You saved me. You loved me. The last ten days have been the happiest. You have to know that."

"And now?"

"I have to go."

"No, you don't. What's his name?" The man leaned on the Buick fender and lit a cigarette and watched them from behind his sunglasses.

"Slava."

"Go tell Slava he just got a divorce." Her husband? How could that be?

"I can't do that."

"Yes, you can. You walk over there, and say, Slava, we're getting a divorce. I'm staying here."

"I can't."

"Yes, you can." Like a schoolyard argument with no winners.

"I can't."

"Well, then, I guess that's it."

She looked into his face, hoping he would soften, and read that it was not going to happen. "All right." She looked once more, and then turned and walked away.

In the dream he had walked after her but could not close the gap, but he did not try to follow her now. In the dream he had called out to her, but he did not call out to her now. In the dream she had turned and waved to him before she got in the car.

Dylan stopped by the car and said something across the hood to Slava. He snapped his cigarette away and got in behind the wheel.

Dylan looked back at him, and, as in the dream, raised a hand. Then she got in the car and drove away.

• • •

Ribera drove Cassidy to the airport, a slow journey through the crowds in the street. More than once they were turned aside by Barbudos holding the main avenues for trucks filled with rebels and their supporters.

"There are almost no planes coming or going. They are using the Cuban airline to bring the freed prisoners from the Isle of Pines, but I managed to find you something."

"Thank you."

"I told you, chaos."

"Yeah, I remember."

"What will you do now?"

"Go home and lick my wounds."

"My advice, my friend, is to find someone else to lick your wounds and anything else you might want licked. Get right back up on the horse."

"Thanks, Carlos. I'll take it under consideration."

"This is advice from a man whose heart has been broken many times. Like everything else, it heals stronger at the broken place. Believe me. I know what I'm talking about. Find some healthy, uncomplicated girl and take her to bed."

Ribera hugged him on the curb outside the main terminal. "I'll see you soon."

"How's that?"

"How can it not be? You and I were meant to be friends." He hugged Cassidy hard, got back in the car, and drove away.

The terminal was crowded with people hoping for a flight off the island. Many of them were Americans, tourists trapped by the revolution. They took up the chairs and benches. Some of them sat on their luggage or on the floor against the wall. They looked tired, forlorn, and a little scared. The party was over.

Most of the Cuban supporters of Batista, the ones who feared they were in danger, had gotten out by boat or had gone into hiding until they saw which way the wind blew.

Cassidy found the desk Ribera had described, in an out-of-the-way corner of the terminal. It was decorated with a small palm tree. A black-haired young woman in a lime green uniform stood behind it.

"Yes, Mr. Cassidy. I have you on my list. We have already boarded. You are one of the last. If you would like to go through that gate, you will see the plane directly in front."

"Thank you." He took the boarding pass and picked up his bag.

"Room for one more?" He turned to the cheerful, familiar voice.

"Hello, Alice."

"Kidder. A friendly face. My lucky day." Her dress had been painted on, and she wore impossibly high heels that allowed her to look him in the eye. She carried a big handbag heavy enough to drag her shoulder down, and a porter waited behind her with a large suitcase.

"Leaving the party?"

"Taking it with me." She turned to the woman behind the desk and rested her handbag on it. "Alice Brooks. I think you have me on the list." She winked at Cassidy.

Alice hooked her arm in Cassidy's, and they went out the gate. The afternoon sun was low, and the day had cooled. A DC-6 waited on the tarmac. Bright green letters on the fuselage spelled *TROPICANA SPECIAL*.

"See? Stick with me. Where I go, the party goes." She bumped him with a hip, and then let go of his arm and went up the ramp first so that he could have the pleasure of following.

PART TWO

NEW YORK DREAMS

6

The dead man sat on a wooden kitchen chair just inside the 72nd Street entrance to Central Park. It was seven o'clock in the morning on a March day, spring a distant hope. Gray clouds scudded low over a waking New York. The pavement was wet from an early-morning rain. A raw day to fit Cassidy's mood as he walked into the park from Fifth Avenue and found his partner, Tony Orso, talking with two uniformed patrolmen. Orso looked crisp and fresh after his daily shave and hot towel in the barbershop at the Park Sheraton. He wore a light wool suit in a tight dark gray herringbone pattern, highly polished black shoes, a Burberry raincoat belted but not buttoned, and a pale gray fedora. He examined Cassidy as he approached, taking in the unshaven face, the pallor, the dark circles under the eyes, the torn pocket on his suit jacket, the lipstick smear on the collar of his creased white shirt.

"Hey," Orso said. "You look like shit."

"Thanks for the kind words."

"You just starting your day, or ending your night?"

"Sometimes it's hard to sort that out."

"Uh-huh. Was it a hit-and-run, or did you actually get her name?"

"Of course I got her name. What kind of asshole do you think I am? It was Corrine, or Mary, or maybe Joan. One of those, I'm pretty sure. What've we got here?"

"Young man over there found him when he came out to walk the dog." Orso gestured to the boy waiting nearby with a big, leashed, dark gray poodle. Striped blue-and-yellow pajama bottoms showed under the hem of his expensive wool overcoat. He wore a blue cap with a white "B" on it and unbuckled galoshes. Cassidy guessed he was about twelve years old.

He looked at the cops, looked at the dead man, and then scratched the dog behind one ear. When he stopped, the dog butted him for more.

Cassidy lit a cigarette as he walked over. The dog looked at him with interest, sniffed his shoes, and then sat back and waited. "Hi, I'm Detective Cassidy. What's your name?"

The dog turned to watch the boy as if curious about his response. Maybe he was. Poodles were supposed to be smart dogs, and he looked smarter than half the dopes on the force. "Seth Rutherfurd."

Cassidy gestured at the cap with the letter "B." "Do you go to Buckley, Seth?"

"Yes." The boy seemed unsurprised at the question. Who knows where adults get their information?

"Is Mr. Mac still coaching?"

That brightened the boy. "Yeah. Did you go there?"

"I did. Tell Mr. Mac that Mike Cassidy said hello."

"Okay."

"Can you tell me what you saw out here?"

"I live in Nineteen East." He gestured toward a building on the north side of 72nd Street. "I have to walk Tinker before I go to school. I always come into the park here. The man was sitting there on the chair. I thought he was waiting for someone, but that seemed kind of weird, sitting on a chair in the park. And when I got close, I thought, whoa, he's got a hole in his head. I ran back to the Nineteen East and had the doorman call the police and then I came back here to wait, 'cause I thought you'd want to talk to me."

"What about your parents? Do they know where you are?"

"I asked the doorman not to call them. They'd make me go upstairs, and I wouldn't see what was happening. I wanted to see."

"Okay." Cassidy understood that. It was what he would have done when he was twelve. He had always wanted to see. "Do you know him? Have you seen him before?

"No. I don't think so."

"Never seen him around the neighborhood?"

"Well, I thought he looked kind of a little familiar, but then I don't think so."

"Maybe in one of the stores? Coming out of one of the buildings you pass on the way to school?"

The boy shook his head.

"Did you see anyone else in the park or on the street?"

"There were some people waiting for the bus at the stop on Seventy-Second. I didn't see anyone when I came into the park. I mean anyone but him. Mostly people come out to walk their dogs when I'm going back in."

"Let me get your phone number in case I have to talk to you again."

"I already gave it to Mr. Orso."

"Okay, then. Thanks for your help."

"May I stay and watch?"

"Not much is going to happen here. They're going to come take the man away, and that will pretty much be it. Besides, you don't want to be late for school, do you?"

"No," he said with perfect insincerity. "I'd hate to be late for school. Come on, Tinker." The boy trudged away, condemned to another day in the classroom. The dog walked beside him, the unnecessary leash dangling between them.

Cassidy squatted in front of the man in the chair to study him. He looked to be in his late twenties. He had the thick body of a former college linebacker now carrying extra pounds. Even in the dull slack of death his face was handsome, though the dark blood–rimmed bullet hole in the middle of his forehead did not add to that. His black hair was curly and tight to his skull like wool. He wore a tweed jacket, a blue button-down shirt, pressed gray flannel trousers, dark wool socks, and polished wing-tip shoes, one of the uniforms of the Upper East Side. His hands rested on his thighs. They were stubby, powerful, and the nails were cut short. Cassidy picked one up and turned it over. It was heavily callused, the hands of a working man, at odds with the clothes.

"What's the thing with the tie, do you think?" Orso asked. The man's tie had been pulled up under his chin and then tied off over his shoulder to the back of the chair.

"Maybe to keep his head up," Cassidy said as he stood.

"Why?"

"Maybe so someone would see him, recognize him."

"A warning?"

"I don't know. Something. Somebody left him here for some reason." What people did to each other no longer surprised him. He had been a cop for a dozen years. He had seen the oven-roasted babies, the mangled women, the shotgun-blasted men, the battered children, bones broken from being thrown against the wall, *because he wouldn't shut up. I told him, shut up, but he kept crying. He kept crying and crying. It was really getting on my nerves,* the raped, the starved, the robbed, the conned, the beaten. That's what a cop dealt with daily, the worst that people did to each other. You had to lean into it or get out. If you stayed in, it wore you down, turned you hard and cynical. He fought against that shell closing over him, fought against losing the outrage.

Orso felt the dead man's jacket. "Dry. When did it stop raining?" he asked the patrolmen. Both of them shrugged. The skinny one said, "We didn't come on till six. It wasn't raining then."

"Around four thirty," Cassidy said. He read Orso's look. "I was out walking."

"Sure. Why not? A nice walk in the rain at four thirty in the morning." Orso shook his head. "So we know he got here after four thirty. Not much, but something."

"Do you think he committed suicide?" the other patrolmen asked. He was a beefy redhead, and he chewed gum openmouthed with an easy bovine rhythm.

"Yeah, I think he did," Cassidy said. "He put a bullet in his head. Then he dumped the gun someplace, walked over here carrying the chair, and sat down to catch his breath."

"Hey, I was just asking." Wounded.

"Easy, Mike." Orso put a hand on his arm.

"Right. Sorry." His anger was hair-trigger these days and had been since Cuba. He bent over the dead man and gently patted his jacket pockets looking for a wallet. There was nothing in the jacket. He checked the man's trouser pockets, but they were empty. "No ID, but somebody's going to miss him sometime. We're going to hear about it."

"How do you figure?"

"He's wearing a wedding ring." A simple gold band on his left hand. It had been put on a younger man's hand years before and would now be hard to get off.

The van from the Bellevue morgue pulled up over the curb and parked near the dead man. A squad car pulled in behind it, and four patrolmen got out. They gathered with the other two uniforms and talked in low voices while they waited for the detectives.

Al Skinner got out of the morgue van, stopped for a moment to look at the body, and then came to join Cassidy and Orso. He was a wiry, spidery man with bright eyes and black hair that was beginning to fleck with gray. He looked at the dead man for a moment and then shrugged. "Well, at least he's fresh. I've got a couple they just pulled out of the river been in the water at least a month. They've got more gas than Con Ed."

"No ID on the guy," Cassidy said. "Get us a picture we can show around. Try not to emphasize the bullet hole."

"Hey, Cassidy, I'm an artist. You don't have to tell me that stuff." Skinner went to get equipment out of the van while Cassidy and Orso talked to the six patrolmen.

"Canvass the area. Talk to doormen. Who walks dogs around this time, who goes to work early, find out who the bus drivers are on this route from four thirty in the morning on. We'll want to talk to them. People walk their dogs a couple or three blocks, so let's check buildings three blocks up, three down, and over as far as Park Avenue. If we get nothing, we'll check another block. You guys know the drill."

The patrolmen split up and went off. Cassidy and Orso watched Skinner take pictures of the dead man from all angles. Two techs brought the stretcher and they slung the body onto it without ceremony, strapped it down, and carried it to the van while Skinner snapped more shots of the chair the man had been sitting on.

"We'll get the chair to the lab," Skinner said. "Maybe the geniuses there can find something. There's some dirt on the legs, looks like, and there are some cracks in the seat, and stuff in the cracks. Who knows?"

The van left. And now there was nothing to show that a dead man had been sitting there for hours waiting for someone to find him.

"How about a cup of coffee?" Orso said.

"That'd be good."

"There's a place over on Lex makes coffee that tastes like the real thing, and if you ask nice, the guy'll put a shot of something in it, give it a little punch. Good muffins too. His old lady bakes them."

"Let's go."

They walked out of the park and east on 72nd Street. This was the gold coast of New York, the neighborhoods where the rich lived in limestone and granite towers with brassbound doors that led to marble-floored lobbies and wood-paneled elevators run by deferent uniformed elevator men who whisked the inhabitants up to the big, airy apartments that looked out over the city high above the smells and the noise and the scuffle of the streets. Splendid isolation.

"It'd be real nice to be really rich, wouldn't it?" Orso said.

"Most people think so."

"How is it that some guys get the money, and some guys don't? One of the mysteries of life. I know which group I'm in."

The coffee shop was on Lexington and 73rd. The counterman nodded to Orso and followed them to a back booth with two mugs and a pot of coffee. He slipped a pint of rye from under his apron and poured a jolt in each mug. Cassidy gestured for him to add a second one to his.

When the counterman went away to get their muffins, Orso said, "You might want to slow down. Don't look at me like that. I'm your partner. I get to say things. You've been on a tear three months now, since you got back. You just might want to take your foot off the gas."

"Sure. Right."

"Okay. I'm just saying. You ain't the first guy to be cut loose by a broad."

"Tony. Drop it."

"Right. Okay. Let's talk about this guy and his little wooden chair and the funny hole in his head. Why's he there, sitting on the chair at Seventy-second Street? And how the hell did he get there? A dead guy and a kitchen chair, you'd think someone might notice someone making the delivery."

"Maybe someone did. Chances are the canvass will turn up something. A lot of eyes in that neighborhood."

"Not so many at night. You ever notice how much of the shit we deal with happens at night? I bet it's seventy percent. They do the work at night, we find out about it during the day." He took a sip of his coffee. "What do you figure? Two guys to get him there?"

"Had to be. He was a big man. Even if they brought him and the chair in a car, they had to get them onto the sidewalk where they left him. Got to be two guys for that."

"A warning you said, but who's getting warned about what? In other circumstances I might say some goombah wants to let some other goombah know, but I can't think of any hoods who live up there on Fifth."

"A business deal gone bad. Maybe someone took someone for a bundle and he didn't like it." Cassidy sipped the loaded coffee and liked the bite and the warmth that spread through his chest.

"Rich people don't do that. They hire lawyers to fight their fights."

"Rich people do what everybody else does. They cheat. They steal. They kill. When I was in eighth grade the mother of one of the kids in my class shot the kid's father with the pearl-handled pistol he gave her. She said she thought he was a burglar when she found him in the hall outside their bedroom at three in the morning. They'd had some break-ins in the neighborhood, in the brownstones up the block."

"What floor were they on?" Orso dunked a piece of muffin in his coffee.

"Twentieth."

"Uh-huh. That was a very ambitious burglar. I don't suppose he asked the elevator man for a ride. Walked up twenty flights. Was going to walk down twenty carrying the loot. Probably doing it for his health. Doctor's orders—get some exercise. Did she go for the high jump, the wife?"

"No. Not even prosecuted. The father owns half of downtown. Family goes back to the Dutch. The old man sat on the Mayor's Commission for This and That, the Policy Board for Such and Such. You know the drill. He didn't want the family name dragged through the dirt of a trial, so it all went away." The people in the towers overlooking Central Park held the same boiling passions as people in the tenements in Hell's Kitchen, but when the lid blew off, there was often someone there to mop up the spill.

"Got away with murder because of Dad," Orso said. "Shit. I knew I should have been smarter about choosing my parents."

7

The doorman at 740 Park Avenue ran an eye over the young woman Cassidy followed into the lobby. He touched the brim of his hat and said, "Good evening, Mr. Cassidy," and raised an eyebrow, a man-to-man gesture of admiration. She was worth admiring. She had auburn hair cut short against the fashion of the day; a narrow, intelligent face; large, dark eyes, a thin-lipped, severe mouth that promised a dark and interesting sensuality; and a lush body in a black cocktail dress enlivened by an embroidered silk emerald shawl. High heels set off her dancer's legs. Her name was Marie (formerly Mary) LaGrange (formerly Kowalski), a Broadway actress who was beginning to excite some notice from the critics and the theater community. She had been singled out as "the only good thing" in *The Belles of Canton*, a sex romp that closed three days after opening. She had parlayed that into the part of the younger sister with the club foot in *Going Around the Other Way*, a turgid but sincere kitchen-sink drama that had lasted a hundred twenty-three performances, and she had auditioned for a juicy part in Tom Cassidy's new play, *A Way of the World*. It was, Cassidy was sure, coincidence that she found the producer's son so fascinating. Cassidy's father was a successful Broadway producer, and Marie was not the first actress who found Cassidy attractive during the casting process. He knew how it would end. If she did not get the part, there would be a couple of weeks of withdrawal, some tears of regret, a promise of continuing friendship to show that it had been him, not the opportunity, that had attracted her. If she did get the part, the break would be quick and surgical. His role was over. The theater was a tough business. A girl had to hustle if she was going to make it. No harm, no foul. Fun while it lasted.

As they rode up in the elevator at 740 Park Avenue, he wondered how the callback had gone. Marie stood close to the door, so the elevator man, a white-haired Irish gnome named Jimmy, only had to turn a little to appreciate her profile.

"How's it going, Jimmy?"

"Great, Mr. Cassidy. Great. You know why?"

"Why?"

"'Cause I realized it's a wonderful world. No matter where you are, beauty is all around us." He brought the car to a smooth halt, clashed the doors open, and gave Cassidy a wink, "Even in an elevator." Cassidy followed Marie out into the chatter and laughter of the cocktail party being given by his sister, Leah, and her husband, Mark Buckman.

The elevator opened directly into the large front hall paved in black-and-white tiles with a staircase that curved up to the second floor. The large living room was off the hall through a wide arched doorway. The furniture was expensive and comfortable, big sofas, deep chairs, American antique tables, some of which held silver-framed pictures of family members. Cassidy stopped in the archway, as he often did, to admire the painting by Claude Monet of *La Gare Du Nord* that hung over the fireplace where birch logs burned. The triangle of the station's roof gave structure to the painting. A train engine was a dark blob in the low center, and behind it was the impression of an apartment building, everything softened by clouds of steam and smoke.

Two maids dressed in black uniforms with white lace–trimmed aprons circulated through the crowd of guests offering hors d'oeuvres from silver trays. A bartender mixed drinks at a small bar in the corner, and a servant in black trousers and a white jacket carried them to the thirsty.

Cassidy's brother-in-law, Mark Buckman, stood near the windows overlooking Park Avenue talking to a group of businessmen in dark suits, and their women in cocktail dresses, girdled and coiffed, and wearing the jewelry one could wear without ostentation this early in the evening. The privileged of New York, secure in their belief that the world was ordered to their satisfaction. Mark was a stocky, powerful man in his mid-thirties. He had an open face and an easy manner. He had gone bald in his twenties and now shaved his head daily, and his skull looked like it could stop a bullet. He was a former Yale hockey star who had the reputation as a player who could see the whole rink, who was aware of all the skaters and where they were going. It was an alertness that he still possessed, and he gave

Cassidy a slight tilt of his head to acknowledge his arrival without losing a beat of what was being said to him. Cassidy had been wary of him when he first dated Leah, but in the seven years that they had been married, he had grown to like him and respect him. Mark had inherited a hundred thousand dollars from his grandfather and had run it into a fortune before he was thirty with the same apparent ease with which he had scored goals. The men around him were older, but it was clear that he held their attention. The ability to make money brought great respect in this crowd.

"There's your father," Marie said. "I'm going to go say hello. Are you coming?"

"You go ahead. I'll see him later." His father waved him over from where he stood near the fireplace. Cassidy waved back and mouthed, "Five minutes." Marie stopped twice, once to air kiss Albert London, an elegant silver-haired man of sixty-five, one of America's greatest stage actors and a director with a string of hits on Broadway, a useful man to know. She stopped again to kiss and body press the best-looking man in the room, a young actor named Newman who had just opened in Tennessee Williams's *Sweet Bird of Youth*. She laughed at something he said, touched him on the cheek, and whirled away. She looked back once to show him how difficult it was to leave him.

Cassidy looked for his sister and saw her coming down the stairs from the second floor. She saw him and posed for a moment with her arms flung wide and her hip cocked and then came down in a rush, a quick switch from elegant sophisticate to tomboy, typical of her, that made him smile. They met in the hall, and hugged and then she pushed back and looked him over carefully.

"Uh-huh."

"Uh-huh, what?"

"Tomcat. I look at you and I think, tomcat, battle scarred and dragging a little, but still howling on the fences at night."

"Thank you. I feel much better about myself now. You, however, continue to be beautiful, though, I suppose, it will all fall away someday and you'll be one of those lumpy old East Side ladies with blue hair and a huge purse eating lunch at Longchamps."

"Oh, you shit. I will get you for that."

She was a beautiful woman. Her hair was as black and smooth as a raven's wing. She wore a blue cocktail dress that matched her eyes, and dark red high heels that matched the small rubies in her necklace and earrings. The planes and angles of her face, so like his own, were more abrupt and prominent than he remembered and it suddenly struck him that she was nearly thirty, that the girl he had grown up with was gone, replaced by a woman of poise and confidence. In the early days with Mark, she had chafed under the restrictions of marriage, and he had half expected her to bolt just to show that she could. Maybe the birth of her children had brought her this new calm. Still, he sensed that there remained something dangerous inside her like an unexploded charge.

"I was just upstairs making sure the boys weren't killing each other." She and Mark had three-year-old twins.

"How are you, really?" He was always aware of how close she was to running off the rails.

"I'm fine. I'm great. How could I not be? I have all this." She waved a hand at the apartment. "My husband loves me, loves our children, loves to make even more money. I think I have that in the right order." She took his cigarette from him for a drag and gave it back. "Have you seen Dad?"

"From across a crowded room."

"Let's go say hello."

But she was distracted by a maid who needed clarification about something in the kitchen.

"Hi, Dad." Tom Cassidy turned from rearranging the burning logs with a poker.

"Michael." He put the poker back in its stand and hugged his son, a holdover from his Russian childhood, a gesture of affection imported to the Upper East Side of New York where men rarely touched except in games or combat. Tom Cassidy had been born Tomas Kasnavietski, but he had changed his name when he made his way to America as a fifteen-year-old fleeing service in the Tsar's army. A new future, a new name.

"A great little actress, that Marie LaGrange. She's going to be wonderful for us. It's as if the part was written for her." His father spoke only in superlatives and with a strong Russian accent. He believed that tomorrow would always be a better day, that every project was due for smashing success. His optimism knew no bounds, and it sometimes grated on Cassidy like fingernails on a chalkboard. "She's a sweet girl. You could do worse, you know."

Sweet girl, my ass, Cassidy thought. *She's about as sweet as a straight razor.* So she was cast. She had the part. Why hadn't she told Cassidy?

"We're doing a stage reading tomorrow. Two o'clock. Can you come?"

"I'm on the job tomorrow, Dad."

"A couple of hours. They'll never know. The first read-through's always exciting. I'd love to know what you think of the piece." His father was always trying to persuade him to give up the cops and come into the business.

"Not tomorrow."

"We're in rehearsal starting Monday. Come soon."

"Sure. Soon." An easy deflection.

"Great. Great. You're going to love this play. Everyone's going to love this play. It's the funniest thing I've ever read. There's a bit in the first act when . . ."

"Tom, we have to go. We're meeting Robbie Lantz for dinner at seven," Tom's wife Megan interrupted. "Hello, Michael."

"Megan." He brushed his stepmother's cheek in a kiss, and as she pulled away she left a trace of perfume. Ma Griffe. His mother had worn it. Did Megan know that? Did she wear it because his father asked her to? Would a man ask his second wife to wear the perfume his dead wife had worn?

Cassidy's mother had died by what Cassidy thought of as accidental suicide. She had taken pills but timed the thing so that Tom would find her when he came home at an appointed hour, find her and save her and love her more for having saved her. But he was late, as he often was, and she died from the miscalculation. Cassidy had found her, and when he did, he realized that he had dreamed of her death a month before it happened, dreamed of finding her. He was sixteen then, and when he'd had the dream, he had dismissed it as an awful nightmare. How was he to know it was prophecy? If he had known he might have been able to stop it. He carried that like a stone in his heart.

"I'll go say good-bye to Leah," Tom said and moved away.

"How are you, Michael?" Megan asked.

"I'm fine."

"Good." Her smile said she did not believe him. She was a striking blonde, a former dancer now in her forties, trim, strong, intelligent, calm, and direct. She was fiercely protective of Tom Cassidy. She organized his life, entertained the people he needed entertained, ran his household impeccably, reminded him of obligations he might have forgotten, sent notes of congratulations or condolence in his name to those who should have them, took an interest in his work without being obtrusive, and checked him subtly when his enthusiasms threatened to run him aground, the perfect wife. For the first few years that she had been with his father Cassidy had fought his instinct to like her. Guilt for his mother's death, rage that someone could replace her, something, a question for a headshrinker, which he didn't care to ask or answer. But the animosity was gone now, anyway. She was a good person, hard to dislike.

"How's the play?"

"Not good."

The answer surprised him, not for its directness, he expected that from her, but because his father's selection of plays to produce was usually flawless. Not every one had been a smash hit, but none had been disasters. "Really not good?"

"Really not."

"Have you told him?"

"Yes. We had a fight about it. We don't usually fight, but that night we did. It's an unfunny comedy about unpleasant people doing unpleasant things."

"That sounds like a great evening in the theater. What made him choose it?"

"The central character is a man who escaped from bad beginnings, is now a big success in America, and has fallen in love with a younger woman."

"Ahh."

"Yes. He reads into it things that are not there but that he wishes were there. And he has hired a young French director, a darling of the avant garde, who has the sense of humor of a toothache and thinks the whole thing is a metaphor for the death of colonialism in the twentieth century."

"Jesus."

"Yeah. It's going to be a great couple of months waiting for the crash."

Tom Cassidy reappeared and put his arm around Megan's waist. "Are we off? We don't want to keep Robbie waiting." This from a man who had never been on time since birth. "Michael, come to the run-through. A couple of hours."

"I'll try. It sounds like too much fun to miss."

Megan winked. Tom Cassidy clapped him on the shoulder, and they left.

Cassidy worked through the room looking for Marie, but the actor Newman and Marie were no longer at the party. So that's why she wanted to come. She must have heard Newman would be at the party. He went to the bar and asked for a martini. So it was done. He had served his purpose. Did he feel anything, a sense of loss? No. He felt relieved. He raised his glass to the bartender. "Happy days."

"Yes, sir. Happy days."

"Frank, make me one of those silver bullets like you made for Mr. Cassidy."

"Yes, sir, Mr. Buckman. Coming up. Twist or an olive?"

"Olive." Mark Buckman took a handful of peanuts from a cut-glass bowl on the bar. "Having fun?"

"I can barely contain my excitement," Cassidy said.

"Yeah. A dull crowd. Well-bred, polite, civic minded, proper, successful, and boring."

"Why do you invite them?"

"It's expected of us. They invite us. We invite them. The iron rules of social intercourse. And I'm making money with some of them. I guess that counts for something. Do you want to stay for dinner? It would liven up the table.

"No, thanks. Thelonious Monk's playing at The Vanguard. I want to catch the early set." He loved his sister and liked Mark, but most of their friends were rich people whom he found insular and self-satisfied, as if the money had sanded off their interesting edges.

"Yeah, I don't blame you," Mark said, as if reading his mind. "I'd go with you if I thought I could get away with it. Come on, one more drink. At least I can send you out of here fueled. And I want to talk to you about something. Five minutes, and then you're free."

The library was a male sanctuary. The walls were lacquered with many coats of a deep red. The chairs and sofa were tobacco leather, and there were hunting and sailing prints in gold frames on the walls. A man named Peter Sanborn, a classmate of Cassidy's older brother Brian, was waiting for them by the windows in the last of the evening light. Sanborn was a tall, narrow-shouldered man with a small, pinched face that always reminded Cassidy of a praying mantis. He tilted slightly forward with his shoulders hunched when he walked or stood, which added to the impression. "Michael, how are you? You look well. How's Brian? Give him my best when you see him, will you? I really must call him. I don't think I've seen him since the last reunion. We should get together." Sanborn had been brought up with all the proper manners: he inquired politely about the lives of others, pretended interest in what they told him, looked a man in the eye when speaking, shook hands firmly.

It was all a lie.

He was a member of a very small club, old New York money, which extended its membership to old Boston money, old Philadelphia money, and a few families from Virginia, and he believed to the bone that he was better than anyone who was not in that club, not that he would ever be so crass as to say it, but it was evident from the thinly veiled contempt he had for almost anyone who came under his eye. He was an arrogant prick, and he had always been an arrogant prick. He had probably sneered at the doctor who pulled him out. There had been a moment, years ago, in a playground in Central Park when Cassidy was ten when Sanborn had explained to a group of older boys that "Cassidy's father is a Russian, but at least he's not a Russian Jew, at least I think not." Cassidy had felt the insult clearly, not so much from the words, but from the complete disdain with which they were delivered, and he had taken a step toward the bigger boy, fists clenched, when Brian stopped him.

"It isn't worth it. He's a jerk. Let it go." That was Brian's way, the conciliator. Cassidy wanted to punch Sanborn in the mouth even if he lost the fight.

As Brian pulled him away he heard Sanborn complain, "What's wrong with him? Their father is Russian, isn't he? And he isn't a Jew, is he? So what's the big deal?"

"How are you, Peter? Still abusing the peasants on the plantation?"

"Oh, no. Father sold the farm two years ago. It wasn't producing financially, and he'd only held on to it for the bird shooting, but since he broke his hip, well, there you are."

So much for Sanborn's sense of irony.

"What's up, Mark?" Cassidy took a sip of the martini. Cold, clear, mineral. Something loosened inside him, and he settled in one of the big comfortable chairs.

"I wanted to pick your brains a bit about Cuba." Mark sat on the sofa opposite and put his feet up on the coffee table.

Sanborn stood rigidly at the end of the sofa as if undecided where to light. "I still don't understand why you think a New York policeman is going to have any insight that might be of value to us."

Mark raised his eyebrows to Cassidy—what are you going to do? Then, patiently to Sanborn. "He was there when Castro took over. He has met some of the players. He's a smart man." To Cassidy, "We have some investments in Cuba. We're concerned about rumors coming out of Havana that Castro is thinking of nationalizing some of the industries, that he is tending toward a socialist view of post-revolution Cuba."

"Socialist? He's a goddamn Communist," Sanborn said.

"He says he isn't," Cassidy said.

"Of course he says he isn't. What do you expect, a confession? He needs our money and support to establish power. After that, he'll do as he pleases. Are you that naïve?"

"Yes," Cassidy said. "It's one of my most endearing traits."

"I have it on good authority that he is hiding his true colors, that he is red through and through."

"What authority?"

"The Dulles brothers. John Foster was at Princeton with Father, and Allen was there with both my uncles." Members of the club. "John's gone, of course, but he was keeping an eye on the situation down there the last few years, and he didn't like it, didn't like it at all, and Allen is in complete agreement."

"Okay. Fine. Who am I to argue with people who went to school with your father and your uncles?"

"The secretary of state and the head of the CIA. The fact that they went to school with my family is beside the point."

Mark Buckman stepped in to calm the waters. "What do you think, Mike? Did you get any feeling for what might happen? You have that friend, the artist, you've talked about. Ribera? What does he think? You said he was involved."

"He believes in Castro. He thinks the man is going to do good things for the people. Socialist? Maybe. Communist? Ribera says, no."

"You're going to take his word over that of the Dulles brothers? For God's sake, most artists are Commies. Everyone knows that," Sanborn said with perfect conviction.

"You really are an asshole, aren't you, Peter. You are one of the few men I know who has learned nothing since he got out of school." Cassidy took another sip of the martini.

"You can't talk to me like that."

"Of course I can." He lit a cigarette and blew smoke at Sanborn. "I have a gun and you don't. The way the world works the guy with the gun gets to say what he wants, and the guy without the gun listens or fucks off."

Sanborn worked his mouth, but nothing came out. He looked to Mark for help, but Mark was busy studying the ice in his drink and trying not to smile. Sanborn put his glass down hard on a table and left the room.

Mark sighed and took a pull at his glass of bourbon. "You're right, of course. He is an idiot. But he's like an idiot savant of finance. What he touches sprouts money."

"Did he take you into Cuba?"

"Yeah. Sanborn had this deal. He invited me and a couple of other guys in." He got up and went to the desk and found a colored brochure and gave it to Cassidy. There was a photograph of the Hotel Nacional on the cover and Paradise One, a Sanborn–Buckman Company. The inside pages extolled the moneymaking certainties of investing in the project, past performance being no guarantee of future performance.

"So what is it?"

"It's a company Sanborn put together to invest in properties in Cuba, hotels mostly, some nightclubs. He used to spend time in Cuba. There was a cousin of some sort on his mother's side who made a lot of money in sugar and introduced him around. Sanborn got tight with a bunch of people in Batista's government, and some of the people who already owned casinos down there."

"Most of the people who own casinos down there are hoods."

"Hey, I'm just a small part of it. I have no control of the daily workings." If there was something unclean about the deal, Mark was holding it at arm's length.

"The brochure's got your name on it too."

"Sure. That's what you do if you're trying to attract investors. You go get a couple of names that are known on the Street. It builds confidence. Sanborn's leant me his name on a few projects. He came to me about this, and I said, okay."

"Do you have any money in it?"

"Some. Nothing like what Sanborn's put in. He sees this as taking him to the next level where he can look down on his father and spit in his eye."

"So why is he so worried?"

"Everyone's a little scared of what might happen down there. If Castro encourages tourism and keeps his hands off the hotels, everyone will make out like bandits. The hotels have casino licenses, and casinos are mints."

"And if Castro is a Communist he might close the casinos or take them over."

"Right. Then everybody takes a bath."

"Would you lose much?"

"A couple hundred thousand. Nothing compared to Sanborn." It wasn't a throwaway number, but it did not seem to bother him much. "If it doesn't completely wreck him, it'll put a big dent in what he's got." He took a slug of his drink. "What do you think? Do you think he's a Commie?"

"I don't know."

"That doctor from Argentina, Guevara, he's a Commie."

"There were Americans fighting on their side too. And Eisenhower wasn't doing a lot to prop up Batista."

"Says who?"

"Brian, for one." Cassidy's older brother was a producer of news for ABC television. "You'd think that if Ike was afraid Castro was a Commie, he'd have done more to make sure Batista stayed in power."

"I should talk to Brian. I hope he's right. I guess we're just going to have to wait and see. Ahh, screw it. Are you sure you don't want to stay for dinner? I'll seat you next to Sanborn and you can stab him with your fork."

8

Diego Fuentes had lost his uniform to the revolution but not his military bearing. He stood ramrod straight with his hands clasped behind his back and watched the seals roll through the murky water of the Central Park Zoo's pool. "Castro comes to New York next month," he said. "He will be some days in Washington, and then here in New York. We will have a week." Fuentes wore a beautifully tailored pale gray suit that accentuated his slimness, an ivory-colored silk shirt, and a raspberry tie decorated with blue birds. He carried a light raincoat over one arm in case the bright sun was a lie and the March day turned cool. He stood back from the iron fence surrounding the seal pool to avoid dirtying his clothes.

Ex-Sergeant Paco Lopato stood next to him. He was dressed in a secondhand suit of some shiny brown material that had been made for a smaller man. His big wrists stuck out below the jacket sleeves, and the trouser hems revealed inches of socks. His shirt was green, and his tie was maroon and made of rayon. Clothes meant nothing to him. He had no vanity about things like that. He had always appreciated the simplicity and lack of choice in a uniform. He was a doer. The action of the mission was important, nothing else. His big hands rested on the fence and he leaned toward the seals. "I have seen an animal like this. My uncle caught a young one in a fish trap when I was a boy in Cojimar. No one had ever seen one before. It tasted like beef. They should clean the water here. Animals like these should live in clean water."

A young couple with a small boy came to stand near them to watch the seals. Fuentes, an instinctive and practiced conspirator, walked away from them and the pool, and after a last look, Lopato went with him.

"A week is not much time," Fuentes said as they walked. "But all we need is one moment in that week."

"What will his security be?"

"We don't know yet. This is not an official state visit. The American government has not asked him to come. He has been invited by something called The American Society of Newspaper Editors. He has come to tell them lies they are eager to hear. We do not think the American Secret Service will be involved. Perhaps the New York Police Department."

"Ah," Lopato said and rubbed his forefinger and thumb together in the sign of money grease.

"Yes. They do not seem to be as corrupt as the Havana Police Department, but we are investigating some possibilities there."

"Does he bring his brother and the doctor?"

"No. Raúl and Che stay in Havana. It's too bad. All three of them in the same room and we take care of our problems in one moment. Still, we should take advantage of this opportunity. Fidel is the head of the snake. Cut it off and the body dies."

They stopped and looked through the black bars of a cage to where two polar bears lay on a ledge of stone above a small pool of brown-green water. A third swam languidly back and forth in the pool, up to one end, a sinuous turn, return to the other, over and over again, its back and head out of the water, its big paws driving it like paddles.

"Do you know where he is staying?" Lopato asked.

"Not yet. We have people working on that. There is much to learn, much to plan."

Lopato nodded. Colonel Fuentes was a smart man. He would get the information they needed. There was no need for ex-Sergeant Lopato to think about it. "I thought these bears would be very white, white like the pictures of snow." The bears' fur had a dingy yellow cast from too much sun, too much city air. Much of New York disappointed him, the cold, the food, the air, the women who shied away from him, the hurrying people, the noise, the anonymity. He was nothing in New York, but soon they would be back in Havana. Soon he would be Sergeant Lopato again, someone to fear, to respect.

They left the zoo through the west exit and walked south. Colonel Fuentes turned onto a narrow, little-used path, and when he was sure they were alone took a folded piece of paper from his inside pocket and gave it to Lopato. "These are the names of people we must deal with before

Castro arrives. There is a number there to call when you are ready." Lopato nodded and put the paper in his pocket without looking at it. They parted without good-byes. Fuentes walked south toward a lunch meeting in the Theater District, a meeting with useful men with similar if not parallel interests, men who knew that rewards came with risks, and did not shy from them.

Lopato watched the Colonel walk away. Lopato was not an educated man. He had left school after fifth grade to fish, and then left fishing to join the army, where he had found his true skill, providing discipline and strength where it was needed. He joined SIM and saved the money that came his way, as money did in that world. He owned three rental houses in Havana, and a small fish processing plant in Cojimar. He was not a rich man by Colonel Fuentes's standards, but he was far richer than his father and uncles had ever hoped to be, and he had been content with that. The revolution threatened to take all that away. There were rumors of confiscations of assets from supporters of Batista. There was a list of names at La Cabaña now, it was said. A list of men from the Batista regime whose turn it was to occupy the cells, to go to the wall. Lopato was on that list.

Colonel Fuentes continued south along the paved path without looking back. Lopato understood the vast chasm between his world and the Colonel's, and he did not resent it. But it occurred to him that the Colonel had not mentioned how he was to get away after he performed his task with Castro. Well, the Colonel had many things of importance to think about. Lopato's father said that the rich use the poor like tools for their own profit, and when the tool is worn out or broken, they throw it away. Lopato would take care of Lopato. He always had. So, perhaps he should know who the Colonel was meeting. Knowledge is power, the Colonel once told him, and the Colonel was a man who knew about power.

Lopato followed Colonel Fuentes through Columbus Circle and down Seventh Avenue through the crowds of tourists headed toward Times Square. He turned west on 54th Street, crossed Broadway, and continued along the block toward Eighth Avenue before stopping in front of a restaurant called Mario's in the ground floor of a six-story brownstone not far from the end of the block. Lopato, following from across 54th Street, watched through the windows of a parked delivery van as Colonel Fuentes selected a cigar from the leather case he carried, bit off the end, and lit it. He turned toward the door and then stopped as a large black sedan pulled in to park next to a fire hydrant in front of the restaurant. Two men got out and surveyed the street for threats and then one of them opened the back door, and a small man in a well-cut gray suit and gray fedora got out. He greeted Fuentes with a smile and an outstretched hand. Fuentes shook the man's hand and offered a small bow, a sign of respect Lopato had never seen him use before. The small man took the Colonel's arm and guided him toward the restaurant door. Lopato recognized him from pictures in the Havana papers, Meyer Lansky, the man Batista had brought in to clean up and organize the casinos in Havana. It made sense that they would meet. There was talk that Castro would take over the casinos. If he did, the men who owned them would lose money. It was better for everybody who had power and made money under Batista that the old ways returned. These men were natural allies. There was nothing new to learn here.

Lopato was about to go when a taxi stopped and a man got out. Lopato did not know him. He was a tall, thin American with a small head and hunched, narrow shoulders. He walked with a stilted forward lean, and he reminded Lopato of a large stick insect as he hurried into the restaurant.

As Lopato turned to go, he bumped into a businessman carrying a briefcase who started to demand an apology, but then took a look at Lopato's face, put his head down, and hurried away. Lopato smiled. At least someone in this fucking city would remember him for the rest of the day.

9

Cassidy woke up with a mouth like dried muck, gummed eyes, and a pounding head in a bedroom he did not recognize next to a woman he did not know. Julie? Jessie? Janice? Would she remember his name? Ahh, christ, what had he said to her? What had she said to him?

Hazed memories of a basement bar full of smoke and boozy laughter, his arm around the woman and a row of shots on the bar top.

The gray early-morning light showed the lines in her face, the dark roots in her blond hair, the bags under her eyes. Well, he probably looked better in bar light too. Could he get out without waking her? The trick, he had learned from experience, was to gather the clothes and shoes quietly and dress in another room, avoid the awkward morning conversation, the hopeful look for assurances he could not give. A coward's retreat. Where was his tie? Who knows? To hell with it.

He went out onto the street, Lexington and 54th, no memory of getting there, and hailed a cab to take him home to a shower and a handful of Bufferin. How many mornings like this had there been in the last couple of months? A lot.

• • •

Orso waited on the sidewalk outside the Bellevue morgue. He held cups of coffee from the Greek across the street, and he handed one to Cassidy after he paid off the cab. "I've got a pint of rye in my pocket. You want a jolt? It might make you feel better."

"What makes you think I want to feel better?"

"Okay, then. Jesus, when did guilt happen to you? Did you suddenly turn Catholic?"

They went into the hospital and down the stairs toward the morgue.

"Did you have a chance to read the canvassing reports on the Central Park guy?"

"No. They came in late. I was out of there early," Orso said. "Mom's birthday yesterday. The whole family goes to dinner in the back room at Pellini's over there off DeKalb Avenue. Like feeding time at the zoo. Thirty-two Italians shouting at each other. My cousin Johnny's there with his new girl; Francine, his ex-wife, is down at the end of the table wondering how she can kill him and get away with it. Pete and his brother Allie are out in the garden having a fistfight over the new lift Allie bought for the garage, didn't tell Pete. Aunt Tess is cold-shouldering Uncle Willy, caught him making a half-assed pass at the neighbor downstairs. Half the people there aren't speaking to each other. Mom's at the end of the table saying isn't it wonderful to have the family together? We all get along so well."

"How is she?"

"Ahh, I don't know. Getting old. She's going to need some taking care of pretty soon. Pop left her a bit of dough from insurance. I got word from a guy who knows his stuff about an investment opportunity, so I took it, a little bit more I scraped up and put it someplace I hope it's going to grow."

"At least she's got the house." Cassidy had been there many times, a modest clapboard-sided house in Brooklyn near Prospect Park usually crammed with members of the extended family. "And it's paid for. Jesus, that was a party." A burn-the-mortgage party that went on until sunrise.

"Yeah, yeah, the house." He said it as if it tasted bad.

"She's got a big family. Won't they step up?"

"Cheap bastards. I mention it, they all say, yeah, whatever she needs, but I ask them to write a check, it's always, it's a tough week, I've got some unexpected expenses, Tommy's got this thing at the orthodontist is going to cost an arm, I'll put a check in the mail tomorrow. It never comes."

They found Al Skinner in his office reading a furniture catalog. A skull on his desk wore novelty Groucho Marx glasses with an attached mustache. A pile of papers was held in place by a skeletal hand with the bones wired together to replace the lost tendons. Skinner tossed the catalog aside when they came in. "Ahh, and I thought I was going to get a couple of minutes of peace and quiet. I shoulda known better. What is it with you two? Do you know how many cops I get coming in here? I get you two. What is it? You can't wait for the report to come over to the squad room?"

"We're eager beavers, Al. We want no delays in our search for truth and justice." Cassidy cleared space to lean against the windowsill and lit a cigarette. "Tell us what you've got on our John Doe on the kitchen chair. His soul cries out for retribution for this foul murder."

"My ass cries out for a three-bedroom apartment with a view. We all face disappointment. Come on. Let's go take a look."

John Doe lay on his back on an exam table. He looked lumpy, like a badly stuffed cushion. His chest and stomach had been split and his organs taken out, weighed and examined, and then piled back into the open cavity without regard to nature's plan, and then the cavity had been sewn up. Al Skinner stood beside the table and indicated the points of interest with a pair of forceps. "What we've got here is a well-nourished male in his late twenties, five feet eleven and a half inches tall, and one hundred ninety-four pounds." He pointed to the small dark hole in the corpse's forehead. "A .32 between the eyes. The slug started tumbling when it penetrated the bone, tore a hell of a path through the frontal lobe, and, as we say in the medical profession, ripped out all the wiring and fucked up the system."

"Did you recover the slug?"

"Of course I recovered the slug. You think you're talking to an amateur?" Skinner pointed to a small glass dish on a nearby metal table near where he stood. The slug was in a clear plastic envelope. "Flattened a bit when it hit bone, but plenty left for comparison if you ever find a weapon. Check the powder stippling all around the entry wound."

Cassidy could see the black speckles embedded in the dead man's skin, burned powder from the gunshot. "What do you think? The killer was about a foot away?"

"About that."

"Probably knew him to get that close with a gun."

"Ninety percent of them do, killer and killed. Friendship's a dangerous thing," Orso said.

"He was killed about twelve hours before he was found in the park. Hypostasis, blood pooling, suggests the guy got shot, sat down, got moved while sitting from wherever he got shot."

"In the chair?" Cassidy asked. He lit another cigarette against the sweet smell of decay and the harsh overlay of chemicals.

"I don't think it was that chair. I think he was sitting on something else, an easy chair, a sofa. Then they moved him to the wooden chair to carry him to Central Park." Skinner looked at them expectantly and waited.

"Okay, I'll bite. How do you figure that?"

"There are traces of urine on the chair, and his trousers were damp. He pissed himself when he got shot, but he was sitting on something that absorbed most of it, a chair or sofa with a cloth cushion."

"That's good, Al. I like that."

"Right. Find the piss-stained sofa and you've got your killer."

"How the hell did he get to Seventy-second Street with no one seeing him?" Orso asked.

No one had an answer.

Skinner touched the forceps to a pale welt on the dead man's abdomen. "Old appendectomy. Not much for an identifying mark, but it might help to confirm if you get a name. Take a look here." He picked up one of the hands and turned it so they could see the back, and pointed out a number of small white scars, healed nicks and small cuts. There were also two recently healed cuts, the scars still livid, and one scabbed-over puncture wound. "The other hand's like that too. The guy worked with sharp tools, machinist, carpenter, maybe a chef, I don't know, but definitely a guy who used blades."

John Doe's clothes hung from a rack nearby. "He dressed well for a workingman."

"I was getting to that. The underwear's from Bloomingdale's. The shirt, trousers, jacket are from Brooks Brothers. The shoes are English, Church's. They've got a store on Madison. I went in and priced a pair when I was pretending I was going to be rich some day. Sixty bucks. The jacket goes for a hundred ten at Brooks. The trousers fifty. At the same time he's wearing a cruddy five-dollar watch. And his socks are crap, worn at the heels, coming through the toes."

"The jacket's new," Orso said. "No cleaner's mark. The soles of the shoes are barely scuffed. Probably new too. Maybe he was stepping up in class. Just 'cause a guy's a working stiff doesn't mean he can't look good." Said by a man who spent all his money on clothes.

"We'll take them with us."

"Fine with me," Skinner said. "Just keep in mind, if no one comes to claim them, the shoes are my size."

Back in his office Skinner produced four copies of a photograph he had taken of the dead man. "Indirect lighting. I used some cosmetics on the bullet hole so it doesn't show up so much. I think he looks pretty good."

To Cassidy he looked like meat, slack-faced, lifeless. He gave two of the photos to Orso and kept two for himself.

• • •

Cassidy went back to the squad room and read the canvassing reports. No one had seen the dead man and his chair delivered to Central Park. How could that be? How do you get a nearly two-hundred-pound man and a chair to that position without anyone noticing? He copied the names and addresses of the people contacted by the canvassing cops into a notebook. He would go talk to them again. Somebody missed something. Somebody had to have seen something.

"Hey, Cassidy, step in here a moment." Lieutenant Tanner beckoned from his doorway and turned back into his office. When Cassidy entered, he was seated behind his desk setting fire to a half-smoked cigar that smelled like burning rope. Tanner was a big, top-heavy man, a heavyweight's upper body on a lightweight's bandy legs.

"What's up, boss?"

"How are you getting on with the dead guy on the chair in the park?"

"Little by little. You know how it is. You begin pulling on the string, pretty soon the whole thing unravels." No reason to disappoint the Lieutenant by telling him they hadn't found the string yet.

"Why'd they leave him out there?"

"We don't know."

"Someone was supposed to find him. Like a warning. Like this could happen to you."

"That's what I think."

"Do you think he did? Find him, I mean."

"I don't know."

"We're getting some pressure. People who live over there on Fifth Avenue don't like dead bodies turning up in their park. They pay for the view, and they don't think stiffs should be part of it. Anyway, some of them know people who know people so, like I said, we're getting some pressure to clear it up. Where's your partner?"

"Checking out the stores where the guy's clothes came from. They were new. We're hoping someone remembers him coming in to buy them."

"Okay. Good. It's a weird one." He looked at Cassidy for a while without saying anything. Then he sighed, put the cigar down in the tin ashtray on his desk, and ran a hand wearily over his face. "You're a good cop, Mike. Some people think you're a loose cannon, a fuckup. Never bothered me. You and Orso get a lot of arrests, you clear a lot of cases. You've got all the right instincts by my lights: fuck up the bad guys, protect the innocent. That's all the job requires, if you look at it right. A good cop. But lately, not so much. Half the mornings you come in you smell like you fell into a whiskey barrel, look like you haven't slept. You let cases slide. You don't follow up. Days I need you, I can't find you. Orso covers for you. I don't know what's eating you, but pull yourself together. Go back to being who you are."

Cassidy said nothing. There was nothing to say. He headed for the door, but Tanner stopped him.

"One more thing. Deputy Chief Clarkson called. He wants to see you down at Centre Street."

"What about?"

"The Deputy Chief did not choose to confide in me."

Cassidy went over his transgressions but could think of nothing that might have provoked someone so high on the food chain as Chief Clarkson. Clarkson ran Special Operations, a unit that worked outside the normal NYPD organizational chart, a kind of flying squad that could be sent to any crisis.

"Ten o'clock Friday. Hair combed, hands and face washed."

"Yes, sir."

"Don't be late for the chief, and by that I mean get there at quarter to ten. He's one of those guys thinks if you're on time it shows a lack of commitment."

• • •

The lab report stated that the kitchen chair on which the dead man sat was mass produced in upstate New York and could be bought at almost any cheap hardware or house supply shop in the city. The chair showed traces of linseed oil, lead-based paint, and varnish, and, as Skinner had said, urine. Sawdust scraped from the cracks came from birch, pine, and cherry. There were trace elements of other woods, but they were too small to identify. The bottom of the chair showed traces of lime. Cassidy picked up the phone and called the lab.

"Geyer here. What do you need?"

"This is Detective Michael Cassidy over at the Nineteenth. We sent a kitchen chair down there for examination a couple of days ago. I want to talk to whoever wrote the report."

"That's me, Detective. What do you need to know?"

"The stuff that's on the chair, the sawdust, the paint, varnish. Where would all that stuff come from?"

"Well, a lot of places. Could be it was used in a hardware store. Could be a home workshop, you know, a guy who likes to take care of his own maintenance around the house. Could be, you know, a carpentry shop, a home or commercial one. Like I said, a lot of places."

"What about the lime? Where'd that come from?"

"It's not the fruit, the citrus, you know. The guy's not drinking gin and tonics while he's fixing the molding."

"No?"

"No. It's the mineral. Crushed limestone, crushed chalk. Inorganic materials with a lot of calcium in them, carbonates, oxides, hydroxides mostly."

"Would that be used in carpentry?"

"Well, you wouldn't use it to fix a table, but it's a construction material, used in masonry work, concrete, like that."

"Okay. Thanks."

"Any help?"

"Could be. I don't know yet."

Orso was coming up from the evidence lockers when Cassidy headed downstairs. "Hey, I was just coming upstairs to find you. Lunch?"

"It's where I was going."

"How about we go over to Victor's, get some of those spiced pork chops?"

"No Cuban food."

"Right. Sure. I forgot. We'll go to Dempsey's. They've got a good macaroni and cheese."

• • •

Jack Dempsey's was full. The Champ was at the rounded end of the bar holding court with Carmen Basilio, the former middleweight champion whose lumpy face looked like a sack full of marbles. They were surrounded by men warming in their light. Red Smith, the columnist for the *Herald Tribune*, caught Cassidy's eye and gave him a nod.

A line of tourists stood like sheep behind the rope waiting to be seated. Frank, the maître d', saw Cassidy and Orso and waved them up. He unhooked the rope and led them to a table near the back, away from the disgruntled muttering and wounded looks of the out-of-towners.

The waiter came and Orso ordered a Schlitz and the macaroni and cheese. Cassidy asked for a double Jack Daniel's on the rocks, water back, and a shrimp cocktail.

"That's it? You're not going to eat anything?" Orso asked.

"I'm having a shrimp cocktail." He read the flicker of concern in Orso's eyes, but then Orso shrugged. *It's your life.*

"I hear Basilio's fighting Fullmer in the summer," Orso said.

"Fullmer'll kick his ass. He's a bull. He's going to push Basilio around the ring, tire him out, and then knock him on his ass in one of the later rounds."

"Bullshit. You know less about boxing than you do about the atom bomb. Basilio's going to hit him from angles Fullmer never knew existed. He's going to stick him with the jab and then hit him with that right hand. Stick him and hit him. Stick him and hit him."

"Did you see him when we came in? The guy leads with his face. Fullmer's not going to have to look for him. He's going to be right there."

"That is one tough wop. A hundred bucks says he's champ again at the end of the night."

"Done. Easy money. Like finding it in the street."

The drinks came.

Cassidy took a slug. The ice banged against his teeth. The smoky whiskey slid down with a cool burn, and things quieted in his head. "What did you find out about the clothes?" Cassidy asked. "Anybody remember him?"

"Nobody at Brooks Brothers ID'd the photo. The jacket and pants were both popular items. They're selling for spring and summer now, and that jacket was probably bought a month ago. They'll check the charge slips, but if someone paid cash it's not going to show up."

"What about the shoes?"

"Maybe we'll get lucky. No one recognized the guy, but the regular salesman is out for the week on vacation, down in Florida someplace. He'll be back in the store on Monday. I'll go back then. God, they've got some good-looking shoes. I'm thinking of asking for the public servant's discount." He winked at Cassidy and looked with satisfaction at the sizzling casserole of macaroni and cheese the waiter slid in front of him. "Did you look at the canvassing reports?"

"Yeah. Nothing there. Nobody noticed anything. Nobody even noticed the dead guy."

"Hard to believe, dog walkers and such, early-morning strollers, guys headed for work. What about Sanitation guys emptying trash cans? What about park workers? Any of them have early-morning shifts?"

"What do you want, Sanitation or the Park?"

"It makes no difference. It's going to be a waste of time. Somebody working for the city sees a dead guy, he's going to call it in. Flip you for it. Heads takes the park."

• • •

It took Cassidy more than an hour at the Department of Parks and Recreation to get the information he needed—half an hour waiting in the outer office of a deputy commissioner, fifteen minutes overcoming the man's bureaucratic reluctance to give out any information, fifteen minutes to track down the duty officer who had the week's work roster and schedule.

"Are you saying one of my guys did something?" Mr. Bruckner, no first name offered, had been checking a delivery of fifty-pound bags of fertilizer when Cassidy found him at a loading dock. The badge did not impress him. Cassidy could have the rest of the city, but this was his territory.

"No. I'm saying he might have seen something related to a crime."

" 'Cause I know my guys. I don't got no bad apples in the barrel. I weed 'em out. Bad apples don't last, and I can spot them." He had the weathered face of a man who spent most of his time outdoors, unusual in the city, and wore corduroy trousers tucked into green rubber boots, a dark blue shirt with a tan wool tie, and a worn tweed jacket with patches at the elbows and cuffs. He wasn't a big man, but he stood with his arms crossed and his legs spread, as if daring Cassidy to challenge him, a man protecting his ground and his people. Cassidy liked him for that. He offered him a cigarette and shook out one for himself and lit them both with his Zippo.

"Thanks. I'm a Camels man, myself, but I like a change." Bruckner drew hard on the Lucky.

"I'm not looking at your guys for this in any way, Mr. Bruckner. I just need to talk to people who might have been in the area between four thirty in the morning and, say, seven o'clock, seven thirty. They might have seen something."

"I got nobody there before five. Shift begins at five."

"Okay, five."

"Barney Rose and Kevin Rotella. They're planting the flowerbeds up to the Conservatory Water. The model boat pool? You know it?"

"I know it." His brother, Brian, had given him a model boat for his eleventh birthday, and he had sailed it there until the discovery of girls refocused him.

"Okay, then. Rose and Rotella. Good guys. You won't find them out there now. Shift begins at five a.m. Five to one. Talk to them."

"I will. Thanks."

"Yeah. Sure. Forget about it."

• • •

Rain began to fall at the end of the day as Cassidy got off the subway at 12th Street, a light misting spring rain that seemed a benediction, a promise of new life. It blurred the lights in the tall buildings uptown and made the streets shine. Cars swished by on the avenues. A couple walking hand in hand stopped to kiss under a streetlamp on the corner of Hudson Street, oblivious to his passing. A white-haired man in a stained apron stood at the back door of a restaurant smoking a cigarette. His eyes were closed and his face turned up to receive the blessing. A stylish woman in a white raincoat with a red scarf protecting her hair gave him a look that on other nights might have turned him from his path. He stopped to buy groceries, and then walked the empty sidewalks the last few blocks west to his building at the end of Bank Street. He owned a loft on the top floor, which he had bought with money his mother had left him. It consisted of a big bedroom and bath and a big living room with exposed brick walls separated from the kitchen by a long black walnut counter.

Cassidy, his hair wet from a long, hot shower, stood at the tall west-facing windows and looked out at the river over the roofs of the piers. The rain dulled the lights of the distant New Jersey shore to a glow. A low barge slipped downstream, its bow tracked by its running lights. It was pushed by a tug with a red-and-black superstructure and a bold white "M" painted on its smokestack. Somewhere upriver a foghorn moaned. He took a sip of his martini, cold and clear, and then another, and waited for that first warming burst of alcohol in the system, the loosening of knots. Was it true what Lieutenant Tanner had said? Had he slipped? Be honest. He probably had. Too many lost nights, nights in bars and clubs, nights in strange beds. Too many lost days, the brain slowed by hangover sand in the gears. Days slid away with little to show for them. The list of witnesses to a liquor store robbery was still in his desk drawer, the people not called, one of the many things pushed off until tomorrow and then tomorrow and then tomorrow. *You're an asshole, Cassidy. Get over yourself.*

Jesus, enough honesty for now. Another drink would take care of that, a drink, and then somewhere cheerful for dinner. Maybe Bello's over on Bleecker, pasta and veal and a bottle of Barolo. Who could he call to join him? Maybe Brian. No. Brian would be home with his wife and daughters. Anyone else? No. All right, dinner alone with the newspaper, and then Toots Shor's. There were always people at Toots's who were glad to see him. They liked him better than he liked himself.

All right. Cut the crap.

In the end he didn't make the second drink. He scrambled eggs and made bacon and toast and ate sitting at the long counter between the kitchen and dining room. Dylan had once handcuffed him to its steel brace so she could make her escape from New York after she had been unmasked as a Soviet agent. He listened to *Steamin' with the Miles Davis Quintet*, one of the last recordings Davis did with Prestige. Davis's long melodic lines intertwined with Coltrane's energetic solos, backed by Red Garland on piano, Philly Joe Jones on drums, and Paul Chambers on bass. He drank a couple of glasses of red wine while he ate and went to bed resigned to spending the night looking at the ceiling and fell asleep the moment his head hit the pillow.

A dream woke him in darkness—*fragments of a fight with his brother who wasn't his brother, gunfire, trees strung with colored lights, the woodshed of the Mexican ranch of his teenage summers, but not the woodshed, a loud, droning voice full of metal.* He lay in the dark reaching for the images, but they faded away.

• • •

Cassidy ate breakfast at four in the morning at the Bickford's on Seventh Avenue. Two cabbies on break played gin at the corner table while a third slept with his head on his arms. An old woman, birdlike in her thinness, with flyaway white hair under a paste and rhinestone tiara, and bright red lipstick that only approximated her mouth, waved wildly from the bulwark of bags that surrounded her at a table near the door. Cassidy nodded to her, nearly a bow, and said, "How are you, Your Highness?" as he went past to take a stool at the counter. She nodded to him regally and made a gesture with her hand, a blessing. She told whoever would listen that she was Anastasia, the lost daughter of the last Tsar of the Russias, and no one in the Village said no.

The waitress brought him a cup of coffee. "What can I get you, Mike?"

"A short stack, sausage, orange juice."

"You got it."

"Kate, has the princess eaten?"

"A cup of coffee, a glass of water. She gives her welfare money to *her people*. No one can get her to stop."

"Get her whatever she wants on me."

The early edition of the *Daily News* groused that Fidel Castro refused to pledge that Cuba would join the U.S. in the Cold War against Russia. Cuba, he said, would remain neutral. A spokesman for the State Department said that there could be no neutrality in a matter this grave. With us or against us—there was no middle ground in American foreign policy.

Cassidy finished his last cup of coffee as one of the cabbies came off break and rode the man's hack uptown. The cabbie was content with silence and Cassidy was grateful for that. He loved the city in the blue predawn hours when it was at its quietest. A few optimistic taxis cruised. Trucks made their early deliveries before rush hour locked down the streets. There was almost no one on the sidewalks, a few drunks tacking home from the late-night bars near Union Square, the night cleaning crews leaving the big office buildings along Park Avenue South, early shift workers headed for the breakfast restaurants. There was more traffic around Grand Central as they went up the elevated street and through the short eastern tunnel and out onto Park Avenue. The cab turned left on 72nd Street and stopped at the corner of Fifth Avenue. Cassidy passed money over the seat back and waited for his change.

"Do you like the city?"

"What?" the driver said.

"I asked if you liked the city. It's beautiful at this time of the morning. Like some big animal just waking up and stretching. We're lucky to live here. I love it," he said. It was easy to confess to a stranger, a man he would never have to talk to again.

The cabbie checked him in the rearview mirror. Love? What kind of whacko did he have in the backseat? "Sure. Greatest city in the world. I've never been anywhere else. Why would I go? What've they got that we don't got?"

A Parks Department truck was parked on the path at the southern end of the Conservatory Waters. A grand name for a shallow concrete oval bowl a couple of hundred feet in diameter. It was bounded by a low, curved parapet against which he used to lie to launch his sailboat, the concrete warm on his belly in the summer, and cool in the fall and spring. The bronze statue of Hans Christian Andersen near the northwestern end had been put in after his time. Two men in khaki work clothes were planting flowers in a broad bed of newly turned earth near the low brick boathouse.

Barney Rose and Kevin Rotella were both in their late twenties. Rose was a tall, bony man with a shock of straw-colored hair, blue eyes, and a narrow face with an overbite that made him look like a hungry chipmunk. Kevin Rotella was a couple of inches shorter and a few pounds heavier. His dark hair was swept up into a pompadour and held in place by some goo that glistened in the light from the streetlamp overhead. He had sleepy brown eyes, bedroom eyes, and his shirtsleeves were rolled up on muscular arms, one of which sported a tattoo of the Marine Corps insignia and the words "Semper Fi."

When Cassidy showed them his badge, Rotella put down a flat of plants he was carrying and lit a cigarette, and Rose got up from where he had been digging in the rich earth.

"What can we do for you, Officer?" Rotella asked. He accepted a cigarette from the pack Rose offered and bent to the lighter.

"Were you here Monday morning?"

"Monday? Sure. We're here, right around here, every morning Monday through Friday. It's planting season. Do you know how many plants we've got to get in the ground? A lot. What do they tell us, Barney? How many thousand?" Rotella was clearly the spokesman, a man who liked the sound of his voice.

"Twelve thousand." Rose's voice was thin and soft, as if he did not use it much.

"There you go. Twelve thousand plants. Takes a lot of time. So why do you ask? About Monday, that is?"

"Did you notice anything out of the ordinary when you came on shift?"

They looked at each other. Rotella shrugged. "I don't know. Out of the ordinary like what?"

"There was a dead man sitting on a chair near the Fifth Avenue entrance. Someone shot him and then brought him into the park."

"You're kidding."

"We figure he was brought here around five in the morning, about when you guys went on shift."

"We heard about a dead guy found in the park, but we didn't see nothing, did we, Barney?"

"No."

"Nobody parked near the entrance, maybe up on the sidewalk for a few minutes?"

"We come in from the west side. The garage where we pick up the truck's over there. No reason to go over to Fifth unless we're putting in new plantings, and that won't happen till next week."

"Okay. If you think of anything, give me a call." He gave each of them his card and walked over to Fifth Avenue and sat on a bench just outside the park entrance. The sun now slanted light from the East River down 72nd Street. People came out of the buildings into the morning, men in suits on their way to work, women herding children off to school, teenagers still half asleep, dog walkers. Delivery vans arrived carrying food from Gristedes, dry cleaning, plumbing supplies, orders from Bloomingdale's and Saks Fifth Avenue. People got off the buses at the stops on either side of the avenue. How many people had he seen in the last two hours? Hundreds. The avenue jammed with traffic as the sun rose higher and promised a warm day.

At seven thirty Seth Rutherfurd and his dog came out of 19 East. They paused for a moment on the corner, ignored the red light, and jaywalked through a break in traffic, a New York kid.

"Did you find the killer yet?" The dog sat and followed the conversation.

"No."

"Do you know who the dead man is?"

"No. Not yet."

"Mr. Mac remembers you at school. He says you used to get into a lot of trouble."

"I did."

"What did you do?"

"I was a wiseass."

"Huh, yeah." The boy grinned in recognition.

"It didn't do me a lot of good."

"No." Recognition again. The dog found little of interest in the talk. It stood and tugged at the leash. "I've got to go."

"Okay." Cassidy watched the boy enter the park. He got up from the bench and walked to the corner where he could see into the park. From where he stood a bush, bright with new green growth, hid where the chair and the dead man had been. Whoever the man had been left for had to go into the park to see him. Then what? You see a dead man you know. What do you do? You don't call the cops. Why not? Because you're scared. You recognize that he was left for you to see by someone who knew you would go by that spot that day. How did he know? Maybe you went by it every day. Maybe you didn't go anymore. Maybe finding the dead man meant you couldn't go back there again.

"Seth." The boy turned to his call and waited for him while the big poodle lifted his leg on a tree. "Do a lot of the people who walk dogs walk them in the park?"

"Some do."

"Do you walk Tinker every day?"

"Yes. Unless I'm sick or something."

"Do you see the same people every day?"

"Mostly, I guess."

"In the last few days has anyone been missing, anyone who usually walks when you do, but you haven't seen?"

The boy thought about it. "I don't know. I mean, we don't always come out at exactly the same time, and I guess I haven't been paying attention. You know, I don't know who they are, a lot of them. They just say hello sometimes if our dogs stop to sniff. I know the dogs better."

"Close your eyes. Think about it for a minute. You come out of your building with Tinker, here. You walk to Fifth and wait to cross to the park. You go. You get to the park and go in. Who do you see? What dogs don't you see?"

The boy closed his eyes and concentrated. The big poodle looked up at him curiously and then yawned showing big, white teeth.

Seth opened his eyes. "The red setter. I haven't seen the red setter for a while."

"Who walks it?"

"A lady."

"Where do you see her? Where does she come from?"

"Up there." He gestured north. "I don't know where, but I see her sometimes coming down Fifth and then going into the park here."

"Where's the next entrance to the park to the north?"

"Up past Seventy-sixth Street."

"So this is the closer entrance, which means she probably lives between here and Seventy-fourth. When was the last time you saw her and the setter?"

"I don't know. A few days ago, maybe a week."

"Since you found the dead guy?"

"No. I don't think so."

"What does she look like?"

"I don't know. A lady. Brown hair. Old."

"How old?"

"I don't know. Like my mother."

"How old is your mother?"

"Thirty-seven."

"Thanks, Seth."

"It'd be cool if I helped you find the killer."

"Yes, it would."

10

Ex-Sergeant Paco Lopato finished his rum and signaled the bartender for another. The man took an unlabeled bottle from the shelf behind the bar and walked down to refill Lopato's glass.

"*Gracias.*"

"*Nada.*" He took a dollar from the change in front of Lopato and walked back to where he had been arguing with two other patrons about the baseball careers of two Havana boys, Julio Bécquer, the Washington Senators first baseman, and Minnie Miñoso, the longtime White Sox utility man now playing left field for the Cleveland Indians.

Lopato picked up the glass between forefinger and thumb, a delicate grip for a big man, and drank half the rum in one. It was the kind he liked, harsh and burning and tasting of the cane. When he turned to look at the clock on the wall the gun in his jacket pocket clunked against the front of the bar.

Five more minutes.

He was not drinking for courage. What he had to do was a simple matter, something he had done before. It needed coolness and confidence, and he had both without liquor. He liked this bar. He liked the rum they served. He had time to kill. What else should he do, read a book? He smiled at the thought and took a leather case from his pocket, selected a thin cigarillo, the same kind of small cigars Colonel Fuentes smoked. The cigars were his only expensive luxury. He had stolen one from the Colonel's desk soon after he went to work for him, had liked it, and had started buying them from the tobacconist in Old Havana where the Colonel bought his. When Fuentes had first noticed he smoked them, he raised an eyebrow but said nothing. Well, let him think what he wanted. Lopato smoked them because he liked them, not because he was trying to mimic his betters.

Lopato finished the drink and went out into the night at Columbus Avenue and 91st Street. A Checker cab was parked in front with the *Off Duty* sign lit. Lopato got in the back and said, "*Vamos.*" The driver put aside his copy of *El Diario,* started the engine, and pulled out into traffic.

The cab came down off the Williamsburg Bridge into Brooklyn and parked on a side street near Grand. Down the block a blue neon sign announced Centro Cubano. The driver turned and put an arm across the back of his seat. He spoke in Spanish. "The bar is on the left as you come in. Then the dining room, then the kitchen. They sit at a table at the back on the left. Always the same table. All the way back and on the left. A table for four. There is a photograph of El Morro on the wall above the table so you know it is the right one."

"Yes."

"There will be four of them. They are there every Thursday night. If they are all there, do it, or if there are three. If there are only two, do not. The others will hide and it will take us a long time to find them."

"All right."

"Go out through the kitchen. No one there will interfere. I will not be here. Go out the back door. Walk to Grand Street. Turn right. You will see the subway entrance. It is the best way to go."

"All right."

"Do not worry. No one will try to stop you. They will be scared. They will think only of saving themselves."

"I'm not worried."

"Have you done such a thing before?"

"Me? No. Why would you think that? Which end do I point at them? Which end has the bullets?"

"You choose to make a joke." The driver was offended. "This is not a joke. This is a serious business. War is a serious business."

"It is for those on the bad end of the gun."

"All right then. Go. It's time."

Lopato took his time getting out to show the driver he was not in charge. The driver took off before the door closed completely. Lopato watched the cab turn left at the corner and disappear. He straightened his jacket and started toward the restaurant in the middle of the block under the blue neon sign.

Lopato stopped just inside the door. The bar was on his left, as the cab-driver had said. The people lining the bar spoke in Spanish with the rhythms and accents of Cuba. The drinkers were mostly men, though there were a few women too. Some turned to look at him and then turned back to their drinks. They didn't know him, and they didn't care, just another Cubano looking for a drink or a meal. He stopped at the entry to the dining room. It was a large room full of people, most of them talking in loud voices, the shouts and laughter familiar to anyone who had spent time in Havana restaurants. People out for a good time. People who liked to live, who liked good food and good drink, who liked the tension a new woman brought to their lives. The smell of the food started the juices in his mouth. He had not found a good Cuban restaurant in the Upper West Side neighborhood where he was living. This clearly was a good one. Well, he would not be back to find out how good, not after tonight's work.

The table at the back on the left was in shadow, but Lopato could see that all four chairs were occupied. He put his hand in his jacket pocket and touched the butt of the gun, a Colt .45 automatic issued to him by SIM, part of the generous supply of weapons sent to Batista's government by the U.S. Army. He walked toward the back, pausing to let waiters with trays get by. The people at the back table leaned toward one another in heated conversation, unaware of his approach. There were three empty wine bottles on the table, and one of the men poured the glasses full from a recently opened one. Lopato glanced at the wall and found the photo of El Morro. No mistake, then. These were the ones. A thin, narrow-headed man with a pencil-line mustache and oiled hair, a white-haired man whose heavy paunch rested on his splayed thighs, a blond with a long face like a horse, and a woman mulatta, her thick gray hair pulled back from her strong face. They hadn't said there would be a woman. Well, there was. So be it. What did it matter? He did not know why this was necessary. It was enough that Colonel Fuentes needed it done.

They looked up without alarm when Lopato neared. Perhaps they were expecting the waiter. He took the Colt from his pocket and shot the man with the mustache in the temple. The shot was shockingly loud in the room, and for a moment afterward there was silence. The man slammed sideways and fell from his chair. Lopato shot the horse-faced man directly across the table twice in the chest, and he was thrown back against the wall. That's when the screaming began. The heavy man began to rise, his eyes wide, his head swiveling for an escape. Lopato shot him in the face, and the heavy bullet threw him into a man trying to flee the neighboring table. The woman sat still, her hands on the table in front of her, her eyes closed so as not to see what was coming. Lopato shot her twice.

He turned, gun ready, but no one came to interfere. The archway from the dining room to the bar was jammed with people fighting to get out. Lopato pushed aside a fallen chair and went through the swinging door into the kitchen. The whole business had not taken more than ten seconds. The kitchen staff stood wide-eyed watching him as he came through the door. A cook in a stained white apron held a big chef's knife. When he saw the gun, he dropped the knife, and it clattered to the floor. Lopato walked through the narrow room past the stove with its steaming pots and sizzling grill. The juices started in his mouth again at the fragrances of the cooking food. The back door was propped open with a milk crate to let in fresh air. He pushed through and went out into the alley and down the street to the avenue. He turned right, as instructed, and walked to the subway station at the end of the block. He would ask Colonel Fuentes. Perhaps he knew of a good restaurant on the West Side.

11

Cassidy read the *Herald Tribune* while he ate breakfast in a diner on Bleecker Street. Ho Chi Minh had gone on the radio in Hanoi to declare a "people's war" to unite all of Vietnam. The Soviet Union announced plans to launch Luna-2, its second spacecraft with a mission to probe the moon. The new Cuban government had nationalized the telephone industry, an affiliate of International Telephone and Telegraph Company. Senator George Smathers of Florida was quoted as saying, "It is clear that Castro hasn't yet learned that you can't play ball with the Communists." Senator Smathers, "Georgie," last seen taking a tour of La Cabaña fortress with his arm around the waist of a pneumatic brunette. What was her name? Alice. If Smathers wasn't qualified to speak on the dangers facing Cuba, who was?

Cassidy finished his second cup of coffee, paid the bill, and went out into a cool morning. White, puffy clouds floated above the city. He lit the first and best cigarette of the day and walked east along Bleecker until he reached Lafayette, and then turned south. It took him twenty minutes and two Luckys to reach 240 Centre Street. Police Headquarters was a massive limestone-and-granite building between Broome and Grand Streets, a monument to power in the Beaux Arts style, designed to impress both the officer and the miscreant with the majesty of the Law. On the streets nearby were the gun shops, saloons, uniform tailors, and restaurants that served the cops, and the reporters, lawyers, and bail bondsmen who fed off them. The Headquarters Restaurant on Grand Street was connected to 240 Centre by a tunnel, a convenience for police brass who did not want to be seen entering the speakeasy during the tiresome years of Prohibition.

The cavernous marble-floored lobby was crowded with uniformed cops, bail bondsmen, lawyers, singly or in disputatious clumps, bureaucrats carrying grease and grit for the government machine in their bulging briefcases, lawbreakers, defiant or cowed, about to be fed into the hungry mouth of the system.

Cassidy rode the elevator up alone, walked the long echoing corridor, and entered Deputy Chief Clarkson's outer office. He glanced at his watch as he did—nine forty-five—right on time. His preference, he knew, would have been to arrive five minutes late, just in case anyone thought he cared what the chief wanted. A childish instinct, but one he found hard to suppress. The deputy chief's secretary, a uniformed policewoman with brown hair like a helmet glanced up from a sheaf of papers she was reading. She examined him for a moment through gold wire-rimmed glasses. "Detective Cassidy?"

"Yes."

She got up, knocked once on the massive wood door to the chief's office, and went in without waiting for a reply. She returned a moment later and shut the door behind her. "Please wait." She sat down at her desk and went back to her papers.

Cassidy wandered the room and looked at the old framed photos on the walls, pictures of police officers from a younger city, some at crime scenes, standing over bodies sprawled on the sidewalk, next to a delivery truck crushed and tilted against a light pole, the broken driver slumped out the window, or leading handcuffed criminals into station houses, the lawbreakers' faces often hidden by upheld hands or tilted fedoras. He sat down on one of the uncomfortable wooden chairs and lit a cigarette. What did the deputy chief want? There was no point in guessing at it. He would know soon enough.

At ten o'clock on the dot, the secretary looked up and said, "You may go in."

Deputy Chief Clarkson's office looked west toward the river and New Jersey and north toward the towers of Midtown. The walls were dark wood paneled but enlivened by large framed prints of Winslow Homer sailing scenes. The carved wood desk was massive, the floor thickly carpeted in dark blue. A comfortable leather sofa and two leather armchairs were grouped around a coffee table with a glass top, but they were not for Cassidy. A wooden armchair, twin to the one in the outer office, waited centered and squared in front of the desk. Cassidy walked to it and sat down.

Deputy Chief Harold Clarkson glanced at Cassidy and then continued to read the papers on his desk. Cassidy had never met the chief before. He was a slight man with black hair painted on a neat, narrow skull, pale skin, dark eyes, and a thin-lipped mouth like a razor cut through the flesh. He wore a white shirt and a black tie with faint red figures, and a black suit. He was as opaque and impenetrable as slate.

"You're an interesting cop, Detective Cassidy." He did not mean it as a compliment. His voice was thin and sharp, his tone cool. It was like listening to a steel needle. "One week people want to give you a medal, the next they want to fire you." Clarkson's hands rested on the desktop. They were narrow and long-fingered, and the nails were cut short, manicured, and buffed. "You grew up on the Upper East Side. You're father's a successful Broadway producer. You went to one of those fancy East Side schools with a bunch of Rockefellers. Why'd you become a cop?" He meant: you had money. People with money don't join the cops.

What could Cassidy tell him? That the war changed him, that he came back from it unable to find traction, that he saw a recruiting poster, walked in and joined up? Did any of that make sense? Only to him. "I wanted to serve." A shading of the truth.

"Sure." Neutral, neither belief nor disbelief. "Are you political?"

"I vote."

"You're not a lefty, are you? There are a couple of notes in your jacket." He tapped a file folder squared to the edges of the desk. "They say you might be a lefty."

"Do they?"

Clarkson waited, but there was no more. "Who'd you vote for in fifty-six?"

"Mickey Mantle. He had a good season. Batted three oh four, had thirty-nine home runs. I figured it was time for him to move up."

"Don't screw with me, Cassidy. I don't give a shit who your rabbi is. I ask you a question, you answer it." He did not raise his voice. "Who'd you vote for?"

"Sanctity of the voting booth. The secret ballot. One of the foundations of Democracy." He did not have a rabbi, a protector, but everyone thought he did, in part because he had thrown another cop out a third-story window, twice, and had never been punished.

"How long do you think you can be a pain in the ass and stay in the Department?" Clarkson showed no anger, only mild curiosity.

"I don't know." Maybe he was reaching the point where he did not care.

"What do you think of the Commies?"

"I don't like them. Dictatorship of the proletariat is still a dictatorship."

"The bastards want to take over the world. At least they don't make any bones about it. Telling it straight out. Khrushchev, Stalin, not an ounce of difference. The biggest mistake we made was not letting Patton push on to Berlin and beyond at the end of the war. We should have stopped the Russians on the Polish border. It would've saved us a lot of trouble. Hell, we probably should have run them back to their own borders, dropped the A-bomb on the bastards before they got one of their own. Let them know how the world was going to work."

Cassidy said nothing. He remembered how tired they'd been after ten months of fighting, those who'd survived D-Day, France, Belgium, the Bulge, Germany—exhausted, running on fumes. Ten days of combat wore you out. Ten months took you someplace you did not know existed. The only ones who weren't tired were the dead. The only ones who didn't remember hadn't been there or had been far enough up the chain of command to sleep in a bed most nights. He wondered what Clarkson had done in the war. A lot of police were declared essential to the war effort and never left home. The war lovers, he had discovered, the most belligerent, were the men who had never seen combat and now suspected they had missed something wonderful.

"Cuba."

"Yes, sir?"

"This fellow Fidel Castro is making a visit to the States on April 15. A couple of days down in Washington, and then he's coming up here. It's not a State visit. He's been invited by a bunch of newspaper editors. The Secret Service will cover him when he's in DC with the help of the DC police and the FBI. When he gets up here, he's our problem. I've been assigned to set up the security detail. You're on it."

"Why me?"

"You've been down there, right? You were there when the shit hit the fan New Year's Eve, right?"

"Yes, sir."

"You speak Spanish."

"Yes."

"You know some of the players."

"I never met Castro. I was out of there a couple of days after they took Havana. He wasn't in the city yet."

"Well, you met someone, because someone asked for you specifically, a fellow named Ribera. Carlos Ribera. Do you know him?"

"Yes, sir." So Ribera had moved into the inner circle.

"Well, there you are. I don't know why they want you, but they do, and we will accommodate them. We'll be setting up a command post down here at Centre Street. You'll be detached from your precinct. Are you working anything right now?"

"A murder in Central Park."

"Wrap it up or pass it off to someone else. When Castro gets here, you're mine."

"Yes, sir." He still had time before Castro arrived. "I'd like to bring my partner on the security detail."

"Sure. We're going to need bodies."

"I don't know much about setting up security."

"I do. I'll be running the show." Cassidy took out a pack of Luckys and started to tap one out. "Please don't smoke. This is not going to be an easy assignment. Castro has made a lot of enemies. Last night we had an incident at a Cuban restaurant in Williamsburg. A man walked into the dining room and shot four people with a pistol. Very cold, very efficient. All four dead. The shooter walked out through the kitchen and disappeared. The restaurant was a known haunt of supporters of Castro. One of the dead was a Castro advance man. He was here to set up hotel rooms, make reservations. Not an important member of the new administration in Havana, and we do not know if he was the target or if the other three were, but we are treating it as an attack on the new regime."

"Any leads?"

"Only a description, and you know what that's like. The shooter is anywhere from five feet six to six feet six, a hundred twenty-five pounds to two hundred fifty pounds, wearing dark clothes, light clothes, red hair, black hair, one gun, two guns, a machine gun. Eyewitnesses." A cop's contempt.

"Do you think there will be an assassination attempt on Castro?"

"We entertain the possibility. Let me assure you that I will be extremely annoyed if anything happens to Mr. Castro while he is in our jurisdiction."

"I'm sure he will be too."

"Cassidy, I'm sure you're a funny man to many people, but I have no sense of humor. You would do well to stifle your instinct to amuse while in my presence."

"I'll do my best, sir."

• • •

He went to bed early and woke after midnight from a splintered dream of Dylan. Not in Cuba. Too much cold concrete for Havana. New York? Maybe New York. *She was crouched over a man lying on the ground. Who was it? Was it himself? No. Someone else.* He lay in the dark trying to pin a fragment that would lead him back into the dream, but they all slipped away and he was left with nothing but an image of her smile, and a hollow feeling. He got up and padded naked through the apartment to the living room and stood at the open window looking out. The breeze brought the salt smell of the river. Just to the north, the El carrying carcasses rattled into the meatpacking district and stopped with a screech of metal on metal. Somewhere uptown a siren wailed. Sleep was gone. He returned to the bedroom, got dressed, and went out into the night.

The taxi dropped him at 28th Street and Sixth Avenue. The neon sign above the White Rose blinked and frizzed, and he went into the saloon and ordered a Jack Daniel's neat and drank it among the late-night drinkers who leaned against the bar in silence, content with their internal conversations with private ghosts. He bought a bottle from the bartender and carried it to 821 Sixth Avenue, a five-story building of dilapidated lofts, and up to the cheerful seething disorder of Gene Smith's apartment.

Some people called it The Jazz Loft, because there was always music playing. Depending on the night you might find Thelonious Monk, Roy Haynes, or Bill Evans jamming, and if they weren't, there would be someone you'd never heard playing like he should have been famous. It didn't matter what time of the day or night, if you were looking for great music and for a lift, you could head to 821 Sixth. It was where disparate strands of the city wound together and produced energy that no one strand could spark by itself. It was a sanctuary for weird talents, thieves, pimps, and whores, artists, con men, known geniuses and unsung ones, teen runaways, and a sprinkling of uptown types, the ones who had a knack for where offbeat life was going on in the city. When Cassidy came in, Zoot Sims was roaming through the higher registers of his alto sax while Roy Haynes leaned over his drums and found a rhythm and urgency that supported and pushed, and some kid who couldn't have been more than fifteen played the upright piano against the wall like he'd invented bebop. The air in the place was the usual fug of reefer smoke, tobacco, and alcohol. It was crowded with people who had lost all sense of time. A dwarf with white hair that sprang from his head as if scared played chess near the window against an impossibly thin Negro man with a head as round, black, bald, and polished as a bowling ball. Three women and two men were dancing to a beat that wasn't coming from the trio with the piano. A woman in a green evening dress and uptown jewelry sat in a chair in a corner and cried as if her heart had broken while a man in blue jeans, work boots, and a leather jacket crouched next to her and tried to comfort her. The walls were covered with black-and-white photographs and unframed canvases of local artists.

The joint belonged to W. Eugene Smith, one of the great war photographers who had been blown up but not killed on Okinawa, a tall, thin man with a narrow mustache and a severe face that had seen more than most men could stand. He was leaning against a wall talking to an up-and-coming bantamweight fighter from Brooklyn named Benny Marquez. Cassidy had seen Marquez spar at Stillman's gym, hands like a snake's strike and vicious intent. Smith, as usual, held a camera down near his waist and was taking photographs from that angle without checking the viewfinder. Cassidy held up the bottle and Smith gave him a nod of thanks. Cassidy headed for the kitchen and the unlikely possibility of a clean glass. As he passed the door to the bathroom it swung open and he had a quick glimpse of a woman with her high-heeled foot up on the toilet, her skirt pulled back above her garter belt while another woman inserted a hypodermic in her thigh.

He found a glass and washed it at the sink and discovered a block of ice melting in a galvanized tub. There was an ice pick stuck in the wall above the tub, and he used it to chip off chunks to fill the glass and then poured bourbon over it and swirled it with his finger to cool it and went back into the big room. A good-looking woman with a white streak in her black hair looked at him with invitation. *Come talk to me. Let's see what happens.* He liked women and they knew it, and on other nights he would have taken up the invitation, but tonight he was not ready for the tension of the new, the feeling out, the exploration, the excitement or ultimate disappointment. Why not? The dream of Dylan? Maybe. It was not a scab he wanted to pick.

The kid on the piano was flying, and Sims and Haynes were drafting in his slipstream exchanging looks of glee. People broke out in applause after one improbable riff that turned back on itself a couple of times, finding seams and strands, following them, and then blowing out the walls, yanking a spontaneous laugh from Cassidy. *What the fuck was that?* And then a hand touched him on the shoulder and warm breath huffed against his ear, and a soft voice said, "Ooooh, I know you. How are you, kidder?"

He turned. "Alice." He was delighted.

"Oh, a girl does like it when a guy she only met a couple of times remembers her name." Alice Brooks, the tall, pneumatic brunette from Havana. He had last seen her when they got off the plane in Miami after the revolution. Her brown hair was now blond and cut in a different way so that it framed her face.

"How could I forget? I've been looking for you all over. Where've you been hiding?"

"Liar. But I do like it." She swatted him gently and took the glass out of his hand and drank from it. Her voice was the same, languid, low, full of easy humor.

"What are you doing here?"

"I came with a guy." She made a face. "He'd heard about the place and wanted to see it, and he heard I'd been, so what the hell? He buys dinner; I bring him here. Here I am. Here you are. It's fate."

"Where's he?"

"Oh, he's around." She blew out a breath of weariness, and drank some more of Cassidy's drink. She looked at him speculatively. "Are you going to save me from him?"

"I think I might." He liked her, liked her cheerfulness, her openness.

She grinned. "I always thought we could have some fun. I was kind of sorry you didn't want to stay in Miami when we got off the plane from Havana. Well, I am a firm believer in second chances. Do you want to get out of here?"

"What about the guy?"

"The hell with the guy. He was a bench warmer. He was never going to make the rotation. But at least I got dinner at 21."

"Cold."

"Hey, it's a cold world. There are only a couple ways for a girl to make her way these days, and I can't type."

They found a taxi on Sixth, and Cassidy gave him the address of his apartment on Bank Street. Alice settled against him and put her head on his shoulder and purred.

They climbed the four floors to his apartment, and he unlocked the door and reached in to turn on the lights, and then stepped back to let her enter. She stood in the center of the living room and took it all in while he went into the kitchen and cracked an ice tray into the bucket.

"Oooh, I like this. Wow, you'd never think the place was so big from the outside." She went to the window and looked out at the distant lights across the river. "Is that New Jersey?"

"Yes." He found the bourbon and poured a splash over an ice cube in a glass. She came to lean on the counter. "Do you want a drink?"

"No, thanks. Which way is the bedroom?"

"Over there."

"Unzip me, will you?" She turned her back and he leaned across the counter and unzipped her dress.

"Thanks." She held the front against her, smiled at him, and walked to the bedroom.

He put the whiskey down untasted and followed her.

• • •

Cassidy made coffee in the morning and was finishing his first cup when Alice came out of the bedroom dressed in his bathrobe with the cuffs rolled up.

"Good morning. Coffee?"

"Please. Cream and sugar if you've got it." She stretched until her spine cracked. The robe's belt pulled loose, and the robe opened to show her heavy breasts, round belly, and long legs. She finished stretching, sighed in contentment, and pulled the robe closed without self-consciousness. She leaned against the counter and watched while he poured her a mug and found the cream and sugar. She took a couple of sips. "Hmmm, good." She took a cigarette from the pack on the counter and lit it with his Zippo. His gun rig was on the counter, and she poked it with a finger. "Going to work?"

"Yes. Can I drop you someplace?"

"Do you mind if I stay and take a bath? I haven't seen a tub that size in a long time."

"Go ahead. Make yourself at home."

She sipped at her coffee and watched him over the rim of the mug while he slipped on the shoulder holster and covered it with his jacket. "So, hit-and-run, or are we going to see each other again? Either way is fine with me. I had a great time." But he could sense a note of anxiety under the brightness. *Does he want me?* No. *Does he* like *me?*

He did like her. "How about dinner tonight?"

"Sure." A big smile.

"Where shall I pick you up?"

"Do you know the Barbizon on Sixty-third between Lex and Third?"

"Sure. What are you doing there?" The Barbizon was a hotel for women, a temporary home for young women starting their adventures in the city.

"Sometimes a girl needs a refuge. You know the rules there—no men allowed above the ground floor, and they have dragons guarding the gates. Sometimes I just want to be someplace where I can close the door and be quiet and no one can get in."

"Seven o'clock. I'll call you if I'm going to be late."

He came around the counter, and she pushed back and straightened, and he slipped his hands inside the robe and pulled her close and felt the heat coming off her and the solid weight of her against him. They kissed and she put her arms around his neck and pressed against him, and he could feel himself rise. She pushed back and laughed and said, "I'll see you tonight."

He walked the blocks toward Hudson Street whistling. For the first time in months he eagerly faced the day.

12

The conference room on the fifth floor of One Centre Street was full when Cassidy and Orso entered. There was a lull in the buzz of conversation as men turned to check them, and then turned back into their groups to exclude them. Orso raised his eyebrows and smiled.

Cassidy shrugged. "That's what happens when you're the best-looking guy in the room. The green-eyed monster of envy."

"Sure. That explains me, but what about you?"

It wasn't the first time Cassidy had walked into a room full of cops and felt the frost. He did not set out to make enemies, but he had a knack for it. He asked questions where others were quiet, pushed when others stood back, disregarded rules and customs that others held dear.

And he did not take the money.

The Japanese had a saying: The nail that stands up will be hammered down. Cassidy understood there were many men on the force who would like to be his hammer. Some he knew about, some he didn't. Some were in this room on the fifth floor of Police Headquarters.

"Check the corner by the window," Orso said.

Two men stood apart from the uniformed cops. They both wore double-breasted suits, dress shirts, and ties, and their fedoras lay on the broad windowsill near them. Carl Susdorf and Paul Cherry, FBI agents he had banged up against before. Susdorf was tall and lanky with a sallow complexion and narrow face, and his brush-cut dirty blond hair had thinned. Cherry was still twenty pounds overweight and wore a suit he must have bought with the idea that he had a few more pounds to gain. His wide hand-painted tie was a mess of purples and yellows. His face was florid, as if there was too much blood below the skin and he looked at the world through angry eyes. Susdorf saw Cassidy looking his way, and nodded. Cherry jerked his head as if inviting a fight.

"Old friends," Orso said.

"Yeah. Well, the Feebles were bound to show up for this one."

Five years before, J. Edgar Hoover had assigned Susdorf and Cherry to bring Cassidy to heel and to retrieve some photographs the FBI Director wanted. They had failed. If Cassidy had any leverage in their world, it was because Hoover and his number-two man, Clyde Tolson, thought he still had the photos. He didn't. He had kept his end of the bargain he had made with Hoover, but Tolson and Hoover were hardened conspirators who could not believe that a man would willingly give up an advantage. If they ever came around to the understanding that he had no leverage, they would probably have him killed.

"Do you know many of these guys?" Orso waved a hand at the men in the room.

"Some, not many."

"Do you see any street cops? I see the Pig and the Nig, but who else?"

"Barzani over by the other door. Wilcox. Dunne."

"Yeah, but who are the rest of these dopes?"

The men in the room were, for the most part, cut from the same cloth. They were alert, bright, trim, with short-cut hair, good posture, and tailored uniforms. Eager beavers, strivers, ambitious men with bright futures in the Department, attuned to every political zephyr that might blow to their advantage. They had spent time on the beat early in their careers, because that looked good on the résumé, but they were office cops, and their goal was to rise in the Department. They paid lip service to the icons of Law and Justice, but they understood that the only mission worth anything was advancement. They were masters of bureaucratic infighting, eager to lick the boot of the man above them and to step on the face of whoever was pushing from the rung below.

"Do you know why we're here?"

"To do the heavy lifting," Orso said.

"Yes. And if something fucks up, they're going to need scapegoats."

A door at the back of the room opened with a bang, and Deputy Chief Clarkson charged in followed by aides carrying charts and notebooks. The room went quiet. Clarkson took a stance behind a lectern. "Seats, please." Chairs scraped as the men settled, and then the room went quiet. Orso and Cassidy leaned against the wall near the door.

Clarkson shuffled papers on the lectern and then looked out into the room without saying anything until he was sure he had everyone's attention. "As you all know, Fidel Castro, who seems to be the de facto leader of Cuba at the moment, will arrive in this country on April 15. He will spend six days visiting our nation's capital, and will come to New York on April 21. This is not an official visit by a head of state. Mr. Castro has been invited by the American Society of Newspaper Editors." He paused. "Guys will do anything to sell a paper, eh?"

Dutiful laughter ran through the room.

"The Department has the job of providing security for Mr. Castro while he is in the city, and we will do that job with the efficiency and professionalism that is the hallmark of the New York Police Department."

Orso leaned over to whisper, "Then the guy's dead five minutes after he hits the streets."

"Mr. Castro's party will consist of about fifty people. We have been informed that nineteen of them will be members of his security detail. We have no idea of their training or competence, and therefore we will proceed under the assumption that they lack both. We will confer with them as a matter of diplomacy, but all tactical decisions will be made by Department personnel. Many of you in this room have worked security detail for visiting dignitaries. You know the drill. However, this situation presents a special set of problems. Mr. Castro, as you know, took power from the elected government of President Batista after a prolonged armed struggle. We have evidence that those animosities have surfaced in New York. Three days ago four people were assassinated in a restaurant in Williamsburg that caters to Cubans. Those killed were supporters of Mr. Castro. There have been rumors, so far unsubstantiated, that there will be an attempt on Mr. Castro's life while he is in this country. I have asked Special Agent Susdorf of the FBI to speak to us on this point. Susdorf."

Clarkson stepped aside and Susdorf took his place behind the lectern. He started to speak, coughed to clear his throat, and started again. "Our Intelligence unit has received reports that former members of President Batista's security forces intend to mount an attempt on Castro's life. As Chief Clarkson said, these are unsubstantiated reports, but we have been hearing of them from multiple sources, and we are not, at this point, willing to discount them. FBI Intelligence units are following up what leads we have, and we will keep you apprised of any new information as we receive it." He nodded to Clarkson and stepped aside to let the chief back behind the lectern.

"As of yet we do not have a schedule for Mr. Castro's visit. We have asked his people to provide us with a list of activities, but beyond a visit to the UN on the Wednesday, and a courtesy visit to Mayor Wagner at City Hall on the Thursday, we have received nothing. We must be prepared for every eventuality. This will be a difficult five days, but we will rise to the occasion. One more thing before we discuss structure and command. There is a rumor that Mr. Castro has Communist sympathies. This will have no effect on this department's resolve to do its duty. We are not here to judge him, God will do that. We are here to protect him. I loathe the Communists and everything they stand for, but I have put aside those feelings for the duration, and I expect every man here to do the same."

As Clarkson droned platitudes, Cassidy let his mind wander. Why listen? No one in the room had any idea of what was going to happen in the week that Castro was in the city. They would flood his movements with cops. They would erect barriers to hold back people eager to see him. They would do what they could. But they knew that anyone determined enough to give up his own life could reach Castro and kill him. The Department could plan. The Department could anticipate. The Department could reassure. But in the moment, it would be up to the men on the ground around the target to react, and few of the cops in this room would be there, and of those who were, fewer still would know what to do.

Clarkson introduced the four captains who would command different aspects of the security structure, and each was allowed his minutes of limelight behind the lectern. Cassidy closed them off and drifted.

Alice lying on the bed smoking a cigarette after making love, one arm behind her head, her big breasts flattened by gravity, one leg across his. Passing him the cigarette and raising herself on one elbow to look down at him. "My lucky night, Michael Cassidy."

"Mine too." Meaning it.

Something had been torn out of him in Havana when Dylan walked away and got in the car. Maybe Alice would close that rip. Could she? Yes. Maybe. *Don't think. Just go.*

"Let's get out of here," Orso said, and Cassidy realized that the room was alive with talk, that the briefing was over, and that most of the men clustered toward the front of the room to bask in the light of Deputy Chief Clarkson.

• • •

Someone called "Hold it" before the elevator doors closed, and the operator clashed them open again. The Pig and the Nig got on.

Alfie Bonner and Clive Newly, the Pig and the Nig, as they were known, though not to their faces. Bonner did not care what you called him, but he would hear no disrespect for his partner. Bonner was an old-fashioned street cop who knew every punk, grifter, con man, pickpocket, stick-up artist who worked Broadway and Times Square. He believed in back-alley blackjack justice, and more than one hood left the city nursing broken bones. Wops, chinks, hunkies, dagoes, niggers, spics, his disdain was democratic, and nobody could figure out how Newly, a Negro, escaped it.

Bonner was built low to the ground, five nine, two hundred ten pounds, square, indestructible. His head was a keg with one blue and one hazel eye, a small nose, a thick-lipped mouth, and fine white hair buzzed short. He looked like someone had built him on a hangover Monday after a long, hard weekend. His usual cologne of whiskey and cheap cigars filled the elevator.

"The guinea and Park Avenue."

"Good to see you too, Bonner."

Clive Newly was a tall, thin black man with a narrow face that rarely changed expression, a mask of calm. Cassidy wondered if the calm was real or cover. Being a Negro was hard enough, being a Negro cop was harder. How did his people think of him, as ally or as enemy? Newly, who lived with prejudice, went about his business quietly and dispassionately and seemed to hate nobody.

"How're you doing, Detective Newly?"

"I'm fine, Detective Cassidy. How are you?" He had a low, smooth voice. Newly had risen to the rank of detective outside the usual quota for Negro officers. He had been the hero in a shootout during an election year, and some bright young politician understood that the Negro vote might swing the election and had engineered Newly's promotion.

"Buy you guys a drink?" Bonner asked.

An unusual invitation.

Orso looked to Cassidy. "Sure," Cassidy said.

Bonner took a cigar stub from his hatband and lit it. It smelled like burning dung.

They walked out of Police Headquarters and across the park in front of the columned arcade at City Hall. An old woman in a stained housecoat and fake fur slippers, her hair wrapped in an orange dish towel, sat on one of the benches and fed the pigeons stale bread out of a brown paper bag. She called them by name, "Here, Florence, you let Peter in to get some. There you go, Henry, there's a nice big piece. Now, Willy, don't be greedy. You have to share." The pigeons didn't seem to be listening.

They went west on Chambers Street, crossed Church Street, and turned into a building halfway up the block. The windows were painted black to keep passing citizens from looking in, and the dingy metal door with small gold letters—Hanno's—did not invite curiosity. The barroom was dimly lighted by the back bar light and hanging globes that had once been gas fixtures. Sawdust and peanut shells muffled the worn oak floor. The place smelled of spilled beer and whiskey, and tobacco smoke trapped for decades. There were a few booths along the wall opposite the bar, and some round oak tables and mismatched chairs in the area between, and if you had the courage, you could order food from the kitchen in back.

It was too late for the graveyard-shift cops who stopped by in the morning for a pop on the way home, too early for day-shift guys, and except for a few timeless drinkers at the far end of the bar, they had the place to themselves. The bartender was an ex-cop invalided out with a hand shredded by a shotgun blast. Everyone called him Hanno, though that was not his name. It came with the place when he bought it, and he soon stopped swimming against the tide. He came and asked them what they wanted. Cassidy ordered a beer. Orso knew better than to order a martini in Hanno's and asked for a gin on the rocks. Newly had Coca-Cola. Bonner ordered a pint and a shot.

When the drinks came, Bonner dropped his shot glass of rye into the mug of beer, and upended the mug and drank till the shot glass slipped down and bumped against his teeth. He banged the empty mug down and wiped his mouth with a bar napkin and belched. "Jesus, that'll knock your dick stiff. Hanno, another." The bartender nodded and reached for a new mug. "So what'd you think of that clusterfuck up there. Jesus christ, I hope nobody goes for this Castro asshole, because anyone really wants him, they're going to get him, and it don't matter how many cops are standing around, and then they'll be looking for someone to blame it on, and it won't be any of that daisy chain over there on Centre Street."

"That's what Mike was saying." Orso tasted his gin and made a face.

"Yeah? Well that's 'cause Cassidy's a bright boy. You're a bright boy, aren't you, Cassidy?" Everything Bonner said had an edge of belligerence.

"That's what my mother always told me, and she was as objective as a mother can be."

Bonner snorted and stuck out his hand to stop the stein of beer Hanno slid down the bar. "The first time I got a look at you, you know what I thought?"

"Yes. You thought what the hell is this Park Avenue kid doing on the job."

"That's right. That's what I thought. You see, Clive? Like I said, this is a bright boy." Newly nodded but said nothing. "I thought what the fuck are you doing coming in to fuck up my police department? I figured you'd be gone or you'd be behind a desk in Centre Street pretty quick, but you fooled me." He poured the shot of rye into his beer and took a slug. "You're out there knocking yourself out on the street keeping the animals in line. Good on you."

"Are you starting a fan club?"

"Yeah, yeah, I know. You don't give a shit what I think. How are you doing with the stiff on the chair in the park? Getting anywhere?"

"No. No ID. His prints don't come up, so he's never been booked, wasn't in the armed services. We're waiting on a guy to come back to work to ask about the clothes he was wearing."

"Yeah, we saw the report. Brooks Brothers, and like that."

"Yes."

"The guy's got workingman's hands and uptown clothes, and he's sitting on a crappy chair on Seventy-second Street with a bullet in his head. Maybe he's working up there. Newly had the idea that maybe he's a bright guy like you. Ambitious. He looks around and sees how people dress up there. He figures if he dresses like that maybe he gets more work."

"What kind of work?"

"How the fuck do I know? People renovate their apartments, you know." He drained the mug, slapped five dollars on the bar, and headed for the door.

Newly said, "Gentlemen," and tipped his hat and followed.

Cassidy watched them leave. He lit a cigarette. "Okay, what was all that about?"

"He thinks you're a good cop."

"Come on. He doesn't think anyone but he and Newly is any good."

"No. He thinks there are maybe twenty good cops on the force. You're one of them."

"Huh." He was unused to praise, and did not look for it. His father showered superlatives on everyone and by doing so cheapened their value, and his mother had been brought up and trained by chilly people who assumed that everyone in *their* family would always do his best and therefore praise was unnecessary. Still, Bonner was a cop's cop, and if he thought Cassidy was a good cop, well, he had to admit, it felt good.

"What do you think of his idea that the dead man was working up there?" Orso tasted the gin again and pushed it aside unfinished. "Hey, Hanno, this stuff tastes like turpentine."

"I've got another bottle tastes like gasoline. You want me to bring you a shot? On the house."

"I think Bonner gave us a hint to see if we'll check it out," Cassidy said. "If we do, even if nothing comes of it, we're okay. If we don't, he'll think we're just assholes like the rest of them."

"Do you care what Bonner thinks?"

"He's a shit, but he's a good cop."

"So what do we do?"

"We check it out."

• • •

Orso went to check on the sanitation men who had worked the early shift the week the man was shot, and Cassidy went to the station house and worked the phones to the Department of Buildings until he had a list of people who had applied for construction permits in a six-block area near where the dead man was found. The first was a town house. It had started out as a single-family town house, was broken into apartments and was being made into a single-family home again. The foreman looked at the photograph and shook his head. "Nah. I mean maybe I've seen him around, but I don't recognize him. You're welcome to show it to the guys inside. Maybe one of them knows him."

They didn't.

The second was in an apartment building on 73rd Street. The doorman swore he had never seen the man, and that if he hadn't seen him, the guy had never been in the building. Cassidy, unconvinced of the man's infallibility, went up to show the photograph to the workers renovating the apartment on the eighth floor. The apartment had a wonderful view over the park, but the three men ripping apart the kitchen did not recognize the dead man. There was nobody home at the third address, a four-story limestone house with an imposing door of glass and black iron near the corner of 73rd and Fifth Avenue. The fourth address held a team of Italian artisans putting in a stained-glass window who passed the photo of the dead man around like a holy relic, discussed it at length in the music of their language, agreed that they had never seen the man, and then crossed themselves in unison. The fifth and sixth addresses produced the same lack of result.

Cassidy sat on a bench against the wall outside Central Park and lit a cigarette. The sun filtered down through the trees behind him and warmed his back. For a New Yorker like Cassidy, the steady rush of traffic on Fifth Avenue was as soothing as the flow of a river. There was something he was missing, something he should have been looking for. What was it? A man is killed and left in Central Park in the early morning. The location is specific. He was put in place so someone could see him. How did the killers know that person would see him? Because it was his habit to go past that spot in the early morning. Who did that? People on their way to work? Possibly. Does someone from one of these gold coast addresses walk through Central Park to work? Unlikely. Who, then?

A young woman in blue jeans and a windbreaker came out of the park pulled by six dogs. Some were large, some small, and some in between, and they all strained forward on their leashes while she leaned back like a water skier. Her piercing whistle brought them to heel at the curb, and when the light changed, a word of command sent them out into the street, and she let them tow her across.

Dogs. What had young Seth said? Someone was missing from the usual dog-walking rotation. A woman with a red setter. How many of the apartments he had just visited had dogs? The first one, the town house, was gutted from top to bottom. No one lived there. No dog. The eighth floor apartment with the new kitchen? There had been a water bowl in the dining room on a rubber mat. For a dog or for a cat? He didn't know. There had been a dog in the apartment with the Italian glass men. He heard it yapping behind a door. No evidence of an animal in the last apartment.

Across the street, the dog walker turned in at the limestone town house and keyed the door while her charges milled about in front of her. One of them was a red setter. Before Cassidy could dodge through traffic and cross the avenue, they had disappeared inside.

Five dogs were trapped in the vestibule between the outer door, with its glass and black wrought iron, and the glass and wood inner door that led to the front hall of the house. The red setter was not among them. When they saw Cassidy climb the steps, they began to bark and circle each other. A small terrier threw itself at the glass three times. Cassidy saw the young woman come into the hall from a room near the back of the house. She opened the inside door and stepped into the vestibule and said something to the dogs that quieted them. She looked out at Cassidy through the glass and bars of the front door, and her eyes widened when she recognized the badge he held up to the glass. She pointed a finger at her chest and mouthed *me*? He shook his head and shouted at the glass, "I need to talk to you." She quieted the dogs again, opened the big door, and slipped out through a narrow opening while holding the terrier back with one foot. "Angus is the curious one," she explained. "He gets into all kinds of mischief if you let him."

Her name was Naomi Stern. She was an athletic young woman with a mass of curly brown hair and guileless brown eyes. She was studying at Hunter College on Park Avenue, and she picked up extra money by walking dogs. She'd been doing it for three years, and she had a group of regular clients. It was clear that she thought of the dogs as her clients, not their owners.

"Do you walk them in the morning?" Cassidy asked.

"No. Usually the owners walk them before they go off to work or whatever, and I come do a late-morning or early-afternoon walk, and that holds them until the owners get home."

"The people who live here"—he checked his list—"Mr. and Mrs. Robert Hopkins? They have the red setter."

"Yes. Lucky. That's his name."

"Do you know when they get home?"

"Why? Did they do something?"

"No. They might have seen something we need help with."

"Oh." She seemed disappointed that there was no greater drama. "Well, they're away, and they won't be back until the end of the week, so I'm walking Lucky three times a day."

"You have a key to the house."

"Sure." The perfect innocence of the innocent. "Why? Oh, I get it. I could run off with all their stuff. Is that what you think?" She was offended.

"No, no. I was just wondering how it worked. They've been having some renovation done, haven't they?"

"A pipe burst upstairs, and when they started to get it fixed, they decided to knock down a wall and do some other stuff. I think it's pretty much done now."

"Did you ever see the men working on it?"

"I saw one of them once when I came to pick up Lucky."

Cassidy showed her the photo. "No. The guy I saw wasn't as big as this guy. At least I don't think so. This guy looks big. The other guy had longer hair. This guy looks pretty strange. What's wrong with him?"

"He's dead."

"Dead? Wow. What happened?" She was still young enough to be surprised by death.

"Someone shot him."

"God, how awful."

"When did Mr. and Mrs. Hopkins leave?"

"Uh, let's see. They left me a note for when I came to walk Lucky in the afternoon asking me to take him out in the mornings too. I was late because I had a Modern History jap."

"Jap?"

"Yeah, you know, a surprise quiz. Like Pearl Harbor?"

"Ahh."

"So it must have been last Friday."

"And they left suddenly."

"Yes, I guess so. I mean they hadn't said anything to me. But they've done that before. He goes away on business, or something, and she decides to go at the last minute. I don't mind, 'cause it means more money for me." The dogs in the vestibule were howling in protest at their confinement. Naomi looked back at them in concern and raised a hand, but it did no good. "Is there anything else? The dogs . . ."

"No. Go ahead."

She released the dogs, and Cassidy watched as they towed her down the block.

13

"Orso talked to the sanitation department guys, the ones who used to work the early shift up there around Seventy-second Street," Cassidy said.

"The ones who wake me up at dawn banging the cans around?" Alice asked.

"Banging cans is part of their job. It lets the citizens know that their tax dollars are being spent on hardworking men."

They were in a wooden booth in Chumley's on Bedford Street in the Village. The old speakeasy had been a literary watering hole since Prohibition, and the walls displayed the book jackets of the writers who came to drown their demons or prime their muses: Eugene O'Neill after he'd made enough money to upgrade from the flop houses and gin mills of the Bowery, Dos Passos, Ring Lardner, Willa Cather, e.e. cummings, Hemingway, the self-proclaimed world heavyweight champion.

The small, shaded lamp on the table cast a golden light, and Alice, half in the light and half in shadow, was beautiful and mysterious. The joint was full. Laughter rose above the hum of conversation, the rattle of silver on china, and the clink of ice in glasses, the companionable New York nighttime sounds Cassidy loved.

"There was a trash barrel twenty feet from where the dead guy was sitting, but of course they didn't notice him when they emptied it."

"How could that be? Twenty feet." She leaned forward to light her cigarette from the match Cassidy held.

"One thing you learn. People are blind. They walk along in their own little worlds, and they don't see anything outside those worlds. And if they do, they don't know what the hell they've seen. Four eyewitnesses will give you four different stories about what happened and four different descriptions about who did it."

"Maybe they should put cameras up."

"Cameras?"

"Sure. Movie cameras or TV cameras or something. On the buildings, so if someone does something you just go look at the film."

"Jesus, what a terrible idea. Do you want them to have a record of what you do out on the street?"

"No." Alice laughed. "God, no. So what do you do now?"

"Well, there are two other places with building permits I couldn't get into. Maybe he was working in one of them. And then the people with the red setter will be back at the end of the week. I'd like to know what made them take off."

"I never would have thought of that, fancy clothes and workman's hands."

"I didn't think of it either." He told her about Bonner and Newly.

"I never saw a colored cop until I came up to New York, not where I grew up."

The waiter brought refills for their drinks, a martini straight up with a twist for Cassidy and a Sazerac for Alice. She took a sip. "Hmm, that's good. This is what my daddy used to drink when he was feeling flush."

"Where was that?"

She scanned his face. *Was he being polite, or did he want to know?* "Cut Off, Louisiana."

"Near New Orleans?"

"No. Well, about seventy miles south, but it might as well have been the other side of the planet, New Orleans seemed so far away. Cut Off. They sure named that right. Lafourche Parrish on Bayou Lafourche. My daddy fished the bayou. My brothers worked the sulfur pit. Have you spent much time in a small southern town?"

"No."

"One main street. Two churches. A crappy diner. A Tastee Freez where everyone hangs out after school. Two garages, a general store, a hardware store, one grade school, one high school, town hall, some houses. A whole lot of nothing. The boys are going to work for their fathers fishing, or in the hardware store or the garage, the sulfur mine. The girls'll be their wives and have babies who grow up to do the same thing. Everybody knows you. Everybody knows your business. They think they know who you are, and that's who you have to be."

"Who were you?"

"Honey, I was the high school slut." She said it with a grin, but when she took a sip of her drink, she watched defiantly over the rim of the glass for his reaction.

"Damn. I kept telling my parents they were sending me to the wrong schools."

She laughed. "Yeah, sure. Every school had one. You must have too."

"Uh-uh. I was locked up in all boy schools from kindergarten through high school. We had to hunt for girls outside the classroom."

"Hunt? All you had to do is stand on the corner and wait. Some girl would come along as hot for you as you were for her. You think we didn't want it? If there was some way girls could know they weren't going to get knocked up you couldn't fight them off with a stick. But I was the town pump, and they were the high school heroes who nailed me. As if I didn't have anything to do with it."

"There were only two conversations boys had in high school—one was sports. The other was girls. What did she let you do? How far did you get with her? First base, second base, third, all the way? Did you stick her? Did you get her? Nobody did, of course, and everybody lied. And we were pretty sure if it was going to happen we would have to trick her into it. No one told us girls wanted it too. The best-kept secret."

Alice rolled her eyes. "At sixteen I decided to stop feeling sorry for who I was and what people thought. I took off with a traveling salesman who sold women's foundation garments. God, did he know women. I guess he would, hands in their underwear all the time. He set me up in a little apartment in Washington and helped me get a job at Berman's Department Store. I loved that place. I'd never seen so many beautiful clothes, shoes, perfume, and women coming in all day long and trying them on. They knocked it down in 1954, city beautification, or something. I never went back to look to see what they put up that they thought was more beautiful."

"What happened to the salesman?"

She shrugged. "He dumped me. I met people and had other jobs. I was a secretary up on Capitol Hill for a while, but I sure wasn't hired for my typing. I met Georgie at a party and went to Cuba and met you, and here we are having dinner."

Dinner arrived with a bottle of wine.

"Fair's fair. I get to hear about you now. Growing up in New York, and all." She leaned forward in anticipation.

"Nothing to tell. I grew up on Sixty-sixth Street. My father's a producer of Broadway plays. I've got a brother and a sister and a bunch of nieces and nephews. I went to school on Seventy-fourth Street, joined the army, came back, joined the cops."

"Wow, you're some wonderful storyteller. I was on the edge of my seat. Some men can't wait to tell you about themselves. You can't shut them up. Some you have to dig it out with a pick. Now I know which one you are."

• • •

Jimmy Greef came into Chumley's through the unmarked door in the little courtyard off Barrow Street. He went to the end of the bar and dropped the leather satchel on the floor and kicked it in under the bar gate. Jamie, the Irish bartender with hair like white cotton, gave him a knowing nod, picked up the satchel, and carried it to the back room. The second bartender, Willie, a slender black-haired man with a mustache clipped so close it looked like a black smear, mopped the clean bar in front of him and said, "How you doing, Jimmy? Get you something while you wait."

"Yeah. Get me one of them, it's like a martini, but made with rye? With the cherry."

"A Manhattan?"

"Yeah, that's it. A Manhattan."

"Up, or on the rocks?"

"Yeah, up. And give me two of them cherries."

"You got it." Willie moved away to make the drink, and Jimmy Greef lit a Chesterfield, inhaled deeply, and blew smoke at the back bar. He could feel some of the tension leave him. Not that he was nervous carrying the bag. Nah, not nervous, but he recognized the responsibility. If they trusted him to carry the bag, it meant he was moving up the ladder. Only six months since he made his bones and here he was doing a thing of trust. Twenty-four years old and on the way up. He took off his fedora and dropped it on the bar and ran a palm over his hair to make sure it stayed slicked back on his skull. His sideburns were long like Elvis's, who he thought he looked like, except maybe his lips were thinner. Not that he admitted it, but a girl he met out at Coney said he did. He wore a dark blue suit from Barney's Bargain Basement with wide chalk stripes, a little too long in the sleeves and the pants, a little too flashy, a look-at-me suit cut a little full in the chest to hide the pistol in its holster under his left arm. Nah, the nerves didn't come from carrying the bag. No one in his right mind was going to try to take it off. No one who knew what was what, anyway. That would mean war. A couple of independents made the move a few years ago, but the word was they ended up in a swamp in Jersey. Still, he always felt good when he came into one of the joints and took a little breather while they got the payment, and he felt better when he dropped the bag at the end of the night at Carmine's. I mean, say what you want, you're carrying fifteen, twenty grand, someone might just try to get lucky. Then how do you explain that to Carmine? You don't. Someone takes the bag, no matter who, you're dead. Don't think about that, man. Don't.

"There you go, Jimmy." Willie slid the Manhattan to him and turned away to serve another customer. Greef ate the first cherry. It tasted like it looked, dark red and sweet. Petey Lick could tie the stem in a knot with his tongue, but Greef couldn't figure out how to do it no matter how many times he tried. He took a sip of the drink, lit another cigarette, and turned and leaned his back against the bar and looked out into the restaurant. He liked Chumley's. A lot of good-looking broads came here to eat, usually with guys, but sometimes there were strays at the bar. College girls came to look at the pictures of the writers on the walls, maybe. He got lucky a couple of times. Chat them up. Buy them a drink or two, let the jacket slip open so they saw the gun. The gun got them hot every time. That one in the red dress over near the wall. Was she eating alone? No, there he was just coming to sit down, back from the men's room or something. Jesus, those were some tits on that blonde in the booth with the black-haired guy.

Wait a minute. Wait a minute. Could it be? He reached into his breast pocket and took out a photograph. It was a color print of a woman facing the camera. There was a palm tree behind her. A man had his arm around her waist, but the man had been cut out of the picture. He looked at the photograph and then over at the woman. The hair's different, blond, not brown, shorter and cut different, but Jesus, it sure looks like her.

A thump on the bar startled him, and he jerked around. "Here you go, Jimmy. All done." Jamie slapped the leather satchel and winked.

"Yeah, good. Put it on the floor back there and watch it for a minute. I've got to do something."

"Sure. No problem." Jamie took the bag and put it on the duckboards behind the bar.

Greef walked with what he thought was nonchalance to look at some of the book jackets on the wall near the booth where the blond sat, and then turned casually and studied her. Yeah. It's her. Jesus Christ. Everybody's been looking for her for months, and I found her. This is going to be good for me. He turned and headed for the phone booth at the far end of the bar.

Alice was aware of the young man with the Elvis sideburns who pretended to look at the book jackets so that he could turn and study her. Men had been looking at her tits since she was thirteen, and very few of them had the courage to do it straight out. She dismissed Jimmy Greef and accepted the cigarette Cassidy offered.

"Do you want a nightcap?" he asked.

"Sure. Here?"

"Is there somewhere you want to go?"

"It's a nice night. We could walk until we see something we like."

"Let's do that." He raised a hand for the check.

"They're paying the check right now." Jimmy Greef stood in the phone booth so he could see the table where Alice and Cassidy sat. "Yeah, I'm sure it's her. What? No. Like I said, she's with some guy. I don't know who he is. What do you want me to do?" He listened for a while. "Okay. Sure. I can do that. Only thing is, I've got the bag with me." He listened again. "Right. Yeah. Sure. Look, Carmine, this is my thing, right? I found her. You'll let people know, right? Okay. Thanks. Yeah. I'll call soon as I know where she goes." He hung up and opened the door to the booth to the hum and buzz of the restaurant and went to the end of the bar where the bartender was opening a bottle of wine. "Hey, Jamie, let me have the bag, huh?"

The bartender put down the bottle and corkscrew and lifted the bag to the bar top. "You could have a hell of a week in Vegas with what's in there."

"Not funny. You don't even want to think that way."

"Just kidding, man." Suddenly nervous. "Just kidding."

"Yeah, well, don't. Okay. I'll see you next week."

Greef waited until Cassidy and Alice went out the Bedford Street door and then followed them up Bedford to Christopher, then over to Hudson where they turned north. In the distance the spire of the Empire State Building was brilliant with colored lights. A taxi slowed in hopes of a fare and then went on. Near Charles Street a man and two women milled in the street, shouting and shoving each other drunkenly. The man fell down.

The women helped him to his feet and they began shoving each other again. Halfway up the block a group of teenagers in blue jeans and flannel shirts clustered on a stoop with a guitar player and sang something about Tom Dooley hanging down his head. A whore in a tight green dress stepped from a doorway and asked for a light, but Greef waved her off and went on. Up ahead the blonde laughed at something the man said and bumped him with her hip. He put his arm around her waist and pulled her close. A few minutes later they went into the White Horse Tavern, and Greef stepped into the phone booth on the corner. He put the money satchel on the floor and closed the door only partway so the light stayed dark, dropped a dime, and dialed. The phone was picked up on the third ring.

"Yeah, it's me," Greef said. "They're in the White Horse on the corner of Eleventh and Hudson. Yeah, I can see them. They're at the bar. She's got her hand in his pocket. The guy definitely thinks he's getting laid tonight, but he's in for a surprise. Okay, okay. I'm just saying. Who are you sending? Yeah, I know them both. Tell them they can park on Eleventh. Plenty of places. Tell them to look for me near the phone booth on the corner. Right. Okay. Hey, Carmine, you told them it was me who found her, right? Okay. Thanks. Yeah, I'll be right here unless they leave. They leave, I'll call you." He hung up and opened the door to the booth and looked through the window of the White Horse to where the man and woman stood at the bar.

At the far end of the White Horse bar three men in orange Con Edison jumpsuits chewed over the Brooklyn Dodgers' move to Los Angeles nearly two years ago, the wounds of betrayal still raw. The bartender, a big Irishman with the face of a basset hound and long gray hair, brought Cassidy and Alice Rusty Nails and said, "Nah, nah. On the house, Mike," and pushed his money back at him.

Alice sipped her drink. "Do you know everyone in the Village? The waiter at the restaurant, this guy, the people who stopped to say hello when we were eating."

"I've lived down here a while. Sometimes I can help someone out. A kid gets in trouble, someone's got a beef with someone and needs someone to arbitrate without getting a lot of other people involved."

"You like being a cop, don't you?" She took the cigarette from between his fingers and took a drag. When he got it back he could taste her lipstick.

"Some of it, I guess." She waited for him to go on. "You get up in the morning, and you go to work. Some days you're hip deep in the really awful things people do to each other. Some days you see how good people can be to each other. Some days you can help. Some you're just shoveling shit against the tide. I don't know if I like it, but I can't let it go."

"Okay."

"I don't like to talk about it."

"No."

"With some things, talking about it doesn't tell you anything. It's blah, blah. Either you know it, or you don't. If you don't, talking won't get you close."

"Men." She said it affectionately, with a small smile. Other women had said the same word to him with different inflections, but they all meant the same thing—you think you hide your secrets from us, you tell us stories about who you are, but we see.

"They don't pay you much, do they, the cops?"

"No. Not much."

"Is that why you live down here, because the rents are cheap?"

"No. I like it here. I grew up on the Upper East Side, but this suits me better. And I own the apartment."

"You do?" Surprised.

"I bought it with money my mother left me when she died."

She snuggled close and hugged his arm. "Oooh, an heir. Better and better." She laughed to show she was kidding. "You know what Billie Holiday said, I've been rich and I've been poor, and rich is better. Well, I've done half of that. I've been poor, and I've seen how the rich live, and Billie knew what she was talking about."

A ten-year-old Ford panel van came north on Hudson Street, blinked its lights once, and turned west on 11th and parked twenty feet down from the corner. Someone had painted it with gray house paint, and through the paint you could dimly see its past as a van for Joe's Fish. The lights went out. The engine turned off, and the metal of the hood pinged and ticked as it cooled. After a while the doors opened and two men got out and walked back toward Hudson. Jimmy Greef flicked his cigarette away and left the shadow of the phone booth to meet them, the money satchel heavy in his left hand. He recognized them both, Junior Carelli and Tommy Longo. They were thick, powerful men in their thirties. They were muscle guys with day jobs running longshoremen shape-ups on the docks, leg breakers, men who were sent to settle disputes with whatever was at hand, bricks, two by fours, a lead pipe, or fists. They both wore cheap double-breasted suits and fedoras, and they walked with the heavy, implacable confidence of men who knew others would clear their path, men used to being feared.

"How you doing, Jimmy?" Carelli's voice was like gravel in a can. He'd been hit in the throat in a melee on the docks when he was starting out, and something broke inside.

"Okay."

"They still inside?"

"Yeah, the right-hand end of the bar. She's the one with the black-haired guy."

The man had his back to them, but the woman was turned in profile to talk to him.

"You sure it's her?"

"I'm sure. Hair's different. A little thinner, maybe. Look at them tits. Those sure as hell are the same."

"Okay. So we wait. We take her when they come out."

"What about the guy?" Jimmy asked.

"What about the guy?" Carelli said. "We ask him nicely, do you mind if we borrow your broad? He says, no, go ahead, take her."

Longo, who had said nothing, snorted.

"What if he doesn't? What if he beefs?"

"What if? There are three of us, one of him. He beefs, we drop him."

"Clip him?"

"Up to him how hard he pushes it, how hard we come back. Up to him, not up to us."

Longo offered a pack of Camels. Greef took one, but Carelli waved it away. "Those fucking things are too strong for me. I think they put some camel shit in there with the tobacco." He looked into the bar. "I could use a drink myself."

Greef bent to the match Longo held. "Thanks."

"What are they offering for the broad? Three grand?" Carelli asked.

"Five," Greef said. "Five grand."

"I could use that dough."

"Who couldn't? That's a brand-new Caddy Eldorado convertible I've got my eye on."

"I figured I was going to find her."

"How'd you figure that?"

"I don't know. I just figured, why not me? You finding her, it's like you're taking money out of my pocket. Maybe you ought to give me some of what they give you."

"Go fuck yourself."

"I'm just saying, since it should've been mine. A couple of grand."

"Go fuck yourself again. What are you, anyway, thinking like that? When was the last time you gave anybody anything?"

"I gave your mother just about everything she could handle only this morning."

"Hey, hey. You keep your fucking mouth off my mother."

"Too late."

"I'm going to . . ."

"Shut the fuck up, both of youse. They're coming out," Longo said.

Carelli moved closer to the front of the White Horse. Longo went with him. Greef dropped the cigarette and ground it out under his shoe. He switched the money bag to his left hand and opened his jacket and touched the gun butt under his shoulder. Show a citizen a gun, and usually that was enough, and if more was needed, well, like Carelli said, it was up to the guy how hard he pushed.

Cassidy held open the front door of the White Horse so that Alice could go first. As they stepped outside, he saw the three men on the sidewalk. The two big ones stood almost shoulder to shoulder, their faces shadowed by their hat brims. The third one stepped away from them and moved to the side. He carried a satchel in his left hand, and his jacket was unbuttoned. Something wasn't right here. He could feel the tension coming off them. Alice tried to take his arm, but he avoided that and turned so she was on his hip and a little behind him. The thin man with the satchel kept moving to flank him. Cassidy unbuttoned his jacket to clear his holster. One of the men moved a step in front of the others. Then he said, "How're you doing, Detective Cassidy?" Did he emphasize *detective*? The big one near him shifted and some of the tension went out of him. The third man took a step south and was almost out of Cassidy's sight unless he turned his head.

"Tommy Longo, right? How's your uncle?" Cassidy asked. The one carrying the satchel took another step. His hand drifted toward his open jacket.

"They moved him up to Attica."

He looked at the other big man. "Carelli, right?" Cassidy recognized the two as muscle for the Gambino crime family. What were they doing uptown outside their usual orbit of Little Italy and the docks? Nothing good.

"Yeah." He stepped out of the shadows and into the light that came through the bar's window.

"Who's this guy? Hey, you, stop moving. You're making me nervous. You don't want to make me nervous." Greef glanced at Tommy Longo and stopped. "What's your name?"

"Jimmy Greef."

"You're carrying the bag tonight, Jimmy Greef. Somebody must like you."

"My laundry."

"Uh-huh." He looked back at Longo. "What's up, Tommy? You guys are a little out of your territory."

"We was coming into the White Horse for a drink. We heard it was okay."

"It is. No better than some of the places down on Grand Street, but what the hell, a change of scene's good."

"Okay. So we'll go in."

"Anything else?"

"Else? Nah. What, a guy can't come uptown and have a drink? Free country, right?"

"So they tell me." Cassidy took Alice's arm and stepped forward, and Longo and Carelli made room, and he led Alice across 11th Street and north on Hudson. He did not look back.

"Who were they?" Alice asked.

"Hoods. Enforcers down on the docks."

"What was all that about?" Alice asked.

"I don't know. My guess is they were about to do something they shouldn't do, and they ran into a cop so they didn't do it."

"Do you think they were going to rob the bar?"

"Maybe. Stickups aren't what they usually do, but maybe. Not something you'd think they'd do with the bagman."

"The bagman? What was in the bag?"

"Money."

"From what?"

"Payoffs. Every Friday a guy goes around with the bag collecting what the bars owe. Some pay for protection. Some are owned by mob guys who skim from the take every week before the tax man gets told how much they made. Some are fairy bars. The mobsters own them too, and they pay off the cops to let the fairies dance together in the back rooms. The money comes out of the till on Friday."

"It's illegal for them to dance?"

"Uh-huh."

"Wow. Why? They're just dancing. They're just having fun." She wrapped his arm tight. "Let's go back to your place, and I'll show you some dancing that's definitely illegal."

"Uh-oh. I may have to use the handcuffs."

"Promises, promises." And she laughed.

Her laughter drifted back to the three men outside the White Horse. "Why didn't we take her?" Greef asked.

"The guy's a cop, or weren't you listening?" Longo said.

"Yeah? So he's a cop, so what? The river's three blocks over. Any luck, he don't show for months. People want that broad. They're paying big money for her so they want her bad. What's one cop?"

"Yeah, well, this particular cop is Frank Costello's godson."

"Oh."

"Yeah. So let me make a call, see what people want to do." Longo stepped into the phone booth and dialed.

"Hey, I didn't know," Greef said to Carelli. "Costello and all. That makes a difference."

"What you don't know could fill a book," Carelli said in his gravel voice.

"Hey, fuck you again, okay? You don't know everything." Greef carried the money satchel away from Carelli and set it down between his feet and lit a cigarette. He watched the people in the bar through the window. Three Con Ed men were arguing about something. Two couples in scrubs from the hospital on 12th were eating at a round wooden table near the window, and two old men in alpaca sweaters were playing chess at a table nearby. *Fucking Carelli. Fucking guy. I was just asking. Thinks he's such a hot shit.* The euphoria of being the bagman, of finding Alice, had vanished, turned to dust. *Shit, fucking guy.*

"Hey," Longo stepped out of the phone booth. "Okay, they say let it be for the moment. Cassidy's got a place over on Bank Street, so that's where they're headed. Junior and me are going to go hang out there, make sure she don't leave. They'll send a couple of other guys after a while. She comes out alone in the morning, they'll take her. Jimmy, Carmine's waiting for the bag."

Longo and Carelli got back into the gray panel truck and went west on 11th.

Jimmy Greef headed south toward Little Italy. After a couple of blocks he began to feel better. Hey, he was the bagman, and he found the broad, and people knew that. Screw those guys. Things were looking up.

• • •

Nobody took Alice in the morning. The word came down from on high, don't mess with her. Follow her and find out where she lives. Now that they knew she was with Costello's godson, people had to talk it over, make sure the next move was the right move.

Shadowing her got easy, because two days later Alice moved in with Cassidy.

14

The day started sunny and then turned back toward winter. A cold, misty rain fell from a gray sky. The tops of the tallest buildings disappeared in the mist. Car tires sang on the wet streets, and people walked with their heads down and shoulders hunched against the weather.

Cassidy and Orso left the station house late in the afternoon as the rain began to let up.

"Taxi?" Orso suggested.

"It's going to stop. Let's walk. I need the air."

Church's shoe store was on Madison Avenue at 62nd Street. The manager of the store was a tall, thin, impeccably dressed man who looked like a roadshow English duke. His name was Caldwell. He noted Orso's lightweight double-breasted suit and polished shoes and welcomed him with polite warmth. He managed to suppress most of his sneer at the scuffed desert boots Cassidy was wearing. His face tightened when Cassidy showed him his badge, but he did not lose his composure. "Gentlemen, how may I help you?" He had the clipped speech and round vowels of someone who had been to a lot of Ronald Coleman movies.

Cassidy gave him the list of people who were having renovation work done on their apartments and asked if he recognized any of the names. Mr. Caldwell picked gold-rimmed glasses from his breast pocket, put them on the end of his nose, and held the list out while he read it.

"I believe we have more than one customer from this list. If you'll wait a tick we can make absolutely sure." His records showed that three names on the list were customers of the store, Grayson, Hopkins, and Milliken.

"Is Mr. Leighton back from vacation?" Orso asked.

"Yes, he is," Caldwell said.

"I want to show him a photograph."

"I believe he's just finishing his break." He came back moments later leading a short cheerful man with a sunburned face.

Orso showed him the photograph of the dead man. Leighton examined it from different angles, and then nodded. "Sure. A pair of the Casual Oxfords in a size eleven D, and pair of dark brown wingtips in eleven E. The wingtips run a little narrower than the Oxfords."

"Did he pay by check or cash?" Cassidy asked. A check would give them his name.

"Oh, he didn't pay. Mrs. Hopkins paid."

"Mrs. Robert Hopkins?" Cassidy asked.

"That's right. She's a good customer. She buys shoes for her husband a couple of times a year."

"This was her husband?"

"Oh, no. No, no. Lord, no. Mr. Hopkins is a very elegant man. This gentleman, well, let's just say that his socks were not up to par. If a man truly cares about his shoes, his socks reflect it. If I might speak out of school, I would say that this gentleman was not accustomed to a store of this quality."

"Did you get his name?"

"She called him Casey."

"Friend? Family?"

"Oh, definitely a friend. Nothing obvious, mind you, but an occasional touch, a smile. People seem to think that when they come into a store they're invisible in some way, and so are the people who wait on them. But we see things. We notice."

"Thank you, Mr. Leighton."

"Not at all."

When they left, Caldwell locked the door and turned the sign in the glass to *CLOSED.*

Cassidy and Orso walked the ten or so blocks to Toots Shor's for a pop. The bar was packed, and a few early diners were at the tables in back. The five-thirty crowd, released from the day's work, buzzed. Toots, big and loud, greeted them as they came in. "Hey, pally, where the hell have you been. I ain't seen you in weeks. What? I owe you money?" He clapped Cassidy on the shoulder and winked at Orso.

"How are you, Toots?"

"I'm great. I'm always great. Hey, Orso, that broad you were in with last week, the brunette with all the equipment, she was in here last night asking for you."

"What'd you tell her?"

"What I tell all of them come ask about my customers. You're out of town and no one knows when you're back."

"Thanks, Toots."

"Any time, pally. Any time." He led them to the crowded bar and ordered people to make room for them.

The bartender brought them martinis, up with a twist for Cassidy, up with an olive for Orso. "To crime," a cop's toast. Then they gave the first sips the attention they deserved.

"God, that's good," Orso said. "It makes the rest of the day worth it if you know you're going to end up with an ice-cold martini." He took another sip. "So here's what I think about Casey and the shoes. He's up there doing the construction work. He and the missus are alone in the house. They begin sniffing around each other. He starts banging her. She likes it. He likes it. She's bored with elegant Mr. Hopkins and likes the rough-and-tough Casey the carpenter. She starts to buy him stuff. He likes that too. He's got it good. He's getting paid, he's shtupping the lady, plus he's getting some expensive presents. We go back to Brooks Brothers, I bet we find out she's buying him stuff there too. Then the old man finds out. He's pissed. He wants to teach her a lesson. He pops old Casey and leaves him out there where she walks the dog. What do you think?"

"Good story. How does he get Casey out there into the park?"

"Walks him out with the gun. Makes him carry the chair."

"Skinner says he was shot somewhere else, remember?"

"Right. The piss-soaked couch. So he kills him in the apartment and carries him out there in the middle of the night when no one's around."

"Casey weighs a hundred ninety pounds, plus he has to carry the chair."

"Two trips, and the guy's desperate, so he's strong, or maybe he's got a bicycle or something he can use to carry the guy."

"Uh-huh. Taking a chance."

"Shoot someone in the head, you're already taking a chance. Besides, he's rich. Maybe he thinks he can get away with it. The rich have been known to skate once or twice, you know."

"I like the story. When they get back, we'll go have a talk."

Orso left to meet a woman at P.J. Clarke's while Cassidy finished his second martini. He paid the tab and then used the phone booth in the corridor by the men's room to call Alice. "What are you doing?"

"Painting my toenails."

"Are you dressed?"

"Come on down and take a look."

He laughed. "Put on some clothes and we'll go out and eat a steak. I'll be there in twenty minutes."

He left Toots Shor's and turned right toward Sixth Avenue, and then stopped. "Ah, hell." Sixth ran one way north now. It had been that way for a year, but he still was not used to it. Why did they have to screw with a city that worked fine? He turned and walked to Fifth Avenue and walked south, glancing behind him every once in a while to see if a taxi was coming. He could have waited on the corner. Walking saved no time, but impatience ruled him. Better to move than to wait. The illusion of progress was often as satisfying as progress itself. The next time he looked back for a cab, he saw a black limousine turn the corner two blocks north. It slid slowly toward him, close to the sidewalk, ignoring the horns of cars caught behind it.

Not for him. Why would it be for him? Still . . . He turned west at the next corner, walked twenty feet, and stepped into the shallow doorway of a closed shoe store. Moments later the limousine turned the corner and idled down the street. Ten yards past Cassidy's doorway it stopped. A man got out of the front seat and walked back toward Cassidy. He stopped ten feet away, his hands well away from his sides as if to advertise peaceful intentions. He was a big man with a hard face, but his voice was mild and polite. "Detective Cassidy, Mr. Costello asks if you wouldn't mind talking to him for a few minutes. We can give you a ride wherever you're going." He jerked his head at the limousine.

"After you," Cassidy said. The man nodded and walked back to the car and opened the rear door. Cassidy stood back and looked in. His godfather waved a hand from the far side of the backseat. Cassidy got in. The door thunked shut behind him. The man got in the front seat, and the limousine moved off.

"How are you, Michael?"

"Fine, Frank. How are you?"

"I'm okay." Maybe he was, but he looked diminished, as if he had not yet recovered from the bullet Big Chin Gigante had fired at his head in the lobby of his apartment building almost two years before. "Where can we take you?"

"I was headed home."

"Okay." Costello leaned forward and gave the driver the address on Bank Street and then closed the window for privacy. "You want a drink?" There was a bar with cut-glass decanters built into the back of the driver's seat.

"No, thanks. I just had one."

"I'm going to have a taste." He poured a glass of bourbon and added ice from a small, zinc-lined cabinet. "Ahh, that's good. How's your father? I know he's in rehearsal. I put a couple of thousand into the show for old times' sake. And I get house seats, so Loretta can comp her friends. She likes that."

Cassidy knew Costello was stalling. "What's up, Frank?"

Costello took another sip before answering. "Do you remember that broad Alice was with Joe Stassi in Havana the night Batista took off? New Year's Eve. Big, good-looking girl."

"Sure."

"You seen her since?" Costello's face was friendly, but his eyes were flat.

"She's in my apartment, and you already know that, otherwise we wouldn't be talking about her."

Costello was unembarrassed about being caught out. "Yeah. Okay. We've been looking for her. Someone saw you with her. They brought it to me, asked me to talk to you. She tell you anything about that last night down there, the night Castro's guys came into the city?"

"No. We haven't talked about it."

"We had a thing, Lansky, Trafficante, Stassi, me, the guys you saw at The Tropicana. We didn't know what was going to happen next down there. You and I talked about it that night. Was Castro a Commie? How was he going to feel about our business? So we picked up the money from all the casinos, brought it all to Joe Stassi's house, packed it up, and got it out to Miami, some that night, some the next day."

"How much?" The limousine stopped for a light, and a couple crossing the street bent to look in to see if the people inside were famous. The man shook his head in disappointment and they went on.

"A lot." The light changed. Costello glanced at Cassidy, but Cassidy said nothing. Eventually the older man would get to the point. "Not all of it made it out of Cuba. A suitcase with half a million in it, give or take, went missing." He stopped again, but Cassidy waited him out. "We think Alice took it. We went back over it as best we could. Who was where and when. There was a time when the money was packed and ready and she wasn't around for a while. Nobody can say where she was."

"What, you guys don't think money's important anymore? You didn't have anyone watching it?"

"Don't be a wiseass, Michael. This is serious. A guy thought another guy was doing what the guy was supposed to be doing. You know how it is when things are a little crazy. Then Alice tells Stassi she's going to catch a taxi back to her hotel, pick up her clothes. Stassi says forget about it. It's dangerous. He'll buy her new clothes in Miami, but she goes."

"Carrying a suitcase full of money?"

"No one sees her get in the cab. We heard a rumor maybe some of Castro's people are coming to the house. Not that it happened, but everyone's running around for a while. No one was looking out for Alice and her cab."

Cassidy remembered the big suitcase Alice brought to the airport the next day. It was heavy, but what did that mean? How much did half a million dollars weigh? It could have held clothes. It could have held the hotel's towels. "What do you want from me?"

"Talk to her. Find out. If she took it and gives it back, then that's the end of it."

"And if she didn't take it?"

"Then we've got a problem."

"With her?"

"We'd go back over it again. We'd check everyone out. But you know these guys, Michael. They can't let it get around that someone's stealing from them and nothing happened. You know how they think. Better to punish somebody could've done it, than punish no one. It's a lesson. Don't even let us think you're stealing."

"She's with me, Frank."

"The only reason they haven't picked her up is she's with you, you're my godson. They came to me, asked me to ask you to ask her. Michael, if the money comes back, everything else goes away. My word on it."

"I'll talk to her."

"It's a bad situation, Michael. No one wants to piss you off." But the unspoken message was that the money was more important and they would deal with Cassidy's anger if they had to.

Cassidy asked Costello to stop the limo on Hudson Street. "I'll talk to her. I'll call you."

"Okay, Michael."

He got out and walked the last blocks west toward the clearing sky and the sunset over the docks at the end of the street. Was Alice stupid enough to steal from the Mob? He didn't think so, but what he thought didn't count here.

• • •

Cassidy took Alice to The Old Homestead on Ninth Avenue and 14th Street. She wore a tight red dress with no girdle and a small black hat with a jaunty white feather, and when the maître d' led them to their table, men turned to watch her pass.

They ordered, and while they waited for their drinks he half listened while Alice told him about going uptown to Lord & Taylor and Bonwits to look at the spring fashions. "I don't know who they design that stuff for. Skinny women, I guess, not for girls like me. And the prices. You'd have to rob a bank or be married to a rich man. But I guess that's it, huh? Good-looking skinny women marry rich men and go there and buy the dresses."

The waiter brought their drinks and went away, and Alice talked on about working at the department store in Washington and how women would come in and buy a dress and bring it back a few days later, and you could always tell that they had worn it, and then one of the girls who had worked there for a while pointed out that it mostly happened when there was a big ball, or a big holiday party written up in the papers. They'd wear the dresses to the parties and then bring them back for the refund. "Kind of dishonest, it seems to me." Cassidy said yes, and no, and asked a few questions just to keep the flow going.

The waiter brought their steaks and baked potatoes, and the side dishes, creamed spinach for him, roasted tomatoes and a salad for her. He ate mechanically, tasting little, and wondered how to start.

Alice solved the problem.

She pushed her half-eaten steak away and lit a cigarette from the pack he had left on the table. "Okay, what's up?"

"What do you mean?"

"Come on, Michael. You sit there while I blab on about fashion and shopping, and things you don't give a damn about, and you say yes, and no, but you're not listening. So what's up? What's on your mind?"

"I have to talk to you about something."

Her face fell, and she stubbed out the cigarette. "Oh, shit, here we go."

"What?"

"You don't think I've heard that before? You don't think I know where that goes? You take me out, feed me, give me drinks, and then you 'have to talk about something.' I get it. It's the brush-off. Do it in a restaurant so the silly woman can't make a scene."

"What?"

"Fun while it lasted, but time to move on." Her face was set and her voice was steady. *We're both adults. We know how this works. No need for drama.* But her eyes glistened.

"It's not that." He reached over the table and took her hand. "It's not." She watched him, waiting for him to go on. "You remember Frank Costello, my godfather. He was down in Havana with Joe Stassi and those other guys." She nodded. "He came looking for me and he found me. He wanted to talk about you. Alice, they think you took money from Joe Stassi's house down there the last night. They think you took half a million dollars."

Her eyes widened, and her mouth formed an "O" of surprise, and then she burst out laughing loud enough to turn heads at nearby tables. "How much? Half a million dollars?" She laughed again until she choked, and Cassidy had to get up and pound her on the back.

A waiter approached nervously. "Is everything all right?"

"Yeah. Just fine, thanks. Fine."

He went away. Alice drank water and regained her breath. She looked across the table at Cassidy, shook her head, and laughed softly. "Half a million dollars. It's true, of course. I mean, look at the glamorous life I've been leading. A hundred bucks a month to stay at the fabulous Barbizon Hotel for women where men are not allowed above the ground floor. And on days when I'm not having lunch with the Rockefellers, I go up to the classy stores and look at the dresses I can't afford."

"It's serious, Alice. The money's important to them, but just as important is showing that people cannot steal from them. If they even think you did it, they'll come after you."

"I didn't take it. If I'd taken it, why would I come to New York? I knew that they come here. I would have disappeared. I've always wanted to go to France. I bet you could live a pretty good life in Paris on half a million." Her face was open, her manner direct. She showed none of the liars' *tells* he had learned over hundreds of interrogations.

"Who else, then? Tell me about that night."

"Well, let's see. You saw us leave the Tropicana. I was with Joe Stassi. We drove downtown to a couple of places and one of the guys from the front seat would go inside for a few minutes, and then we'd go on. There were people in the streets shouting and dancing. Men firing guns in the air. That was pretty wild. It made Stassi nervous, so after a while we drove back to his house. Everybody met there. Men kept showing up with bags and boxes full of money. They'd take it into the dining room and they had a couple of men counting it and putting it in suitcases."

"Were you in the room?"

"No. The women were all in the kitchen making sandwiches and stuff. Doreen, Marsha, a couple of others. Peggy. One, I never got her name, a bottle blonde with one of those overbites men find so sexy."

"So how did you see the money?"

"Oh. Okay. I took a plate of sandwiches into them, but they chased me right out."

"Then what?" Cassidy poured wine into her glass and took some for himself. She smiled in thanks.

"Then what? Let's see. I don't like to sit around doing nothing, so Joe came into the kitchen and I told him I was going to get a cab back to the hotel and pack my things. He didn't want me to go. He said it could be dangerous, that he'd buy me new stuff in Miami, but you know what? I know how that goes. *Here you are, honey. Here's a hundred bucks. See you around.* Uh-uh. I had some nice things back at the hotel, and I wasn't going to leave them. I figured, how dangerous could it be? They weren't shooting women down in the streets, were they? So I went back down there, and the front-desk guy liked me, and he called someone at The Tropicana about the plane the next morning, and there you were." She lit a cigarette and took a sip of the wine and waited for Cassidy.

"Okay."

"You believe me."

"Yes, I do."

She smiled in relief. "Thanks."

"I'll talk to Frank." Would that be enough? He didn't know. How much influence did Frank still have? He was getting out of the rackets. Other men were moving in to fill the power vacuum. They would be the ones who made the decisions on this.

15

When Cassidy rang the bell at the big limestone house on 73rd Street, the red setter came scrabbling down the marble-tiled hall and stood looking at him through the glass. Moments later a man appeared carrying a coffee cup. He opened the door and stepped into the vestibule and looked at Cassidy through the bars and glass of the big exterior door. The red setter followed him and stood at his knee. The man was in his early forties, tall, thin, already losing his sandy hair. He had a bony, patrician face and looked at the world through gold-rimmed glasses. He wore suit pants held up by dark green suspenders with embroidered silver whales, and a crisp white shirt with gold cuff links. He did not look like a man who had carried a two-hundred-pound corpse a couple of blocks to the park. He raised his eyebrows in question, and then nodded when Cassidy showed him his badge. When he opened the door, the red setter pushed its head through and sniffed Cassidy's knee.

"Come here, Lucky, that's enough," the man said and pulled him back by his collar. "Can I help you, Officer? I'm afraid I've already given to the fund. The precinct sent someone around about a month ago." He had a soft, reedy voice and a mild, accommodating manner.

"Are you Robert Hopkins?"

"I am."

"Do you recognize this man?" Cassidy passed him the photograph of the dead man from the park.

"Yes. Of course. Casey Allen. He's been doing some renovation work here at the house. Why? What has he done, Officer?"

"Detective Cassidy. When was the last time you saw him?"

"About a week ago. He was supposed to finish up the work he was doing, but he didn't show up. Very unlike him. He's usually very reliable. If he can't be here he calls. Then my wife and I went away for a few days. Casey has a key to the back door, and I assumed he would come in and finish up while we were gone, but when we got back last night, it was clear that he was never here. What exactly is the problem with him? Why are you asking about him?"

"Is Mrs. Hopkins here?"

"She is."

"I'd like to speak to her."

"Is that necessary?" A bit of steel showing through the soft exterior.

"Yes."

"Why?"

"He's dead. We're trying to discover how and why."

"Dead. I see." But if he was surprised, he covered it well. "I'll go speak with her and see if she's available."

"She has no choice."

Hopkins raised his eyebrows. "Yes, she does. She has a choice about when she speaks to you and who is with her when it happens. If you'd like, I can call our lawyer and he can clarify her rights for you." More steel. Cassidy admired him for it even though it checked him, kept him from what he needed to know.

"Does she have something to conceal?" Cassidy asked.

Hopkins smiled and shook his head. "Oh, that's a cheap ploy, Detective. If she doesn't speak to you it's because she's hiding something." He laughed at the absurdity. "Jane is not hiding something. She's protecting something, her rights, her constitutional rights. You do remember those, don't you? We have not yet become a jackbooted country where the police have the rights and the citizens have none. If you suspect her of a crime, state it, and we will get on with that. If you just want to speak to her about Casey Allen, there are better ways of approaching it than barging in here at eight in the morning demanding a meeting." The red setter barked twice, upset by his master's agitation.

"All right. Let's take a step back here," Cassidy said. "You're absolutely right. There is no need to bother Mrs. Hopkins right now. I can come back at a more convenient time."

"Please call first."

"Of course. Why don't you give me your phone number here and at your office, and I'll need Mr. Allen's phone and address as well."

"Fine. Come in, and I'll go write them down for you." He opened the inner door, and Cassidy followed him into the front hall. The setter went with them. "I'll be right back." Hopkins went down the hall and into another room.

The front hall was two stories high. Its wide floor was laid with black-and-white marble tiles like the ones in Leah's apartment. A marble staircase with a dark red runner held by brass rods led to the upper floors. A large mirror in a carved gilt frame hung over a delicate cherry wood side table, one last look to see if the tie was straight, the hair combed, the lipstick on right before going out to face the world. Cassidy looked into the large living room off the hall. The fireplace was surrounded by a marble mantel. The furniture was expensive and comfortable. He recognized some of the paintings on the walls, a Picasso, a Matisse, a small oil of fruits in a bowl that he was pretty sure was a Cézanne. The house had been rubbed with money until it glowed.

When he went back into the hall, the setter came to him carrying a leash in his mouth and sat down and looked at him expectantly. "Not me, boy. I'd like to, but you're going to have to ask someone else."

"Ask about what?" Robert Hopkins came toward him carrying a piece of paper.

"The dog and I were talking about going for a walk. I told him I couldn't."

"I see." No smile. Hopkins was impatient to see him go. "Here are the numbers. My office, the house, Casey Allen's number and address."

"Do you walk the dog?"

"On weekends. Jane walks him during the week. Now if you'll excuse me, I'm already late for work."

Cassidy took his dismissal and left. He crossed Fifth Avenue and found a place in the shadow of a big tree that grew near the wall to the park that gave him a view of the front of the Hopkins house. He looked at the piece of paper Hopkins had given him. It was a letterhead from Brown Brothers Harriman. Robert Hopkins, Vice President, was circled with a pen. The circle included his private number. Brown Brothers, Cassidy knew, was one of the largest private banks in America, and its officers were masters of the revolving door between Wall Street and Washington. Averell Harriman, the founding father, had been Franklin Roosevelt's personal envoy to Winston Churchill during World War II, and had run unsuccessfully for the Democratic presidential nomination in 1952.

Was Hopkins trying to tell Cassidy that he was too well connected to fuck with? Probably. But the fucking with was unavoidable, because Hopkins had forgotten to ask one question. He had forgotten to ask how Casey Allen died. Did he not care, or did he already know?

Casey Allen's address and phone number were written in a tight, round, neat hand at the bottom of the page. He had lived in Queens.

Cassidy was on his second Lucky Strike when a black Lincoln Town Car stopped in front of the Hopkins house. Cassidy made a note of the company name stenciled on the trunk. Robert Hopkins came out armored in a pinstripe suit, got into the car, and went off to tend the money fields. Fifteen minutes later Mrs. Robert Hopkins was pulled out of the house by an eager Lucky, who dragged her to the nearest tree, lifted his leg, and sighed. She and the dog walked to the corner, waited for the light to change, and then crossed Fifth Avenue to the broad sidewalk that ran along the park. Lucky, maybe out of habit, turned south toward the nearest entrance, but she pulled him back and turned north, away from where Casey Allen had been found dead on a kitchen chair.

Cassidy followed.

Jane Hopkins was a tall, slim woman in her mid-thirties, a few years younger than her husband. She had shoulder-length honey-colored hair held in place by a black velvet headband. She wore tailored, high-waisted charcoal gray slacks that emphasized the length of her legs, black leather boots, and a green-and-black jacket with a high, Chinese collar. She walked fast and went into the park at the entrance on 76th Street, and he followed her till the dog stopped her at a particularly interesting smell near the Conservatory Waters boat basin.

"Mrs. Hopkins, I'd like to talk to you for a minute."

She looked up, startled from the cigarette she was lighting, and then her face cleared. "Michael, how nice to see you. What are you doing here?"

That threw him, and she recognized his confusion.

"Jane Hopkins. We met at Leah's party before Christmas. You told me a very funny story about working on a ranch in Mexico when you were sixteen. Don't tell me you don't remember."

A vague memory poking up through the mist of holiday booze. A good-looking woman, flirtatious, one of those women who touches you while she talks, a hand on the arm, a nudge, a finger on the chest, leaning in for a moment at the punch line.

"You don't know how devastating it is to a woman's ego when an attractive man forgets her."

"Jane, of course. I didn't forget you, I just didn't put it together this far out of that context."

"Hmmm, not a bad recovery. I've heard better, but not bad. But what are you doing here, and approaching me as Mrs. Hopkins with that very serious tone of voice?"

She was a woman who was used to being admired by men, used to disarming them with her looks and her charm.

"I want to talk to you about Casey Allen."

That checked her. "Oh," Then, "Oh, my god, were you the cop downstairs grilling Bob earlier? He was very pissed off, going on about invasion of privacy, and the nerve of this and the nerve of that. Secretaries and junior partners are going to suffer today." It was delivered with a practiced breeziness, but there was something brittle and strained just below the surface. "Poor Casey Allen. Bob told me he was dead. What happened?" At least she asked.

"He was shot."

"Shot? Who did it? Was it a robbery? That's awful." Her eyes were wide in surprise.

"We don't know yet. I'd like to ask you some questions about him. Do you mind?"

"No, not at all. Bob thinks I should have three or four lawyers hovering, but then he didn't realize you were Leah's brother and Mark Buckman's brother-in-law. He's done quite a bit of business with Mark." What she meant was that they were all in the same club, as if, therefore, there could be no rudeness, no friction, no unpleasantness. "Do you mind if we walk while we talk?" She gestured to the dog tugging at the end of the leash.

They walked past the newly planted flowerbeds near the boat pond, the earth turned up dark and rich, the plants vibrant, hopeful green. "Tell me about Casey Allen," Cassidy said. What would she volunteer, what would she leave out?

"We brought him in to do some work in the house. We had water damage upstairs, a burst pipe. We'd been talking about knocking down a wall, making our bathroom bigger and giving me a proper dressing room, and since we were going to have workers in anyway, we decided this was the time to do it. Casey was recommended to us by the Millikens. You know them, don't you? He's with Sullivan and Cromwell. Anyway, Casey was exactly what we wanted. He was prompt, efficient, he did most of the work himself, so we weren't tripping over people. If he needed help, he brought in his brother-in-law or someone else."

"What was he like? What did you know about him?"

"Not much. He was one of those cheerful Irishmen. Always a smile on his face. Whistled while he worked, if you can believe it." She laughed and touched Cassidy on the arm, a fleeting brush of fingers, but still a gesture of intimacy.

When Lucky was finished, they moved on. Jane took Cassidy's arm as if it were a perfectly natural thing to do, more intimacy. "Did he tell you anything about his life? Did friends come by, anything like that?"

"Just the brother-in-law when he needed help with the work, and no, we didn't talk much about his private life. He was married, but I don't think he had children. You know how it is when someone is working for you. You make polite conversation, but no one let's down his hair."

"What can you tell me about the brother-in-law? What was his name?"

"His name. Oh, god. What was it? He was only there a few times, and sometimes I was gone. Let's see, Casey, and Curt, Carl? No. Cameron? That sounds close, but it's not quite right. But it was something like that, a hard 'C' sound. I didn't like him much, so I didn't pay attention. He was one of those men who thought he was God's gift to women, undressed you with his eyes. Not that women aren't used to that, my god." She laughed and squeezed his arm. "Still, one wants to choose, and I found him kind of creepy."

"Did you ever see Casey outside the house, outside of work?"

"What do you mean?" A glance and a touch of frost.

"I don't know. Bump into him on the street, see him in a restaurant, that kind of thing."

"I don't think Casey Allen and I eat in the same restaurants."

"So, no."

"No. Just at the house. Or on the block, coming or going."

"Uh-huh. What about at Brooks Brothers or Church's shoe store over on Madison?"

She yanked on the leash to pull Lucky away from a piece of trash. "No, Lucky, no." And it covered any reaction she might have had to Cassidy's question. When the dog obeyed, she started walking again. "Oh, yes, that.

Of course." Easily said, with almost no tension. "Casey was an ambitious young man. He wanted to better himself. He'd ask what books to read and how people behave in certain situations. He paid attention to how Bob dressed. He seemed genuinely interested in learning things. Bob and I both admired that. I told him about Brooks Brothers and about Church's, but he seemed a bit intimidated by them, so I said I'd go along and help him choose." She checked him for his reaction. He smiled encouragement. "He asked me. I thought, why not?"

"Expensive stores for a man in his line of work."

"That's what I told him, but he quoted one of the homilies Bob loves so much: 'You have to spend money to make money.' Bob's talking about spending millions to make millions, but I suppose the principle is the same. Casey thought that if he presented himself correctly he might get more work in our neighborhood. I think he was right."

"And he had the money."

"No, no. I paid. We had an agreement that involved dropping his hourly wage on the work he was doing until he paid off the debt."

She had an answer to everything. Or she was telling the truth.

They walked on for a minute without speaking, and then she put a hand on his arm and stopped him. "You think I had an affair with him."

"It crossed my mind."

"And what, Bob found out and killed him in a jealous rage." She laughed. "That is priceless. One, I was not having an affair with Casey Allen, the hunky construction guy. That is just too *Lady Chatterley's Lover.* And two, Bob doesn't do jealous rage. Bob does cool and calculated. Bob does cost-benefit analysis. Bob weighs avenging honor against going to Sing Sing. Guess which comes out on top? Uh-uh. Sorry."

"A week ago Friday, did you see him?"

"We left a week ago Friday. We went to San Francisco."

"Did you walk Lucky before you went?"

"I don't remember. I assume so."

"Where do you usually walk him?"

"Here, in the park."

"Here, or down at Seventy-second Street?"

"Sometimes here. Sometimes there. Why does it matter?" She tried to make it casual. The dog tugged at the leash, and she jerked him back abruptly and he yelped in surprise.

"Casey Allen was shot and left on a chair near the Seventy-second Street entrance to the park. We think he was left as a message to someone who was used to going in there in the mornings."

"Me? What could the message possibly be to me?"

Cassidy shrugged.

She opened her purse and thrashed through it until she found her cigarettes. She lit one and slammed the pack back into her purse.

"Oh, I get it. This would be Bob's way of telling me he disapproves. Is that the best you can do? Why couldn't it be some business rival? Why not someone he had a fight with in a bar?"

"Was the trip to San Francisco planned, or spur of the moment?"

"Bob does not do things on the spur of the moment."

"What about Lucky? What happens with him?" He scratched the dog's ears, and it butted him on the leg for more when he stopped.

"We have a dog walker who takes care of him. It was arranged before we left."

That, he knew, was a lie. Naomi, the dog walker, said that they had left unexpectedly and had left her a note about walking the dog.

Cassidy walked back to the precinct and called the company that sent the town car to pick up Robert Hopkins. The day Casey Allen was found, the driver arrived at the regular time, but instead of taking Mr. Hopkins down to Brown Brothers Harriman, he took Mr. and Mrs. Hopkins to TWA at Idlewild Airport. Cassidy called TWA. Mr. and Mrs. Robert Hopkins took the morning flight to San Francisco. They made their reservations by phone at seven thirty the same morning and paid for the tickets with cash at the airport desk.

16

Cassidy and Orso walked the platform under Penn Station as the train pushed in slowly and stopped, hissing steam. They nodded to the uniformed patrolmen spaced every ten feet. The doors opened, and passengers disembarked, and the two men worked against the tide of people headed for the exit stairs.

"How many have we got?" Orso asked.

"Twenty uniforms down here. A hundred in the concourse, a hundred outside. Twenty plainclothes here and there."

"Jesus. They must really think someone's going to go for this joker."

Ahead of them a knot of cops blocked anyone trying to get back to the last car. A tall, thin lieutenant with red hair and a freckled face as Irish as a shamrock separated from the group. "How're you doing, detectives?"

"Connolly, right?" Cassidy asked. "Do you know Detective Orso?"

"Yeah, sure. I came up through the academy with your cousin Frankie." The three men shook hands. "I sent Perez in to tell Castro and his people they were going to have to hang back till the other passengers cleared the platform. I guess we're pretty much good to go now."

"How many of them?" Cassidy asked.

"Thirty-two."

"They told us fifty," Cassidy said.

Connolly shrugged. "They sent an advance party on an earlier train without telling us. Thirty-two here including Castro."

"Shit, it's going to be like herding cats," Orso said.

"Could shoot 'em all now, save everybody the trouble," Connolly said. The men who heard it laughed. "Perez, go back in there and tell them they can get off."

Fidel Castro's followers straggled out of the doors at either end of the car and coalesced near the middle around the tall figure of their leader. Like Fidel, most of the men were bearded, and most of them, like their leader, wore khaki fatigues as if about to go out on patrol. There were a number of women in the group, and all of them were dressed in fatigues. Some of them glanced at the cops who watched them and looked away again, and their laughter had a nervous edge of bravado. Cops had never been their friends in Cuba. Castro seemed unaffected. He looked out over their heads with genial curiosity, a large cigar clenched in his teeth.

"All yours, Detective," Connolly said. "And good luck to you."

Cassidy approached the Cubans with Orso at his shoulder, and people stepped aside and nodded to them, deferring, but when they got close to Castro, two men stepped in to block them. Cassidy looked past them to Castro and said in Spanish, "My name is Michael Cassidy. I'm a detective with the New York Police Department. We're here to escort you to your hotel."

Castro gestured to the two men, and they stepped aside. He stepped forward and offered his hand, taking the cigar out of his mouth with the other. "Michael Cassidy, you are a friend of Carlos Ribera, my friend. He said you are a good man. I am happy to meet you." His English was heavily accented. He was a big man, tall and bulky, and his beard, though full, was scraggly and unkempt. His hand, when Cassidy shook it, was surprisingly soft, the hand of the lawyer he had been, rather than the guerrilla fighter he had become. His fatigues showed no insignia of rank, but the way people looked at him, waited for him, moved around him made it clear that he was their leader.

"Is Carlos here?"

"He is somewhere. He was on an earlier train. You know Carlos. He goes where he wants when he wants." He laughed. "So, show us where we are to go."

They went up the stairs to the main hall, cops at the front and at the back, leading fast and pushing hard. They wanted Castro and his party across the street and under cover in the hotel, but he did not seem to feel their urgency. He stopped in the middle of the vast main concourse and looked up at the vaulted ceiling. He raised his arms wide as if to embrace it all and told his followers in Spanish, "It was modeled after the Baths of Caracalla in ancient Rome, and is as big inside as St. Peter's." Then he laughed. "Of course this was not built to the glory of God, but to the glory of commerce." He waved his cigar like a baton, and charged the wide marble steps that led to Seventh Avenue, and his police escort hurried to keep up.

When Castro led his followers out onto the sidewalk at Seventh Avenue, they found thousands of people packed behind the wooden sawhorses the Department had set up for crowd control. At the sight of Castro cheers exploded, "*Viva la revolución!*" "*Viva Fidel!*" "*Cago en la leche de Batista!*" "*Arriba el Movimiento 26 de Julio!*" Signs and placards supporting Castro and the 26th of July Movement danced and swung above the heads of the crowd that surged against the barriers and the uniformed cops who manned them. Among the shouts of approval, Cassidy heard other voices of protest. "*Abajo Fidel.*" "*Donde esta mi hermano?*" "*Asesino, asesino.*" A fight broke out deep in the crowd. A man went down with his head bloodied by the wooden pole of a placard that read, "*Fidel brings peace and prosperity.*"

"This way," Cassidy said, and took Castro's arm to lead him through the cleared area between the barriers and across Seventh Avenue where four cops wearing white gloves had brought traffic to a halt. Horns blared in protest. Castro pulled away and plunged into the crowd grabbing hands, hugging, kissing women. He was quickly surrounded by people, cut off from his escort. Past him, Cassidy could see two men fighting through the crowd toward Castro. One of them carried a placard calling for Castro's death. The other held a heavy pole from which he must have ripped a sign, because pieces of white cardboard were still stapled near the top. The man swung the pole like a bludgeon, and two people went down, and the path cleared in front of them. Cassidy pushed into the crush, but the dense pack of admirers trying to get near the Cuban leader held him back.

"Orso! Orso!" His partner saw the problem and slammed into the crowd. His charge threw people back, but the two men coming for Castro were going to get there first. Cassidy dug for his gun, but someone hit him hard on the ear, and the only reason he did not fall was there was no room. And then in front of him a man drew a silver revolver from under his shirt. "Gun! Gun! Man with a gun!" He threw himself forward. Someone grabbed his jacket. He jerked an elbow back and it smacked something hard. He heard a grunt of pain, and whoever it was let go, and he plunged ahead. Where was Castro? There, head and shoulders above the crowd, an easy shot, not twenty feet away. The gunman struggled to turn. Cassidy grabbed the back of someone's collar and jerked him to the ground and went into the gap the man left and jumped on the gunman's back. He crooked his left arm hard around his throat. As he rode him to the ground he reached over the man's shoulder with his right hand and clasped it over the gun. The gunman pulled the trigger and the hammer came down on the web between Cassidy's thumb and forefinger, tearing the flesh. Cassidy ripped the gun from the man's hand and slammed it against the side of his face, and he grunted and tried to throw him off. Cassidy hit him again; the man sagged. He pulled his handcuffs from his belt, jerked the man's hands behind his back, and cuffed him.

Orso put a hand under his arm and pulled him to his feet. "Are you all right?"

"Yeah. Castro?"

"Not a scratch. Looks like he didn't even know it was happening."

Castro was still glad-handing his admirers. "There were two guys who were headed for him, one with a sign, one with just the post."

"I guess they took off. You're bleeding, Mike. Your hand."

"Yeah. Goddamn it. Here, give me your handkerchief, will you?"

Orso hesitated. "It's silk."

"Oh, for christ's sake."

"Yeah, yeah. Here."

Cassidy wrapped his hand. The man on the ground groaned and tried to roll over. Cassidy got his good hand under the man's arm and levered him to his feet. There was blood, and dirt from the street on the side of his face. He glared at Cassidy. "*¿Por qué hiciste esto a mí?*"

"Shut up."

"What'd he say?" Orso asked.

"He wanted to know why I did it to him."

Orso laughed.

Castro was suddenly at Cassidy's shoulder. "What happened to José?" He looked concerned. "He's bleeding."

"You know this man?"

"He is one of my bodyguards."

"He had a gun."

"As I said, he is one of my bodyguards."

"He can't carry a gun in this city. How many other of your men are carrying?"

"I don't know. Some." Castro shrugged it away as unimportant.

"Okay, let's get everybody over to the hotel and sort this out." It was going to be a long week.

• • •

"We'll give the guns back to your men when you leave New York," Cassidy said. "You won't need them here. You'll be covered by a hundred cops every time you leave the hotel." They were alone together in the bedroom of Castro's suite in the Statler Hilton across from Pennsylvania Station. The window was open, and the traffic noise drifted up from the street.

Castro shrugged. "*Bueno.* It is all unnecessary. I am sure there are many things the police could be doing in this city besides watching me." Cassidy noticed that Castro used Spanish when he wanted to assert his authority, English when he wanted to please. "I do not need your protection." He took a long cigar from a box on the table, flicked a wooden match with his thumbnail, and carefully applied the flame to the cigar end, rolling it until he had an even burn.

"We have information that there may be an attempt on your life." *Attempt on your life* sounded formal, bland, without danger.

Castro dismissed the idea with a wave of the cigar. "They can't kill me. Batista and his army tried for three years and could not. Thousands of men with thousands of guns. Do you believe in destiny, Detective?"

"No."

"I have a destiny to lead my people out of the poverty and despair they have lived in for generations, to free them from the oppression they have suffered. This cannot be done in a few months. It will take years and years. No one is going to kill me before I fulfill that destiny."

"No one's going to kill you in New York, because we're going to make sure it doesn't happen. After that, you're on your own."

Castro smiled and opened his arms. "Very well, I am in your hands. I could not feel safer if I was home in my own bed."

The living room of the suite was crammed with Castro supporters, and they burst into cheers when he appeared in the bedroom door. Women presented themselves to be kissed, and men moved close to warm in his presence. Castro worked the room, hugs for the women, strong handshakes and clasps of the arm for the men. Smiles through the beard. Laughter. Occasionally he offered a cigar or bent to whisper in an ear, marks of favor, of intimacy, and those who received them glowed when he moved on. Three young women dressed not in fatigues but in tight cocktail dresses watched him with proprietary interest and glared at each other. Cassidy knew Castro was married but, what the hell, surely the revolutionary leader of a country should be granted some leeway in such mundane matters as women.

The door opened at one side of the room and Susdorf and Cherry came out of the bathroom. "Don't you think that's carrying the partner thing a little too far?" Cassidy said. Cherry flushed with anger, his automatic response to most things.

Susdorf, a man with a literal bent, said, "It's hard to find a private place to talk here. We just stepped into the bathroom for a moment to share some information."

"Are you afraid the NYPD is going to leak something?"

"No, no, of course not. Director Hoover has put protocols in place that we have to adhere to. We've received some information pertinent to the operation here, and we needed a couple of minutes to talk it over." A serious business carrying the burden of the Director's directives.

"Are you going to tell me, or am I outside the protocols?"

"No, no. We were going to reach out for you."

"Shall we step back into your office?"

Susdorf looked around at the people in the room. "Yes, I think that would be a good idea."

The bathroom was barely big enough for the three of them. Cassidy went in first and leaned against the sink, forcing Susdorf and Cherry to stand one behind the other, and Cherry had to butt up hard against his partner's back to make room to close the door. Susdorf flinched and then leaned past Cassidy and flushed the toilet and spoke over the rush and gurgle of water. "We've been running down those reports of an assassination attempt. What we've got so far is three men headed north in a Cadillac or a Lincoln sedan with Florida plates. We've alerted Highway Patrol and State Police and our local FBI offices."

"That's it?"

"At the moment, but we're confident we'll have more information soon." He didn't look like a man who was confident.

"Florida?"

"Yes."

"There are a lot of Cubans in Miami, people who took off when Batista got kicked out. I'm sure some of them want Castro dead."

"We have no information that the men coming are Cuban, but if we learn something, we'll reach out to you."

"Terrific."

Susdorf checked him for sarcasm.

"I guess we can go now if Agent Cherry would open the door."

Cherry pushed up against Susdorf again while he opened the door, and Susdorf gave Cassidy a pained smile and started to back out of the room. Cassidy stopped him. "Anything else you want to tell me?"

"No."

Cassidy spoke to the cops manning the door to the suite and then stopped by the room down the corridor the Department had set up as command headquarters. A metal coffee urn sat on a folding table next to a plate of doughnuts. There were ten uniformed cops in the room, and their conversations died when Cassidy entered. He picked up mimeographed copies of Castro's schedule and took the elevator to the lobby while he read one.

He went to the desk and showed the clerk his badge and asked for the manager. The desk clerk went away carrying one of Cassidy's business cards and came back with a tall, dignified man with the wary eyes of someone who was called when there was a problem. He wore a tailored black suit with a white shirt and a dark blue tie swimming with small yellow fish and he held Cassidy's card between his thumb and forefinger. "I'm John Quincy, the day manager. May I help you, Detective Cassidy?" Helpfulness and reserve. *Tell me your problem and I will do everything I can, but some things cannot be solved. We both know that.*

"Eight twenty-four, the suite where Mr. Castro is staying. Did the Cubans send an advance party to the room before Mr. Castro arrived?"

"An advance party? No."

"Nobody went into the rooms after they were cleaned."

"Nobody but the FBI agents."

"Tell me about the FBI agents."

"An Agent Susdorf and Agent Cherry. They had two other men with them who they did not introduce. They said they had to make a security check. Is there a problem?"

"No. No problem. Thank you very much."

"You're welcome."

Cassidy found Orso in the bar off the lobby. It was too early for the evening drinkers, and the room was empty except for the bored bartender, elbows on the bar, reading *The Racing Form,* and one cocktail waitress with dyed blond hair and eyebrows plucked to thin curved lines. She sat beside Orso in a booth while he read her palm. He held her wrist and traced a line on her hand, which made her giggle and jump. "And this one," Orso said, "means you are adventurous in love. Hmm, I could use a little adventure."

"You be careful," she said, not meaning it.

"And this one," he ran a finger lightly over her hand, and she twitched and sucked in her breath. "Whoa, this one."

"What?"

"I probably shouldn't tell you about this one."

"You better."

"Hmmm, later."

"What you mean, later? I've got to go to work."

"I'll pick you up when you're done. What time do you get off?"

"I don't know. I mean, I don't even know you."

He still held her wrist, and he ran his finger over her hand again, and she giggled.

"Don't you want to know what this one means?"

"Maybe I do, maybe I don't." She gave him a look up from under her fake eyelashes.

"What time?"

"Eleven."

"I'll see you then." He released her hand.

The woman stood up and said "Excuse me" to Cassidy, and stilted off on high heels, smoothing her skirt with her hands.

Cassidy sat down across the table in the booth and told Orso about the meeting with Susdorf and Cherry in the bathroom of Castro's suite.

"What's that all about, the bathroom and all?" Orso asked.

"They've got a bug in Castro's suite."

"Okay. Why does that put them in the bathroom?"

"They don't want to be on tape saying something Hoover might not like."

"Like what?"

"I don't know, and neither do they. He might not like their tone of voice. He might not like their use of the passive voice or the subjunctive. Who knows what God likes or doesn't like? Better safe than sorry."

"Jesus. And I thought working for the Department was a pain in the ass. What's our deal with Castro?"

"We're with him tomorrow for lunch at the Overseas Press Club, and then the Bronx Zoo." He slid Orso a mimeographed copy of Castro's schedule. "Let's get out of here and find a real bar and I'll buy you a drink."

Orso pocketed the schedule. "Thanks, but I can't. I've got to meet a guy about something."

"I'll walk with you, buy you a drink when you're done."

"No. Thanks, Chief, but I better not. I don't know how long this is going to take. Could be a while. I'll see you in the morning." A half smile that was not a smile at all, and he got up and went out. Cassidy watched him go. Why was he lying? What made him so nervous? The hell with it. Orso led a complicated life. If he didn't want to tell, why should he? Let it go.

17

The Bronx Zoo on a cool, gray day. The animals paced metronomically behind their bars. On the weekend the zoo would be crowded with families showing their children the exotic beasts trapped on the dreary concrete, but it was the middle of the week, and there were few children there. What few there were Castro found. He lifted the boys onto his shoulders, and hugged the girls, and talked to their parents as if they were old friends. Cassidy admired his easy way with them, but it put the cops on edge. How do you guard a man who won't be guarded?

Castro paused for a long time in front of the tiger cage. The big cat walked to the bars and stared through yellow eyes at the men gathered there, as if assessing their protein value. It yawned to show them its teeth. Then Castro reached through the bars and patted the animal on the head. People around him gasped. The tiger submitted without moving, and Castro withdrew his hand and turned away. A compact between predators, Cassidy thought. Professional courtesies.

Castro and his entourage drove back to Manhattan in their Cadillacs escorted by squad cars, lights and sirens to clear the traffic. Cassidy and Orso watched them go and then walked to where their car was parked in the shade of trees just beginning to push out their spring buds, the season of hope. A man waited in the shadows near the car. "Do you see him?" Orso said.

"Yes."

"Do you know him?"

"I can't tell yet."

They separated. Orso went toward the back of the car, Cassidy toward the front. The man saw what they were doing and stepped into the light and put his hands on the car hood.

"Carlos," Cassidy said.

"Michael." Ribera came around the front of the car and hugged Cassidy.

"Tony Orso, Carlos Ribera." The two big men shook hands and looked each other over warily the way men often do when they first meet someone a friend has talked about.

"What are you doing here?" Cassidy asked.

"I go early where he is going to go later. I like to walk around before he gets there. Sometimes you see something that shouldn't be there. Sometimes you feel something that isn't right."

"Are you any good at that?" Orso asked.

"I don't know. Maybe. There was a day in Santiago a month ago. Fidel was there for a speech. His men had searched the hall and found a bomb, but I felt something was still not right. How was it that the bomb was so easy to find? I went back. There was another in a light over the stage." He shrugged. "So, just a feeling, and I was lucky. Let's get out of here. I don't like zoos. I don't like the way men cage wild things to feel better about their own limitations. Buy me a drink, and I'll show you something."

They drove back to Manhattan and left the car in a no-parking zone with a police plaque on the dashboard and went into the Oak Room of the Plaza Hotel and took a table near the windows. Dusk darkened toward evening. Across 59th Street a young man handed his date into one of the horse-drawn carriages and drew the blanket up around them for a romantic ride through Central Park. Men hurried by on their way home from work, disembodied heads under fedoras as they passed the high windows.

A waiter brought their drinks. When he went away, Ribera took a sheaf of photographs from his pocket and pushed them across the table to Cassidy. "Do you recognize anyone?"

Cassidy spread the black-and-white prints out on the table and examined them. They showed crowds in a street. In one he could see the columned façade of Pennsylvania Station. "This was the day Castro arrived."

"Yes."

"You were taking pictures. I didn't see you."

"No. But I saw you."

Cassidy looked back at the photographs. "Ahh."

"Yes. You remember him."

"The colonel from La Cabaña. Fuentes."

"Yes, Colonel Diego Fuentes, lately of SIM."

"Do you think he was going to try for Castro?"

"That day? Maybe. He was far back in the crowd and he did not try to get close. I think we was just scouting."

"Who are we talking about here?" Orso asked. "The guy you told me about clipped what's his name, Echevarria, you took down there on the extradition?"

"Yes."

"You think this guy wants to try for Castro."

"Yes," Ribera said. "I do."

"Why?"

"Because he and his friends don't think the war is over. They think a few well-selected deaths will put them back in power."

"Do you have any ideas about where they might be in the city? With the émigré groups, Batista supporters?"

"We're asking. So far, nothing."

• • •

Nine hundred miles to the south, a police cruiser pulled into the parking lot of the train station in Atlanta, Georgia.

It had rained off and on for the last twenty-four hours in Atlanta, a fine, soft, warm, misty rain that lured children out to slide on lawns, and drew flowers up out of the ground. The weather cleared in the evening just about the time Cassidy, Orso, and Ribera ordered their second drinks in the Oak Room of the Plaza Hotel in New York City. The cruiser pulled to a stop in front of the station doors, and two officers got out. Arlie Spencer hitched up his gun belt where it sagged below his gut and started walking to the station. "You want anything, Lloyd? Coffee or anything? Maybe a slice of pie. Maryellen said she was baking today."

"No, thanks. I'm just going to stretch my legs. Been cooped up in that car all day." Lloyd Fairchild was half an inch over the five foot six minimum requirement of the department, and he weighed just over the hundred-thirty-pound cutoff. His beaky nose supported horn-rimmed glasses, and his uniform hat hid a skull that was nearly bald three years before he was due to turn thirty. He knew he didn't look like a cop, and so he worked twice as hard to be the cop he knew he was. He wore black half boots with lifts in them, and he carried himself tall and walked with a swagger that was just on the right side of comic. He lit a cigarette and strolled the parking lot, happy to be out of the car. They'd kept the windows closed while it rained. The cruiser was not one of the new ones that had air-conditioning, and by the time the rain stopped the air inside had been thick. Arlie was a good partner, but Jesus, it was like whatever he ate came back out through his skin when he sweated.

Lloyd spotted a '48 Ford sedan with a broken taillight and a '56 Impala with an expired registration and left warning notes under their windshield wipers. What was it about the Lincoln parked in the far corner of the lot? He walked over and examined the car. Florida plates. Wasn't there something about a Lincoln with Florida plates that came in over the wire? He hurried back to the cruiser and pulled a sheaf of mimeographed bulletins from the glove compartment and fingered through them. There it was. A '55 Continental with Florida plates, three men riding. Do not approach. Notify the FBI. Okay, then. He picked up the radio handset and called it in and was told to stand by. A few minutes later the radio crackled. Officers Fairchild and Spencer were to secure the car and to wait for the arrival of Special Agent in Charge Harmon of the Atlanta FBI office.

SAC Harmon looked like a professor at a small liberal arts college. He was a tall, sandy-haired man in a gray wash-and-wear suit and a straw Panama hat with a red hatband. He clenched a briar pipe in his teeth. "Checked the interior?" He asked mildly.

"No, sir. We were told to secure the car and wait for you," Lloyd said. "But the car's been here since yesterday morning."

"Is that so?"

"Yes, sir. It's been raining off and on since early yesterday afternoon, but the tar underneath is dry."

"Hmmm, good, good. Let's take a look, shall we?" It was not a question and the "we" was royal, because when the two cops moved to help, the FBI agent checked them. "Why don't we let me do this one? Less complicated that way." Harmon said it with a smile, but it was an order. He opened all four doors and the trunk and then slowly and methodically searched the car. He found Coca-Cola bottles, waxed paper sandwich wrappings, a broken fountain pen, a pack of condoms in the glove compartment, and under the passenger seat a single shell for a .30-06 rifle.

"Thirty ought six," Officer Spencer said when he saw the brass rolling in Harmon's palm. "Good deer rifle. My uncle Boley had one. I prefer the thirty-thirty myself."

"Fascinating," Harmon said. "Let's go see whether the gentlemen with the deer rifle took the train."

The ticket office clerk remembered them. "Three of them together? Sure. Yesterday. Three of them got on the Crescent Limited. They took two double sleepers for the three. Money to burn, I guess. Last people I sold tickets to before I went to lunch."

"Where were they headed?" Harmon asked.

"End of the line. New York City. Got in there this morning."

"Can you describe them?"

The clerk thought for a while. "Well, I only really saw the one bought the tickets. The others stood back a ways with the bags. Now that fella who bought the tickets come up to about here on the cage." He indicated a height on the bars that separated him from Harmon. "A couple of inches shorter than you."

"About five nine, then," Harmon said.

"If you say so. Wore a seersucker suit and one of them straw hats with a feather in the band. Not so wide a brim as on yours. Mustache and chin whiskers. What do they call that where the mustache is part of the beard? Kind of thin, the mustache, not the man. Not that he was fat, you see. Ordinary, I'd say."

"And the others? Anything stick in your mind?"

"I can't say it did. Just looked over to see there was two more of them over there for the tickets."

In the parking lot Harmon stopped near the cruiser and shook hands with the two policemen. "Thank you for your help, gentlemen."

"What's this all about?" Lloyd asked.

Harmon took time to load his pipe and light it while looking at the two cops over the bowl. He shook the match out and ground it under his shoe. "Well, as much as I'd like to tell you, I'm afraid I've been told to keep this one under my hat. I can tell you it's a matter of national security and falls under the jurisdiction of the Bureau. I wish I could tell you more, but I can't." He smiled genially, gestured good-bye with his pipe, and walked back to his car.

"Wishes he could tell us, my ass. When was the last time the FBI shared any information with the local cops?" Lloyd asked. "I'll tell you when.

Never. Jesus, that chaps me." They watched Harmon's car turn out of the parking lot. As it went, his arm came out the window and he waved. "The fucking FBI."

SAC Harmon went back to the office and put in a call to FBI headquarters in Washington, DC, where he spoke to Deputy Assistant Director Cavanaugh, as high up the chain of command as he was allowed to go. Cavanaugh carried the message upstairs and waited patiently in the anteroom outside Associate Director Tolson's office until the severe gray-haired secretary who guarded the double doors allowed him to enter. He went in and closed the door behind him and glanced at the door in the east wall that led directly to J. Edgar Hoover's office, a holy place he had never had the privilege of seeing. Tolson let him wait in front of the desk until he finished reading a report. He pushed it into a manila folder, squared it on the desk and looked up.

"Yes?"

"I had a phone call from SAC Harmon in Atlanta. He believes he has found the car we've been looking for, the Lincoln from Florida."

"And the three men?" Tolson spoke softly with a Missouri twang.

"They took the Crescent Limited yesterday. They would have arrived in New York this morning."

"I see." Tolson ran a hand over his hair while he thought. "Write up the report. Bring it to me. No copies. Call SAC Harmon. Tell him I want his report in the pouch tomorrow, the original, no copies, my eyes. Is that clear?"

"Yes, sir."

"Thank you, Agent Cavanaugh."

Dismissed, Cavanaugh left, and as always after an interview with Tolson, he felt like he had barely passed a test whose questions he had not been allowed to see.

Tolson waited until the door closed. He got up and took his suit jacket from where it hung on the back of his desk chair. He stopped in front of the mirror on the back of the door to Hoover's office and checked his appearance. He was six feet tall and reasonably trim for a man who spent much of his life behind a desk. He had a high forehead, a fleshy nose, and a heavy chin. He would be fifty-nine in May, but the hair he smoothed with the palm of his hand was still dark. He checked to make sure that his tie was straight and pulled on the hem of his jacket to make sure it hung right. Eddie was a stickler for neatness, and there was no point in starting this conversation off on the wrong foot. He adjusted the handkerchief in his breast pocket, rapped once on the door, waited until he heard the word "come," and then opened the door and went in.

J. Edgar Hoover stood looking out the window. His bulldog face was clouded with a frown. "Clyde, how many people do you think pass this building in the evening on their way home from work?"

"I don't know," Tolson said. "How many?"

"I don't know the number. Tens of thousands, I suppose. Now, how many of them do you think are criminals of one kind or another? How many criminals walk by the Bureau every day? I would like to know. We would be a much stronger and finer country if we could spot the criminals in our midst and remove them from our society before they do damage instead of waiting until they commit their crimes."

"I'll have a word with Research. Maybe they can come up with something." Eddie got bees in his bonnet sometimes. After a while they stopped buzzing, and he forgot about them. Know who the criminals were before they committed their crimes. A wonderful idea, but how the hell would you do it? Tap everyone's phone, maybe. You'd be sure to pick up word of crimes before they happened, but where would you get the manpower to listen to all those calls? Forget about it. "We got a report from SAC Harmon down in Atlanta. It looks like he found the Lincoln we've been looking for. The men took the train to New York yesterday. They'll be there by now."

"Ahhh," Hoover said and went to his desk, sat down, and folded his hands on the leather-backed blotter, the pose he often took when he was thinking.

Tolson knew better than to speak. Eddie would formulate his thoughts, and then they would talk. Tolson sat in a wooden armchair across the desk from Hoover, lit a cigarette, and waited.

"We're at war, Clyde, at war against godless communism. It is a war being fought in the shadows. Many people in this country still don't understand that, but you and I do, because the Bureau is on the front lines of that war, and winning it is our number-one job. Nothing is more important. We must stand strong, because we are good, and they are evil. It is as simple as that."

Tolson said nothing. He had heard these sentiments before, and Eddie knew he agreed with them.

"I spoke with Vice President Nixon after he talked with this Castro fellow. He spent hours with him, and what he told me is that the man is either very naïve about communism, or he's a Commie. I do not believe he is naïve. A naïve man does not win a war against Batista's army. A naïve man does not surround himself with Communists like this fellow Guevara. No. He says he is a democrat, but he is a wolf in sheep's clothing, and I see through him." He paused to light a cigarette from the silver box on his desk. "Can you imagine the danger of having a communistic country ninety miles from Florida? We cannot let this happen." He stubbed out the cigarette in agitation. "Who are these men from Florida?"

"We don't know exactly who they are. We haven't been able to identify them. We believe they are connected to people in Tampa and Miami, Mr. Trafficante, Mr. Lansky. We understand that some people are worried about losing their investments in Havana to nationalization. Our informants tell us they think Castro's nationalization of the telephone company is just the beginning of his government's takeover of industry."

"In war," Hoover said, "we cannot always choose our allies."

"No."

"Of course, the Bureau cannot go off half cocked in a situation like this. We should take some time to substantiate who these men are who went to New York and if they truly present a danger to Mr. Castro. And, of course, the ultimate jurisdiction in a matter like this resides with the New York Police Department. After all, Mr. Castro is not here on official business. He is here as a private individual, isn't that right?"

"Yes, Eddie, it is."

"Then I think it would be best if we do not overstep our bounds and trespass on the New York Police Department's territory. If we can help them, we will, but let's not be premature about it. Let's substantiate that these men are a threat to Castro before we interfere with New York police procedure. We don't want them to shift focus and manpower to individuals who may be innocent of any criminal intent."

"I've asked SAC Harmon to send me the only copy of his report. I'll hold on to it until such a time as it might be useful to send it along."

"Who's heading the New York office?"

"SAC Susdorf."

"No need to bother him with this yet. Best to be sure of the information first. As to dinner tonight, I was thinking of trying that new Italian restaurant in Georgetown, but now I think not. Let's just go to Harvey's. We'll have a steak. I feel like a steak."

"Harvey's is fine, Eddie."

"He's a Commie, Clyde. I feel it in my bones. The man's a Commie, and we can have no mercy."

18

A maid in a gray uniform with white lace accents greeted Cassidy when he entered his sister's apartment on Park Avenue. He found Leah on the terrace off the living room. She was wearing blue jeans tucked into rubber boots, one of Mark's cast-off white shirts with the sleeves rolled high, and a red bandanna around her hair. There was a smudge of dirt on her cheek, and her gloved hands were deep in the earth of a planter that ran along the terrace wall. The other planters on the terrace were empty. A man in khaki work clothes was removing sacks of dirt and fertilizer from a handcart. He nodded at Cassidy and trundled the empty handcart back toward the open door at the end of the terrace that led to the freight elevator landing.

"Hi," Leah said. "What are you doing here?" She wiped her face with the back of her glove, smearing more dirt across her cheek, and offered herself for a kiss.

"I came to watch you do the spring planting."

"Yup. We're putting in wheat on the north forty and four acres of corn down by the creek. There is no rest for a woman farming a Park Avenue duplex." The man in khaki pushed the handcart back toward them. Now it was loaded with boxes of spring flowers. "Fred, this is my brother Michael. Michael, Fred Tyler. He's the green thumb. I just do the heavy lifting."

"Pleased to meet you," Tyler said. "I'd shake, but . . ." He showed a dirt-encrusted hand. He was in his forties, sturdy and compact, and weather-beaten.

"Good to meet you too," Cassidy said.

Leah scooped up dirt from a planter against the wall between the two sets of doors that led into the living room. The thick, dark root of an espaliered rosebush grew from the planter and spread branches up and out in a fan shape against the wall. Wires fixed to bolts driven into the bricks held the branches. Leah rubbed the dirt between her hands and sifted it back into the planter. "Fred, we talked about replacing the dirt in here. What do you think?"

"I'm going to add some fertilizer, Mrs. Buckman. I checked the pH, and it comes out a bit acid. The lime will take care of that."

"Whatever you think best. Michael, you have to come when the roses are in bloom. They are so beautiful."

"I'll clear my calendar."

She jabbed him with an elbow. "Come on, I'll buy you a glass of iced tea. Fred, would you like a glass of iced tea?"

"Thank you, Mrs. Buckman, I would."

"I'll send it out."

The maid brought three glasses of iced tea to the library on a round silver tray. She left two, and carried the third to the gardener on the terrace. Cassidy picked up one of the glasses and went past the desk to look out the window overlooking Park Avenue. Below him the planting season in New York continued. Teams of gardeners were putting flowers in the beds between the southbound and northbound lanes, the yearly ritual that transformed the parkway from the dull brown of winter to the vivid colors of spring, a celebration of life.

Leah came in. She had washed her face and brushed her hair and exchanged her boots for polished moccasins, and she looked beautiful and composed. She picked up the waiting glass and took a long pull. "Ahh, that is good. Do you want something stronger?"

"No, thanks. This is fine."

"Michael, did you drop by because you missed me, or because you had something you wanted to talk about?"

"Both."

"Liar. What do you want to know?"

"Tell me about Bob and Jane Hopkins."

"Which one are you really interested in?"

"Both."

"I'll start with Jane, then. How's that?"

"Fine."

"Personal or official?"

"Official."

"What'd they do?"

"Nothing. They're just a small part of a larger investigation."

She studied him for a moment while she drank some of the iced tea. "You know, when you were a kid you were a lousy liar. I think because you didn't give a damn whether people knew you were lying or not. Being a cop has made you much better at it."

"I always know where to come for a compliment."

"Anyway, Jane Hopkins, Jane Delano when I first knew her. Some collateral connection to the Roosevelt family. She was a few years above me at school here and then at Farmington. She was one of the cool beauties, always going out with boys who were older. You know, the sophomores at college while she was still in school, very sophisticated. A good student, but a wild one under the cool exterior. You know the kind, the one who shows you where to smoke illegally, who knows how to sneak off campus. The girl who always takes the dare, is always the first to jump off the bridge into the river. The one the adults always think of as the perfect young lady and the girls know as the one who gets away with murder." She saw his expression change. "What?"

"Nothing. What about him?"

"Mild-mannered Bob? A good family, but not much money left. His father was a drunk who ran through it all. Bob made it back and then some according to Mark. Mark calls him the Wall Street assassin. Apparently he is a ruthless dealmaker."

"What's their marriage like?"

She thought about it for a moment. "Who knows what goes on in someone else's bedroom? She's a major flirt. She was all over you at our party before Christmas. Did you get the feeling that it was real?"

"I barely remembered that I'd met her."

"That doesn't speak well for her powers of seduction."

"Would he be jealous?"

"I've heard they have an open marriage."

"You mean they can take lovers and it doesn't matter?"

"Something like that. I think there are some rules, like you can't make a public spectacle and you can't bring it home."

"How do you know this?"

Leah was embarrassed, a rare moment. "We had lunch one day last year. She called out of the blue and asked me. We went to one of those dark little French restaurants in the mid-fifties where men take women who aren't their wives. Martinis and then wine with the meal. The talk was all over the place—people we knew, places we'd been, but toward the end she got around to it, how sophisticated our family was because we grew up in the theater. How worldly all that must have made us. Fewer rules. A broad-minded understanding of how life really works. And then a very deft and subtle suggestion that Bob found me fascinating and she found Mark fascinating, and we were all intelligent, mature people who didn't need to be bound by the mundane rules that shackled most people."

"God, I didn't know we were that cool. Did you tell Mark?"

"Of course."

"Was he tempted?"

She grabbed a magazine and swatted him. "Ooohh, you bastard. Of course he wasn't tempted. He laughed. What's this all about, anyway?"

"Do you think Bob Hopkins is capable of violence?"

She looked at him seriously. "You're not going to tell me, are you?"

"No. Not yet. It's all guesswork right now. There's nothing to tell."

"Okay. Bob, violent? I don't know. Half the women I know have been hit by their husbands. Has he hit Jane? A fifty-fifty chance."

"Come on."

"Why are you so shocked? Men think it's a God-given right to smack their wives."

"Mark?"

"No. Not Mark. He doesn't have the instinct, and he knows that if he did do it, I would be out the door so fast. Speaking of which, I've got to go pick up the boys. Do you want to walk with me?"

"I can't."

"Okay. Was this a help?"

"Yes, I think so. What do women do when their men hit them?"

"I don't know. Maybe a few slip a little ground glass in the guy's hamburger, but most of them just take it."

She found her purse and they rode down in the elevator together. "I hear you have a new woman in your life," Leah said.

"Where'd you hear that?"

"We were at Peter Sanborn's for cocktails. Somebody mentioned it. I can't remember who. New York's a small town, Michael. You can't get away with anything. Do we get to meet her?"

"Sure."

"When?"

"I don't know. I'll talk to her. We'll figure something out. You and Mark can come slumming to the Village."

They kissed, brushing cheeks, under the awning outside the building. Then she went north to pick up the twins at nursery school, and he walked south to the precinct.

19

It was long after midnight when ex-Colonel Diego Fuentes turned west on 54th Street away from the lights of Broadway and the people looking for one more drink, one more laugh before heading home. By the time he reached Eighth Avenue he was alone on the street. He stopped in front of the six-story brownstone just east of Eighth Avenue, where the Italian restaurant called Mario's occupied the ground floor. Unlike the last time he had been here, the restaurant was closed. Looking past the artificial plants in the darkened window he could see the chairs turned upside down on the tables. There was one light left on behind the bar so the beat cop could check for intruders as he made his rounds. Fuentes checked his watch. He was on time, one thirty in the morning, a conspirator's hour.

Voices, laughter. Fuentes stepped into the shadowed doorway. A couple stopped on the corner of Eighth Avenue for a clinch and then crossed the street, wobbling a bit, their arms around each other. He waited until they were out of sight and then rapped on the glass of the door. Nothing. He rapped again, harder. A door opened at the back of the restaurant and light spilled into the front room. A man threaded through the tables and came to the front door. He examined Fuentes through the glass, and then unlocked the door and opened it. He turned without saying anything and went back through the room. Fuentes closed the door and followed.

There was a dinner table for twelve in the back room. It was covered with a red-and-white-checked tablecloth. Candles in straw-covered Chianti bottles ran down the center. Between them were open bottles of wine and bottles of water. Men occupied all the chairs except one. They did not look alike, were of different sizes and shapes, but all were stamped with a competent brutality. They glanced at Fuentes when he entered and then went back to their conversations and the plates of antipasto in front of them. Santo Trafficante sat at the head of the table. He glanced at Fuentes through his black-rimmed glasses, nodded, and then turned to talk to Joe Stassi, who sat on his left. Fuentes sat down at the empty place in the middle of the table. The men on either side of him checked him briefly but said nothing to him. He assumed they were ignoring him to unsettle him, to put him on the defensive, to make him more amenable to whatever was going to be discussed. He had used the same techniques himself. He ate a piece of salami, and tasted the red wine in the tumbler in front of him. Not bad. He liked Spanish wines better, but this was not bad. He ate a pepper and an anchovy and some cured meat he could not identify, sipped the wine, and listened to the talk around him.

He had met here before, but usually with two or three men with common interests. The meetings had been exploratory to see whether their common interests could lead to joint action. This was different. Something had been decided and Fuentes had been called here to learn what that decision was.

The small man to his left jiggled with energy, and his leg jerked up and down in quick rhythm. He cut small bites from the plate in front of him and stabbed them into his mouth with his fork, talking all the time across Fuentes to the man on his right, a big, stolid guy with a face like a ham under a cap of curly black hair, who offered an occasional grunt to hold up his end of the conversation.

"I don't get it," the little man said. "I get out of the joint, I ask them to put me back to work. They give me a job. That's okay. But I'm a little guy, right? So what do they give me, a fucking guy's built like an elephant, makes you, Alfie, look anemic, you know what I'm saying? Okay, the job's the easy part. It don't take more to drop a big guy than a little guy, but then I'm out in some Jersey swamp for the rest of the night digging a hole big enough to bury a horse. Why is that? Why don't I ever get a little guy? Some sort of joke or something? I don't get it."

Fuentes assumed the story was told for his benefit. Maybe it was true, maybe it wasn't. It amused him that they would work so hard to show him how dangerous they were. He knew they were dangerous. Did they understand that he was too? Three women came out of the kitchen to clear plates and serve new ones. He picked at the ravioli, tasted the veal, ate half the cannoli, and drank some more of the wine but stopped when he began to feel it.

The women cleared the table. The men got up and left and went into the front room to the bar, except for Santo Trafficante and Joe Stassi, who remained. Stassi gestured and Fuentes went down to the end of the table and took a chair next to Stassi. A woman brought a bottle of clear liquid and three small glasses. "Grappa," Stassi explained, and poured. They raised their glasses. "Salute," Stassi and Trafficante said. "Salud," Fuentes replied.

"Now," Trafficante said. "How are we going to kill this motherfucker? Your guy? Our guys? How?" He poured another glass of grappa and drank half of it, and Fuentes realized he was drunk. "It has to be here. It has to be this week, here in New York. If he gets back to Havana we'll never get to him. He has too many friends. If he gets back there the first thing he's going to do is take the hotels and casinos. Jesus christ, we're already down forty percent just on the take 'cause Americans are scared to go over there. Bunch of fucking bearded guys walking around with guns. Who the hell needs that on vacation?"

Stassi took a sheet of paper out of his pocket and pushed it across to Fuentes. "This is Castro's schedule in New York."

"How'd you get it?"

"We've got a guy." He left it at that.

They didn't trust him. Well, he didn't trust them. He studied the schedule. "Your men are a rifle team, yes?"

"Yes."

"So, when he comes out of the hotel? From a building across the way?"

"Sometimes the cops take him out a side door. Sometimes they've got the car pulled right up tight and you don't get a look before he gets in. We were thinking about the thing he's doing in Central Park."

"It will be night."

"Castro will be on stage under the lights."

"Where will your men be?"

"There's a place. We've looked it over. It'll do."

"How far?"

"Three hundred yards."

"Ahhh." Meaning, a long shot at night. "I've done this work. I've done security. President Batista had many enemies, but he is going to die in bed. The first thing the police will do is check every place a man with a rifle can hide inside a five-hundred-yard perimeter. If you've found such a place, so will they."

"We have that covered," Stassi said. Trafficante said nothing. He drank more grappa and watched Fuentes with cold eyes.

"You have it covered?"

"Yes."

So, they own some cops. "It's still a three-hundred-yard shot."

"These guys are good. We've used them before. Even if the trigger-man misses," Stassi said. "There'll be a lot of confusion. A perfect opportunity for a guy who's in close. Your guy. He could take advantage."

"I see." Their man shoots. If he misses, Lopato finishes the job. And if he is caught, well it would not be a problem for these men.

"Can your man do that?"

"Oh, yes."

They talked details for a while, and then Fuentes stood to go. Trafficante struggled up from his chair and needed a hand on the table to steady himself. "The next time I see you, Colonel, we'll be back in Havana, and everything will be back the way it was."

The three men shook hands, and Fuentes left. No one spoke to him as he went through the barroom and out into the night.

"Fucking spic. Do you trust him?" Trafficante asked.

"No. But he'll be useful."

Fuentes stopped outside the restaurant to light a cigarette and then turned toward Broadway, where he knew he would find a cab. *Back the way it was?* No, it would never be back the way it was, not if he could help it. Colonel Fuentes would be General Fuentes, and that was just the beginning. He went over what they had talked about. Their man taking the shot from a distance. Three hundred yards at night with thousands of people milling around, and Castro moving on the stage. What were the chances of hitting the target? Slim. And then Lopato was supposed to step up and finish it. Typical. The American *chulos* manipulating from a distance, and the Cubans doing the dirty work. Maybe there was a better way.

20

Having Alice in the apartment was like living with a big cat. She bathed and washed often and would stand near the tall windows, one hip cocked, running a brush through her hair over and over again while she looked out at the river. She often lay curled on the sofa reading a book or a magazine, and when she turned, she would stretch luxuriously and then resettle with a sigh. She padded around the apartment in bare feet wearing only one of Cassidy's shirts, and if she passed near him she would drape an arm over his shoulder, rub against him, and then move on. He found her spoor everywhere—a stocking hanging on a lamp, panties on the bathroom floor, a half-eaten apple on the arm of a chair. If she ate something that really pleased her, she would let out a low moan, almost like a purr.

She was an active, greedy lover who sought her pleasure openly, *do this, and that, no over here, more, more, oh god, higher, there, there.* She never said no to anything. Do you want to go . . . ? Yes. Do you want to see . . . ? Yes. Would you like to try . . . ? Yes.

And yet sometimes he would catch her looking at him with the impenetrable marble gaze cats have, as if thinking *what is this thing, and what is it doing in my world?*

Cassidy came out of the bathroom dressed. He moved quietly so as not to wake Alice. She slept on her side, her hip a round swell under the sheet that covered her to the waist. As he started past, her eyes opened to slits, and she reached out and caught his hand. "Where are you going? Castro?" Her voice was heavy with sleep.

"Yes."

"Forget him. Come back to bed."

"I can't."

"Yes, you can." She rolled over, and the sheet fell off and showed him what was waiting for him.

"No."

"Coward."

"I'll work up the courage by tonight."

"Tonight? That's a long way off. Who knows? I may have found a new lover by then."

"I'll arrest him for poaching."

"Ahh, well, no point then, I guess." She pulled the sheet up and turned over and burrowed back toward sleep.

• • •

Cassidy sat on the porch of Gracie Mansion and read a copy of the *New York Post* he had found on a table. Castro was inside the Mansion for a courtesy meeting with Mayor Robert Wagner. Some of his men walked around outside the house, incongruous in their fatigues, as if transported by magic from some jungle fight to the manicured grounds. They held themselves with the stiffness of men who felt out of place and were determined not to show it. Carlos Ribera came out of the house and took a chair at Cassidy's table. He offered a cigar and lit one for himself when Cassidy refused. Ribera wore linen trousers and a pale gray silk guayabera shirt. He leaned back in the chair and extended his legs to rest his soft leather half boots on the porch railing. He was, as always, a man at ease in his surroundings no matter how foreign.

"I love New York," Ribera said. "If I did not live in Havana, I would live in New York. Except the winter. I do not like the winter. But six, seven months of the year . . . There is so much art here, so much, what? Ferment. Things are happening here. You sense it everywhere you go. Something new is about to break loose. Do you feel that? I feel it all the time. I think if I am not here I am going to miss something wonderful."

"Would you be willing to repeat that on television for the New York Tourist Bureau?"

Ribera laughed. "Sure. Why not?" He looked out at the men in fatigues on the lawn. One of them was doing a handstand while his friends applauded. "Who would have believed this six months ago? Eh? Fidel Castro meets with the Mayor of New York City. Six months ago there was every chance that he would be dead in the mountains, but now, *Cuba Libre* finally." He looked over at Cassidy. "What? What?"

Cassidy pushed the newspaper across the table. It was folded open to the story he had been reading. Ribera picked it up and started to read. His face stiffened. He looked at Cassidy, glanced at the paper again, and then put it down on the table and pushed it away, dismissing it. The banner headline read *EXECUTIONS IN HAVANA.* "So?" he said.

"Funny way to start a democracy," Cassidy said. "Fifteen-minute trials and then out to the wall."

"These men put many people in front of the same wall."

"And you hated them for it."

Ribera took that like a punch, and then shook his head as if to clear it. "Every historic change is messy. And Castro offered people the choice. A million people came out in Havana to hear him, and when he asked if they should continue with the revolutionary tribunals and the executions, do you know what the people yelled? They yelled '*Sí!*' A million voices cried, yes. That is democracy."

"Jesus, Carlos. Come on." He could see the anger rising in Ribera.

"Who are you to criticize? The United States of America, the beacon of democracy and freedom? Unless you are a Negro, or a *bracero* who has come to pick your vegetables, or someone who joined a group that is now called Communist. You prop up dictators like Batista because it makes you money. You get rid of heads of state you don't like, Arbenz in Guatemala, Mossadegh in Iran, why? Because they were socialists. But they were elected by their people and thrown out by your CIA. Democracy. Freedom. America." He stood and leaned over the table and poked a finger at Cassidy. "We will be better than you. We will show you how democracy works." He threw his cigar out into the lawn and stalked away.

Ribera's anger had the heat of a man who had been betrayed and could not admit it.

Orso came up the steps to the porch. He gestured at the disappearing Ribera. "What was all that about?"

"I suggested that standing a few hundred people up against the wall wasn't the ideal start to democracy."

"I don't know. You shoot us; we shoot you. Seems democratic to me. You shoot us but we don't get to shoot you, now that's undemocratic."

"I'm glad we've had this conversation," Cassidy said. "It's cleared up a lot of my confusion."

"Bonner and Newly just got here to relieve us. Let's get out of here."

"Give me a minute."

Cassidy looked around for Ribera. He wanted to make it right, but the big man had disappeared.

• • •

Cassidy and Orso picked up an unmarked car at the police garage and drove to Queens where the late Casey Allen had lived before someone shot him and left him in Central Park. The car was a 1956 Ford lugging eighty-six thousand hard miles. The worn shocks transmitted every bump and pothole to the spine. There was a lateral crack across the top of the windshield. The passenger seat sagged, tilting Cassidy against the door, and the perp seat in back smelled of vomit and disinfectant. Nothing but the best for New York's finest.

Casey Allen lived on 145th Street, a blue-collar neighborhood of single-family houses off the main drag of Jamaica Avenue. The Allen house was a two-story wooden building halfway down the block whose first-floor exterior walls were covered with vinyl sheets patterned as bricks. Orso found a parking place between a three-year-old Studebaker and a Nash Rambler, and they got out and walked back to the house. Cassidy rang the doorbell. They waited under the shade of an aluminum awning painted to match the dark red of the concrete walk. "The old biddy up the way is giving us the eyeball," Orso said. A woman at a house two doors down turned away and went back to trimming bushes in her front yard when Cassidy looked over at her. A moment later the front door opened a foot and a woman looked out at them through the gap.

"Yeah?" She was a good-looking woman in her late twenties. She had a fierce, strong-boned face with dark eyes deep set under heavy, black eyebrows. Her thick, dark hair was barely controlled in a ponytail by a strip of yellow cloth. She held a feather duster in one hand and wore a yellow rayon blouse with a round collar and tight, dark green Capri pants that showed off her narrow waist and good legs, and matching green sandals with high wedge soles. "Whatever it is I don't want it."

"Mrs. Allen?"

"Yeah. So what?"

"My name's Cassidy. I'm a detective with the New York Police Department."

Her fear was almost instant. "Oh, no. Oh, shit. Is it about Casey? What happened to him? Is he all right?" One hand flew to her throat in a gesture of panic, and she dropped the feather duster.

"May we come in?"

She stepped back. Her eyes were wide. Cassidy and Orso stepped into the narrow front hall, and Orso closed the door.

"Is he all right? Tell me he's all right."

"Mrs. Allen, is this your husband?" Cassidy showed her the photograph of Casey Allen.

She stared at it and then looked up, stricken. "Yes. What's wrong with him? He's dead, isn't he? He's dead." She crumpled the photograph and slammed her clenched fists against her temples and howled like an animal and then turned and stumbled away.

Cassidy started after her as Orso said, "I'll go get her some water," and went down the hall in search of the kitchen. Cassidy found her in the living room, a fifteen-by-fifteen-foot box dominated by a large mahogany-cased television facing two Barcaloungers, clues to how the Allens spent their evenings. Sliding pocket doors were open to a small dining room with a Formica-topped table and four chairs. Mrs. Allen was curled on the living room sofa, her howls of anguish somewhat muffled by the back cushions where she had buried her head. Cassidy crouched by her and put a comforting hand on her shoulder. "Mrs. Allen . . ." She flailed backward blindly and hit his arm, and he gave up and backed away.

Orso came in with a glass of water. Cassidy gave him a look and a shrug. *What do you do with a hysterical woman?* Orso went to the sofa and crouched down by her head and began to talk to her softly in Italian. After a while she calmed. When she sat up, her eyes were swollen and her face was puffy and raw. She took the glass from Orso and drank some of it, and gave it back to him and sighed heavily. Orso nodded to Cassidy. Cassidy sat close to her on the narrow coffee table in front of the sofa, knee to knee, reducing the space between them to intimacy. "Mrs. Allen, what's your first name?"

"Theresa," she said dully.

"Theresa, tell us about Casey. When did you see him last?"

"I don't know."

"Think back. Was it last week? The week before?"

"I don't know. The week before, I guess."

"Do you remember what day?"

She took the glass out of Orso's hand and drank some more, and then put it on the table and turned to look at Cassidy. Her dark eyes were glazed with tears and impenetrable. "Thursday, I guess. Thursday night, because we like to watch *The Untouchables,* and then he went to bed, 'cause he had to get up early. I watched the news, and then did the dishes. He was already asleep when I went up, and then he was gone in the morning before I got up."

"Do you know where he was going on Friday?"

"He had work in the city. He was doing renovations for some rich people over there near Central Park, tearing down a wall and building, like, a dressing room for the woman or something."

"What'd you do when he didn't come home that evening?"

"What'd I do? I went nuts. He calls if he's going to be late. I called the place where he was working, but there was no one there, just one of those answering things you can talk into. I tried the next day. Same thing. I called the hospitals. I went down to the police station, but, like, that was a waste of time. They patted me on the head and told me to go home, he'll show up. You know what they said? They said *sometimes men roam.* What the hell does that mean?" She gulped air. "What happened to him?"

"Someone shot him."

She wailed and put her head down on her knees. Cassidy reached over and patted her on the back to comfort her. "Theresa, did he have any enemies?"

"No." Head down, muffled.

"You're sure? No beef with anyone? No arguments about work?"

"No. He was a good worker. No one ever complained."

"Did he owe anybody money?"

"No. We were doing good. We were saving. He was going to buy a pickup or a van so he could haul stuff himself and not pay." She straightened. "Who did it? Why would anyone do that?"

"Do you know the people he was working for, Robert and Jane Hopkins?"

"Me? No. How would I know them?"

"Maybe you were in the city and you went over to say hello to Casey."

"Uh-uh. Nah."

"Did he talk about them at all?"

"No. Not much. I mean, he said they were fancy people with a lot of money. He said the guy had really nice clothes."

"Did he say anything about her?"

"No. Not really. He said she was nice. She wasn't stuck up or anything."

"That's it?"

"Yeah. That's it." Flatly. Looking straight into his eyes the way people do when they want to convince you they're not lying. Orso saw it too, because he gave a tiny gesture with his head. Cassidy got up from the table in front of Theresa, and Orso moved in and began to talk to her quietly in Italian as Cassidy left the room.

He walked down the hall to the kitchen and drew a glass of water from the sink and stood looking out the back door while he drank it. The yard was half concrete and half grass, and flowerbeds ran along the wooden fences that separated it from the identical yards of the neighbors. The grass was sparse and weedy, but the flowerbeds were newly planted with flowers. He had never noticed so much spring planting in the city before. Now everywhere he looked someone was putting in flowers. Had it always been like that? His mother had planted flowers in the backyard of the brownstone on 66th where they had lived until her death, but he had paid no attention and he could not name the ones planted here, though they seemed familiar. Where had he seen some just like them recently? At Leah's? Yeah, maybe there. He opened the door and went down the steps into the yard and ducked under the laundry hanging on clotheslines and walked out to the small garage that backed the yard. The garage was Casey Allen's carpentry workshop. A workbench ran along one wall. Hand tools hung from a pegboard above it. Paint cans lined the shelf underneath. A drill press, band saw, router, and table saw stood along the opposite wall. Double doors gave out to an alley.

When Cassidy came back into the house, Orso was waiting for him in the front hall. Theresa Allen lay on her back on the sofa in the living room with a wet towel on her forehead.

"Her sister's coming over. Be here in ten minutes. She'll be okay. Wops are tough."

"And?"

"I told her we'd let her know the minute there was anything."

"All right. Good." He gestured with his head toward the door. Orso nodded.

"*Theresa, addio.*" She did not answer and did not watch them go.

They walked to a bar Orso had noticed on Jamaica Avenue. It was a workingman's joint, quiet, dark, smelling of spilled beer and ancient tobacco smoke. At this time of the day the place was almost empty. Four men playing dominoes at a table near the back of the room slapped the tiles down with sharp cracks. A solitary drinker nursed a beer at the far end of the bar. The bartender slid a cloth back and forth across the polished wood while he watched them come. He was a sharp-faced, foxy-looking man with fading red hair.

"What'll it be, Officers?" He wore a slight grin as if savoring a private joke.

Orso studied him for a moment and then nodded in recognition. "O'Malley, right? You worked the Seventy-ninth in Bed-Stuy back in, what? Forty-eight."

"Yeah." He pointed a finger. "Orso, right?" His grin got wider. "Yeah, I never forget a guy I worked with. So you must be Cassidy. Threw that fuck Franklin out a window. Twice!" He laughed. "What a fuck that guy was. Running whores and working Vice at the same time. I mean, pick a side of the street and work it, but don't do both. Beating up those women too, wasn't he? What a shit. Too bad you weren't a couple of floors higher when you tossed him. What can I get you?"

"Beer for me," Cassidy said.

"Yeah," Orso said.

"Knicks okay?"

Both men nodded and O'Malley went to the cooler to draw a couple of bottles, brought their beers, and then went off to carry drinks to the dominoes players.

Orso and Cassidy banged bottles and then took the first long, cool pulls.

"What'd you get from her when you were speaking Italian?" Cassidy asked.

"I don't know. Nothing much. She said she loved Casey Allen more than anything in the world, but every once in a while, something really angry would come through. Nothing specific, but I bet that one can go off like a rocket. Sicilian. Man, some of them have tempers. She seemed pretty goddamn torn up."

"Do you believe her?"

"Yes. At least until I saw the sofa. Did you notice?"

"I can't say that I did. What about it?"

"It's new."

"No."

"Not new, new. New to the house. There are deep dents in the rug where the old sofa used to be. The new one doesn't match them."

"Wow. Sherlock fucking Holmes. No detail gets by you."

"Elementary, my dear Cassidy."

"Maybe they just moved it around."

"No. It can't match them. The new one's legs are much farther apart."

"The piss sofa."

"Could be." Orso looked pleased with himself.

"I'll give you one more. The garage out back is a workshop. Paint. Sawdust. One thing's missing. There's no chair. If you had a workshop you'd want a chair for when you got tired, a chair you didn't care about. Get paint on it. Sawdust. It wouldn't matter."

"The chair he was sitting on in the park."

"Could be."

"She did it. She popped him."

"Maybe. But how did she get him from a Hundred forty-fifth and Jamaica Avenue to Central Park and Seventy-second?"

The bartender brought them two more beers and a bowl of popcorn. "On the house. You guys on the job?"

"Yeah," Orso said. "You been in here long?"

"Bought the joint the year after I put in my twenty. Six years ago."

"Do you know Casey Allen lives over on a Hundred forty-fifth?"

"Sure. Good-looking Irish guy. Drinks Jameson, beer back, sometimes a Guinness stout. He comes in a lot, except lately I ain't seen him."

"Do you know his wife, Theresa?" Cassidy asked. "Does she come in here too?"

"Oh, yeah." He shook his head wearily. "Times I wish she didn't."

"Why's that?"

"That woman's got a temper on her. Casey lived around here all his life. He's got friends. Some of them are women, you know, but friends. I mean, who knows what went on in the past, but now friends. They come by to say hello, it don't matter if they're with husbands, boyfriends, Theresa goes nuts. She went after one with a beer bottle. I finally had to tell her to stop coming in here."

"What about him? Did he play around?"

"If he did, I never saw it. Man, he couldn't get enough of her. What do they call it? Besotted? The way he talked about her, it was like he couldn't believe how lucky he was. Loved her. Loved her. What's this all about?"

"Somebody shot him."

"No shit? You think she did it?"

"It's beginning to have that smell."

"Did she grow up around here?" Orso asked.

"Nah. Bushwick, Rego Park, somewhere over there where the Italians live."

"Keep this under your hat, okay, Tim? We don't want to spook her."

"Yeah. Sure. I can keep my mouth shut."

After the gloom of the bar, the afternoon sun was like a slap in the face. "Do you think he'll talk about it?" Cassidy asked.

"I don't know. Probably not. He was a good cop."

"Okay."

They walked back to 145th Street where they had parked the car. The old woman was still tending her front yard a few doors down from the Allen house. She stopped what she was doing and watched them as they came down the street. Cassidy veered over to speak to her. She stood ramrod straight with her hand clenched around the top of her rake handle like a warrior with a spear. She was tall and lean, and her sharp, pointed face was topped by a cap of gray curls sprayed to the hardness of china. Her mouth was a smear of dark red lipstick. She wore trim blue cotton trousers and a white shirt open at the collar that revealed a gold crucifix on a thin gold chain.

Cassidy stopped at the metal gate. "Ma'am, my name's Michael Cassidy. I'm a detective with the New York Police Department. This is my partner, Detective Orso. We'd like to speak to you for a moment, if you don't mind." He flipped his wallet to show her his ID.

"Kelly," she said. "Moira Kelly. I saw you speaking to that Theresa Allen. What has she done?"

"What can you tell me about her?"

"God forbid that I should say something bad about another person"—she touched the crucifix for support—"but she is not a good woman."

"How's that?"

"She is short-tempered, unfriendly, and she is unkind to her husband, Casey, who is a good man, always a friendly hello, or an offer to help carry something. Last month he came over and dug up a small tree that died in my backyard and refused to be paid. God forbid that I should judge"—another quick hand to the crucifix—"but she does not deserve him."

"Have you seen him lately?"

"No. Not for two weeks. Two weeks ago Thursday."

"You're sure?"

"Of course I'm sure." A certainty that brooked no argument. "God forbid that I should gossip, but they had a big fight that night."

"What about?"

"I don't know. I couldn't hear." Her mouth tightened in disappointment.

"Is there anything else you'd like to tell us? Has she had any visitors?"

"I wasn't here for a few days. I went to see my sister in Armonk, but the day I left she had a sofa delivered. They took away one and brought in another. The only reason I noticed is they bought a sofa from the Parkers across the street when they moved to Florida and that was only last year. God forbid that I should tell others how to live their lives, but that seems extravagant to me."

"What can you tell me about the delivery? Could you see a company name on the truck?"

"The truck was green, that green like an army truck. I remember that. It wasn't very big. Usually the furniture companies send those great big trucks and they block the street. I don't know why they do that. It had writing on the door, but I couldn't see what it said. I came out with my reading glasses on." She shook her head in exasperation at that slip. "I was going to get my distance glasses, but . . ." She shrugged.

"You didn't want to miss anything," Orso offered.

"Don't be silly. I do not pry into my neighbors' lives." The phone began to ring in the house behind her. "If you'll excuse me, I have to answer that."

Cassidy gave her one of his cards. "If you think of anything else, call me. Thank you."

Orso rattled the car back toward Manhattan. "She did it. The broad clipped her husband. For what, getting a piece off the reservation? Shouldn't be a hanging offense." It was clear what side of that conflict Orso was on.

"We're not going to nail her with what we've got. We need to find who helped her move the body. She didn't shoot him, stick him in her purse, and carry him over to Central Park."

"A friend with a car."

"That'd be some friend. And besides, how do you drive a car into the park and pull out the body and chair and no one notices? Even at five in the morning people are walking around."

"If we could find the guys who delivered the sofa and took the other one away. We get ahold of the old one it's going to have piss stains and maybe some blood. That would nail her."

"How many used furniture stores do you think there are in Brooklyn? A store like that is more likely to use a small truck for delivery."

"Too many. We're going to be on the phone for the rest of the day."

They were, and at the end of the day they had nothing.

21

Drago Peck was a doorman at an apartment building at 73rd and West End Avenue. Peck was the shortened version of a Balkan name that was unpronounceable to the immigration officer who signed him into the country. Drago was a thin, pale man of indeterminate age, opaque nationality, and elastic ethics who had washed up on the shores of America in one of the waves of refugees after World War II. He had never thought of himself as a lucky man, and most of his life had proved him right, but what luck he found landed him in an internment camp in the American Zone in Austria after the war where he had learned English and the useful lesson that Americans were susceptible to flattery and the well-tuned sob story. For a man with no traceable history it was easy to become a victim of Nazi oppression and easier still to exaggerate the dangers that awaited him if he was repatriated to Poland. When offered alternatives, he chose emigration to the United States, the land of milk and honey and easy marks.

Drago held the door for General Alfonso Garza y Mendoza and followed him out under the awning where General Garza y Mendoza bent over with a fat man's groan and put Mitzi down. Mitzi was a four-year-old white Pomeranian bitch a little bigger than the General's shoe and as fluffy as a dandelion. She skittered around the General's feet and demanded attention with a high-pitched yap. "*Basta, Mitzi. Basta ya.* She knows we are going to the park, and it makes her excited."

"She's a lucky dog," Drago said, who had a mimic's perfectly colloquial English but spoken with a heavy Balkan accent. "I don't know no one in the building loves his dog the way you love Mitzi." Drago had a match out and lit it before the general had bitten the end from his cigar. Garza y Mendoza bent to the light and puffed his cigar till it drew. "Well, Mitzi, where shall we go?" The little dog cocked its head to the side at the sound of its name. "To Central Park, or to the river? Ah, no. Not Central Park, Mitzi. They are setting up for that *cabron*, Castro. Do you know this *maricón* Fidel Castro, Drago?"

"I've heard of him," Drago said. *Say nothing till you know which way the wind blows. You don't make any money disagreeing with the tipper.*

"The son of a bitch has stolen my country." This from a man who owned a house in Miami and paid a thousand dollars a month rent in New York on the nine-hundred-dollar salary of a Cuban Army Lieutenant General, a salary he had not drawn in the three months since the revolution. "He is going to turn it over to the Communists. He is going to turn paradise into a shithole."

"I hate the Communists, General. When I see what they've done to my beautiful country . . . I don't know. I wish I could go back there with a gun."

"A gun, yes. It is the only argument they comprehend. You're a good man, Drago. You understand these things." Garza y Mendoza took a dollar bill from his pocket and pressed it on the doorman.

"No, General, you don't have to do that," in perfect imitation of sincerity as his hand closed over the bill.

"I do it because I want to. I do it to show my appreciation. Come on, Mitzi."

Drago watched as they walked to the corner, the big man and the tiny, fluffy dog. *What the hell's a man doing with a little faggot dog like that?*

• • •

General Garza y Mendoza walked Mitzi in Riverside Park in the glory of a spring morning. The trees were budding. Flowers had begun to sprout in the beds. The sun was warm. The tall apartment buildings looked as permanent as mountains. It was a day to feel hopeful, strong, full of life, but the thought of Castro in Central Park turned it all dark. Who was it who said that God is on the side of big battalions? They had had the battalions, and Castro had nobody. What had SIM reported? Eighty-two men had landed with Castro. Many of them had been killed or captured in the first twenty-four hours. Only twelve had gotten away to the mountains. Twelve men. How could twelve men defeat an army? It was against the natural order of things. He threw away the stub of his cigar and sighed. How could such a thing happen?

Mitzi tugged at her leash. "Yes, I'm coming, Mitzi. I'm coming. We'll go home and have something to eat." He turned south toward 73rd Street.

A car pulled to the curb on Riverside Drive. A man got out of the passenger seat and went into the park and turned down the path behind Garza y Mendoza. He was a tall, powerfully built man. He wore rubber-soled shoes, khaki pants, a white wash-and-wear shirt, and a windbreaker. His hair was as pale as ice. He walked just fast enough to close the distance without appearing to hurry.

Mitzi stopped to sniff at the base of a streetlamp. General Garza y Mendoza felt a presence and turned to find a tall man with pale eyes a few feet away.

"Do you have a match?" He held a cigarette between two gnarled and twisted fingers that looked like they had been badly broken and never properly set. His accent was similar to Drago's, from somewhere east of Europe, somewhere cold.

Mitzi strained at her leash and began to yap at the man. She bared her teeth and scrabbled at the pavement in her fury to get at him. Garza y Mendoza looked down at her in surprise and never felt the blow that dropped him into darkness.

• • •

Drago Peck handed Mrs. Rothman into the taxi as if she were a delicate and valuable package. He palmed the quarter she gave him, closed the door, tapped on the roof of the cab to let the driver know, and turned away, flipping the coin in the air as Mitzi came around the corner of the building trailing her leash. She ran past him to the door and stood there barking for entrance. He looked around for the general, but he was not in sight. She must have pulled loose from him. He would be hurrying up the block from Riverside Park, frantic that Mitzi would dash out into traffic. So, Drago would save her from the crushing wheels of a truck and return her unhurt to her master. Surely worth a dollar or two. When he stooped to pick up the trailing end of the leash, he saw that the white fur on her shoulder was matted with blood.

• • •

Cassidy and Orso pushed through the crowd of onlookers held back from Riverside Park by police barriers and uniformed cops. Why did violent death attract people? Did the butchery of others make them feel more alive, or were they just drawn there for a possible glimpse of the mystery?

They walked toward the group of cops and coroner's crew clustered at the far side of the grass in the shadow of the West Side Highway. FBI Agents Susdorf and Cherry kept a Federal distance from the other cops.

General Garza y Mendoza lay on his back in a patch of green spring grass near the river behind a pile of sand and gravel to be used for resurfacing the park's paths. His face was battered, and the one hand Cassidy could see was ripped and broken, and he could smell burned flesh. "Who found him?" Cassidy asked.

"A couple of kids playing. One of them chased their ball over here and saw him." The beat cop's name was Wangold. He was a short, dark man with a severe widow's peak and arched eyebrows that gave him a permanent look of surprise. He held a cigarette between his thumb and forefinger, dragged on it luxuriously, and looked down at the dead man. This wasn't the first body he had seen in the park.

"Where's Skinner?" Cassidy asked. A coroner's office assistant flicked his cigarette away and pushed away from the coroner's van. His name was Brackett or Hackett, Cassidy could never remember.

"He's out on another call."

"Cause of death here?"

Brackett or Hackett crouched by the dead man and pulled back his shirt collar. There were livid marks on the dead man's throat. "Strangulation. Whoever did it had a hell of a grip. Take a look here. Only three fingers of this hand got a real grip. A couple of marks here, but the other two didn't really dig in."

"Okay, thanks." Orso trailed him to where Susdorf and Cherry stood. "What've we got?"

Susdorf flipped him a black leather wallet. The surface was covered with fingerprint powder, and he could see where the lifts had been made. He went through the wallet while Susdorf talked. "General Alfonso Garza y Mendoza. One of Batista's boys. He's on our list, so when they got an ID, we got a call. We called you."

"Why's he on your list?"

"Number two in Batista's secret service. SIM, you know it?"

"Yes."

"We like to keep our eye on guys like that. The Director says that sometimes they forget they're in our country, not theirs. They kill this guy, kill that guy, bring their war into our towns. We watch who they meet. If it looks like they're getting too excited, someone goes and says something to them."

"Not a robbery," Cassidy said. The wallet was thick with money. "Castro's people?"

"Maybe. Maybe retaliation for the four killed over at that restaurant in Williamsburg last week. The wallet was lying open on his chest. The cop didn't have to touch it to get the ID."

"Someone wanted someone to know he was dead," Cassidy said.

"A lot of that going around," Orso said. "He must have screamed when they were working him. Nobody heard him?"

"Yeah, they heard him," Cherry said. "Some guys fixing potholes up the next block said they thought it was kids playing. Kids, Jesus." He shook his head at the stupidity of citizens.

Cassidy put the wallet in an evidence envelope and slipped it into his jacket pocket. "His apartment's around the corner."

• • •

Orso stayed downstairs to talk to the doorman. Cassidy and the two FBI agents went up to the fifteenth floor and opened the door with the dead man's keys. They walked through the apartment, getting a feel for the place and the people who lived there. They would do a proper search later. The rooms were crammed with gilded, overstuffed furniture. A big radio-phonograph in a blond wood case dominated one corner of the living room. There were silver-framed photographs on every flat surface. Many showed General Garza y Mendoza with a plump big-haired woman and three plump daughters on beaches, at the racetrack in Havana, on the deck of a ship, at a swimming pool, on horseback in a cane field above men stooped to cut cane. There were photographs of the general with other uniformed officers, with Batista on maneuvers in the country, seated with their wives in a nightclub smiling widely at the photographer, shaking hands at what looked like an awards ceremony, at a formal dinner, a long table with a white tablecloth freighted with dishes and bottles, the men leaning forward or backward to make sure they got in the photograph. Meyer Lansky, a small, gray figure among the glittering uniforms, was at the end of the table near Batista. Colonel Diego Fuentes was in a number of the pictures, never in the front, always at someone's shoulder, often angled away from the camera, a man more comfortable in the shadows. In one photo Sergeant Lopato was standing back against the wall. The camera had snapped just as a waiter passed him with an empty tray, leaving the illusion that Lopato's head was on the tray, like John the Baptist's.

The master bedroom was up a narrow flight of stairs. The big bed was canopied in white and pink and covered with matching throw pillows. There was a thick white rug on the floor, a pink-cushioned wicker bed for a dog, and a series of large gold-framed oils on the walls showing country and sea views of Cuba, the sun too bright, the colors too rich to be real. Decoration by the absent Mrs. Garza y Mendoza, Cassidy guessed. And where was she? Well, that would be someone else's problem.

Downstairs again Cassidy found Susdorf going through the desk in the living room while Cherry took the tops off bottles on the bar and sniffed the contents. Cassidy followed the hall to a bedroom at the back, a guest room, he supposed, since there were none of the frills and frou frou of the other bedrooms, the ones he assumed were for the general's daughters. It was spare and orderly. The bed was made with military tautness. Three pairs of shoes were lined up next to the closet. When he opened the closet door he found three suits, three sports jackets, six pairs of trousers, a pair of highly polished black boots, and the uniform of a colonel in SIM. A .45 automatic in a polished leather holster hung in a gun belt from a hook next to the uniform. He opened the desk drawers but they contained nothing but a colorful brochure with the Hotel Nacional in Havana on the cover. He recognized it as a duplicate of the one his brother-in-law, Mark, had showed him—Paradise One, a Sanborn-Buckman Company. He tossed it back in the drawer. The general was an investor or maybe one of the men who greased Sanborn's wheels.

The elevator doors clashed. A key grated in the lock. The door opened, and Colonel Diego Fuentes walked into the apartment. If he was surprised to see Cassidy walking toward him he covered it well. Fuentes wore a well-cut black suit, a pale yellow shirt, and a paisley tie aswirl with red and yellow. He took off his dark Panama hat, put it on the table in the hall, and looked in the mirror above the table while he smoothed his hair with a comb from his pocket.

"Detective Cassidy, how nice to see you again." As cool as a blade.

"Colonel Fuentes." Neither man felt the need to shake hands.

"I understand from the doorman that something has happened to General Garza y Mendoza."

"He's dead."

"Ahh. How?"

"Someone strangled him."

"I see." What he saw did not seem to disturb him much. "And do you know who did it?"

"No. Do you?"

"The Communists, of course. The general was an enemy of communism. He understood the dangers it presents to people who love freedom. And they are ruthless with people who oppose them."

"They tortured him. What do you think they wanted to know?"

"I have no idea. Perhaps nothing. Perhaps they just wanted to hear him scream. They're animals. They have no humanity." He stopped in the open arch to the living room and looked in at Susdorf and Cherry.

"Special Agent in Charge Susdorf and Special Agent Cherry. FBI. This is Colonel Diego Fuentes. He worked for Batista's secret police. He's a friend of the general," Cassidy said. Susdorf looked up from the letter he was reading. Cherry put the cork back in a bottle and turned away from the bar, satisfied that the bottles held nothing of national importance.

"Continue, gentlemen," Fuentes said. "I'm sure the general would want to hold nothing back from the FBI." He took out a leather case, selected a cigar, lit it, and blew smoke at the ceiling, all the while watching Cassidy with cool amusement.

"Where are the rest of the family, his wife and daughters?"

"Out of the country at the moment. They are visiting General and Mrs. Batista in the Dominican Republic, old friends. Your government did not allow the Batistas into the United States, even though they own a house in Fort Lauderdale. It is a disgusting way to treat a man who has been your friend and ally for years. You Americans are so shortsighted. Everything you do is because of the next election. Every decision your government makes is because of the moment now, with no thought to tomorrow. Only what works today. You have no long-term vision. General Batista's usefulness is over, so you throw him away so as not to offend Castro. A year from now, you will understand who Castro is. Do you think his nationalization of the telephone company is the end? It's the beginning. And when you finally see that, then you'll start looking for some way to replace him. You'll look for allies, but you won't find them, because you betray your allies so quickly. It is no wonder you are becoming hated by so many people around the world." The elevator stopped on the fifteenth floor and Orso came into the apartment. He nodded toward Fuentes and raised his eyebrows in question.

"Colonel Fuentes, my partner, Detective Orso." Orso recognized the name. Fuentes turned and the two men checked each other for a moment. "We've received a report that someone's going to try to take Castro out while he's here in New York," Cassidy said.

"Good. Let us hope it's true."

"Do you know anything about it?"

"No." What other answer could there be?

"Is Sergeant Lopato in New York?"

"I have no idea. Sergeant Lopato is no longer under my command. Now, if you'll excuse me, I have things to do."

"I want you to come down to the station house. We need to talk to you about General Garza y Mendoza and who might have killed him."

"Communists, as I told you. I have nothing more to add."

"Is that your room at the end of the hall?"

"Yes."

"Everything in it is yours?"

"Yes."

"Tony, do me a favor, keep the colonel company for a moment. I'll be right back." He came back carrying the holstered pistol. "This is yours?"

"Yes."

"Do you have a New York license for it?"

"No." Fuentes was wary now.

"You're under arrest under the Sullivan Act for owning an unlicensed gun small enough to be concealed."

"Why are you doing this?"

"Tony, could you take him over to the house for me and book him? I'll finish up here."

"I want to speak to my lawyer." Fuentes was losing some of his calm.

"Let him call his lawyer after he's booked, then bicycle him."

"Sure."

"What is this, *bicycle*?" He looked alarmed.

"Nothing that'll hurt. It's not *paredón.* We're just going to move you from precinct to precinct for a while, give your lawyer some exercise."

"Why are you doing this?"

"Because I don't like you, and you piss me off."

"Do you think it will make any difference? You are involved in something much bigger than you can understand."

"What's that?"

"No," Fuentes sneered. "What's the point of saying anything to a man like you? You have the small mind of a cop."

"He's all yours, Tony."

"How long do you want him on the bike?"

"A couple or three hours. Enough time to go through here without interference, see if we find anything interesting."

"All right. You've got it." He took the gun belt and draped it over his shoulder and then clamped a hand on Fuentes's arm. "Let's go, pal." Fuentes tried to jerk away, but Orso's grip tightened, and the blood drained from Fuentes's face. Orso turned him toward the front door, looked back at Cassidy, and winked.

Cassidy knew that arresting Fuentes was nothing more than petty revenge, but fuck him. It felt good. Put him at the wrong end of power for a while and see how he liked it.

• • •

Cassidy, Susdorf, and Cherry searched the apartment, but they found little of interest unless you counted the list of people slated for execution when Batista returned to power that Cassidy discovered under the paper liner of a drawer in the desk. Carlos Ribera was on it. So was Dylan under her work name of Selena Perez. He gave the list to Susdorf, who looked it over, nodded, and said, "I'll pass it up the line." It was information above his pay grade. Best to shove it off on someone closer to the holy of holies at the top.

"Any news on the three guys in the Lincoln coming up from Florida?" Cassidy asked.

"No. I checked with Washington this morning. They've got people watching the roads coming into New York, but nobody's spotted them yet."

The elevator arrived and a uniformed patrolman came in through the open door to the apartment. "Detective Cassidy?"

"Yes."

"You're supposed to call the house."

"Okay."

"Wow, some joint, huh? Mind if I look around? I've never been in a penthouse before."

Cassidy went into the living room and dialed the precinct, identified himself, and asked for the captain. "What's up, boss?"

"Orso's in the emergency room at Roosevelt."

"What happened?"

"Apparently he was bringing in a prisoner, and the guy took him out."

"I'm on my way." Fuentes got away? How did that happen? And why did he run? His lawyer would have had him out in a few hours even if they moved him around for a while. Now if they caught him he was in real trouble. Assaulting a cop. Why? What was so important? Was there something he couldn't afford to miss?

The Roosevelt emergency room was in Hell's Kitchen, and it saw more gunshot and knife wounds than any other in the city. It was a place of despair and fear—fear of mortality, fear of medicine, of the unknown: *What's going to happen to me now? Will I heal? Will I live?* A large man in a ragged raincoat leaned his forehead against the wall near the door and sobbed while a small gray-haired woman in a bathrobe and slippers patted him on the back and whispered words of comfort that could not penetrate his grief. A young woman in a flowered rayon dress sat on a bench next to a ten-year-old boy who was clearly her son and smoked a cigarette in short rapid puffs. The woman wore only one stocking. The other, bloodstained, was wrapped around the boy's knee below the hem of his cut-off jeans. The boy was absorbed in a comic book, oblivious to his surroundings and his mother's anxiety. Two teenagers in motorcycle boots, pegged black jeans, and leather jackets leaned against a wall in studied nonchalance while they answered questions from a uniformed cop who took notes in a lined book. A third teenager lay on a bed in an open cubicle behind them. The side of his face was bloody, and his eyes were closed.

A triage nurse directed Cassidy to a curtained cubicle at the back of the room where Orso, naked to the waist, lay on a cot and held the hand of a nurse with short black hair. She laughed at something Orso said, and then he saw Cassidy and said, "I'll see you later, honey. My partner's here."

She gave Cassidy the once-over and said "Hi" as she left.

Orso's head was bandaged above the right temple. He had the beginnings of a black eye, and there was a dark line of stitches at the corner of his mouth.

"What happened?" Cassidy asked.

"Ahh, shit, I wish I knew." He pushed himself up to a sitting position, winced, and closed his eyes. "Worse than a fucking hangover. I don't even know what he hit me with." He scrubbed his face with his hand. "We come out of the building. The nearest call box is over on Broadway, so I figure we'll take a cab to the house rather than make the walk then wait around for a squad car. But there are no taxis coming down West End, so we'll walk, take whatever comes first, a taxi or the call box. Right on the corner he turns an ankle and goes down. My first instinct is to reach for him. When I do, he comes up with something from the gutter, slams me in the head, a brick, maybe a piece of wood. Hits me again, and I go down. When I wake up, he's gone, and a couple of people have called an ambulance. Here I am."

"He wasn't cuffed?"

"No, he wasn't cuffed. I mean, what's he going to do, run? I told him if he tried, I'd shoot him." Orso was embarrassed. He knew the prisoner should have been handcuffed to him.

"Shit, Tony."

"I know. I know." He put up a hand to ward off any more comments and was saved by the doctor who picked the clipboard off the cot rail, glanced at it to make sure he knew what was what, and then flipped it on the bed near Orso's feet. The doctor was a man in his thirties, but emergency-room duty sucked something out of him, and he looked worn and tired and older than his years. There was a big smear of blood on his white coat, and his fingernails were bitten to the quick. His manner was brisk. He had no time to waste. "Okay, Mr. Orso, you've got a mild concussion, nothing to worry about unless someone hits you in the head again pretty soon. Contusions around the eye. You're going to have a shiner. Nothing much to do about that. Put a piece of steak on it if it makes you feel better. It won't make much difference. Go see a doctor in a week and have those stitches removed. Do you drink, Mr. Orso?"

"Yeah, I've been known to take a pop."

"No liquor for twenty-four hours. If your vision suddenly blurs or the headache gets worse, go see your doctor. Go home and lie down. Take it easy." He tapped Orso on the knee and left.

"Let's get out of here," Orso said. He swung his legs to the floor and got up and had to steady himself for a moment on the bed rail. He waved away the hand Cassidy offered and went to where his clothes hung. He took his shirt off the hanger and examined it. "Shit, look at that, a fifteen-dollar shirt and I've only worn it once." There was blood on the collar and on the front of the shirt. His tie was stained with blood, but he put it on and pulled up the knot. He shrugged into his jacket. "You know they say you can't get blood out, but it's not true. I've got this Chink down on Canal Street can get any stain out you want."

"I try not to bleed on my clothes," Cassidy said.

"Yeah, but sometimes you've got no choice. Then you need the Chink. Let's go up to Dempsey's and get a drink. They don't mind blood on your clothes in there."

"The doctor said no booze."

"Yeah, and my mother tells me to wear galoshes when it rains, but I don't do that either. Are you coming, or am I drinking alone?"

22

Cassidy went up the stairs to his apartment singing, "Hey, bird dog get away from my quail . . ." The phrase kept running though his brain on a loop he could not stop. *Jesus Christ, is that what music is coming to?* The cabdriver had found the song on three different stations on the radio on the way downtown, and had been offended when Cassidy asked him to turn it off. And now the damn thing was stuck in his head. *Who the hell are the Everly Brothers and why don't they go screw with someone else's mind?* He scraped the key across the lock and missed the slot. Maybe that third martini had been a bad idea, but it hadn't seemed like it when Orso ordered it. He tried again. Ah, hah! Dead eye. He unlocked the door and pushed it open. "Honey, I'm home."

Alice screamed.

She was tied to a chair near the windows. The liquor slowed his reactions. When he started toward her someone blindsided him and bulled him into the wall; someone else pulled a big sack over his head and down over his arms, binding him. "Don't hurt him," a man said. Someone punched him hard in the stomach and sent him looking for breath in the bottom of his shoes. His knees buckled and he went down hard, unable to break his fall. *Don't hurt him, remember?* Hands pulled the sack down over his thighs. The cloth was rough and smelled of grain like the feed sacks he had humped on a ranch in Mexico as a sixteen-year-old summer cowboy. Someone wrapped a belt or rope around his thighs, and he was trapped, unable to move his hands or legs more than a few inches. His own breath was hot in his face and for a moment he panicked that he was going to suffocate, but the weave of the bag was coarse, and light came through it, and if there was light, there was air.

He heard the crack of an open hand on flesh. "I told you not to make any noise." Alice moaned. The hand cracked again. *She had tried to warn him.*

"Where is it?" Was the man's voice familiar?

"I don't know. I don't know what you're talking about." They must have already been at it for a while, because her voice was weary, resigned, getting to that point where you didn't give a damn anymore; you just wanted it to be over.

"Look, you stupid bitch, you tell us where it is, and we go away. If you don't, we kill you."

"Okay."

"Okay, then. Where?"

"Kill me." Hollow, like a voice down a pipe.

"Let me," someone said, and a moment later Alice screamed. The scream broke off into bubbling sobs.

Cassidy shouted, "I'm going to kill you fuckers. I'll find you and I'll kill you." His voice sounded muffled to him, without real threat. He shouted again, trying to distract them. "I'll hunt you down. I'll find you."

Footsteps, and then someone kicked him in the ribs. "Shut the fuck up." He did not know the voice.

He heard someone say, "Give me that candle."

"No!" he shouted. "Don't. Don't burn her."

The scrape of a match, and then a moment later Alice screamed.

One of the men giggled and said "Jesus," but it wasn't a prayer.

"She passed out."

"Wake her up."

Cassidy rolled over and tried to sit up, but it was no good. He could see light through the coarse weave of the cloth, and sometimes the men, but they were just blurred shapes. One passed near him, and he lashed out with his feet. The man stumbled away and then came back with a kick to reward him for his effort.

Alice screamed. "Please, please, please."

"Just tell us, and it'll be over."

"Please."

A key scraped in the lock and then the front door opened.

One of the men said, "Who the fuck are you?"

The gunshot was loud in the room, and one of the men yelped in pain.

"I'll kill the next one who moves."

He knew that voice. Was he dreaming?

"Hey," one of the men said. "You don't know what you're getting into here. You were smart, you'd leave."

"No. I'm going to stay."

Cassidy could feel a hand working on the rope that bound him. It came loose. "Can you get out of there now, or are your hands tied?"

"I can get out." He worked the bag up above his waist until he could get his hands on the bottom edge, and then he pulled it up and off, and as it cleared his head, the world was suddenly clear and bright.

Dylan looked down at him. "Is this what they call a pig in a poke?" She held a black automatic in a steady hand. It was pointed at Junior Carelli and Tommy Longo, the muscle guys Cassidy had last seen outside the White Horse Tavern. They both looked unafraid but sullen. They'd been interrupted in their work, and that was going to cost them when they reported back to their masters. Any harm Dylan offered was of secondary importance. The third man was the young bagman who had been with them outside the White Horse. *What was his name? Jimmy Greef.* Blood dripped from Longo's left hand. His right was clamped on his shoulder where Dylan had shot him.

Dylan glanced at Cassidy and then brought her eyes back to the three men. She was tan and had lost the prison gauntness and the trapped look in her eyes. She was beautiful, and Cassidy found it hard to look at her and breathe.

Alice was slumped in the chair near the window, held on to it only by the rope. There was blood on her blouse. Cassidy went to her and ripped at the knots in the rope, but her struggles had tightened them, and they would not give. He went into the kitchen and came back with a knife and cut the cords holding her arms and legs before he cut the one around her chest. When he did, she slumped further and he took her weight. He threw the knife into the kitchen and picked her up to carry her to the bedroom. "Can you hold them?"

"Yes."

He put Alice on the bed and covered her with a blanket and then sat on the edge of the bed and called a doctor he knew who lived over near Washington Square. "Frank, it's Michael Cassidy. I've got a woman in my apartment who has been beaten and burned. Can you come?" He listened. "No, I can't take her to St. Vincent's. Too many questions to answer. No, I didn't do it. Jesus, Frank." He listened again. "Let me look." He turned to Alice. "Her breathing is steady. Okay, hold on." He put the receiver down on the bedside table and leaned over Alice and gently raised her eyelid with the tip of her finger. He let it droop again and then he raised the other one. He picked up the phone. "As far as I can tell both pupils are the same size. When I lifted her eyelids, the pupils got smaller. All right. Thanks. Just ring the bell." He put the phone down. Alice's breathing was shallow but steady. There were burns on her arms. A blow had puffed her eye. Slaps had turned the side of her face livid, and it was beginning to swell. He leaned down and kissed her and then got up and went back into the living room.

No one had moved, but Longo was looking paler. He swayed once and had to take a step to steady himself.

"Is she all right?" Dylan asked.

"I've got a doctor coming. He'll tell us."

"What are we going to do with them?"

"I'd like to kill them."

"Not here. I could take them someplace and hold them for you. There's a warehouse I know. No one's using it. It's on Duane Street. I could take them there. You come when you're ready." She watched him without losing sight of her prisoners. She was steel. When he first met her almost five years ago, she had been tough but full of laughter. Things had happened over the last few years that had tempered her to a greater hardness.

"No. Let them go. They won't be back." He walked over to the men and looked each one in the eye. Longo and Carelli looked back. Greef shied away. "If she had it, she would have told you. Don't come back. This is finished. Tell them if something happens to her, I'll come after them." They would report what he said, but if they were told to come back, they would come.

Carelli put an arm around Longo's waist and helped him toward the door. Greef followed.

"Are you sure?" Dylan asked.

"Yes."

She stepped aside and let them pass. The door closed behind them, and they were gone.

Dylan slipped the gun into the big leather purse that hung from her shoulder. They looked across the room at each other, currents flowing, no language available to explain what had happened to them, to say what was between them now, what held them at a distance, and drew them close at the same time.

"You still have your key."

"Yes."

"Why?" Was this important? It was the only question he could think of.

"I don't know. I just kept it." She shrugged. "You never changed the lock."

"No." For the same reason, maybe: a thread back to what they were in the past, or toward a forlorn hope for a future.

And Cuba, a loop out of time, a moment on a different planet. Were they going to talk about that?

"Will you make me a drink?"

"Sure." He went into the kitchen and began to build a martini. She leaned on the counter and watched him and noticed he took only one glass from the cabinet.

"You're not going to have one?"

"No." Adrenaline had chased the alcohol from his system, but one drink and he'd be over the edge again, and he wanted to stay clear. "What are you doing here? Why did you come?"

"I don't know. I've been in New York for a week. Today I opened my purse and I saw the key. I came. I wanted to see you." She ducked her head away nervously and lit a cigarette.

"And your husband? Where's Slava? Does he know you're here?" Just the tip of the knife under the skin. He slid the drink across the counter to her.

She flinched. "You're not going to make this easy, are you?"

"Should I?" What was driving him, anger, sorrow, or green-eyed jealousy?

"I loved you. I was in love with you. And then you were gone and I was gone, and we were never going to see each other again. I met someone. We got married. What did you expect?" He said nothing. "And then there you were, like magic, like a dream. I didn't know, Michael. How could I know? We talked about this in Cuba."

"And then you walked away."

She jerked as if slapped, and then her face set hard. She pushed back from the counter. "All right. I'm sorry I came. You're right. It was a mistake. I'll go." She picked up her purse and headed for the door.

Whatever it was, anger, sorrow, jealousy, a corrosive combination of all, drained out of him, and he was ashamed. "Wait. I'm sorry. Stop. Don't go. Don't leave. I was being an asshole."

"Yes, you were." Almost a smile. "I can't help what happened. It's done. We are as we are." She gestured toward the bedroom where another woman lay.

But where were they going? That was the question he wanted to ask, but the doorbell rang. Frank said, "House call for Michael Cassidy," into the intercom. Cassidy pressed the buzzer and opened the door. They could hear his steps as he climbed and they said nothing to each other, grateful for the interruption.

Frank Kotter's curly hair lay thick and close on his skull. A perfume of whiskey followed him into the apartment. He wore blue jeans, a T-shirt, and a windbreaker and carried a black doctor's bag. He had the open, friendly face of a man who liked people, and it lit up when he saw Dylan, because he liked women most of all, and they liked him back. "Ahh, the patient. You better get your clothes off, my dear, and let me examine you."

Dylan laughed.

"She's in the bedroom, Frank," Cassidy said.

"Well, if you insist, but I still think we should examine this one while we're here. A bird in the hand. Will you still be here when I finish in the other room?" He asked Dylan.

"Probably."

"Oh, good. We'll talk then."

Cassidy took Frank into the bedroom. When he came out, Dylan was sitting at the counter sipping her drink. He sat on the stool next to her with his back against the counter and lit a cigarette.

"She was in Havana on New Year's Eve, wasn't she? With those gangsters at the Tropicana," Dylan said.

"Yes."

"I thought I recognized her. What did those men want from her?"

"Some money went missing that night, casino money. They thought she might have it."

"Does she?"

"No. They were just making sure."

"Uh-huh. And they liked it. Men like to hurt women, like to beat them. When I came in, those guys were having a good time. The younger one was grinning. How can you have a good time beating a woman?"

"I don't know."

"You're a cop. You must see it all the time."

He did see it, all the time, the battered, the broken, raped, and beaten. *I didn't do anything, he just exploded. The food was too cold. There was starch in his shirt. There was no starch in his shirt. I forgot to hang up his towel. He'd been drinking and he just came at me.*

And, *She pissed me off. She's always whining. I didn't like the way she looked at me. What the fuck do you care what I do, she's my wife.*

"I think we scare the hell out of men."

"Scare us how?"

"I don't know. But what else could it be?"

He had seen the results, but he had never thought about the cause. "I've never thought about it."

"No. Most men haven't. When I went back to Russia and they locked me up, they would come beat me once or twice a week. I could see that they liked it, and I began to wonder why. I began to think about it a lot. The two great mysteries are life and death. Women hold the key to life, and you hate that power." She finished her drink and pushed the glass away with the tips of her fingers. "That was good. You always made a great martini."

"Dylan, why are you in New York?"

She took a deep breath and switched gears. "We have information that someone will try to kill Castro while he's here. There are people who don't think his security is up to the job of protecting him, so they sent us."

"You and Slava?"

"Yes."

"You're better than his security team?"

"We are."

"Castro's surrounded by New York cops whenever he goes out. You know that. You've seen it."

"Yes."

"But you don't think it's enough."

"No."

"You think you're better than we are at this."

"Yes."

"Do you know who's coming for him?"

"Not exactly."

"The three men in the Lincoln from Florida?"

She almost suppressed her surprise. "We don't know about them. Who are they?"

"We don't know. The FBI has an alert out for them. They say they'll pick them up before they get into the city."

She smiled her disbelief. "What do you know about them? Are they anti-Castro? Are they working for someone?"

"That's all we know. Three men in a Lincoln coming to kill Castro in New York. There may be nothing to it at all. It may just be a rumor. What do you have?"

"Members of anti-Castro factions. Revisionists."

"Who?"

"There's a general named Garza y Mendoza."

"Not anymore. Someone killed him this afternoon."

"Ahh. Who did it?" Wariness in her look and voice.

"We don't know yet."

"No witnesses? No leads?"

"No. Not yet. Where was Slava this afternoon?"

"No, Michael. Don't."

The general was strangled. The man who did it only used three fingers on one hand. There's something wrong with one of Slava's hands, isn't there?" She said nothing. Her face was still, her eyes unreadable.

"Diego Fuentes was staying in the general's apartment. We had him in custody, but he got away."

"That's unfortunate. He's dangerous. Fuentes is a killer, and he brought men out with him who are killers." She lit a cigarette and passed it to him and lit another for herself, a familiar intimacy from the past.

"The general was tortured. Whoever killed him wanted information. Maybe he wanted to know where Fuentes was."

"Maybe he wanted revenge for what Garza y Mendoza had done in Cuba." They were sparring without inflicting damage.

"How will they try for Castro?"

"What we worry most about is the man who doesn't care whether he gets caught or killed. Someone who is willing to give up his life to do it is hard to stop if he picks the right moment."

"He'd have to get through a lot of cops." But he knew she was right.

"We're worried about the evening in Central Park. There'll be thousands of people there, and Castro wants them close. He wants to be able to touch them, to shake their hands. It'll be a security nightmare."

"Will you be there?"

"Yes. I'll be close to him. I'll be there as Selena Perez." There was a challenge in her look. *Will you give me up?*

"No guns, Dylan. If they take you with a gun, there's not much I can do. There are people in the Department who remember you from before. Your cover won't hold up. They'll identify you as KGB."

"Some things are worth the sacrifice." He could see that she meant it.

Frank Kotter came out of the bedroom and dumped his black bag on the counter. "What does it take to get a drink around here?"

"How is she?" Cassidy moved around the counter to the kitchen and showed the doctor a bottle of Ballantine's scotch.

Kotter nodded. "She's got some nasty bruises, maybe a cracked rib, a couple of minor burns. Some teeth are loose, but they'll set up again. They split her lip, but it's not big enough for stitches. It might leave a scar, but you'd have to work damn hard to make that woman unattractive. Personally, I like a scar. It adds a little, I don't know what, danger or something. The only thing I'd worry about is if she pisses blood. I gave her a sedative. She'll sleep till morning. I left pills on the bedside table. If she has pain when she wakes up, she can have one every four hours. Thanks." He took the glass, rattled the ice to cool the liquor, and inhaled half of it. "God, that's good." He turned to Dylan. "Tell me your name."

"Selena Perez." A glance at Cassidy to make sure he would back her lie.

"Whoa, Selena Perez. I like that. And you are a wonderful-looking woman. Do you like to dance? You look like a woman who likes to dance. Selena Perez must love to dance. Let's go dancing, you and I. I know a place on Eighth Avenue in a basement you'd swear you were in Buenos Aires, or someplace. The tango. All the women smolder. All the men carry knives."

She laughed, charmed and amused, and touched his arm with her fingertips. "Not tonight, but some night. Do I carry a rose in my teeth?"

"Absolutely." He finished his drink and banged the glass on the counter. "Bartender, one for the road. I have to be up at six for an appendectomy."

Cassidy refilled his glass. "Remind me to book my operations later in the day."

"Hey, I could do this one in my sleep with a butter knife and a spoon." He drank the whiskey and put the glass down with a sigh. "Everything I like is bad for me. Michael, are you going to get the guys who did this to her?"

"Yes."

"Good. Hurt them, the fuckers. Selena, you'll be in my dreams until I see you again." He lifted her hand and kissed it, and pressed it against his heart, picked up his bag, and went out the door.

Cassidy went into the bedroom to check on Alice. She had turned in the bed and the covers were awry. He pulled them back around her and turned off the light on the bedside table and crouched down for a moment to smooth the hair back from her face. When he stood, Dylan was watching from the doorway. She turned away abruptly.

When he came into the living room, she had her bag over her shoulder and her hand on the door knob. "I'll see you, Michael."

"Dylan, wait. Where are you going? Stay."

"No. I don't think so."

"How do I get ahold of you?"

"Uh-uh. It's okay. Everything's okay." But her smile held regret and then she was gone.

23

Cassidy woke at first light, gray dawn in the windows of the bedroom and birds trilling from the cornice that ran just below the sills. Spring is here, they were insisting. Alice groaned in her sleep next to him. He slipped out of bed, careful not to wake her, and padded naked into the kitchen and put the coffee on before taking a shower. He stood by the window, a towel around his waist, and drank coffee as the sun touched the tops of the trees on the Palisades across the river. A black-and-red Moran tug had the river to itself as it towed a barge downstream toward the ocean. Seagulls circled and dove over the roofs of the piers. Early morning, when the world still seemed at peace.

Alice cried out his name from the bedroom.

He put the mug down and went to find her curled in a fetal position, her arms clasped around her stomach. He knelt by the bed and put a hand on her shoulder. She flinched and looked at him with wide, frightened eyes. "I thought you'd gone. I thought I was alone."

"No."

"Alone." Full of anguish. The worst thing in the world.

"No. I'm right here." He put an arm around her and she buried her face against him, and he could feel her tears on his chest. When he shifted his arm, she gasped in pain. "I'm sorry," he said, no comfort at all.

"They hurt me. They really hurt me. They wouldn't stop. I told them I didn't have it, but they wouldn't stop."

"It's all right. They won't be back. It's over. You're going to be all right." Silly, useless words against her pain and fear. "Here, the doctor left you some pills. Take a pill. It'll help." He refilled her glass from the jug on the bedside table and supported her while she sat up and took the pill.

"I have to go to the bathroom." The pain drained the blood from her face when he helped her out of the bed, and he could see that she clenched her jaw against crying, but a moan escaped. He put an arm around her waist, and she leaned against him as they navigated to the bathroom. When she saw herself in the mirror, she gasped. Her face was swollen and livid, and one of her eyes was blackened, and there was dried blood at the corner of her mouth. Her torso and stomach were bruised and there was a place on her arm that looked like someone had ground it with a rasp. She put a hand on the sink to steady herself and pulled his arm from around her waist. "Go away. You can't look at me like this. Go away."

"It's all right, Alice. Just let me . . ."

"Go away, Michael. Go away. Leave me alone. Don't look at me. Don't look at me. Just please go away."

He started to protest, to offer help, but he saw that she did not want it, so he left, closing the door as he went. He heard the shower start as he was dressing. It was still running when he went into the kitchen and poured another cup of coffee. The men who had come to beat her here in his apartment had no fear of Cassidy as a cop and no fear of Frank Costello, so Costello's power in the Mob was waning. Other men were rising, Vito Genovese, who had tried to have Costello killed in 1956, Carlo Gambino, once a Costello underboss who wanted to move up, and Meyer Lansky, always Meyer Lansky, the little man who loved numbers.

He heard the shower stop. A few minutes later she called for him. She was in bed propped up on the pillows. The shades were down and the curtains drawn, and the room was as dark as she could make it, but there was still enough light to see the bruises on her face. He sat on the side of the bed and she took the mug of coffee he had brought her. "Thank you."

"How are you?"

"Better. The hot water helped, and the pill is working."

"Good. You'll hurt today and maybe tomorrow, and you'll be stiff, but it will get better every day." Knowledge hard won from beatings he had suffered. What he knew and what she now knew was that the beatings connected you back to the animal we were before we had the language to talk about fear and death, when waking moments were spent attuned to threats, the rustle in the underbrush, the click of shifting pebbles, the hints of dangers that were waiting to snatch you out of life. Once you had been there, it was hard to come all the way back. Once you had been there, you were forever aware that the veneer of civilization was too thin to trust.

She sipped the coffee and studied him over the rim. "Will they come back?"

"No, they won't, but just to be sure I'll call the precinct over on Perry and have them station a patrolman outside the building."

"Thank you." She drank more of the coffee and then handed him the mug to put on the bedside table. "The woman who came in, the one with the gun, she was with you in Havana at the Tropicana on New Year's Eve."

"Yes."

"Who is she?"

"Her name is Dylan McCue."

"She saved my life. I was about to give up. I was just going to let go. I could feel myself slipping, and I was just going to let go, because I couldn't take it anymore. And then she came in. Michael, why did she have a gun? Who is she? Is she a cop?"

"Yes. In a way." How to explain Dylan? Best to let it go.

She yawned. "Wow, that pill is strong." Her voice softened and slurred. "You won't go until you call for a cop, will you?"

"No. I'll stay until he's downstairs."

"Michael."

"Yes."

"They really hurt me." She sounded almost surprised.

"I know."

"I want to thank her." Her voice blurred.

"I'll tell her."

"Good." She closed her eyes.

• • •

Cassidy met Orso at the coffee shop on Lexington with the good muffins and the counterman with a pint of rye in his apron. Orso was in the back booth hunched over a mug of coffee. He had the sullen look of a man with a hangover. His face was raw from Fuentes's assault, and the line of black stitches made the skin at the corner of his mouth seem paler than usual. He still wore the suit he had worn the day before, and there were dark patches of dried blood on his shirt. He was usually a fastidious man, and Cassidy wondered what was making him slide. "What the hell happened to you?" He asked as Cassidy slid into the booth across from him.

Cassidy reflexively touched the abrasion high on his forehead. "Somebody kicked me while I was tied up in a sack."

"One of those nights, huh? You've got to find a better class of people to run around with."

The counterman came with a basket of muffins and a mug of coffee for Cassidy. He slipped the pint of rye from his pocket and put it on the table. "You guys look like you could use this." Then he went away.

Orso poured whiskey in their mugs. "So, tell."

Cassidy told him about the missing half million, the men trying to beat information out of Alice, and Dylan's rescue.

"Who were the three guys?" Orso asked.

"Longo and Carelli, and the new bagman, Jimmy Greef. Do you know him, Greef?"

"Jimmy Greef? There was a Big Sal Greef ran numbers for Anastasia awhile back. He ended up in the river. I think he had a son. Could be this guy. You going to go back at them?"

"Yes. When I get the chance, I will."

"Half a million dollars. Jesus, what I could do with that." He shook his head, a mistake that made him wince.

"Yeah, wine, women, and song, and then you'd waste the rest."

"You don't know what the fuck I'd do with it. You've got money, so the stuff doesn't matter to you. You don't have a fucking idea what it's like not to have it."

"Whoa, easy. I was just making a joke." Where'd that anger come from?

"You think I can get anyone in the family to help with the old lady? My mother's going to end up in some fucking county ward."

"I thought your father's insurance money was going to take care of that."

"Yeah? Well, it's not. Okay? It's not."

"Tony, if you need help, come to me."

"Yeah, right."

"I mean it."

"Okay. Yeah, I know you do. I'm sorry. That fucking spic kicked the shit out of me yesterday. I had a couple too many pops at Toots's and slept in the back room there. I woke up feeling like shit. I'm sorry."

"It's okay. Any word on Fuentes?"

"No, he's still on the dangle."

"I'm going to go talk to Jane Hopkins about Casey Allen. I've got a few questions. Other than that we've got nothing till this evening. Why don't you take the day, get some rest?"

"Yeah, I might do that."

"I'll check with Clarkson's office, but I don't think we're on till five. We can meet at the house and walk over to where they're setting up for Castro."

"Yeah. Good. Okay. Look, I'm sorry about going off on you. I've been kind of nervy these last few weeks."

"Don't worry about it."

"All right. Thanks." Orso heaved himself to his feet, touched Cassidy on the shoulder as he went by, and left the diner. Cassidy watched him go and wondered what was eating him. It couldn't just be his mother's finances. Even if the insurance she got from her late husband wasn't much, she owned her house outright, and that had to be worth something. But what did he know about the pressures of too little money? He had always had more than enough, and he had been brought up to regard it with a certain disdain. It was hard for him to believe that money was grinding Orso, but it didn't matter. He would cover for his partner the way Orso had covered for him during the first couple of months when he came back from Cuba and was trying to drive Dylan out of his head with booze and women.

Dylan. Where was she? He wanted to see her. He wanted to talk to her, to be with her. *Stop. Don't think about her. There is nothing there but pain.*

He returned what was left in the bottle to the counterman, paid the bill, and went out into a day that was turning warm. Big cotton clouds floated above the building tops, and the breeze that came off the river was warm. He stopped at a phone booth on the corner and called the hotel where Castro and his people were staying and asked for Ribera's room. His excuse was to talk about Castro's rally that night in Central Park, but he knew that the real reason was to ask Ribera how he could get in touch with Dylan.

Which rules, the head or the heart?

Ribera did not answer the phone.

• • •

Cassidy rang the bell at the Hopkins house on 73rd Street. A maid in a black uniform appeared from the back of the house. She opened the barred front door, and Cassidy explained who he was, and she let him wait in the living room while she went to find Mrs. Hopkins. The room was dim and cool, and though the traffic on Fifth Avenue was no more than twenty yards away, it could barely be heard through the thick stone walls. The house was in the middle of a big, raucous city, but it was as quiet and private as a hilltop in the country. If you had enough money you could live like this where nothing could touch you. An illusion, he knew, but it was an illusion people wanted and paid for.

The scrabble of toenails on the marble of the hall announced the arrival of the red setter, Lucky, who approached Cassidy eagerly, sniffed him to make sure he was not an impostor, and then butted his hand for affection. Cassidy scratched his head and watched Jane Hopkins enter the room. She wore a dark green dress of some light material. The top was cut low and held up by two straps, and the full skirt molded to her legs when she walked. She looked bright, fresh, and clean, as if she had just been taken out of the box. Lucky saw that he was going to be ignored, and went to lie on a throw rug in front of the fireplace.

"Michael, how nice of you to drop by. To what do I owe the pleasure? Have you come to accuse me of bank robbery or murder?" She threw it away like a bright line from a Broadway play. She brushed his cheek with a kiss, sat down on the sofa, and leaned forward to take a cigarette from the silver box on the coffee table, giving him a chance to look down the front of her dress. She held the cigarette expectantly between two fingers until he dug his Zippo from his pocket and lit it. "Now, darling, don't loom over me. Come sit." She patted the sofa cushion next to her, but Cassidy chose a chair across from her where he could watch her face while they talked. She looked disappointed and said, "I don't bite, you know."

"That's not what I've heard."

She smiled, and then snapped her even, white teeth together with an audible click. She was used to tipping men off balance, and she enjoyed it. "What happened to your face? Have you been in a fight? Should I ask how the other guy looks?"

"I never saw him."

"What an interesting life you lead, Michael Cassidy."

"Let's talk about Casey Allen."

"Fine. Let's."

"The day that he was killed, Friday, you told me you and your husband left on a planned trip to San Francisco."

"Yes."

"That was a lie. The driver who picks him up thought he was going to the office, but took you to the airport. The tickets were reserved that morning at seven thirty."

"Well then I guess we hadn't planned it for long." She smiled.

"It's not a joke."

"No. Of course not. I'm sorry." Serious now, like a schoolgirl called to task for talking in class.

"You took Lucky for a walk like you usually do in the morning." The dog raised its head at its name, and then flopped back down. "You went into the park at Seventy-second Street like you usually do, and you found Casey Allen sitting on a kitchen chair with a bullet hole in his head."

She watched him for a while without speaking while she calculated. *If I say this, then what? If I say that?* "Even if I did see him, I didn't have anything to do with it. You don't think I killed him, do you?"

"No."

She came to a decision that cleared her face. She nodded and shrugged. "Yes. I saw him."

"Then what?"

"I thought he was dead. I mean, I'd never seen a dead man before, but he was so still, and he wasn't breathing, and he was very pale. And there was that hole in his forehead. I just knew." She took a deep breath at the memory and let it out in a rush.

"And?"

"I came back here and told Bob what I had found. He told me to go pack a bag. He called the airline. We left. He thought there was a good chance that Casey would never be connected to us. And if he was, we weren't here."

"Yeah. That worked well."

"Bob's very smart about a lot of things, but dead men are outside his areas of expertise. And he was probably right to take the chance. Not all policemen are as smart as you are. We might never have been connected."

"It didn't occur to you to call the police?"

"What for? He was dead. Someone was bound to call. Why did it have to be me?" A woman used to having her problems solved by other people.

"You may have been partially responsible for his death."

"Me? Don't be ridiculous. How?"

"You were having an affair with him."

She laughed. "I was not having an affair with him. I might have an affair with you, Michael, because you are an interesting, dangerous man.

Casey Allen was a great big boy, enthusiastic, sweet, but simple. With him I got laid." She laughed again. "Oh, the look on your face. Are you shocked?"

"Not really. I've heard about the Hopkinses' open marriage."

"Oh, you've been out gossiping with the ladies, or was it the men? It's hard to know who finds it more exciting. I do know when I go to a party these days, I am never without male companionship." Cassidy sensed defiance behind her smile.

"Did Casey's wife ever show up here?"

"His wife?" One of those questions asked to buy time to think. "Yes. Once, as far as I know. She brought him a sandwich."

"After you started screwing him?"

"Now you're being unpleasant."

"Answer the question."

"After."

"And while she was here, did you flirt with him?"

"No. Of course not."

"No gesture, no hand on his shoulder, tap on the arm, one of those things where you pat a man's chest?"

Her eyes were wide and her face was serious. "I do that to everybody."

"No, you don't. You do it to men you're attracted to. And she got the message. And you meant her to get the message. You just wanted to mark the territory a little, didn't you?"

"Don't be stupid. I did not," she protested, but he could read the lie.

"Then he began showing up at home with all the new clothes. That must have gotten her attention."

"I was trying to help him out. He asked me." She lit another cigarette, oblivious to the one smoldering in the ashtray, and took a couple of fierce puffs.

"It turns out she's a very jealous woman. She attacked an old girlfriend of Casey's with a beer bottle for the crime of saying hello."

"It's not true."

"Yes, it is. She shot her husband because she was jealous of you, and somehow she moved him to where you would find him. She wanted you to see."

"No. I don't believe it." But she did. She stubbed the cigarette out hard in a crystal ashtray, saw there was another burning and said, "Goddamn it." She looked at Cassidy and her face was stiff. "I'm going to call our lawyer. Bob said he should be here if you came back, and he's right."

"Don't bother. I'm leaving." He stood up.

"What's going to happen to me?"

"Nothing. I guess I could work up some sort of obstruction charge against you, but it wouldn't stick."

"And her? What about her?"

"We'll probably get her. Everything she did was on the spur of the moment. There are bound to be some loose ends. But then again, she might get away with it. Who knows? Maybe she'll come see you." Jane's eyes widened, and for a moment her composure dropped away and she looked scared.

Cassidy stopped on the corner of Fifth Avenue to light a cigarette. He looked back at the house he had just left. It was five stories of gray limestone with the entry blocked by the iron-barred door. The light reflected off the big, deep-set windows so they looked impenetrable. It was a fortress, a sanctuary, and the people who lived in it expected to be insulated from the dirtier problems of the world.

His comment about Theresa showing up here was a thin blade under Jane's guard, enough to prick her into fear, and he was glad that he had done it, but he knew it was cheap and petty revenge. The wound would close quickly. Careless people like Jane Hopkins sailed on untroubled by the wreckage they left in their wake.

24

The three men who had left the Lincoln in the parking lot of the Atlanta train station had two adjoining rooms in the Bradford Hotel on West 70th Street. The Bradford was a mid-range apartment hotel of no special distinction whose clientele consisted for the most part of businessmen in town for a week or two who, seeking economy, appreciated the kitchenettes in the rooms that allowed them to cook simple meals for themselves rather than eat in restaurants. The three men from the Lincoln were not interested in economy, since they were spending their employers' money, not their own. They appreciated the hotel's anonymity and its proximity to Central Park, half a block away, where they would do their work.

Two of the men from the Lincoln were twins, Terry and Jerry Brasoli. The third, Will Horner, was their first cousin. The three of them had grown up in Ybor City, the cigar-making section of Tampa, Florida. Their mothers, who were sisters, held jobs in the Arturo Fuente cigar factory, and their fathers, petty gangsters in the Trafficante mob, had died stupid, violent deaths. Pete Brasoli bled out on the floor of a dive called the Blind Pig with a hatchet buried in his neck after calling a cross-dressed Cuban meat cutter a fucking faggot. Tim Horner went down at the wrong end of a sawed-off shotgun that ended an argument about whether the Florida state bird was the pink flamingo. The boys, joined by blood and an instinct for mayhem, had grown up rough and wild. When they were in their late teens, a judge took a dim view of their joyriding through an upscale neighborhood in South Tampa in a stolen car and offered them the choice of enlistment in the Marines or three years in jail. They had opted for the military on the assumption that they could run when they got tired of it, but discovered, to their surprise and satisfaction, that the

Marines would train them to kill people efficiently. They practiced their craft for a year in Korea and then came back to Tampa and offered their services to Santo Trafficante, Jr., who had a need for their talents.

Terry Brasoli, the most orderly and precise of the three, favored a Winchester M70 target rifle as opposed to the M1903 Springfield he had mastered in Marine Corps training. He mounted a Unertl 8 power scope with a one-and-a-half-inch objective lens and a fine crosshair reticle. He used M72 match ammunition and at six hundred yards he could group his shots in a four-inch circle. He preferred to work closer, because he liked to see the impact.

His brother Jerry had discovered an affection for explosives and could shape a charge in such a way that the target would lose his foot, his hand, or his entire being when he turned the key in his car. Cousin Tim was a more straightforward goon who liked to work in close with a knife or a handgun, and he favored the short, brutal Uzi the Israelis had developed. "A pretty goddamn good weapon for a bunch of yids."

The three men ate pizza and drank Coca-Colas and watched a black-and-white rerun of Roy Rogers and Dale Evans chasing bad guys around a mythical Wild West where Jeeps, telephones, and the rest of the twentieth century coexisted happily with cowboys and cowgirls riding horses and sporting six shooters. The men wore the Parks Department uniforms they had found in the closets when they checked into their rooms. They had scouted the target area and were satisfied the plan would work as outlined. The rifle, wrapped in a couple of layers of cotton cloth, was in a wheeled canvas bucket surrounded by rakes, shovels, and hoes in the short hall near the front door. Roy Rogers leaped from Trigger and dragged two fleeing rustlers from their saddles and rode them to the ground. Dale Evans lassoed a third, and Pat Brady subdued a fourth with the front end of his Jeep. Roy and Dale sang "Happy Trails to You," and they cut to a Jell-O commercial. Jerry stacked the plates and carried them to the kitchen and dumped them in the sink. They would not be coming back here tonight. Someone else could wash up.

• • •

Cassidy was restless. They had been over the plans for the rally in the park three times in the last three days. Who went where. Who was responsible for what. What to do if this contingency arose, or that one. Now all they could do was wait, and Cassidy was no good at waiting. He would meet Orso at the station house at five, but there was time to kill, and it died slowly for him if he did not have something to do. On the off chance that Fuentes was stupider than he seemed, Cassidy went back to the apartment building on 73rd and West End Avenue.

Drago Peck leaned against an awning pole and smoked a forbidden cigarette hidden in a cupped hand. When he saw Cassidy coming up the block, he flicked the cigarette out into the street, straightened, and smiled a tip-sucking smile. "How're you doing, Detective? What a day, huh?" He gestured proudly toward the blue sky and white clouds as if he had summoned them himself.

"I'm going up to the general's apartment."

"Sure. Whatever you want. That Fuentes guy hasn't been back. I've been keeping my eye out. I told the other doormen, the elevator men, I wanted to know if he showed."

"Thank you."

"Just doing my job. The good of the tenants is my concern."

The apartment looked much the same as when Cassidy last saw it, but it already had the musty, airless smell of an uninhabited place. He did not expect to find anything of note, but there was always the chance that Fuentes had slipped in. He walked down the corridor to Fuentes's room. As far as he could tell no one had been there since the day Garza y Mendoza had been killed. He opened bureau drawers and closed them again. He looked in the closet. The clothes still hung neatly and nothing seemed to be missing. He sat at the desk and let his eyes drift over the room. Sometimes if you did not look directly but let your glance slide, you picked up something out of place. Not this time. He checked his watch. Okay. You came. You looked. You didn't find anything, another long shot fired and missed. Time to go.

Drago Peck opened the front door with a flourish. "Everything copacetic, Detective?" The slang sounded weird coming with a thick Balkan accent.

"Yes. Everything's fine."

"Let me get you a taxi."

"No, thanks. I'm going to walk for a while."

"What is it with cops? You don't like taxis?"

"What do you mean?"

"When that other cop came down with Mr. Fuentes, I had a cab right here. Mrs. Mendelstein was just getting out. I said, here you are gentlemen. He said, no thanks. They were going to walk. What is it with you guys, walking when there are perfectly good cabs to carry you where you want to go?"

Cassidy turned away without answering. He went back over his conversation with Orso in the hospital after Fuentes escaped. Orso said there had been no taxi outside the building when they came down, so they walked toward Broadway and the nearest call box. *Did I get it wrong? No. That's what he said. Why the lie?*

• • •

Cassidy found Orso on one of the cots in the co-op room behind the squad room. He sat up rubbing his eyes when Cassidy came in.

"Time to go," Cassidy said.

"Any coffee left in the pot?"

"I think so."

"Give me a minute. I've got to splash some water on my face. Man, I was deep down." He got up and stretched and shuffled to the bathroom. He came out to the squad room a couple of minutes later carrying a cup of coffee. Cassidy sat with his feet up on his desk smoking a cigarette and watched him come. Again he noticed that Orso, usually sleek, and fastidious, was pasty and tired-looking. His hair was hastily combed, and his suit coat was wrinkled.

"What's with you?" Orso asked.

"Nothing."

"The way you're looking at me."

"Tony, nothing. I was just thinking."

"About what?"

"Casey Allen."

"Yeah? Did you talk to the Hopkins broad?"

"I did."

"What'd she say? Was she banging the carpenter?"

"Yup. And the wife came by one day."

"Oh, boy. She got a whiff, huh?"

"It's what it looks like."

"Broads, man. What are you going to do?" As if that said it all. He checked the clock. "We better get out of here. If we're late Clarkson's going to get his panties in a bunch."

"Yeah, let's go." Cassidy stood up and ground the cigarette out in the full ashtray on his desk.

"Are you okay?"

"I'm fine," he lied.

Orso studied him and then shrugged. "Okay."

They did not talk much on the walk to Central Park. Orso seemed preoccupied and nervy. Once he said "Ah, shit" under his breath, and when Cassidy asked what was up, he said, "Nothing. Nothing. Hey, after this is over, let's go to Toots's and get shitfaced."

"Sure."

Orso smiled and said, "Okay, good." But worry came off him like heat.

• • •

The twins Terry and Jerry Brasoli and their cousin Will Horner made their way toward the Central Park Mall and the Naumburg Bandshell. They were dressed in their Parks Department uniforms. Terry wheeled the tall canvas bucket that concealed his rifle among the rakes and hoes. Will pushed a wheeled garbage can. Every once in a while he paused to stab a piece of trash with the nail end of his pickup stick. Four times he stopped at trash cans the Parks Department maintained in the hope that people would take the trouble to drop their trash there rather than on the ground. At each one Jerry and Terry shielded Will while he removed a small package from the wheeled garbage can and placed it at the bottom of the trash can and covered it carefully with trash.

• • •

A hundred uniformed cops had gathered on the vast paved terrace in front of the Naumburg Bandshell by the time Cassidy and Orso got there. Television crews from the local networks set up their cameras and strung cable out to generator trucks. Police barriers had been erected to limit the entry points for people who were coming to hear Castro speak. Even though he was not scheduled to arrive for two more hours, people were already there. Some brought signs saying *Viva Fidel*, *Viva La Revolución*, or *M-26-7*, commemorating the 26th of July Movement. Folding chairs had been set up on the pavement, but many people chose to sit on the grass or on the park benches that surrounded the paved area. Some brought picnics. Children played games among the trees. Three men with guitars and a trumpet played mambos while a fourth added percussion with *claves*, short, thick dowels of wood. Men and women danced in front of them to rhythms rarely heard on the Upper East Side.

Cassidy and Orso walked the perimeter. They were not looking for anything specific, just something out of place, something that did not belong. They had been cops for a long time, and they had learned to trust instinct. If it felt wrong, it probably was wrong. Four men in Parks Department uniforms were loading bags into a green Parks Department van. Cassidy showed them his badge. "Guys, you're going to have to move this van outside the perimeter."

"Sure, Officer," said a tall, sharp-faced man with a salt-and-pepper buzz cut. "We're all done here." He gestured to a strip of turned earth with freshly planted bushes. "Acid soil, man. You've got to throw the lime at it." He picked up a last bag of fertilizer and threw it in the back of the van. The tall man stripped off his gloves and stuffed them in his back pocket. "What've you got going here, a concert or something?"

"Castro's going to give a speech."

"Who?"

"Fidel Castro."

"Who's he?"

"The Cuban guy. The revolutionary."

"Huh? Never heard of him. Well, take it easy." The men got in the van and drove away. Cassidy stared after it.

"What?" Orso asked.

"I don't know. Something he said, but I can't get ahold of it."

"It'll come."

They found a small duffel bag a couple of hundred yards from the bandshell stage, but all it held was an old baseball glove, cleats, and a well-used sweatshirt. A Parks maintenance shed sat on a knoll a little farther on. "I've got it," Orso said.

He opened the door, blocking the entry with his bulk. It was dark inside the shed and it took a moment for his eyes to adjust.

Three men in Parks Department uniforms looked back at him. One of them held a brutal-looking machine pistol.

"Anything?" Cassidy asked from behind him.

"No." Orso picked up something from the floor, and turned and shut the door. "A padlock on the floor. A good place for it, huh? I'm going to lock it up." He ran the lock through the hasp and snapped it shut, and rattled it as if to make sure it was solid. The screws that held the hasp were loose in their holes, and one good kick from inside would open the door. He took a roll of orange police department sealing tape out of his pocket and slapped it across the padlock and door frame.

25

Castro's motorcade drove through the 72nd Street entrance to the park, lights and sirens, as the sun set over the buildings on the west side burnishing the roofs and spires with golden light. The cars parked inside the perimeter, and Castro led his fatigue-wearing entourage toward the bandshell as the crowd began to cheer. Chief Clarkson walked at Castro's side, and the group was flanked by Headquarters' cops, crisply dressed, square-jawed, clear-eyed, commanding presences coincidentally in range of the TV and press cameras.

Cassidy did not like it that the cops in front of the bandshell were as relaxed as if they were guarding a Boy Scout picnic rather than a controversial foreign dignitary with dedicated enemies. At the briefing the day before Chief Clarkson had announced that the FBI was discounting the rumor of the three men in the Lincoln and the assassination attempt. They would still be on guard for disruptions and possible violence from Batista loyalists, but it had been decided on high that a professional hit was unlikely. When Cassidy joined the blue-coated crowd, Carlos Ribera was asking Clarkson to remove the barriers that had been erected to keep people back from the front of the bandshell and Castro.

"It is not going to happen, Mr. Ribera. It is a basic rule of crowd control in a situation like this to keep people a safe distance from the principal," Clarkson said.

"Fidel wants the barriers down. He understands the risk, but he wants the people close."

"It is not Mr. Castro's decision. It is a matter of New York City Police Department protocols."

Ribera rolled his eyes at Cassidy. *What do you do with an idiot like this?*

Castro appeared at Ribera's shoulder. "Why are the barriers not removed?" He asked in his heavily accented English.

"I explained to Mr. Ribera that Department protocols require the crowd be kept back a safe distance," Clarkson explained.

"*Que cabron. Que mariconada,*" Castro said. And then in English as he loomed over Clarkson, pressing him with his bulk, "I am not a man on a balcony. I am a man of the people, and I will speak to my people in the way that is right. If you do not remove the barriers, I will not speak here. I will go to the newspapers and tell them how this country that talks about freedom of speech refused to allow me to speak to my people in a free way."

The muscles bunched in Clarkson's jaw. He was used to command not being commanded, and he loathed the threat to his authority, but he was a political animal and he weighed the embarrassment of Castro leaving against the unlikely threat of assassination. "Captain Moore, please have the barriers removed. And I want ten men stationed along the pavement in front of the bandshell." The last was an ineffective measure of security, but at least it gave him a gesture of control. He turned to Castro. "Will that satisfy?"

In reply, Castro smothered him in a hug and rubbed a bearded kiss across the top of the smaller man's head. "You are a good man, and a democrat, and I salute you." He released him, and Cassidy could see he was amused and pleased by Clarkson's discomfort.

Ribera took Cassidy's arm and drew him aside. "One more night, and then we are out of here. Boston, Canada for a few days, and then home. I will be able to breathe again when we get him to Havana." He offered Cassidy a cigar from his leather case, but Cassidy lit a cigarette and then offered the match until Ribera's cigar was drawing well. "Michael, I want to apologize for my anger the other day."

"Not necessary. I was talking out of turn."

"No. I confess the executions at La Cabaña trouble me, and I make excuses for them. I understand the need for revenge, for blood. We are not so civilized that we can always be true democrats, and the men who go to the wall there deserve their deaths for the things they have done. It troubles me, because I hoped we would be better than they were. But things will be better. They have to be. I have to believe in this man, because if not Fidel, I am without hope for my country and my people again." He put an arm around Cassidy's shoulders and hugged him hard. "You and I will always be good friends, Michael. At least we have that out of all the politics and lying and crap."

"At least we have that," Cassidy said. "Carlos, I saw Dylan the other day."

"Yes, she told me."

"Is she here?"

"I don't know, but probably."

"And her husband?"

"Yes." He put a sympathetic hand on Cassidy's shoulder. "Let it go, Michael. She is not the same person she was when you met her. You are not either. You cannot go back."

"Tell her I want to see her."

"Michael, don't do this to yourself."

"Tell her."

"All right. I'll tell her." He squeezed Cassidy's shoulder and shook his head in mock despair. "The heart wants what the heart wants. Who can deny it?"

Someone called for Ribera. Cassidy watched him walk away, a big bear of a man trailing smoke and rum and energy. He wondered how long it would be before Castro broke his heart. Then, spurred by a sense of unease he could not stifle, he walked back into the crowd.

• • •

Ex-Sergeant Paco Lopato stood in the shadows of a tree on the north side of the plaza and watched Cassidy walk away from the front of the bandstand. He should have known that this man would be part of the security around Castro. He had been a stone in his shoe since the first meeting in Havana. He looked at the men and women in fatigue uniforms crowding around Castro. Did he recognize any of them? He did not think so, and he did not think any of them would recognize him. Many of the men he had dealt with at La Cabaña were dead, and besides, he did not look like the fearsome Sergeant Lopato, who they had only seen in the uniform of SIM. He had cut his hair short. He wore a red, black, and white guayabera shirt, the colors of the 26th of July Movement, black trousers, and canvas shoes with rubber soles good for running. It would be so easy to walk over with a smile on his face, offer greetings in Spanish, and then pull the big .45 from where it was hidden under his shirt and shoot Castro *boom, boom, boom.* But it would not be as it was in the restaurant. These men and the police would not freeze or run at the sound of the gun. They had heard guns before. They would have him before he ran ten yards. No, he would do as Colonel Fuentes had suggested. He would wait to see if the gringos' killers did what they were hired to do. If they did, then good, there would be nothing for him to do. If they missed, and if in the confusion the opportunity presented itself, he would kill the man. It would give him pleasure. But he would not do it if there were a chance of being caught. He had learned that caution from Colonel Fuentes, who, he knew, was nowhere near the killing ground in Central Park that evening. What had the priests said when he was small? *Work hard and enjoy the fruits of your labor.* Difficult to enjoy if you were dead. Still, if the thing were possible, he would be ready, and if he missed him here, there would be another time.

He checked to see that the gun did not show under his shirt and joined a group of people who were moving toward the newly opened space in front of the bandshell.

• • •

Night came. The stage where Castro would speak was bathed in hot light from banks of spots. Technicians set up a microphone and a podium. The streetlamps that lined the park's paths came on, and there were colored bulbs strung through the trees. Cassidy moved through a crowd that had grown from hundreds to thousands, a crowd that gave off an electric hum of excitement that rose and fell in pitch.

More musicians had joined the small band of guitars and trumpet, and a hundred people were dancing in front of them. Onlookers ringed them. Some of them swayed and moved to the rhythm, and every once in a while the music would seize one or two of them and pull them out of the circle of watchers and into the dance. Cassidy turned away and pushed through the throng. What was it that made him uneasy? There was a dream fragment waiting tantalizingly at the edge of consciousness. What was the dream? It remained beyond his capture.

• • •

Waiting did not bother the three men in the maintenance shed. It was part of the job, and they were used to it. Each went about his business silently, automatically. If they had to speak, they did it in whispers. They used penlights, shaded to narrow beams to help with their preparations. Jerry pinned black cloth squares over the glassless windows to block anyone looking in. Will pushed the wheeled trash can in front of one of the windows and wedged it so it would not move. He piled bags of fertilizer on top until the last was level with the windowsill.

Terry removed the rifle from among the rakes and hoes. He unwrapped the cloth that cushioned the gun and laid it across the fertilizer bags while he hunted for the second wrapped tube at the bottom of the bag that held the Unertl 8 power scope and the suppressor that would reduce the sound of the shot to a cough. He clicked the scope home and threaded the suppressor onto the barrel. He took five shells from his pocket and pressed them down one by one into the magazine. The bullets were hollow points designed to spread on impact and smash their way through flesh and bone for maximum damage. They had agreed they would wait until Castro had spoken for ten minutes, enough time for the latecomers to settle in, but not so long that people in the crowd would get bored and begin to move around. Castro would be in his rhythm then. They would know how he moved on the stage. Did he leave the podium and walk while he talked? Did he hold still, and if he did, was there a rhythm in that, a predictable moment in his movements where he paused to gesture, to emphasize a phrase, a moment where he would be easy to kill?

The crowd quieted when Castro moved to the podium and began to speak. His amplified voice sounded metallic from the speakers hung in the trees. His English was heavily accented, but slow-paced, and clear. "We wish to express our sympathy for the American people which we have always loved and are fond of. All Americans in the last months congratulated us, have seen how much freedom and happiness there is in Cuba. I have sincere sympathy for the people of the United States and I am grateful. Things have been said about our revolution which are not true, that we are Communists, that we are the enemy of Democracy. Many times in the history the truth is now known, many times in history the lie is more powerful than the truth. In this case the trust is opening its own road by the help of the people. The American people say how can they help us. I can answer. There are many ways, their friendship, their sympathy, and many other ways. We are not asking for money from the U.S. government or anybody. We are trying to solve our economic difficulties by only working in Cuba."

Cassidy only half listened. He smelled tobacco smoke, and rum, and burning charcoal and grilling meats from small braziers people had brought to the park, smells that reminded him of Havana rather than New York. Was Dylan somewhere among the mass of people? Would he find her? The crowd shuffled and sighed like a huge animal. Occasionally Castro's voice rose in passion, and when it did, people cried out in agreement. Cassidy looked for Orso, but he could not find him. He saw Bonner and Newly and recognized a few other plainclothes officers. Uniformed cops moved through, spinning their nightsticks down on their lanyards and snapping them back up to meat-slap their palms, the beat cop's visible tic of authority meant to suppress any thoughts of disorder.

• • •

"He's been going more than seven minutes now," Jerry Brasoli said. "Fucking guy loves the sound of his own voice."

Terry Brasoli had cut a hole in the cloth covering one of the windows and had been watching Castro on the stage of the bandshell. "He doesn't move much. A lot of waving the hands around, but he doesn't move the body much."

"Head shot?" Jerry whispered at his shoulder.

"No. He moves his head while he talks, ducks forward sometimes. Body shot." It was what his instructors at sniper school taught him. If you're not sure of a head shot, go for the center mass of the body. Better to knock the target down than to miss completely. You might have a chance to put another round into him while he's on the ground. If he hit him in the chest, the hollow points would blow out his heart and lungs, a sure kill. No reason to fuck around with a head shot. "Let's do it."

Jerry took a remote-control garage-door closer out of his pocket and put it on the stack of fertilizer bags where he could reach it easily. Will took down the black cloth in front of the rifle rest and then pulled the Uzi around from his back so that it hung by its strap across his belly. He pushed the selector lever at the top of the grip behind the trigger group forward from safety to single shot to fully automatic. "Okay."

Terry took a stance with his elbows planted firmly on the top fertilizer bag. Will slipped a small sand bag under the forestock to steady it. Terry put his eye to the scope, and the side column of the bandshell jumped into view. He adjusted left, and the people seated on the stage swung quickly past. He hit the podium, went by, overcorrected and went by the other way, and then found his target and steadied. Castro's face was clear in the scope, his bushy, untrimmed beard and mustache, his heavy-lipped mouth and prominent, fleshy nose. There was a slight time lag between the movement of his lips and the words that came tinnily from the speakers hung near the maintenance shed. Terry adjusted the rifle. Castro was a big man, and the podium rose only to his stomach. The microphones on the podium would not interfere with the shot. The scope slid to Castro's chest. His shirt was open at the throat. Terry settled the crosshairs on the first button below that vee. There was no wind that evening, nothing to affect the bullet's flight. Three hundred yards of open space to a big stationary target; the man was as good as dead.

• • •

Cassidy stood on a park bench and looked over the heads of the people listening to Castro's speech. If Clarkson and the FBI were wrong and there was a three-man team in the city to kill Castro, this is the time for it. He was as exposed as he ever would be. One shot, and then disappear into the crowd. Where would they set up to shoot? His back and sides are protected by the bandshell. The shot would have to come from in front. They would need a little elevation to be above the crowd. He turned his head and something about the colored lights in the trees pricked his memory. The dream—*lights in the trees, the droning voice, fighting with his brother who was not his brother, the woodshed in Mexico.*

Jesus, the shed. The fucking shed. He turned on the bench. *Where was it? There.* It was about fifty yards away. *No. We checked it. It was empty. Orso sealed it, padlocked it and sealed it.*

Orso.

With a sick feeling, he suddenly knew what was going to happen. He jumped down and began to force his way through the crowd toward the shed on the rise of ground under the trees. *Above the crowd. A clear shot of maybe three hundred yards. Movement. There, in the window. There's something in the fucking window.* People in the crowd were intent on Castro, and they did not want to move for Cassidy. Someone elbowed him. A big man in a guayabera shirt shoved him with his belly and called him *cabron.* He stepped on someone's foot and drew a shout and a shove. He was not going to get there in time.

Cassidy pulled his gun, but he could not take the shot. There were people in the line of fire. *Don't let him shoot yet. Give me time. Give me time.*

• • •

Terry Brasoli worked the rifle bolt and chambered a round. He moved his head forward toward the scope until his right eye was just behind the ocular lens. Both eyes open. It was one of the first things his instructor told him. *You don't drive with one eye shut, do you, son?* Terry minutely ticked the rifle left and up until the crosshairs centered on the first button of the target's shirt. He touched the trigger with the first pad of his index finger. He focused on his breath and listened to his heartbeat and shut out all things that did not belong in the moment. All that was left was the target and the trigger, his breathing and his heartbeat. Three breaths, and then at the bottom of the third, between heartbeats, squeeze the trigger and let the shot be a surprise to you and the target. One . . .

• • •

Cassidy stumbled over someone's leg and almost went down. He saved himself by grabbing a man's shoulder. "Sorry," and lurched on. *Too far away. Too far away.*

• • •

Two . . . Terry's finger took up slack on the trigger. In the scope, the target licked his lips. Terry took in the third breath and started to let it out, his heartbeat a steady thump in his ears. Three . . . Now.

The rifle slammed back. The back end of the scope drove into Terry's face, cutting him above the eye. The rifle spat, and the bullet went high into the night sky.

• • •

Cassidy saw a man step up next to the window and drive the rifle barrel back with palm of his hand. The man put his back against the wall between the window and the door. He was tall and broad-shouldered, and his hair was white in the backwash of light from the bulbs in the trees and the streetlamps. Slava.

• • •

"What the fuck?" Jerry grabbed his brother to steady him.

"Go, go!" Terry yelled and swung the rifle toward the door. He could feel the blood flowing down his face and blinked to clear his eye. His heart hammered in his chest.

Will swung the Uzi around and fired a burst through the door and then kicked the door open and went out hard and low. Slava stepped away from the side of the shed and shot him twice. Will staggered and turned and tried to bring the Uzi up. Slava shot him again, and Will tripped over death and went down.

A man with a rifle appeared in the door of the shed and shot Slava. The man came out of the shed working the rifle bolt, and Dylan stepped around the corner of the shed and shot him twice. The man dropped the rifle, touched himself lightly where the bullets had entered his chest, said "Shit," sat down hard, and then tipped over on his side.

Jerry grabbed the garage door remote and pushed the button. The four explosive packages he had left in the trash cans near the perimeter went off one by one. He jerked a .45 automatic from his belt and followed his brother and cousin out the door with a scream of rage and fear.

• • •

Cassidy saw the explosions jerk Dylan around in surprise. The man with the gun burst out of the shed.

"Dylan! Gun! Gun!"

She started to turn. The man brought his gun up.

Cassidy shot him. The bullet took Jerry high in the left shoulder and turned him. Cassidy shot him again. The bullet hit him in the chest and knocked him back a step, but he did not go down. Cassidy shot him again, and he fell, twitched, and lay still.

The crowd ran in panic from the gunfire and explosions.

Dylan knelt next to Slava, who rolled over with a groan and tried to sit up. *That was part of the dream too.* She put a hand on his shoulder and said something to him in Russian, maybe *stay down*, because he lay back breathing hard. Cassidy picked up his gun and pocketed it. "Where is he hit?"

"His leg." She pulled a scarf from around her neck and wrapped it around his thigh and tied it off.

"How did you know they were in the shed?"

"Where else could they have been? I walked by once and saw there was something over the windows, maybe black cloth, and I wondered why the Parks people would go to the trouble. So we watched. When the cloth came off, we saw the gun."

Cassidy heard shouts of men approaching. If they were running toward the danger they were cops. "Dylan, you've got to go. You're cover won't hold. There are people here who know about you from last time."

"What about Slava?" He was jealous of the concern in her voice.

"How's his cover?"

"Good. Iron. Cuban passport."

"Then go. I'll look out for him." She hesitated for a moment, then touched Cassidy on the hand, got up, and walked away into the darkness.

• • •

Ex-Sergeant Lopato had worked his way down toward the front of the stage and was only ten feet from the line of cops guarding it when the four explosions went off. Unlike the people around him, he did not turn to look back. He put his hand on the gun under his shirt and watched what happened in front of him. The cops tensed. Some of them drew their guns. There was no panic onstage. Some of the fatigue-wearing *barbudos* moved in close to Castro and pulled him back from the podium. A man Lopato recognized as the artist Ribera said something to Castro. They argued for a moment, and then Ribera and the other men herded Castro toward the back of the bandshell where there was an exit door. Lopato saw there was no chance of an action here. He would report back to Colonel Fuentes. They would have to do it another way. With luck there was still a good chance of success.

26

No one wanted to be in Deputy Chief Clarkson's office at eleven thirty at night. It was the time of postmortem, a time to assign blame, a time for alliances, a circling of wagons. An assassination attempt on a visiting dignitary, Commie or not. Three dead men. Heads would roll, but if you could place yourself correctly in the drama, the less likely it would be your head. They had already gone over the events from every angle, but to Cassidy they were like the blind men trying to describe the elephant. People had their individual pieces, but when you put them together there was no clear picture of what they were looking at.

Yes, Orso had padlocked the shed door and taped it. Yes, other cops had seen the tape intact minutes before the shootings. How did the three men get into the shed? A mystery.

A detective from the 22nd said he saw a woman with a gun, but no one could corroborate and it was dropped, so maybe Dylan was in the clear.

Slava was identified as one of Castro's security men.

Susdorf and Cherry and the FBI came in for abuse. They were the ones who had first identified the possible assassins, three men in a Lincoln. How did the FBI drop the ball? But Susdorf had spent years in bureaucratic skirmishes, and he was quick to point out that the FBI had been allowed no role in Castro's security setup. They had been granted status as observers only. If the FBI had been in charge, the security cordon would have been very different. Clarkson recognized this line of argument as unproductive for the Department, and cut it off. He left the room to confer with his masters on the top floor and reappeared to dismiss the gathering with the warning that they were not to discuss what had happened until further notice, which meant the official version had not yet been massaged into an acceptable shape.

Castro was to remain under hermetic security until his train left the next day and he became another city's problem.

Cops gathered around to congratulate Cassidy on his shooting. When he got clear, Orso was gone.

• • •

Alice was asleep when he got home, but she woke when he came into the bedroom carrying the glass of bourbon he had craved over the last tedious hour in Clarkson's office. She sat up and turned on the bedside light. "I tried to stay up, but I fell asleep." She pushed the shade down so her bruised face was in shadow. "You look tired."

"I am." He sat on the edge of the bed.

She reached for the glass and took a sip of his whiskey and then a drag off his cigarette. "Bad day?"

"You have no idea."

"Do you want to tell me about it?"

"First tell me how you are."

"Not too bad. I actually worked up the courage this afternoon to go look at myself in the mirror." Her laugh was bitter.

Cassidy leaned forward and kissed her, and the ends of the stitches at the corner of her mouth pricked his lip. "You're going to be fine."

"Hmmm." Not agreement or argument. "Tell me about your day."

They drank the bourbon and smoked the cigarette, and he told her the short version of what had happened in the park. He did not tell her about Dylan.

Later Alice cried out in her sleep. Cassidy put his arm over her, and she woke enough to say "I'm all right. I'm all right," then moved closer to him, held his hand, and went down into sleep again while he lay awake staring at the ceiling and thinking about what had happened that evening and what would happen tomorrow.

27

Cassidy rode the subway south just after rush hour. The *Daily News* gave him the official version of what had happened the night before in Central Park. Anti-Castro Batista supporters had disrupted the rally by setting off small explosive charges in trash cans near the Naumberg Bandshell and firecrackers in the trees nearby. Twelve people, including a member of Mr. Castro's entourage, had been hurt in the ensuing panic. Authorities were pursuing a number of leads. No shootings. No dead men.

The Orso house was on a tree-shaded block in Brooklyn that was a five-minute walk west of Prospect Park. It was in a tidy, blue-collar neighborhood of modest, well-cared-for three- and four-story houses owned by house-proud people who devoted much of their spare time to upkeep and maintenance. The Orso house was in the middle of the block. It was three stories of freshly painted white clapboard fronted by a small concrete yard with a black iron fence. There were pots of geraniums near the stoop, and an American flag on a staff flew from a fixture on one of the burglar grates that protected the ground-floor windows.

Cassidy rang the bell. Moments later he heard the shuffle of feet inside. The door opened a couple of inches against the safety chain. "Detta, it's me."

The door shut, the chain rattled loose, the door was thrown open wide, and Orso's mother, a small gray-haired woman, grabbed Cassidy in a hug. "Michael, Michael, where've you been? How come you don't come see me no more? Come in. Come in." Detta Orso dragged him into the house by one hand. The dim front hall smelled of the polish that made the floor slick enough to skate on. She pulled him down the hall and into the kitchen that smelled of baking, talking all the time. "Look at you. Don't you eat? Tony's upstairs. I heard him moving around up there, but he hasn't come down yet. You want a cup of coffee? I just made it fresh. Here, eat this, *cornetto alla marmellata.*" She pushed a plate with a flaky pastry at him. "I make the jam in it. I make the pastry. You don't get this in a store." She wore a flowered housedress with a yellow apron over it, and her gray hair had been recently permed. She was a small, thin-faced, birdlike woman, and it was hard to see how she could have produced Orso. "I'll call Tony. I'll tell him you're here."

"Why don't I go up?"

"Sure. Go on up. You know where he is. Tell him to come down, I'll make you both breakfast."

Cassidy's feet made little noise on the worn stair runner. He climbed past colored reproductions of Naples harbor scenes to the landing where a blond Jesus raised a hand and looked at him benignly from a gold frame. He went down the corridor to the bedroom at the back of the house, knocked on the door, and pushed it open. Orso sat on a wooden chair at a small round table in the windowed alcove that overlooked the backyard and the newly turned spring earth of Detta's vegetable garden. He wore the trousers from the suit he had worn the night before with the suspenders hanging down, and an undershirt. His feet were bare. The bed held an impression from where he had spent the night on top of the covers. The ashtray on the bedside table was full of butts. Cassidy sat down in the chair across the table. A pack of Chesterfields and Orso's service revolver lay between them. Orso glanced at him when he sat down and then went back to staring out the window. Cassidy took one of the cigarettes and lit it. "How're you doing?"

Orso did not look at him. "Great. Yeah, great. Never better."

"Who approached you? Sanborn?"

Orso looked at him without surprise. "Yeah."

"Is my brother-in-law in on it?"

"No." Orso turned back to the window when he answered.

"Sanborn wouldn't know how to get it done. Who'd he go to?"

"That guy from Tampa, Santo Trafficante. He met him while he was down in Havana. And Meyer Lansky. He made some money for Lansky on some real estate deal."

"Does Sanborn owe those guys money?"

"I don't know. Could be. He talked about how he and Lansky were friends and Lansky had a lock on all casino licenses through Batista. Not much good if Castro took over the casinos."

"How much were you in for?"

"About thirty-five grand. That was Dad's insurance, some savings she had, I took another mortgage on the house." Orso breathed a deep sigh. "I gave it to Sanborn last summer. He was pretty goddamn sure Batista was going to kick Castro's ass."

"But he didn't."

"No. I told them I needed to get the money back. I wanted out. I just wanted to make it right for her." He glanced at Cassidy to see if he was believed, if he was understood. "Sanborn said it wasn't that easy. I'd signed papers saying I'd leave the money in for two years."

"What'd they ask for to let you out?"

"I was to let them know Castro's schedule. I was supposed to make sure the maintenance shed was clear, make sure no one but me checked it. That was all."

"But you knew what they were going to do."

"Sure I knew, but I wasn't going to let myself look at it hard." He looked over at Cassidy. "You ever do that, not look at something hard 'cause you don't want to see what you're going to see?"

"All the time."

"How'd you figure it out?"

"I didn't, really. But you've been fucked up all week, and you've been worrying about money in a way you never did before. Then I went back to the general's apartment to see if Fuentes had been back. The doorman let it drop that there was a cab in front when you came out with Fuentes, but that you didn't want to take it. That's not what you told me, so I thought about that for a while."

Orso reached for a cigarette from the pack on the table. His hand brushed his service pistol. When he drew his hand back, he pulled the gun toward him. "Did they send you to bring me in?"

"No. I came on my own."

"Because I'm not going in, so you might as well take off." His hand covered the gun.

"She gets to clean it up, I guess. The blood all over the wallpaper, the shit and piss on the floor. Gets to look at you and then clean it up."

"Fuck you. I can go to the park." His grip on the gun was white knuckled.

"Sure. Why not? Some mom and her six-year-old can find you." Cassidy pulled another cigarette. "You're not going to do Detta any good dead."

"I'm not going to do her any good in jail."

"Who says you're going to jail?"

"Don't fuck with me, Mike. You can get away with a lot of crap in the Department, but they can't let this slide."

"The shooters are dead. The hoods and Sanborn aren't going to talk about it. I'm the only one who knows."

Orso looked at him with the beginning of hope.

"Have they contacted you since last night?"

"No."

"Castro's leaving on an afternoon train. Do you think they'll try for him again?"

"I don't know. Maybe. They've got a lot at stake."

"That's what I think."

• • •

Cassidy left. Orso sat at the table and pulled the gun close. He stuck his finger in the trigger guard and spun the gun on the tabletop. It stopped with the barrel point at the bed. He spun it again. It pointed at him. He spun it again. It pointed at him again. He lit a cigarette and thought about his choices.

28

Castro's train was scheduled out of Penn Station at four o'clock. The security briefing took place in his suite in the hotel on Seventh Avenue. The living room of the suite was thick with cigar smoke and crowded with bearded men in fatigues and with cops. There had been a few women in cocktail dresses when Cassidy arrived. They popped up like flowers after a rain wherever Castro went in the city. One of them was in the bedroom with Castro, and the others, exotic birds among the khaki and uniformed men, ignored each other and focused on the closed door in nervous anticipation of a summons. Cassidy knocked on the door and announced his presence and with Ribera's help shooed the protesting women out. "Sometimes," Ribera said, "I think he is trying by himself to father an entire new generation of free Cubans."

"Pleasant work if your back holds out," Cassidy said.

"Until recently I did not understand how strong an aphrodisiac power is. They come scratching at his door at night like cats. I'll be happy to get him back to his wife and mistress. Let them sort him out."

"I'll be happy to have him on a train out of here."

"Sometime you will have to tell me what happened last night. We'll get drunk on good Cuban rum and tell each other the truth about things. I will explain to you about art and love, and you will tell me how three assassins were able to hide inside the security perimeter."

"I have no idea. It was lucky I was close by."

"It will take a lot of rum, I suspect. *In vino, veritas.* Was Dylan there?"

"Yes."

"But you made her go."

"Yes." Ribera put an arm around Cassidy's shoulder and hugged him. "You're a good man, Michael. Slava is in Roosevelt Hospital speaking Spanish, very little English, and no Russian."

"Get him out of town before I have to arrest him."

• • •

Assistant Deputy Chief Holloway was in charge of the briefing. The consensus among the street cops was that Chief Clarkson was keeping his distance in case there was another fuckup. Chief Holloway looked like everything you would want in a cop. He was tall, broad-shouldered, flat-bellied, trim in his tailored uniform. He had thick, dark hair with elegant flecks of gray at the temples. He was square-jawed, and cleft-chinned, and when he smiled, his teeth were as even and white as Chiclets. He clapped his hands twice for silence.

"Gentlemen, after last night's incident, the New York City Police Department feels that we should take extraordinary precautions to make sure that Mr. Castro's departure from this city is a safe one. You've all been briefed on the plan, and we think it will minimize any danger to Mr. Castro. Sergeant Olotka, would you stand up, please. A large man rose from a chair in the corner of the room. His beard was not as long and scraggly as Castro's, but he was about the same size as the Cuban leader, and in the fatigues he wore he could easily be mistaken for him from a distance. "Sergeant Olotka has volunteered for duty as a decoy. He and the rest of the Cuban group will leave the front of the hotel on my signal. Uniformed officers will escort them quickly cross Seventh Avenue and into Penn Station. They will proceed directly to Track Nine, where the train is waiting and will enter the second-to-last car, which has been reserved exclusively for them. They will be covered all the way by more than sixty officers. We feel that this public display will draw the attention of anyone out there who means to harm Mr. Castro. At the same time, those people will have no access to their target. Mind you, after last night's incident, we do not believe that there is another threat. This is purely a precautionary measure. At the same time, the real Mr. Castro, with a small escort, will take a separate elevator to the basement of the hotel, access the steam tunnels that connect it with Penn Station, and will proceed to Track Nine unseen. Any questions?"

There were none.

"Thank you, gentlemen. I will see you downstairs in the lobby in ten minutes." Chief Holloway smiled, touched a finger to his forehead in salute, and left the suite.

"We're going to adjust a couple of things about that plan," Cassidy told the assembled crowd after the chief left.

• • •

The tunnels that led from the hotel basement to Penn Station were dim corridors lit by wide-spaced, naked bulbs. The walls were brick and stone, and the floors were concrete. Asbestos-wrapped pipes carried water and steam from generator plants buried fifty feet below the streets. The pipes were old and some of them leaked at the joints, so the floor was wet in places. The air was thick and it smelled of mold and hot stone and the tunnels echoed with mechanical clicks and bangs and the hiss of steam. Every once in a while, Orso could hear the scratching run of rats along the asbestos wrappings.

Orso stood in a deep alcove in one of the tunnels. There was a metal door at his back, and behind it he could hear the whirr and clank of machinery, but he had no idea of what it was or what it did. He stubbed out a cigarette and resisted the temptation to light another. He checked his watch. *Maybe he isn't coming. Maybe this was over. Ahh, fuck, man. How did I get here? Little by little, and then in a rush, the way most bad things happened. Maybe he isn't coming.*

He heard the scrape of shoes on concrete. Moments later Diego Fuentes stopped just down the tunnel from the alcove. He held a stubby, black machine pistol that Orso did not recognize. When he saw that Orso was alone, he let it dangle.

"Detective."

"Colonel."

"Is everything in order?"

"Yes."

"Show me."

Orso led him along the tunnel toward the hotel basement, coldly conscious of a man with a gun at his back. He stopped where two more tunnels came in from the left and the right. "One of us on either side."

Fuentes nodded. "And the stairs you told me about? The exit?"

Orso led him ten feet into the right-hand tunnel. An iron gate blocked metal stairs that rose toward the distant thump and rush of traffic on the street. He pulled on the gate, and it opened. Fuentes stepped in and looked up the stairs. "Where does it end?"

"In the lobby of a building on Thirty-first Street."

"Very good." He stepped aside and let Orso lead them back to the intersection of the tunnels. "How far are we now from the hotel kitchen?"

"About twenty-five yards. I paced it off like you asked."

"So, in the end now, who will it be? How many?"

"Detective Cassidy. Mr. Ribera. Castro."

"Only three? You're sure?"

"Yes."

"Why not more? Why not ten men around him? If it was my operation, I would have many men." He watched Orso closely.

"Cassidy knows you're working for Lansky and Trafficante, and they've got lines into every precinct in town. He's pretty sure there's a leak in the security detail. He's afraid that if he involves a lot of men, it'll get out."

"Yet he told you."

"I'm his partner."

"Yes. Lucky for us." Contempt in his voice.

"Fuck you."

Fuentes ignored him. He looked back down the tunnel toward Penn Station and whistled shrilly. Moments later there were footfalls in the dimness, and then a man dressed in a Con Edison jumpsuit appeared. He carried the twin of Fuentes's machine pistol. He was a big man with wiry black hair hacked short and a broad, flat, high-cheekboned face. "Detective Orso, this is Sergeant Lopato." The big man stopped, nodded to Fuentes, and then turned to inspect Orso carefully as if weighing how much trouble he would offer if it came to that. The machine pistol looked small in his hand.

"I thought you said it was just the two of us," Orso said.

"Yes, well, when a man offers you a plan, it is always better to change it a bit so it becomes your plan, not his. What kind of gun do you carry, Detective?"

"A Smith and Wesson thirty-eight."

"May I see it?"

Orso pulled the gun from the holster on his hip and held it with the barrel slanted toward the floor at Fuentes's feet. Out of the corner of his eye he saw Lopato shift the muzzle of the machine pistol toward him.

"May I look at it?" Fuentes held out his hand.

"Sure." He turned the pistol around and handed it to Fuentes butt first. Fuentes dropped it in his jacket pocket. "If you don't mind. Until this is over."

Orso shrugged. "Colonel Fuentes, we have a deal, remember. Castro, okay, but not my partner."

"It is up to him, not to me. If he is sensible, we will have no problem, but he must be sensible, otherwise . . ." He shrugged away his responsibility in the matter. Now, we will change the plan a little more. The basement is this way, no?" He inclined his head up the tunnel.

"This is a better place. We take them from both sides. There'll be people in the kitchen down there."

"Yes. I know. Still, I think we will go to the basement." Lopato led. Fuentes went last. Orso was sandwiched between them.

• • •

Cassidy used his left hand on the control lever to start the service elevator down from Castro's floor. After a minute, he took his pistol out of its shoulder holster and held it down by his side. The two men behind him felt the tension too, and both of them breathed heavily. One of them had had garlic for lunch.

"This is what happens when an artist becomes involved in politics," Ribera said. "Instead of studying the beauty of a nude model in his studio, he is riding down in an elevator that smells of garbage to meet a man with a gun."

"Twenty-two yards from the elevator to the tunnel intersection. Orso'll be in the left-hand tunnel, Fuentes in the right," Cassidy reminded him.

"Tell me again why we are doing this."

"You said that Colonel Fuentes was dangerous. If he missed here, he'll try again in Boston. If he missed there, he'll try again in Canada. This way we know where and when he's coming."

"I get no comfort in knowing this."

"Orso will have him covered, but we need him to make the attempt, otherwise he walks away."

"Yes, you told me all this. So why is it that I want to throw up?"

"Olotka, are you okay?"

"Yeah, Mike, I'm good." The big bearded detective laughed. "First time I ever volunteered to get shot at."

"Almost there."

• • •

Orso could hear the elevator grinding down. They were in a wide, short hallway outside the kitchens. Three serving carts loaded with dirty room service dishes were against one wall. He could see into the kitchen through the glass panels in the big double doors. Men in white moved past the windows carrying pots or roasting pans or dishes. A man walked by bent under the half side of beef on his shoulder, another followed with a metal tray of raw chickens. They moved quickly, concentrating on their tasks, and no one looked back at him through the windows.

The elevator whined down the shaft.

Fuentes and Lopato stood on either side of the elevator doors, Fuentes on the left, Lopato on the right. Their machine pistols were centered on the doors. Orso knew they would shoot as the doors opened and the passengers were still trapped in the car. Fuentes ignored Orso, but Lopato watched him.

• • •

"Two more floors," Cassidy said. "When the doors open, we go out fast. Turn right, and there's a door, then steps down to the steam tunnels. I go first, Olotka next, Ribera last. The steam tunnel is badly lighted, and I think he'll let us close before he makes a move, but if he sees it's not Castro, he'll go for Orso and try for the stairs, so keep your head down, Olotka, and stay close behind me. He's expecting Castro. He'll see Castro."

• • •

Fuentes hissed at Lopato and jerked his head toward the elevator. The elevator indicator showed the car a floor above them. Lopato set himself in a shooter's stance, feet at shoulder width, knees bent, left hand to guard against the gun barrel's need to rise as it fired.

Orso wondered that they did not hear his heart pound, that they weren't warned by the noise. Tension squeezed him breathless. The elevator was seconds away from arriving. When the doors opened, the men in the elevator would be slaughtered. And it was on him, all on him.

Orso shook a cigarette loose and put the pack back in his pocket. He pulled out a book of matches and dropped it. "Shit." Lopato threw a look his way as he bent to pick it up, saw what he was doing and turned back to the danger of the elevator.

The elevator arrived. Whoever was running it missed the landing, and they could hear it maneuver up and then down again.

Fuentes and Lopato snicked off their safeties.

Orso pulled his hideout gun from its ankle holster.

The elevator came to rest.

Orso stepped forward and shot Lopato in the head. The hideout gun was a little Browning .25 automatic, and it made a high, flat crack like someone snapping a shingle. He turned and fired two shots at Fuentes as fast as he could pull the trigger. The first hit him in the cheek and blew a spray of blood against the wall. The second hit him in the chest. A .25 has little stopping power. It rocked Fuentes, but did not put him down. Orso fired again and missed. Fuentes turned and triggered his machine pistol. Three bullets hit Orso. They smashed him back against one of the service carts and he went down in a wreckage of dirty dishes and silverware.

The elevator doors started to open. Fuentes swung the machine pistol toward them. Cassidy, warned by the gunfire, filled the gap between the doors, and as the gun tracked toward him, he shot Fuentes twice in the chest. In reflex Fuentes's finger tightened on the trigger, and bullets stitched up the wall next to the elevator and across the ceiling. Cassidy shot him again.

The bullet Orso had fired into Lopato's head had not penetrated his thick skull. It had hit the bone and then torn a groove under the skin around to his forehead where it exited over his right eye. He pawed at his face, trying to clear the blood that poured into his eyes so he could see to shoot. Cassidy stepped out of the elevator and shot him, and Ribera and Olotka cleared on either side of him and shot Lopato again and again until he slammed against the wall and slid to the floor.

The room stank of cordite, and the blast of shots made Cassidy's ears ring. As he went toward Orso, he was vaguely aware of the faces that crowded the glass panels of the kitchen doors. "Tony, Jesus, Tony." Orso made a gesture with one hand to show that he was all right. Then he slipped away into darkness.

29

"Is he going to be all right?" Alice asked.

"They don't know. He's still unconscious. They got the bullets out, which they say is a good thing, but they don't know."

Raindrops pecked at the bedroom windows and slithered down the glass. The lights across the river in New Jersey were muted to a glow. A foghorn moaned somewhere as a ship slid down the tide toward the open sea. Cassidy could feel Alice's warmth down the length of his body. He took the cigarette back from her, took the last drag, and stubbed it out in the ashtray on the bedside table. He offered her a sip of his bourbon.

"No, thanks. Not now. Maybe later."

He was desperately tired, but he could not sleep, and the bourbon did nothing to blunt the jaggedness inside him that kept him awake. The liquor and the darkness let him talk, and the story came out slowly, and to him it sounded like something that had happened to someone else.

The sudden flood of cops into the basement of the hotel, and then the cops pushed aside as irrelevant by the emergency medical crews who had been on standby to care for Castro in case someone managed to get a bullet into him. They were quick and efficient with Orso, but their faces were grave as they carried him to the elevator on a stretcher. The dead, broken bodies of Fuentes and Lopato were photographed, mapped, sketched, and then carried away. The bullet holes in the walls and ceiling, and the brass shell casings that littered the floor were marked with red circles and photographed.

Deputy Chief Clarkson and Assistant Deputy Chief Holloway arrived together followed by two assistants, Headquarters detectives, as lean and nervy as whippets. One of them loped off to find a private room while the two chiefs surveyed the wreckage. The assistant came back and said something to Clarkson, who nodded in approval and then barked, "Cassidy, Olotka, Ribera, you're with us."

"Ribera went to talk to Castro before his train leaves," Cassidy said.

"Parker, go find him. Bring him back." The detective nodded and left in a hurry. The other detective led them through the kitchen where the chef was ringing his hands and trying to explain to cops questioning his staff about the disaster that was imminent if he could not have his people back to prepping for the evening meals. Dinner would be ruined. The hotel guests would be disappointed. There would be hell to pay.

The detective led them into the kitchen manager's office and then stood with his back to the door as if barring escape.

Deputy Chief Clarkson started with, "Who the hell came up with this fucked-up plan? Who the hell let you think you were in charge of this security detail?" And it went downhill from there. The very professional reaming included threats of dismissal from the Department, loss of pension, and possible prosecution.

Then Ribera arrived to hear the tail end of it. He read the anger in the room. "Ah, Chief Clarkson, I am so glad to find you. I have a message from Fidel." He wrapped the startled officer in a hug. Clarkson held himself stiff with his hands at his sides. Ribera kissed him on both cheeks and then stepped back. "He insisted. He is awed by the courage and sacrifice of the officers of the New York City Police Department, and intends to publicly thank the Department and to award medals for bravery to all the officers who took part in the operation that saved him from assassination. I am to tell you that he is impressed that the police department leadership has trained its men to abandon set plans and take the initiative when necessary." Cassidy could see that he was riffing, but both Clarkson and Holloway were absorbing Ribera's bullshit.

One of the detective assistants was sent to find a stenographer, who took down Ribera's description of the events. Clarkson warned Cassidy of punishments available and imminent, but Cassidy suspected he had weighed Castro's public praise against his private need to punish, and his heart was not in the threats.

There was rain in the evening sky when they left the hotel, but it had not yet begun to fall. "Let me buy you a drink," Ribera said.

"I'm going up to the hospital."

"Of course." Ribera nodded in understanding. "Michael, when I was seventeen, my brother, Ricardo, and I, and our cousin Manuel attacked a small police outpost in a little town east of Havana with hunting rifles we had stolen from our fathers. Who knows what we were thinking? Revolution. Anarchy. Romance. Something. The confused brains of teenage boys said this was what we should do. So, bang, bang, bang. One policeman shot in the leg, and then the others replied with a machine gun. We ran. One bullet, one bullet out of the hundreds they fired, clipped my brother's hand and took off three fingers. Blood, fear, screaming. I have never been so scared until we rode down in the elevator today, and we heard the shots, so we knew someone was waiting. You could have taken the car back up, but I watched you. You did not even change expression. The doors opened, and you went out. You are a brave man and a good man. Cuba is in your debt, and I am proud to be your friend."

"I'm proud to be yours." They hugged, and people passing on the sidewalk looked at them curiously. Cassidy raised his hand for a taxi, and one pulled to the curb. "Are you going to Boston to rejoin Castro?"

"No. I'll take care of some things here, tell my version of the glorious heroism of the New York City Police Department to the newspapers, and then, in a day or two, I will go back to Cuba, and back into my studio, and to hell with politics."

"Can I drop you anywhere?"

"No. I'm going to walk, and stop for a drink, and walk, and stop for a drink. And so on. Take care, Michael. We will see each other soon."

• • •

The uniformed cop outside Orso's hospital door recognized Cassidy. He nodded toward the room. "He's still out, but the doc's in there. Man, you've been busy, last night and today. I've been on the Force nineteen years. I've drawn my gun three times and never fired it."

"That's the way it should be."

"Yeah? I don't know. Seems to me there are a lot of scumbags out there could use a little instant justice."

The door opened, and the doctor came out followed by a nurse. The doctor was a tall, thin man with a kind face and the long, strong hands of a pianist. "How is he, Doctor?"

"And you are?" A raised eyebrow, and a smile to disarm the question.

"Michael Cassidy. I'm Tony Orso's partner."

"Ah, family, then. Would you like to take a look in? He's unconscious, but if you want to see . . ."

Cassidy stepped inside the room. Orso lay on his back. His face was pale and slack. His hair, normally slicked, stood out randomly from his head. Tubes ran from IV stands into his arms. Wires ran from his chest to monitors. His chest rose and fell in slow, shallow breaths. He was a man balanced at the edge of the drop.

The doctor touched Cassidy on the shoulder, and they went back into the corridor.

"I'm Dr. Trager, by the way. Do you mind if we walk while we talk?" They set off down the corridor. "He was hit three times. We had a bit of trouble with the bullet in his shoulder. It lodged against the brachial plexus. This is a network of nerves that comes from the spine. They pass through the armpit, and run down the arm. I'm a little worried that we're going to see some nerve damage. The major concern would be damage to the median nerve, because it branches down into the hand and serves the thumb, index, and middle fingers. He's right-handed, isn't he?"

"Yes."

"So that might be a problem, but of course the biggest concern we face is that his body has received a massive insult, and there is no real way to predict how it will react. Some people absorb this kind of punishment and two days later they announce they want to go dancing. Some people take a minor hit, and just like that they're gone. Were you in the war, Detective Cassidy?"

"Yes." They stopped in front of double doors marked AUTHORIZED PERSONNEL ONLY.

"Then you've seen that. You know what I'm talking about. But Orso seems a vigorous man, so perhaps it rests with how much he wants to live. You know him. Does he want to live?"

Cassidy thought about Orso sitting at the table in his bedroom, his hand on the gun. "I don't know. I hope so. When will you know more?"

"The next twenty-four hours should tell. I'll leave your name with the nurses as family so you can call in. I have to go. I'm due in surgery." He smiled encouragement. His handshake was firm and brief. The doors flapped behind him.

Cassidy patted his pockets for cigarettes and found he had none. He set out to look for a cigarette machine and was told by a janitor mopping the floor at the open door to a ladies room that there was one in the waiting room at the end of the corridor.

Dylan stood next to it feeding quarters into the machine.

• • •

They sat at a table in a corner of the basement cafeteria and drank weak coffee and smoked, and he told her what happened in the basement of the hotel across from Penn Station. When he finished she reached across the table to squeeze his hand. "You saved Castro's life."

"Did I? I don't think Fuentes would have tried when Castro was surrounded by cops. We could have gotten him to the train without incident and sent him off to Boston. But I wanted Fuentes. I used Castro like bait to bring him in. I wanted him for what he did to you. I wanted him for killing that shit Echevarria who I despised, but I despised how Fuentes killed him even more. I may have gotten my partner killed. I almost got another good cop and Ribera killed. I never stopped to think that Fuentes would not come alone, that he would have Lopato at hand somewhere. I never stopped to think that he would have his own ideas about how things would happen. You know why I didn't think about it? Because I didn't want to look at all the reasons I shouldn't do what I wanted to do."

Dylan pushed her half-full coffee cup away. "God, that stuff is foul. Why can't they make good coffee in America?" She took a cigarette from the pack on the table and lit it. "You're right. You made some stupid choices."

"Now I feel better."

"But Castro's alive, and Fuentes is dead, and if he was still alive, he would have gone to Boston, and if he missed there, he would have gone to Canada and tried again. Maybe someone some day will get Fidel, but it won't be that son of a bitch. So thank you. And I'm sorry about Orso, but he's not dead, and maybe he'll be okay. There's no way to go back and undo what you did. Leave it. Move on."

Dylan was at the hospital, because Slava was on the floor below Orso's recovering from his gunshot wound. "The bullet went in and out. It didn't hit bone. They'll let him go in a couple of days. Carlos will get him on a plane." She read something in his face. "What?"

"We have some eyewitness descriptions of the man who was with General Garza y Mendoza the afternoon he was killed. Tall, strong, fit, very pale hair. They all remarked on the hair."

Dylan became still, and tried to show him nothing, but her eyes were worried. "What are you going to do?"

"Get him out of here as fast as you can. Some other cop might put two and two together."

"Thank you." She took his hand. "I know you're doing it for me, Michael."

"Yeah, well, if I'm going to fuck up, I might as well get it all done at once." He took her cigarette and took a drag and then gave it back to her. "I want to see you again."

"I don't think that's a good idea."

"What are you going to do now?"

"I told him I'd bring him some cigarettes before I left the hospital. He must be wondering where I am."

It was not what he meant by the question. He meant, where would she go, what would she do next, where would he find her if he looked for her? But her answer showed how empty his hopes were.

They stood up from the table together. They knew they had to go, and neither wanted to be the first. Cassidy put out his hand. Dylan took it and used it to pull them together. A good-bye kiss that went on longer than good-bye. Dylan broke it, turned, and walked away quickly.

So that was that.

• • •

"She loves you, you know," Alice said in the darkness of the bedroom.

"I don't think so."

"Trust me. She does."

"Is that one of those secrets women know and men don't?"

"Yes."

"She married someone else."

"Women marry men for all kinds of reasons. Love isn't always one of them."

"She'll be in Cuba in a few days, and then who knows where."

"That's just geography." She rolled closer and put a leg over him. "We're going to stop talking about your other women now, okay?"

"Okay."

" 'Cause talking to your guy about other women who love him does not make a girl feel all sexy and interested, so I'm going to sleep, and when I wake up, I'm going to have a whole new attitude about that." She rose on one elbow and kissed him on the corner of his mouth, and then turned over and was asleep in minutes.

The dream woke him at dawn.

Dream mosaic—fragments and bits, but never the whole picture. Orso and gunfire, and a garden somewhere with someone he could not identify asking if he wanted lime with his drink. But he wasn't drinking. A dog, and the boy in a Buckley School hat laughing and pointing at someone. At who? At Cassidy sitting on a kitchen chair, and then the elevator doors started to open, and a woman turned around and pointed a gun at him. Cassidy lurched up out of sleep with his heart pounding.

Alice slept deeply beside him. He got up and went into the living room. The dream still held him, and his heart would not slow. Who was the woman with the gun? He stood at the windows and looked out through the gray light of dawn over the tops of the piers to the river beyond, but he did not see it, because the dream fragments were fading and he concentrated on trying to hold on to them.

Lime. There was something he knew about lime. What was it? Don't think about it. Maybe it will come.

He went into the kitchen and filled the coffeepot with water, put grounds in the basket, and set it on the stove to perk while he took a shower.

How does the brain work? Hot water to relax it, coffee to stimulate it, and the memory of being on his sister's terrace bubbled up unbidden. The gardener, Fred, saying something about putting lime in one of the planters to correct the balance in the soil.

Jesus Christ, it's been right in front of you all the time, and you couldn't see it. Maybe you're getting too stupid to do this job.

He knew how they had moved Casey Allen on his chair to the park where Jane Hopkins would find him.

30

The rain was gone by the time Cassidy left the apartment. The rain had washed the city, leaving crystal air the traffic had not yet dirtied. The sun was still low down in the stone canyons to the east, but it promised the first really hot day of spring.

He spent an hour in the squad room on the phone and then went out into the warming day and walked north to 72nd Street and west to Central Park. He did not see Jane Hopkins and her red setter, and it was too late for Seth Rutherfurd and his dog, Tinker. He would be in school. No sign remained of murdered Casey Allen sitting on his chair.

Cassidy walked out onto Bethesda Terrace. The trees in the park were now thick with new green leaves. When he turned, he could see the maintenance shed where the gunmen had waited to kill Castro. The only sign of that explosive night was the length of yellow police tape hanging from the door. Time helped nature cover all scars.

He turned away and walked down the wide stairs and along one of the paths to the Conservatory Water, the shallow concrete-rimmed pond where people sailed model boats. The children who used it most were in school, and the few people there were serious enthusiasts who spent their days as they wished. He watched an elderly man in a well-cut coffee-colored linen suit use a bamboo pole to turn his six-foot-long model of an America's Cup defender J-boat to catch the wind. It was an exquisite replica, so beautifully made to scale that you expected to see a tiny crew working the deck. The sails filled and the boat heeled and slipped across the pond as if friction had been abolished. At the other side of the pond, a man who could have been the first man's twin turned the boat with his bamboo pole and sent it back. A puff of wind tightened the sails, and it came across fast. It was the largest boat on the pond, and if it encountered another boat it pushed it aside, *force majeure.* When the J-boat reached the shore, the elderly man beckoned and a man in a chauffeur's uniform stepped forward and lifted it from the water. It was too heavy to hold away from him, and the front of his uniform was quickly wet. The elderly man walked away and the chauffeur followed carrying the boat. When they reached the other side of the pond, the man's twin fell in step and they strolled toward Fifth Avenue talking quietly with the chauffeur trailing.

Barney Rose and Kevin Rotella were planting a tree near the north end of the pond. The tree was nearly six feet tall, and its root ball was bound in burlap. It lay on the floor of the army green Parks Department van parked on the sidewalk six feet from the hole they had dug for the tree. Their pickaxe and shovels leaned against the end of the bench where the two men took a cigarette break.

"Can I get a light?" Cassidy asked.

"Sure," Rose said and handed him his cigarette. Cassidy lit his off the burning coal and handed it back. "Thanks. How are you guys doing?"

"Yeah. Fine. Hey, wait a minute. I know you." Rotella was the smarter of the two. "You're that cop, right?"

"Right."

"What's up? They got you patrolling the park these days?" Rotella offered him a wiseass grin.

"Actually, I was looking for you two." He caught the worried look that passed between them. "I wanted to ask you a question about fertilizer." They both relaxed.

"Yeah, sure," Rotella said. "What do you want to know?"

"Do you use lime to balance soil?"

"Yeah. I mean if you've got too much acid in your soil, you add lime, otherwise you might add gypsum if you've got, like, too much clay or maybe too much salt."

"How does lime come, in sacks?"

"Yeah. Twenty-five pounds. Fifty pounds."

"Do you use much?"

"All the time, right, Barney?"

"Yeah. High acidity in the soil all over the park." They both had settled back in the bench, lulled by the innocence of the questions, happy to show their knowledge.

"Is it tough on the hands? Do you have to wear gloves, or what?"

"Yeah, gloves. Otherwise you can burn your skin."

"Can I see? I might as well buy what the experts use."

"Sure." Rose found his gloves on the bench and tossed them to Cassidy.

Cassidy examined them. "These look pretty worn. Do they last?"

"I've had those, I don't know, three months? That's pretty good." Whatever had worried them had slipped away.

"What about you," Cassidy said to Rotella. "Do you use the same kind?"

"No. I like these." He tossed his to Cassidy.

"Do these last?"

"Yeah. Three or four months."

"So you guys were wearing these gloves when you carried Casey Allen on the chair out of the van and put him down where she told you to." A quick "what the fuck" look passed between them. "You probably should have thrown them away, because we're going to find that the fibers and lime from these gloves are going to match the fibers and lime on the bottom of the chair you took out of his workshop." Rotella started to make a turn toward the pickaxe next to him. Cassidy stepped back and opened his jacket so they could see the holstered pistol. "Don't. Don't do anything stupider than you've already done. Which one of you shot him?"

"We didn't shoot him." Rose's panic was too close to the surface to hold in.

"Shut up, Barney," Rotella said.

"You can still hang for it."

"We didn't do it. She did it."

"Shut up."

"Kevin, it took fifteen minutes on the phone to find out that Theresa Allen's maiden name was Rotella and that she has a brother working for the Parks Department. A neighbor saw you two taking away the old sofa from Theresa's, piss and blood all over it, I guess, and bringing in the new one. She's going to be able to identify you and the van. When the science guys go over the van, they're going to find blood, and it's going to match Casey's. Do yourselves some good. Talk to me."

• • •

Cassidy picked up a car from the car pool and drove it out to Queens. He parked it in front of Theresa Allen's house, walked up the stoop, and rang the doorbell. After a while, the peephole darkened as someone looked out, and then the locks rattled, and Theresa Allen opened the door and looked out at him. She was dressed for widowhood, a long black skirt, a black blouse, a black velvet ribbon holding back her hair.

She was the woman in his dream who stood outside the opening elevator doors holding a gun. Now, her right hand was hidden behind the door. His hand was a long way from his gun under his arm. What would she do if he reached for it? "Mrs. Allen, may I come in?"

In answer she turned away and walked to the living room, leaving him to come or go as he pleased and to shut the door. Her hands were empty.

The fallibility of dreams.

When he entered the living room, she was standing near the sofa, hip cocked, smoking a cigarette, her left arm across her stomach, her right elbow resting on it, arm up, cigarette near her mouth. "Where's your partner?"

"He's in the hospital."

"What happened?"

"Someone shot him. There's a lot of that going around right now."

"I'm sorry."

"Uh-huh."

"Have you found out anything about Casey?"

"Yes, quite a bit. I just had a long conversation with Kevin and Barney."

"What do you mean?" She tried to throw it away, but her sudden stillness betrayed her.

"Theresa, you don't have a play here. You got into a fight with your husband over Jane Hopkins. You shot him while he was sitting on the sofa. Then you called your idiot brother and his dim friend to come help you. If you'd just had them dig a deep hole for him, you might have gotten away with it. Probably not, but who knows? But you had to let her know."

"I don't know what you're talking about."

"Sure you do. Do you think Kevin and Barney want to take the fall with you? They told me everything. What bothered me was why no one saw him being delivered to the park. People saw the Parks truck, but they didn't think anything of it, because it was always around. It was invisible."

She did not flinch. "He was mine. She had no right. He knew what would happen if he cheated. I warned him. He knew." As if that made it right.

"Sure."

"What happens now?" No anger, no defiance, no resignation, no tears. Sometimes an arrest was like that. The crime was too heavy to carry, and arrest was a relief.

"You'll have to come into the city with me."

"Can I get my purse?"

"Go ahead."

She stubbed her cigarette out in an ashtray on the coffee table and opened the sliding doors between the living room and the small dining room enough to slip between them. Cassidy could see her purse on the dining room table. She turned back toward him, and she approached the doors again, he could see only part of her body.

The dream. The elevator doors sliding apart. The woman in black with the gun. Not the elevator doors—these doors.

He heard the thump as she dropped the purse, and she came out of the dining room with a small silver automatic out in front of her. He was already moving when she pulled the trigger, and the first shot smacked into the wall over the sofa. The second broke a window. He chopped her wrist hard, and she dropped the gun and went at him with fingernails, knees, and feet, screaming. He tried to fend her off, but she was wild, and strong with rage. A fingernail ripped a gouge down the side of his neck. She jerked free, pushed him off balance, and darted away through the dining room toward the kitchen. He went after her, unnerved that she might have another gun there.

He found her scrabbling at a drawer in a counter, and she turned with a large carving knife and came hard at him. Her lips were scraped back from her teeth in a snarl, her eyes were mad, and she howled while she slashed at him. He barely eluded the first thrust as he backed away in the small kitchen. He threw a chair in her path. She kicked it aside and came on, thrusting and slashing. He grabbed a glass from the counter and threw it at her, and she let it bounce off her chest. She stabbed at him again, and for a moment she was off balance. He knocked her knife hand aside and punched her in the side, and she gasped in pain and surprise and sat down on the floor. The knife fell out of her hand, and he kicked it aside. Her legs splayed, she tipped forward from the waist, trying to find breath, her black hair fell over her face, and she began to wail.

• • •

"Nice work," Lieutenant Tanner said.

"Thanks," Cassidy said.

"Did you put some iodine on those scratches?"

"Yes."

"Buy you a drink?" He gestured with his head toward his office.

"Sure." Cassidy got up from his desk where he was writing the arrest report and went into Tanner's office. Tanner closed the door and took a bottle and two glasses from the bottom drawer of his desk, poured the drinks, and pushed one of the glasses to Cassidy.

"To crime," Tanner said, and they both drank. "God, that's good." Tanner lit the stump of a cigar that was waiting in his ashtray.

Cassidy lit a cigarette and blew smoke at the ceiling and took another sip of the whiskey.

"So what the hell was she thinking, leaving him out there in the park? It was like a warning, right? Don't fuck him again. Seems to me when she shot him she took care of that part of the equation. Jesus, broads." Tanner got the bottle out and poured more into their glasses. "The hospital called. Orso woke up for a while. It's still touch and go, but they say it's a good sign."

"Good. I'll go on over after I finish my report."

"What the fuck were you thinking, Mike, a plan like that?"

"It seemed smart at the time."

"How many people have we put in jail had the same thought? And going out there to Queens to arrest a murderer without backup. Are you all right, Mike?"

"I'm fine."

"Are you sure? We talked about this before. You've got to pull yourself together."

"I'm all right, Boss."

"Watch yourself, okay? You made enemies with Chief Clarkson and Chief Holloway with that stuff at the hotel. They turned it around so they looked good, but they didn't like it. They're looking to get you, so try not to be too big an asshole for the next few months."

"I'll do my best."

"Thank you. Here's an order. Take the rest of the week off. Get out of here. Go see Orso. Get drunk. Get laid. Do something productive."

• • •

Cassidy did not like hospitals, did not like how they smelled of medicine and plastic and floor polish, did not like the quiet desperation and hushed voices of people worried about their loved ones, and the cool distance of the hospital staff who had seen it all time and again, sickness and recovery, sickness and death, and had grown armor against it that allowed them to work efficiently, with compassion, if that was their nature, and brusquely if it was not. He recovered and was discharged? Mark the chart, change the bed, clean the room. He died? Mark the chart, change the bed, clean the room.

Detta Orso was in the waiting room at the end of Orso's corridor. She sat in a chair with light from the window, knitting something that was still without shape. Her fingers and the needles moved as if on their own while she looked out the window without seeing, her face drawn and worried.

"Detta," Cassidy said.

"Michael, Michael." She put the knitting down carefully on the chair next to hers and got up and went to him and hugged him. The top of her head did not come to his chin. "He's going to be all right. I just know it. They've got a chapel downstairs, and I went down and prayed for him. God's going to take care of him."

"Did you see the doctor?" Cassidy had more faith in him.

"Yes. What a nice young man. He seems very young to be a doctor. Do you think he's young? Do you think an older man should see Tony?"

"Detta, I saw him yesterday. I liked him. I think he's a good doctor. He's not too young. He's just the right age."

"Okay. You think so. Maybe you're right. You know better."

"Was Tony awake?"

"For a little while. Then he went back to sleep. You go see him, Michael. He'd like to see you. He loves you."

"I'll go down and then I'll come back and find you."

A nurse left the room as he arrived. "Is he awake?"

"He just woke up. Go ahead in, but don't stay long. He's very weak. Just a few minutes."

"Yes, ma'am."

Orso's eyes were closed. He looked pale and shrunken. Someone, probably Detta, had combed his hair. There was a vase of spring flowers on the windowsill. The machines to which he was attached blinked and whirred. Sickrooms made Cassidy feel helpless and uneasy. Orso did not move, and Cassidy thought of retreating and recognized it as cowardice. He sat in the plastic armchair next to the bed and watched the slow, shallow rise of his partner's chest.

Orso opened his eyes. "Hey." He flapped a hand in welcome. "Light a cigarette, will you? They won't let me smoke. I just want to smell it." His voice was as light and dry as dust.

"How do you feel?" Cassidy took a pack of Luckys from his jacket and lit one.

"I feel like shit. I mean, I don't hurt 'cause they got me juiced with drugs, but I feel, I don't know, hollow, or something." He closed his eyes for a moment. "Hey, Mike, what happened? I hit that fucker twice, but he didn't go down, and when that gun started to turn, I knew I was done. I've got to dump that twenty-five, get something that will hurt a guy."

"I killed him. You saved us, Tony, taking the shots, so we knew they were there. If we hadn't known and opened the door, we would have been dead. I almost got us killed, but you saved us."

"Yeah. Some hero I am." He stopped talking and closed his eyes for a moment to gather strength. "Ma was here."

"She's down at the end of the hall in the waiting room."

"Make her go home when you leave, otherwise she'll sit there all night."

"I will."

"What am I going to tell her about the money? You know, I thought, well if I'm dead, I don't have to tell her anything. I don't have to see her face. I don't have to know."

"Not so good for her, though, is it?"

"At least she'd have the Department insurance. Ten thousand. It's not much, but it's something. Make her go home, Mike." Orso turned his face away.

He took Detta downstairs and waved a Yellow Cab up from the rank that waited near the entrance.

"It's all the way to Brooklyn, Michael. It's too dear," she protested. "I can take the subway."

"Detta, let me do this for you. I told Tony I would." He gave the cabbie a ten and the address and watched while the cab pulled out into traffic and turned downtown.

He wondered whether Orso could will himself to death like an animal in a trap.

31

They went to dinner at Fiorello's. It was the place to go in the Village that year if you wanted the romance of candles, white tablecloths, private booths, discreet waiters, murmured conversations, delicious food, good wine. Alice's choice, Alice's treat, over Cassidy's protest that women did not pay for dinner. She took the advice of the sommelier, who beamed when she ordered a twelve-year-old bottle of Vino Nobile di Montepulciano.

She savored everything put in front of her and ate with a delight in every taste and texture. Sensing his mood, she worked hard to make him laugh with stories of women smuggling men into the forbidden upper floors of the Barbizon, and of the peculiar habits of senators and congressmen she had met while working in Washington, including one from Hershey, Pennsylvania, who begged to be allowed to strip her naked and cover her with chocolate. She slipped off her shoe and slid her stockinged foot up under his cuff. When the waiter stopped by to ask if everything was to their satisfaction, she moved it up and pressed her toes against his balls just as he was saying, "Yes, thank you. Everything's great." They drank champagne with dessert and grappa with their coffee. They necked in the taxi going home, and in their eagerness, left most of their clothing on the floor between the front door and the bedroom.

She teased him and then stopped just when it became unbearable, and let him in. After the first collision, they slowed to enjoy each other, each having learned what the other liked and, by the end, he was weightless, adrift, freed of the anger and guilt that had been corroding him.

"You like me, don't you, Michael." Her leg was over his and her head was against his shoulder. He could see the shape of her face from the glow of the cigarette in her mouth. She was stating a fact, not fishing for a compliment.

"I do. I like you a lot." So easy when it was the truth.

"Good. I like you too." She turned enough to kiss his ear. "I always knew it would work if you just gave me the chance. From the first time I saw you on the plane to Cuba when you were handcuffed to that guy. Removing the mattress tag." She laughed at the memory. "Kidder. That's what I called you."

"I remember." He took the cigarette for a drag and then handed it back.

"It's not really enough, is it?"

"What's not enough?" He was adrift on the edge of sleep.

"To like someone. You need more, 'cause after a while maybe he doesn't like you as much, or you don't like him as much. It's not like love. Love lasts."

"Does it?" This was beginning to sound like good-bye. He sat up and lit his own cigarette and saw her face for a moment in the flare of the match. She was smiling, so whatever was coming would not be with tears.

"I lied to you."

"About what?"

"About the money."

"What money?"

"The money. The money from Havana. The money they thought I stole. I did. I stole it. I lied to you about it."

"You're kidding."

Alice laughed. "Stay there." She turned on the bedside light and got up, hunkered down, and pulled a suitcase from under the bed. It was heavy, but she heaved it up on the bed, clicked open the latches, and threw back the lid. The suitcase was full of packets of money banded with paper strips or rubber bands.

Cassidy laughed. "Jesus Christ. Under the bed? You hid it under the bed?"

"I didn't know where else to put it."

He picked up a couple of packets and flipped them in the air. "This is goddamn wonderful."

"You're not angry?"

"No." How could he be angry? A big, beautiful, naked woman and five hundred thousand dollars on his bed.

"It was New Year's Eve, remember? Out with the old. In with the new.

I took it, because I knew I couldn't go on like I've been going. I saw a play once in Washington where the lady says 'I depend on the kindness of strangers,' or something like that. Well, maybe it wasn't kindness with me. They got what they wanted, but I began to see I wasn't getting what I wanted. So I figured if no one was going to give it to me, I was going to have to take it. They took the money from the suckers, and I took it from them."

"You took a hell of a chance."

"It was my chance to change my life. I had to take it. Then when those three men came here and began beating me, I was going to give it to them. They were hurting me, and I thought if I give it to them they'll stop. It's just money. Give it to them. But the young one liked what he was doing. Do you remember him? You called him the bagman when we were at the White Horse."

Jimmy Greef. He remembered Jimmy Greef.

"He liked it." She winced at the memory. "The other two, it was like it was their job and they had to do it, but he was smiling all the time that he was doing things to me, and he laughed, and so I started thinking, fuck you. I'm not giving it to you. It's my money. If you hurt me and I don't give it to you, I've earned it."

Cassidy got up and went to her and hugged. "You're great. You're fucking wonderful, and you deserve every penny."

"Yeah? Really?"

"Really."

She grinned at him. "Hey, have you ever gotten laid on half a million bucks?"

He pretended to think about it. "You know what? I don't think I have."

With a laugh she upended the suitcase, and money flew all over the bed.

In the morning they drank coffee standing together at the counter that divided the kitchen from the living room. She stood with her hip pressed against his as if unwilling to break contact. She wore a suit he had never seen before. It was beautifully tailored to subtly display her body without being obvious, dark green to flatter her complexion and her blond hair. She wore high heels that made her as tall as he was, an impressive package. Two big suitcases stood near the front door.

"You look like half a million bucks."

She laughed. "It's hard to believe that tomorrow morning at this time I'll be in Paris, France. Paris. It's supposed to be the most romantic city in the world. Do you think the French will like me?"

"The French will love you. A couple of weeks from now, you'll probably own the Eiffel Tower." She had confessed that she had no idea what she would do in Paris, but she wanted to go. She was a woman who had made her way by herself in a harsh world that did not treat women kindly, but she was beautiful, rich, and tough. He knew she would be fine.

"I'm kind of scared, and I'm kind of excited. But I'm going to miss you, Michael. You've been the best."

"I'm going to miss you too." Cassidy called a town car to take her out to Idlewild. He carried the suitcases downstairs when the car came. The driver turned away discreetly while they kissed. She clung to him for a moment, took a deep breath, showed him a smile and tears, got in the car, and left with one last hand wave out the window.

32

Friday night. Jimmy Greef leaned against the bar at Chumley's and drank a Manhattan while Jamie carried the bag to the back office to pick up the week's take.

"Heavy tonight," Jamie said when he picked up the bag. "What's up, they been paying off in quarters?"

"Silver dollars, mostly," Greef said, going with the joke. He wasn't about to tell Jamie he was carrying more tonight than he'd ever carried before.

"Stop at Rosie Blue's over there on Broadway and West Third, the candy store there," Carmine said just before Greef started out. "Pick up the numbers tote."

"Sure. Is this going to be a regular thing?" Picking up the numbers money was a step up the ladder. Numbers money ran five, six, ten times what Greef took from the bars.

"Nah. A onetime. Paulie's sick."

"Will do." Not a step up, but a sign that people had their eye on him.

Greef signaled the second bartender for a refill and checked out the Friday-night crowd. There were a couple of broads at a table for two, college girls, maybe, or secretaries out on the town. One of them was dark-haired and a little chubby for his taste, but the other was a cute little strawberry blonde with big tits. Jesus, he'd like to get her unwrapped. He wondered how she felt about the rough stuff. He'd been thinking about that since they'd worked over the big broad at the cop's apartment. Jesus, that had been something. Some broads liked the rough stuff. That was a known fact. He wondered if the strawberry blonde was one of them. He'd been thinking about some things he'd like to try. The thought of it gave him a hard-on, and he had to turn to the bar and rearrange himself. Yeah, he'd stop back after he dropped the bag, and if she was still here, he'd make a play, get her back to his apartment, and see what was what. She looked like she'd probably love it. And if she wasn't here, he'd find someone else, because he and some broad were going to have some fun tonight.

Greef came out of Chumley's carrying the bag. *Fucking thing was heavy.* He headed south on Bedford figuring he'd find a taxi on Seventh. There was no point in breaking his back humping the thing down to Carmine. Besides, if he got back to Chumley's fast, the strawberry blonde might still be there.

Cassidy followed Greef and took him just south of Commerce. He bull-rushed him into an alley, slammed his head into the brick wall, pulled it back and did it again. Greef sagged to the pavement unconscious. Cassidy picked up the leather bag of money and walked away.

• • •

The morning rounds were over, and Orso was asleep when Cassidy arrived at the hospital. He sat on the uncomfortable chair next to the window and looked out across the river to Welfare Island and the redbrick lunatic asylum building abandoned five years back. *They probably should have kept it open for me.* He thought about what he was doing and realized there was no rational explanation. He was working on instinct and trusting that what he was doing was right on some scale. *The hell with it. It's in motion, so go with it.*

"Jesus, you again. Can't I ever get rid of you?" Orso's light, dusty voice.

"Tanner told me to take the rest of the week off and go do something productive. I couldn't think of anything, so I came here to make sure you were behaving."

"Yeah, I've been running up and down the halls chasing the nurses."

"I thought I might see Detta."

"Nah. I told her to stay home today. Some of the cousins are going to take her out for lunch. She needs the break."

Cassidy got up and carried the canvas duffel he had brought to the bed.

"What's that?" Orso asked.

Cassidy opened the duffel and showed him the money.

"Jesus Christ, what's that?"

"It's money, Tony."

"Yeah, I can see that." He waited for Cassidy to go on.

"Forty-one thousand dollars."

"Okay. What are we doing here?"

"Does that get you healthy, the mortgage and your father's insurance?"

"Yeah. A bit more." Orso was clearly puzzled.

"Okay. You come pick it up when you get back on your feet. I'll hold on to it till then."

"What the fuck are you talking about? Where did that come from? Is that your money?"

"I took it off Jimmy Greef for what he did to Alice."

"You took the bag off Jimmy Greef?"

Cassidy nodded.

"No matter what he tells them, they're going to think he had something to do with it. He's in trouble."

"Yes. But you're not."

"You do this after what I did?"

"We can talk about it when you're out of here, if you want, but we're not going to talk about it now."

Orso closed his eyes and made a choking sound, and tears squeezed out and ran down his cheeks.

"Okay," Cassidy said. "I'm not staying around here while you leak water."

Orso scrubbed his eyes with the back of the hand that was unpenetrated by tubes. "How do I pay you back for this? How do I thank you?"

"Buy me a drink at Toots's."

Cassidy held the duffel on the seat next to him in the cab on the way downtown. He wondered where he should store it until Orso came to pick it up and decided that what had been good enough for Alice was good enough for him. He would shove it under the bed.

When he entered the apartment, Dylan was standing by the window smoking a cigarette. She turned at the sound of the door and watched him come in. Her stance was relaxed, but her eyes were wary, as if she was unsure of her reception.

His heart rose at the sight of her.

"She's gone, isn't she?" Dylan said.

"How did you know?" He put the duffel down.

"I'm a spy, remember?"

He lit a cigarette and noticed his hands shook. "Where's Slava?"

"Ribera took him to Havana this morning." She stubbed out her cigarette but did not move away from the window. Neither one could take the first step.

Cassidy saw the suitcase near the door to the bedroom. "Are you staying?"

"May I?"

"For how long?" Nothing he said made any sense to him. They were just words that covered all the things unspoken.

"I don't know. Let's not talk about that. Let's just be together. Let's have what we can have for as long as it lasts. Is that all right?"

"Yes."

When they met in the middle of the room, they waited for as long as they could stand it before they kissed.